Finding *Utopia*

A Novel

LINDA WEBER

BOOKBABY PUBLISHING
FINDING UTOPIA
Linda C Weber

Copyright © 2023 by Linda C Weber

ISBN (Print Edition): 978-1-66789-694-6
ISBN (eBook Edition): 978-1-66789-695-3

First BookBaby Trade Paperback Printing April 2023

For My father, William Echols Jones, Jr.
"Little Dubbya'E"

I tried to find out "why," but there was no answer.

And to my daughter, Stacey Ladd Jennings,
who never stopped believing I could do this.

CHAPTER 1

Utopia Texas
April 1917
MAIZELLE

The day I met Will Jones, Leila and Papa were having words, or it might never have happened.

Papa was distressed with her for being too strict with my little brother, Samuel. Papa calls him Sambo, and it makes Leila real mad. I think that's why he does it. My little sister is Edra, after Leila's mother, but Papa nicknamed her 'Toofy'.

That's the one thing I agree with my stepmother about. I don't care for those nicknames, either. I only use them because it gets her dander up. My name is Maizelle Nannie Clarke, but most folks call me Maidee, and I don't mind.

Leila shouted at Samuel and slapped his hand for taking a cookie without permission.

He cried, and I hugged him. He's only five. When the little ones hurt, I hurt.

The next thing I knew, she backhanded me across the face. I think my head spun clear around. She clinched my shoulder in such a tight grip I knew it would bruise. "Do not interfere when I am disciplining my son," she said right into my face, spraying me with spittle.

I twisted out of her grasp as Papa came into the room. "What's going on?" he asked, scowling at Leila.

"Your daughter thinks it's all right to interfere when I scold Samuel."

Papa shot me a stern look and said, "What'd he do?"

Before I could answer, Leila snapped, "He took a cookie off the counter without permission," and tipped her head back with her nose in the air, like what Samuel did stank to High Heaven.

Papa said, "You might take it as a compliment to your skills as a cook."

"You think I should let him eat cookies whenever he feels like it? I allowed them one each, and he stole another." Leila's voice rose, and Papa's eyes narrowed.

Samuel looked from one to the other and began to cry. He doubled up his little fists and shook them. He didn't like it when they quarreled, and neither did I.

Papa said, "Maizelle, take Toofy and Sambo and get in the car."

I glanced at my stepmother. She turned away and stared out the window, her face a hard mask.

I pushed the little ones out the door and we ran to the car. They scrambled into the back and I scooted in upfront.

I rubbed my cheek to calm the prickling as I listened to Papa's deep voice and Leila's shrill replies grow louder by the minute. I ducked, afraid to watch.

Papa jerked open the door on the driver's side, and I held my breath until he closed it.

Leila stood flat-footed on the front porch with her lips pursed and both hands on her bulky hips. My stepmother found most everything distasteful: father, the little ones, and me. But nothing in her life is as bad as mine. I hate my stepmother.

We motored up the lane and pulled in behind Will's Central Garage. A tall, gangly guy in overalls strolled up to the car wearing a smile that lit up my whole afternoon.

His light blue eyes danced and sparkled as he admired Papa's automobile. When he leaned on the open window to speak with Papa, he caught sight of me.

I stared him full in the face, and my stomach flipped. I got goosebumps and a trill up my middle. My cheeks burned, but I smiled.

His mouth hung agape, halfway between a smile and a laugh.

My hair was pulled back, revealing my widow's peak. I hardly ever wear it that way, and I felt exposed.

The intensity of his gaze embarrassed me and I lowered my eyes. When I raised them, he was still fixed on me.

Later, after we started sparking, he said my face held an unmistakable invitation. I don't know about that, but I knew right then and there I wanted to marry him.

"Will" was embroidered in red on the coveralls of the man who rested his arms on the edge of the window. Papa turned to explain his complaints about the automobile and when he saw Will ogling me, his mouth clamped shut, and his face flushed red.

"What are you staring at, boy? Haven't you ever seen a girl? I'm here to have my car fixed, not entertain you."

Will wiped the smile off his face and straightened. "S...s... sorry, Dr. Clarke," he said in a soft drawl, like music from heaven. "It's...your daughter, sir... she's all grown up. She's beautiful..." His voice trailed off when it dawned on him that Papa appeared ready to explode.

My face burned. My body prickled from my toes to the top of my head. *He is so cute*, flashed through my mind.

Papa wrestled the handle and shoved the door open. The sudden thrust knocked Will to the ground. "She's barely fourteen! Children are not beautiful." Papa said, stepping out of the car.

It was too late. From that moment on, all I thought about was Will's compliment and the new stirrings I experienced every time I let him into my mind.

CHAPTER 2

End of May 1917
MAIZELLE

I spent the last two months of ninth grade daydreaming about the cute mechanic at Will's Garage. I knew he was Will Jones, and his brothers, Calvin and Alvin Jones, went to school with me. Anyone watching could tell I was distracted. My attention to my lessons waned to the point of nonexistent.

Today Miss Miller stopped me as I was leaving for lunch and said, "Maizelle, I've noticed your interest in class has lapsed. Are you not planning to continue next year?"

"I'm not sure," I said. "Papa might send me to school in San Antonio where Julia's in business college."

"I'm sorry to hear that. Your thoughtful contributions always add so much."

"Thank you," I said, in a hurry to join my friends.

"Could you run a little errand for me?"

"I guess so. When?"

"Now. I need someone to go to the basement and give Jimmy his slate. He left it when he brought me a goodbye gift earlier. You wouldn't mind, would you?"

She held it out, and I couldn't think of any reason to refuse, so I took it. I didn't want to miss lunch with Katherine and my friends, so I ran to the basement and took the stairs down three at a time.

"Jimmy?" I called down the stairway, "Miss Miller wants me to give you this."

Our deaf and dumb janitor pulled his head out of the bin where he fed coal into the chute, his mop of white hair smeared black with the dust. His smudged face and ghoulish smile made his teeth shine like lights in a jack-o'-lantern.

I offered the slate, but he didn't take it.

"M'zl," he muttered, "pr'ty g'rl."

"Thank you," I said, "here's your slate."

Jimmy reached for me like he wanted to hug me. I shoved the slate into his outstretched hands and bolted for the stairs.

"Wa't, wa't."

I paused to see what he wanted.

"Pr'ty, pr'ty."

The hunger on his face scared me. I've never been afraid of Jimmy, but something in his eyes made my insides crawl.

"I need to go. I can't stay. Katty and my friends are waiting. Sorry."

"Don' go." He grabbed my arm.

"Let go!" I twisted away and bolted up the steps.

Katherine and the other girls were sitting in a row on the teeter-totter like always.

"Where have you been?" she asked.

"I ran an errand for Miss Miller. Jimmy left his slate in her room. I took it to him."

"You went down in the basement with that creep by yourself?"

"He's not so bad, Katherine. He looked spooky with coal dust all over his face and hair, but I'm not afraid of him." I decided not to tell her about him grabbing my arm. I didn't think he meant to scare me.

"Ewww," she said. "My mom says he's an Albino. I wouldn't touch him with a ten-foot pole."

"I don't think it's catching."

I turned to the other girls and said, "What are you guys talking about?"

"Sue Ann has a crush on Cal Jones," Lula Mae teased.

"Do not. I just think he's cute."

"Not as cute as his brother," I blurted out as the warning bell rang. "I better hurry and eat my sandwich, or my stomach will be growling all afternoon."

The bell stopped our conversation about which Jones boy was the cutest. I was happy not to have to explain what I said without thinking.

Now that school was out for the summer, I was desperate to see Will again, but I doubted someone so much older would return my feelings. I hoped to run into him by inviting my little sister and brother to walk to town for an ice cream soda. We went almost every day.

I steered clear of his garage, but I held conversations with him in my head. I flirted, and he flirted back. Thoughts of him gave me little rushes, like squeezing whey through a wad of cheesecloth. I obsessed over these new feelings and the memory of the day at his shop—the way he stared at me and how it made me feel when our eyes locked. Remembering gave me courage.

One day, I altered our route to a path along the alley behind his business. I scooted past the open bay and spotted him. He was carrying something in his arms, and he caught my eye when I stole a glance. I quickly shifted my eyes, tugged the kids, and hurried out of sight.

"Don't pull my arm," Toofy whined.

It turned out that when he saw me, he stumbled and dropped a heavy tractor part. When he fell, he tried to catch it and smashed his thumb. That was a stroke of luck for both of us because he ran to Upton's Pharmacy for bandages, where I perched on a stool at the fountain.

Will's aunt, Elizabeth Upton, was making our sodas. She glanced up when the bell on the door jangled, dropped the ice cream scoop and rushed from behind the counter. "Will, bless your heart. Whatever happened to you?"

"I had an accident in the shop. I need antiseptic and something to wrap this."

It was Will.

I spun around, and there he stood, with a dirty, blood-soaked rag wrapped over his hand.

Mrs. Upton reached for him and removed the makeshift bandage. Will grimaced when the air hit his smashed thumb, and blood dripped onto the floor. The nail had started to turn black.

"Oh my, I should say you do. I'll be right back." She scurried off.

Will glanced at me, and our eyes locked. It was like the other time. A force I couldn't resist pulled me off the stool. "Toofy. Sambo. You stay put and wait for your sodas. You hear?" I stepped over to Will.

"Let me see," I said, taking his injured hand in mine to examine his thumb. I don't know what possessed me to take his hand like that, but when I raised my eyes to his, the rest of the room disappeared. We stood fixed on each other, lost in a silent waltz, until Elizabeth returned with a wet cloth, disinfectant, and bandages.

Whatever had possessed me when I took his hand got hold of me again. I lifted the items out of her hands and began wiping the blood from his fingernail.

Mrs. Upton opened her mouth like she wanted to say something, but she didn't.

Once I'd cleaned the wound, Will's aunt applied the dressing and said, "I better finish those sodas for Toofy and Sambo before the ice cream melts."

I nodded.

When I looked at Will, my heart lurched, and a voice I didn't recognize said, "Would you want to join the little ones and me for a soda?"

A slow, lopsided smile spread across his face. The mischievous look in his eyes answered before he said, "Why, I'd be honored, Miss Maizelle." His voice teased and sparked hope at the same time. He added in a more solemn tone, "On the condition you allow me to pay as a thank you for your nursing care."

My face grew hot. I nodded and reclaimed my seat next to Toofy.

Will sat on my other side, rested his arms on the counter, and tilted his head. There was a question in his eyes.

I wanted to say 'yes, yes, yes' to whatever was on his mind. I stared at the marred wood and picked at a divot where someone had carved their initials.

Will's Aunt Elizabeth raised an eyebrow when we both ordered strawberry sodas. Her eyes caught mine, and there was no mistaking what she was thinking. Will appeared unaware of her interest.

He said, loud enough for her to hear. "I work late at the garage lots of nights, and I walk past your house to take the river trail."

I seized on that. "What time?"

"Around eight-thirty or nine. Sometimes I stop at the Spanish Bridge and have a smoke before I head home."

I stole a glance. "That's a beautiful old bridge. The way it curves up on the sides, the cool grassy area underneath the arch. It's one of my favorite places. When the moon is bright, I can see it from my bedroom window."

His face took a puzzled expression with a half-smile as if he didn't quite believe me.

Toofy and Sambo slurped the bottoms of their glasses to let us know they were empty. Then, they began spinning on their stools. I put a hand on Samuel's arm to stop him and said, "They're getting restless. I think I'd better get them home."

Will and I hurried to finish. I lifted the kids down, taking each with a firm hand.

"I think we should walk you back to your work and make sure your wound doesn't start bleeding," I said, sounding much braver than I felt.

"That would be mighty nice," Will said as we headed out the door.

Angelic Toofy, with her straight blond hair and round blue eyes, gazed up at me. Her mop-headed brother twisted his hand, trying to extract himself.

"Can we race to O'Brien's?" Toofy asked.

When Sambo succeeded in pulling his hand free, he announced, "Girls can't run as fast as boys. I can beat you."

"Cannot. I can beat you," Toofy spouted back.

"Hunh, uh," Sambo whined. "Cannot."

Already running, Toofy shouted, "Ready, set, go!"

"No fair! You got a head start," Sambo hollered.

"Wait for me at O'Brien's gate," I called after them.

"Okay," Toofy said, glancing over her shoulder.

I didn't want Leila to know I let them out of my sight.

Will and I turned into the alley behind the businesses along Central Street. We walked shoulder to shoulder in silence. Electric shocks ran up and down my spine every time our arms brushed. My mouth was dry, and my throat was so constricted I couldn't talk. My heart pounded until my chest hurt.

I glanced up, wondering if Will would say something.

He had his head down, and his jaw clenched. The cords in his neck pulsed in rhythm with his step.

I opened my mouth but couldn't think of what to say.

He cleared his throat.

I glanced at him and waited, but nothing followed.

When we reached the open garage bay, we stopped, rooted to the spot. The tension between us sparked like a loose connection.

"You left the door open."

"My thumb hurt. I forgot."

We stared.

Will opened his mouth. Closed it. Opened it again, and spit out, "Your papa."

"My papa?"

He wrinkled his brow and made sad eyes. "He warned me not to have anything to do with you."

My face flushed with humiliation. Tears stung. I turned toward the street and lifted my hand in a little wave, unable to speak.

I heard a voice say, "Miss Maizelle, I'll be stopping at the bridge about nine tonight to have a smoke. Maybe your face will be in the window you told me about."

I turned, lowered my chin so he wouldn't notice my tears, and summoned my courage. "I might be there myself. I like to sit and listen to the cicadas sing." My voice squeaked, and I lifted brimming eyes.

His face flushed pink as a new piglet.

I jumped off the raised wooden sidewalk and skip-hopped along the dirt street toward our house with burning cheeks.

What have I done? Does Will want to see me alone?

My mind raced from one question to another, and I chided myself. I sounded so stupid.

Listen to cicadas sing? I'll bet he thinks I'm simple. Am I brave enough to show up? Is he?

I flushed cold when I realized I'd have to think up a story to tell my sister. I hugged my body with both arms and danced side to side as I skipped down the street.

I scanned the length of O'Brien's picket fence for Toofy and Sambo. When I didn't spot them, a chill ran down my spine. Then I spied them at the other end— about as far from the gate as they could be without leaving the property. I was too happy to scold. "Come here," I said and wrapped them in my arms, squirms and all.

CHAPTER 3

Early June 1917
MAIZELLE

After we got back from town, I went to my room and closed the door. I needed to be alone to figure out all these new feelings. I felt full in a way I couldn't ever remember. My tummy fluttered every time I recalled bumping Will's arm or hand. It was the same feeling I got in the car the day Papa took us to the garage. I didn't know what to call it, but I liked it a lot.

My sister, Julia, and I shared a small bedroom behind the kitchen in what had been the maid's quarters—Leila's room before Mama died and she married Papa. The room was crowded with both our beds, but we liked the privacy.

Nervous as a barn cat, I jumped whenever someone walked into the kitchen. I felt like I was going to get caught doing something I shouldn't. But who could catch me? Anyway, I wasn't doing anything I shouldn't—yet.

When Julia opened the bedroom door and peeked in, I lay on my bed writing in my diary. I slammed the cover shut. That was so stupid. Of course, she said, "What are you doing? You've been holed up in here for two hours."

"Nothing. Writing in my diary."

"What about? Did something happen?" She stepped inside and plopped down on the edge of her bed.

I scrambled for something to say.

"You're blushing," Julia announced as if she'd caught me red-handed. I suppose, in a way, she had.

"I am not." I turned my head.

"Yes, you are. Now tell me what's going on." Julia reached over and grabbed my diary.

I snatched it back and swallowed hard against telling a lie. There was no way I was going to explain Will to my sister. Julia's never had a suitor. She wants a career despite the fact she's always making something for her trousseau and storing it in her cedar chest.

"Nothing. Nothing's going on. I just got an idea, and I was writing it."

"Let me see." She reached for the diary.

"Don't." I jammed the little book under me and flattened myself on it. "It's not your business."

"Let me see, Maidee." She softened her voice to put me off guard.

"No. It's private."

Julia planted her feet on the floor and stood. She plucked a book off the foot of her bed and said, "It's almost time for dinner. You should come set the table for Leila."

I collected myself, hid my diary under the mattress, and went to help. At dinner, my throat was so tight I couldn't swallow, so I pushed my food around to make it look like I was eating.

"Maizelle," Leila said, looking down her nose like I smelled, "is there something wrong with my cooking tonight?"

"No. It's too hot to eat. I guess I'm not hungry."

"If your father were here, he'd make you eat whether you're hungry or not. You won't have any apple crisp with us."

"Well, he isn't here, is he?" I shot her a look. I knew he stayed away to avoid her. We all knew it. "Besides, I don't mind missing the apple crisp. Toofy can have mine."

"I want it," Sambo chimed in.

"You stop it now. The both of you," Leila said through gritted teeth.

"Yes. You may both leave the table...and the sooner, the better," she said under her breath.

Our brothers, Jamie and Bowen, stared at their plates, hoping to avoid Leila's bad temper.

Toofy and Sambo bounced up and down in their chairs, singing, "I get Maidee's apple crisp," and "no, you don't, I do."

Leila reached over and grabbed Toofy by the arm.

"Ouch!" She wailed. "Let go."

The action stopped Sambo, and his eyes went wide.

Julia and I pushed our chairs back, picked up our plates, and headed for the kitchen. Neither of us spoke as we cleared the dishes and set them on the counter for Leila to wash.

Julia poured a glass of sweet tea and went out on the back porch, carrying her book.

I went into our room and closed the door. I heard Leila in the kitchen serving the apple crisp and wondered who was getting my share, wishing I hadn't been so quick to give it up.

It took forever until nine o'clock. The big hall clock chimed to note the quarter-hour, and I slipped out the back door at exactly eight-forty-five. My heart hammered so hard I thought Julia would notice the rise and fall of my blouse. My stomach turned flips with anticipation that I might see Will alone.

As usual, Julia sat sipping tea with her nose in her book. She looked up, scowled, and said, "Where are you going?"

"The river," I shot back over my shoulder, "to cool off." I avoided eye contact and didn't stick around to see if she swallowed my story.

The sun dipped low on the horizon, painting the sky a wild mixture of orange, pink, and dusky blue. My nerves jangled as I hurried along. A chorus of frogs, cicadas, and crickets filled the evening air.

I didn't see anyone when I broke out of the trees and scanned the bridge. I bent forward and slid beneath the cool stone arch. Only someone looking for me might see me in the shadows.

The shaded grass felt moist as I stretched my legs and laid my head back. The sluggish river sloughed past with a sloop, flub, sloop, flub. A loud plop broke the silence, and I watched ripples spread across the water where a bullfrog made a dive for supper.

The anxiety of waiting all afternoon, hoping and not knowing, had me turned inside out. I didn't really believe he would come. To calm myself, I concentrated on the water and the quiet sounds the evening made as night fell.

My eyelids drifted shut. I startled when I heard a soft whistle and quick foot-steps on the bridge. They stopped overhead. Jolted to full consciousness, I bolted upright and smoothed my skirt down over my rough sun-browned knees.

Whoever was on the bridge slung one leg over the wide stone railing, then the other, and slid into a seated position with feet dangling.

I rolled onto my side and peered up at the bottoms of what I hoped were Will's shoes. The man rustled around, and his legs kept swinging this way and that. I wondered if he was going to jump. Then he got still, and a bright flare from a match lit the sky. I could see a profile against the gathering dusk.

It was Will.

I saw his outline like the shadow dancers we made in school—his narrow nose curved slightly upward at the end. I whistled as I scooted out from under the bridge.

Will dropped his cigarette, and it landed in front of my face. I picked it up and carried it up the grassy slope, holding it as if it were about to bite.

He scrambled off the high rail and rushed to meet me.

When I reached the top of the slope, I could see he didn't quite believe his eyes.

We both stopped stone still and stared. I held my breath. Blood rushed to my head, and the thumping in my ears deafened me. I swooned.

Will stepped forward and caught me.

I let out my breath and inhaled a lung full of air.

With his arm still around my waist, Will lifted me. When he had me upright, our faces were nearly touching, and he cupped my chin with his other hand and kissed me on the lips.

I leaned into him and returned his kiss until my knees collapsed.

He held me up very close to his body, and I didn't resist. I felt weak all over and happier than I'd ever felt. His lips were soft and tentative against mine. He seemed as unsure and shy about the kiss as I was.

Suddenly, he let go and stepped back.

I thought I had done something wrong until he reached for me and pulled me to him again, pressing my head against his chest. I could hear his heart hammering.

He stroked my hair and kept a small space between his body and mine. Truth to tell, I think we were both badly shaken by that impromptu kiss.

Much to my surprise, I still gripped his cigarette in my trembling hand, which I held straight out at my side. How had I not dropped it?

Will took it, and I let my arm fall. He put the smoke to his lips and pulled hard on it, blowing a white cloud over my head before stubbing the cigarette out on the parched grass with the toe of his boot. He took my shoulders and gently pushed me back, gazing into my eyes. I could see those same questions that were there this afternoon still troubled him.

He leaned down and picked a lavender-tinted bluebell from the wildflowers along the riverbank. "A pretty flower for a beautiful lady," he said, and my throat swelled.

He shook his head and said under his breath, "You fool."

I knew he scolded himself, but I giggled and asked, "Who?"

"Me. I know I'm playing with fire. Doc Clarke won't be happy if he finds out. But watching you skip away today—I knew I couldn't help myself."

I didn't know what to say, so I blurted, "I think I'd better scoot on home. My sister will get suspicious if I'm gone much longer."

"I suppose so," he said, sounding deflated. "Miss Maizelle, I'm sorry... you know... about kissing you. I had no business." He looked real sad and dejected.

"It's okay. It took me by surprise, is all." I hesitated, then added under my breath, "I liked it. It's just... I've...never been kissed by a boy."

"It might have been better if it had been a boy. Me being twenty-four puts a different light on things."

"That's not what I meant. I mean...it was special, is all. I don't mind that you're older than me."

"You might not mind, but your pa does."

"Doesn't it matter what I think?" My voice sounded shaky, and my chin quivered.

"'Course it matters what you think," he said, taking my hand. "Can you risk another couple minutes...so we can settle something?"

I nodded and pulled a sad face. I knew he was going to tell me there couldn't be a next time.

"Sit," he said, motioning to the grass.

I sat, and he plopped down beside me, hugging his knees.

"Look, Maizelle, I don't know what's going on between you and me, but I think we need to get a few things straight."

"You can call me Maidee," I said, "everyone else does." I stared hard at Will, waiting for him to say something. If he could read minds, he would have heard me imploring him to kiss me...beg me to stay...want to see me again.

He looked into my eyes and said, "I mean to say...well...I don't know what I mean to say. I guess I am attracted to you, and I'm not sure that's a good thing... you bein' so young and all."

My eyes brimmed, and what Papa calls my 'intractable stubbornness' took over.

"I'm almost fifteen."

"And I'm twenty-four." He said it like it was a crime.

I set my jaw and let fly. "I've never been sweet on anyone before. The boys at school don't appeal to me at all, but... something's different about you. I go all soft inside. I can't think. I make a fool of myself. In my head, I can talk, but when I'm near you, I can't untie my tongue."

I sucked in a big breath. My eyes shifted across his face. When he didn't say anything, I jumped to my feet and said, "I should go. You can think about whatever needs straightening out and let me know." I knew if I didn't leave right then, I'd have more to answer for than coming in after dark.

"Wait," Will said, scrambling upright, "can you come back tomorrow? That'll give us both time to think."

"If I can get past Julia," I said, running up the bank. "See ya."

CHAPTER 4

WILL

And she was gone. Just like that. She hightailed it up the hill. I rolled another cigarette and sat to ponder her outburst and my feelings. The night had grown still by the time I unspooled my legs and stood, half hoping she would materialize out of the dark. I walked to my folk's place, running over the whole thing in my mind.

Maidee met me at the bridge the next night, the next, and the next. We never spent more than a few minutes together, talking casually, as if we had accidentally run into each other in case anyone came along. Our ease with each other grew, and I decided to broach the subject that had sent her packing a few days before.

"Maidee, remember when I said we needed to straighten some things out?"

"I remember." Her voice caught, and I could tell she was nervous.

"This isn't good, us meeting every evening. I'm sure your pa or Julia will get the idea something's going on and follow you one of these nights."

She looked down and said, "I know. I guess you don't want to see me anymore?"

"That's the trouble. I very much want to see you. I just think we should not make it every evening. Maybe if we took a small break, we could do something together, like go to the Rodeo and Fair at Tip Toe over the fourth. Would you be willing?"

Her head popped up, and she searched my face. Her forehead crinkled with concern. A smile of disbelief crept across her face. "Would it be a date?"

She sounded scared to death.

"I suppose you could call it that."

"I'd love to go with you. I don't think you should call for me at the house, though. If Papa's home, he might not let me go. Could we just meet up by accident?"

"Sure. If that's the way you want it. I'm not afraid to call for you though."

"No. Not yet. Please?" She pleaded with her voice and doe eyes, and there was no way I could let her down.

"Okay. We'll meet by the livestock barn at ten o'clock—before it gets too hot to enjoy the day." I leaned in and gave her a quick peck on the cheek. "See you Wednesday at the fairgrounds."

CHAPTER 5

July 1917
WILL

Holy moly, it's hotter than a blister bug in a pepper patch. I rolled out from under the car and pulled my shop rag out to wipe sweat off my forehead. It was too hot to work. I couldn't concentrate on repairs when all I could think about was seeing Maidee again. I decided to close up early and head home.

It occurred to me that July had rolled in like a tornado spawned in Hell as I walked in the sweltering heat. I'd lived in Texas all my life and never felt heat like this. The drought that had plagued the canyon for a third straight year was all anyone talked about. The rest of the world might be talkin' about war, but in Utopia, the only war was tryin' to save livestock and crops.

The farms and ranches needed every able-bodied boy and man right here at home. It was easy to put the niggling thoughts that I might get called up into the back of my mind until I stopped at the post office and saw the color poster they were hanging.

It showed Uncle Sam in a white top hat pointing his finger and saying, "I Want You for the U.S. Army." Next to it was the law Congress passed to conscript all men eighteen to thirty-one.

Despite the heat, I felt chilled. I read the notice and saw there would be local Draft Boards. There would be few exemptions.

I stepped to the counter to collect my mail. Mrs. Burns nodded when she handed it to me. I nodded in return and stepped outside. It was too hot to make small talk.

Shimmering waves of color rose from the hard-packed street. Heat hit me like a blast from a coal furnace, and I sucked in my breath. The air was steamy and close, the humidity so heavy I could almost touch it. Nothing stirred. No birds sang. The street was empty, the silence palpable.

Uncle Sam wants me, but Utopia grinds on as if the outside world doesn't exist.

I reached the end of the raised wooden walkway and stepped off. The bottoms of my feet burned through my boots. I headed toward my new lodgings with my cousin Bobby and his wife, Emma, thinking about the plan Maidee and I made for Fourth of July week.

I'd been turning over in my mind this thought that Maidee didn't want me to come by the house for fear her pa wouldn't let her go with me. What if Doc Clarke gets wind of it? It's stupid to pursue this friendship. Her pa objects to me, and the Army is knocking on my door.

I hated the idea of leaving my business when it was just getting going, and I still owed my brother-in-law, Fred Brown, a considerable amount of money. I knew I'd be hard-pressed to avoid service since I'd been in Cadet Corp at A&M, but that didn't stop me from wishing. I didn't want to miss out on a possible romance with this young beauty either. Some other guy will be sure to snap her up as soon as I board the train out of Utopia.

When the morning of our date rolled around, I was nervous as a long-tailed cat in a room full of rockin' chairs. I sauntered onto the fairgrounds, scanning the area for Maidee. I spotted her leaning against the livestock barn, nervously shifting her weight from one foot to the other. She acted as jittery as I felt. I moseyed in her direction, tipping my hat to folks I knew, swallowing the lump that kept rising in my throat.

Maidee saw me and turned to go into the building.

I stepped up my pace.

As she started through the doorway, I bumped into her.

We pretended running into each other was a surprise and stood staring like a pair of startled calves. I found my voice first and said something brilliant like, "Aren't you Maizelle Clarke?"

Maidee laughed and ran an arm under her mane of honey-colored hair, tossing it over her shoulder. "Ah suppose Ah am," she drawled, "you're that Will Jones from the garage, aren't you?"

I chuckled and stuck out my hand, but when she put hers in mine, I flushed hot and lost my voice. All the sounds from the bustling crowd faded to a faint hum.

From somewhere, a voice said, "Nice to see you, Mr. Will. Why don't we go inside where it's cooler?"

We stepped into the barn and walked along the rows of stalls, making sure we didn't touch shoulders or hands. Whenever someone came close, we slipped apart to look at different exhibits. It would have been hard for anyone to say for sure we were together. Eye contact was out of the question. It was a dead giveaway we had feelings for each other.

Walking next to this girl, I felt the sweat under my arms and knew it was forming a telltale ring on my shirt. I was so tense I could barely swallow.

I looked at Maidee and saw her shoulders pulled up almost to her ears. Her arms hung still at her sides.

I touched her arm and whispered, "Relax your shoulders. You look like you're about to lift off."

She glanced up and smiled. Her shoulders dropped.

Several people entered the barn, laughing and pointing at the animals. Maidee moved to the right side of the aisle, and I stayed left.

I was looking at a Nanny goat with a pair of kids when the placard wired to the gate caught my eye. As the newcomers passed, I stooped down to get a closer look. The card said, "Exhibitor: Alvin and Calvin Jones."

Maidee moved up behind me just as I raised my head and stood. I bumped her, and she stumbled. I grabbed her arm. "Sorry, ma'am," I muttered, and she said, "Excuse me," at the same time. The physical contact knocked both of us off our pins. Our eyes locked while the world drifted around us like a fine morning mist.

It was dark in the barn. The odor of goat dung, straw, fresh-cut alfalfa, and well-used leather drifted up my nose and brought me back to my senses.

Maidee looked star-crossed. Her breathing was rapid and shallow. "Are you okay, ma'am?"

Her eyes shifted, and a smile spread like warm molasses. When she spoke, her whisper sounded thick and smoky. "They're gone. I'm just fine. How nice of you to catch me."

Her sultry smile had an inviting slant, and I felt the uncomfortable rise in my groin. I dropped her arm and turned back to the goat pen. "Look here." My voice was too loud, echoing through the barn. I dropped it a notch. "These goats belong to my twin brothers."

Maidee leaned down and peered at the placard. "Al and Cal Jones," she read aloud.

I chuckled. "Do you know them?"

"Of course, I do. We go to school together. Well, not exactly together. They're two grades ahead of me, but we shared a room when I was in fourth and seventh grade, and we'll be in the Upper Room together this fall." She prattled on until I interrupted.

"They're rascals. If they find out we're sweet on each other, they'll make sure the whole town knows."

"In that case, we'll have to make sure they don't find out." She leaned in and focused on the nanny and her young 'uns. "Oh," she cooed, "the kids are *nursing*."

My heart melted. When Maidee turned back, her eyes were bright with joy, and I thought, she'd make a great mother. I stepped away to get control and moved to the opposite side.

We continued up and down the lanes of goat pens, chicken cages, and cattle stalls, admiring the blue-ribbon champions and commiserating over the Johnny-come-latelies.

Whenever she came close, I felt her body heat like a warm sunbeam. I inhaled the fragrance of Lavender from the oil she brushed through her hair. I didn't need to talk to her, but I needed her near.

We reached the end of the livestock displays in the far corner of the barn. Maidee stepped close to me and asked a question that caught me off-guard.

"Will, why'd you leave home and go live with Robert and Elizabeth?" Her soft voice made my stomach clutch. I wasn't sure how to answer.

"I had a bit of a row with Pa over me wantin' to go to A&M."

"Didn't he want you to get an education?"

"No. He thought I should stay here and help out."

"What happened?"

I was surprised by how roiled up I felt. "I don't like to think about it." I turned away and mumbled, "It was a long time ago."

Maidee tilted her head with a determined set to her chin. "I want you to tell me. I'd like to meet your ma and pa."

I searched her face. I saw she had her heart set on knowing the details. "Maybe someday. Not now, though. Let's just enjoy our time together." I placed my hand under her elbow and guided her toward the light.

The sun momentarily blinded us, and we stopped to let our eyes adjust. When my vision cleared, I saw my cousin and his wife standing under a live oak by the picnic tables.

Bobby raised his hand and motioned us over.

"Maidee, there's someone I'd like you to meet. Come on," I said, starting toward them.

She spotted Bobby and Emma waving in our direction. "Who is it?" I heard hesitation as she squinted into the sun.

"My cousin, Bobby, and his wife, Emma. You know Emma, don't you?"

"Not really. She was a year ahead of Julia, but I know who she is."

"Well, I live with them, so I think we'd better say hello."

"Do you think I should come?"

"Look, Maidee, they're here, and we're here. I don't know how to avoid seeing folks we know when almost everyone in town is here."

"Do you think she'll tell Julia?" The confident, flirtatious young lady from the barn dissolved into a shy, apprehensive girl right before my eyes. I tried to sound confident and unconcerned. "I suppose she might if they're friends. You didn't think we'd make it through a whole day here without seeing anyone we know, did you?"

Her voice wavered. "I don't know. I guess I didn't think much about that part. I was mostly just thinking about how nice it would be to spend time with you."

I smiled. "And it is nice, isn't it? We can act natural, or we can hide, but I think natural is best."

"Okay." She agreed, sounding unconvinced. I guided her toward Bobby and Emma, who were eating hotdogs and potato salad.

Bobby jumped to his feet. "Hi there." He sized Maidee up, his eyes all twinkly with mischief. "Who's your friend?"

"This here's Miss Maizelle Clarke, Doc Clarke's daughter. Maizelle, this here's my cousin Bobby Upton."

Maidee dipped her knees and bobbed her head as Bobby put his hand out to shake. When she put her fingertips into his hand, her face colored like a fall apple. One pump, and she pulled her hand back. "Pleased to meet you," she whispered.

Bobby laughed and said, "I know who you are. You're Julia's baby sister, right? Now I know who Will's been hiding from us, and I can see why. Does your daddy know you're out with this rascal?"

Maidee's eyes darted in my direction.

"Stop it, Bobby," I said. "Maidee and I ran into each other in the livestock barn. You're embarrassing her."

"Likely story," Bobby said. "I've seen you two having sodas at the pharmacy. I see what's going on."

"Stop, Bobby," Emma chimed in. "Come here, Maizelle. Sit next to me."

Maidee managed a weak smile and slipped onto the bench next to Emma.

I glared at Bobby.

"Sorry," he muttered. "I thought she was your date."

"Not to disappoint you, Pal," I blustered, "but Miss Clarke is a good friend. She helped Aunt Elizabeth doctor my thumb when I smashed it. I offered to buy her a soda to thank her. If you'd been paying attention, you'd 'a noticed her brother and sister were with her."

Maidee shifted her gaze and smiled the sweetest smile I'd ever seen. "Thank you, Mr. Will."

"Don't feel like you need to stay and be embarrassed by this scoundrel if you have someplace else you want to go."

"I appreciate your concern. But after that long walk through the barn, I'm enjoying the rest."

She sounded confident again. I felt my chest swell with pride.

"When is Julia leaving for business college?" Emma asked.

"Right before Labor Day," Maidee said, and the two girls were off chatting like two old friends.

I sat opposite Bobby, who kept looking at me, asking questions with his eyes. His eyebrows bobbed up and down like a cork in the river. I refused to take the bait.

Finally, there was a lull in the chatter, and I said, "Miss Maizelle, would you like a hot dog? I'd be honored if you would let me buy you one."

"Honored?" Bobby blurted out with a big guffaw.

I leaned over the table and punched him in the shoulder.

Maidee ignored the scuffle. "That would be nice, Mr. Will. I suppose you heard my stomach grumbling."

"No. I just thought I'd like one myself and hoped you'd do the honor of eating lunch with us." I unwound my long legs from under the attached bench and headed across the dry grass to the food stand.

When I returned, Maidee and Emma were laughing and chatting like the best of friends, even though Emma was five years older.

Emma was excited about winning a red ribbon for her prickly pear jelly, and Bobby had spotted a new piece of farm equipment he wanted to show me. We soon discovered that wandering through the exhibits with another couple was a great way to go unnoticed. Since they'd already seen the displays in this building, it wasn't long before they left us on our own.

Solid works of art hung on three sides of the quilt exhibit. Maidee and I stood close together to examine the handiwork. Sparks flew between our bare arms, and Maidee jumped. A lump rose in my throat, and I reached for her hand to give it a quick squeeze. "Would you like to watch some of the rodeo?"

Three older ladies came into the booth, nattering on like magpies, oohing and awing over the quilts. Maidee stole a glance, and we turned to leave. She went left, and I went right.

"I'll meet you at the double doors," I said under my breath, nodding my head toward the east wall. When I reached the doorway, I saw her hurrying with her head tucked into her chest.

We started through the doorway at the same time and bumped shoulders. "Miss Maizelle," I said, "are you headed for the rodeo?"

"Yes, I am," she said, flashing a big smile. "Is that where you're going?"

"It is. Care to join me and watch a few cowboys bite the dust?"

She laughed and said, "I'm lost at the rodeo. It would be nice to sit with some-one who knows what's happening." She fell into step with me, her head high.

Dust billowed as we walked toward the bleachers circling the arena. We found seats near the center aisle. People didn't pay us much attention beyond an occa-sional nod or smile.

Maidee and I watched the quarterfinals of the bull riding competition. The finals would be tonight under the lights. I hoped we would be secreted away from the crowds by then. The sizzle that ran through me every time she brushed my arm had me on edge.

We feigned interest in the rodeo. She asked questions, and I offered answers as if I were an authority. After a couple of hours, Maidee whispered she needed to use the privy. That created the perfect opportunity for us to leave.

"I'll just wait here for you," I said, nodding my head to an area between the privy and the exit gate.

"Why don't I meet you behind the stock barn?" she asked, sounding innocent of the possibilities that conjured.

"Sounds like a plan," I said, hoping she didn't catch the excitement in my voice.

The things I imagined could lead to trouble, so I put my mind elsewhere. I stopped and rolled a cigarette before I headed behind the barn. As I rounded the corner, I caught a glimpse of the river. It occurred to me that we might slip away and sit by the water with no one the wiser.

I tucked the cigarette into the corner of my mouth and relieved myself. I but-toned my trousers and leaned against the old barn while I waited.

Maidee poked her head around the barn wall, and I made a grab for her. She giggled and dodged before stepping into my arms.

I'd waited all day for this. I held her close and nuzzled her hair. I wanted to remember her smell and the way she felt. Her body was so slight I thought this must be what it's like to hug an angel.

I pulled her hair back from her face and whispered. "Let's go down to the river and sit in the shade." I felt her body press against me ever so slightly before she stepped back and took my hand. Without another word, we headed for the water.

We'd never taken much time just to sit and talk. Seemed like we always had one eye open and our ears on high alert in case someone spotted us. It would be nice to have this time together.

We found a grassy spot under the shade of a giant cypress tree. I took Maidee's hand and scooted close. Her body radiated warmth, and the sparks between us sent chills along my arm. She leaned against my shoulder as we listened to the river burble and the cicadas sing.

"Will?" Her soft voice caused my stomach to lurch.

"Hum?"

Maidee lifted her head and looked at me. "I want you to tell me what happened with your pa. I can't imagine what it would be like never to see Papa again."

I didn't want to talk about this. Maizelle was from a different world. She wouldn't have any way to understand what my brothers and I went through with Pa.

"Aw, Maidee, it's not that interesting."

Maidee shifted so she could see my face. Her eyes were clear with resolve.

I hadn't thought much about my leavin' in the five years since it happened. I shook my head, trying to clear the cobwebs and figure where to begin.

"Well, let's see. Pa and I were working the goats, tryin' to get the kids separated from the nannies. It was gettin' on in the day, and Pa said, 'Let's knock off. We can corral the rest of 'em tomorrow.'

"I had exams comin' up. I told Pa I needed to stay late at school every day to study, and he told me I didn't. Said I had all the schoolin' I needed. I told him I wanted to go to A&M and study Mechanical Engineering. He laughed and said, 'Don't go gittin' above your raisin'. You ain't goin' to no college.'"

I glanced at Maidee. Her eyes were wide. I looked at my feet. "That's about it."

"What happened then?"

"I smarted off."

"What did you say?"

"I told him he didn't know the first thing about college, seein' as how he never got out of primary school...or somethin' like that."

Maidee gasped. I shook my head. "I was a bit of a hothead, I guess."

"What'd your pa say?"

"Not much. He balled up his fist and punched me in the gut. I bent over double, and he got me in the chin with an uppercut."

She clapped both hands to her face. I pulled them down. "Sugar, this is upsettin' you. I don't think we should spoil our day by gettin' all worked up about something that happened a long time ago. I couldn't do nothin' about it then, and I can't do nothin' about it now."

Maidee didn't miss a beat. "Did you hit him back?"

"No. Pa said, 'Don't you go mouthin' off to me, boy. I know enough to support a family and run a ranch.' Then he stomped off, and I knew what that meant."

"What?"

"It meant he was fixin' to give me a strappin'. I wasn't sticking around for a whuppin'."

Maidee's eyes glistened. "A whipping? I've never known anyone whose pa whipped them. Does it hurt a lot?"

"Your darn tootin' it hurts...a lot. And it hurt a lot when he punched me. When I could stand straight and finished spittin' blood from biting my tongue half off, I walked to the house and told Ma I was leavin' for good."

Maidee shuddered. Tears rolled out and fell into her lap. "No one should ever hit a child—even a nearly grown one."

"I agree, Sugar. I'll never strike one of my children. Ever."

Maidee threw her arms around my neck and said, "Thank you. I can't bear it when Leila slaps Edra or Samuel, and I'd just die if someone hurt one of *my* children." When she pulled back, she said, "What'd your ma say?"

"You mean when I told her I was leaving?"

"Yes."

"She said, 'You don't mean it. Your pa needs you.'"

"I looked her in the eye and said, 'I do mean it. He's hit me for the last time. I'm not waitin' around for more.'"

"I don't blame you," Maidee said, her voice soft and sympathetic. "Didn't your ma ever try to stop him?"

"No. She kept her peace and stayed out of his way. But she helped the girls leave as soon as they were old enough and encouraged Thomas and Irv to leave the farm. My Aunt Elizabeth said if his meanness ever got so bad I couldn't take it anymore, I should come live with them. So that's what I did."

I reached for Maidee, pulled her close, and dabbed her cheeks with my handkerchief. I stroked her hair and brushed it back from her face. "Don't feel bad. I don't even think about it anymore. My pa is a hard man. I was lucky I had Elizabeth and Robert."

She sat back and touched my face. This girl was tender-hearted, I could tell. I moved her hand from my cheek and held it.

She squeezed my fingers. "Don't you ever want to see your ma again?"

From the tremor in her voice, I knew she couldn't imagine anyone not wanting to see his ma. I clenched my jaw and tried to think how to answer. I loved my ma, but sometimes it *was* hard to separate her from Pa. When I did think on it, I wondered how she could have let him use the strap on us kids and keep silent. She doctored our welts, covered them with ointment, and hugged us after, but she never tried to stop him.

I decided a small fib wouldn't hurt, so I said, "I miss my ma. Someday I'll take you out to meet her. Her name is Sarah. I think she would take to you."

Maidee smiled and looked at me with hope in her eyes. I didn't want her to press me for a specific time, so I kept talking. "It's funny how it all happened. I ended up working on Uncle Robert's ranch, and I got a following with folks for having a knack for fixin' things. Seems I had a 'natural aptitude.' When I left for A&M, most ranchers and farmers were already calling on me to repair whatever broke. When Uncle Robert bought the Packard, I saw my future. I fell in love with that car. I figured if I got the right education, my fortunes would grow with the popularity of the automobile."

I put my arm around Maidee and turned her. She looked up, and her eyes told me everything I needed to know. I kissed her in a way I never had before, parting my lips and putting them to her mouth. I teased the space, and she let her mouth open a bit so I could touch the inside with my tongue.

We clung to each other like pitch on tree bark, and I felt the swell of her breasts against my chest. I slid my hand under the back of her chemise and ran my fingers up and down her bare skin.

She arched her back, and a tremor traveled up her spine. Our hearts pounded so loudly they threatened to drown out the Cicadas mounting their final mating call.

I slipped my hand around the front of her chemise and cupped her breast.

She pulled away, and I let her go. There was too much at stake for me to lose control.

As dusk gathered, we heard the crowd roar in the distance as riders were bucked off bulls or managed to ride until the buzzer sounded. I don't think I'd ever felt as comfortable and relaxed with this girl as I did then.

I stood and pulled Maidee to her feet. We walked in silence toward the arena and arrived as the last cheers echoed off the walls of Sabinal Canyon. The crowd poured out of the small stadium. Without a word, we parted and disappeared into separate groups of people making their way home.

What we shared on the riverbank was deeper than anything we had experienced in our brief encounters under Spanish Bridge. I knew I shouldn't be, but I was in love.

CHAPTER 6

WILL

Keeping a secret of our romance made it all the more exciting. We met under the bridge almost every evening in July. Maidee conjured up a barrel full of excuses for being away from the house. Her creativity impressed me, although the specter of discovery loomed.

Each forbidden encounter found us more in love. We talked, laughed, and teased until the stars came out, and she scooted off home again. One night she said, "Julia's leaving soon. Papa spends more time away than he does at home. I think it's to avoid Leila. But also, I think he's upset about Julia."

"Where does he go?"

"I don't know, but when he's gone, Leila is so mean to Jamie and Bowen I can't leave the house for fear of what she'll do to them."

"Does she ever hit on them the way she does you?"

"No, but she threatens. She locks them in their room and tells them they can't have any dinner. She always says she will tell Papa what awful boys they are, and he'll take the switch to them when he gets home."

"Does he?"

"No. He threatens sometimes, but he's never done it. I sneak them some food when she's out of the kitchen or in her room with the door shut. If she catches me, I'll be the next one locked up."

Maidee rested her head against my shoulder. She wanted the Leila problem to go away, but she didn't know how to fix it. I wasn't much help. My relationship with my own ma isn't good. All I could do was hold and comfort her.

I liked those times when she spilled her troubles. I felt needed and enjoyed the closeness. It was easy to listen with my arms wrapped around her.

One night in late July, we lay tangled under the safety of the bridge later than usual. Maidee recalled sad stories. To cheer her up before she headed home, I tickled her. She laughed hard enough to gasp for breath and cried, "Stop, help!"

Footsteps overhead brought our play-wrestling to a halt. I clapped my hand over Maidee's mouth. We quieted, hoping whoever it was would move on. The steps paused, reversed, and left the bridge. Dry grass crunched.

I rolled away from Maidee, tucked her behind me, and rose on my forearm to face the intruder.

My cousin, Jimmy Calvert, peered into the dark, where we huddled. There was no mistaking who it was, with his shock of white hair and pale skin lighted by the moon.

I whispered, "Be still."

Jimmy strained to see who was in distress. "Hu, th'r?" he said in his garbled speech. "Hu n'd he'p?" He squatted and started toward me.

I pushed myself to my knees. "It's me, Jimmy, Will. Havin' a smoke. Nobody needs help. Move along."

He stared, and for a minute, I had the unsettling thought he could see in the dark. "G'rl'?" he muttered. "He'p?"

"Nope. No girl. Move along now." I shifted position to plant my feet.

He squinted, and his expression changed. "M'zl?" he said, "Ma'de?"

I crouched, ready to push him if he came closer.

He noticed the change, and his body tensed.

"Get lost," I threatened.

Jimmy didn't budge. Still crouched, I chicken-walked toward him, my hand stretched out to make contact. At the edge of the overhang, I stood.

He straightened, and we met eyeball-to-eyeball.

I gripped his shoulders and turned him away from the bridge, saying, "Keep on goin'," as I gave him a shove up the bank.

He resisted and twisted to release my grip. "Ma'de? He'p?" he called over his shoulder.

I tightened my grasp and put my mouth close to his ear. Through clenched teeth, I said, "No. No Maidee here. Nobody needs he'p." My imitation of his garbled speech mocked. I knew it would make him mad. I didn't care. I pushed and prodded the interloper until we reached the bridge. "I'll stand here and make sure you get to the other side. Keep right on goin' and forget this ever happened, ya hear?"

Jimmy peered around me and over my shoulder. He looked confused and uncertain about what he'd stumbled on.

"It's okay, man. Go on home now." I turned him toward the other side of the river and gave him a shove.

He walked with his chin tucked into his chest. His white head bobbed up and down with his uneven gait, like a piece of flotsam floating on the current.

I waited until he walked off the other end and disappeared. Once I was sure he headed toward his ma's place, I scrambled down the bank and met Maidee emerging from the shadows.

"I better get home," she whispered. "If Jimmy decides to tell anyone what he saw, we'll both be in a pickle."

"I don't think he will. I scared him plenty. Anyway, nobody can understand him."

"He has trouble talking, but he's not dumb," she said, sounding defensive. "He knows a lot more than folks realize."

"Now you're startin' to sound like my ma. I been hearin' it all my life, 'Jimmy ain't dumb,' he just can't talk right.' Sometimes I think she'd a been happier raisin' that mute than raisin' me."

"Don't be silly—and don't be unkind."

Chastened, I gave Maizelle a quick hug and pulled her up the bank to the pathway. I plucked a blue bell off its stalk and tucked it into her hair to make amends. She smiled and smooched me on the cheek before she slipped into the dark

CHAPTER 7

MAIZELLE

I crept into the room and slid beneath the covers without bothering to undress. Holding my breath, I buried my face in the pillow to let the air out, trying not to disturb my sister. When I sucked in another lung full of air, I made a loud flub-ba-ba noise. My eyes flew open, and I stared through the darkness, afraid she heard.

I couldn't let her catch me—she might rat to Papa. Papa would not consider Will Jones a suitable match. He made sure Julia knew none of the boys in Utopia would be acceptable, so she kept to herself and planned for a future in the city.

I doubt he thought it necessary to warn me. He still thinks of me as a child.

I was just a long arms-length away from Julia. My heart almost stopped when she said, "Maidee?"

My whole body jerked at the sound of her voice, and I almost fell out of bed.

"What?" I said, scrambling to come up with an excuse for coming in so late. I didn't want to lie to Julia, but no way I was going to explain Will to her.

"Nothing. Just checking to make sure it was you."

I heaved a huge sigh, relieved I didn't have to concoct a lie. *Why didn't she ask, where have you been?* "Yep. Just me."

Julia planted her feet on the smooth pine-board floor and stepped across the narrow space to wrap me in her arms. I buried my face in her clean cotton nightgown and inhaled the fresh smell of sundried laundry and rosewater perfume. Relief flooded through me and tears fell.

Julia cradled me. I thought *I'm losing her in the morning. First, my mama, now my sister. Why didn't she ask where I'd been?* A jumble of questions pelted my mind.

"I'm going to miss you, Honeybee," she said, wrapping me in a tight hug. "Can I sleep with you tonight?"

So, we slept in my narrow bed, locked together in mutual gratitude—me that my secret was safe—Julia that she was escaping Leila and her responsibilities to three siblings.

CHAPTER 8

August 3, 1917
MAIZELLE

The next day, Julia stepped onto the porch shortly after dawn and hugged me extra tight. "Maidee," she whispered against my ear. "Mama would be proud of me for going to school. She wanted the same for you. I know you've been sneaking out to spoon with Will Jones at night."

Stunned, I stiffened in Julia's arms.

She loosened her grip but kept her mouth close to my face. "I wish I'd said something last night, but I didn't have the courage. You were losing so much with me leaving. I didn't think I should pile on more worry."

She pulled me in tight and whispered, "Please don't do anything to disgrace Mama's good name. Remember, Honeybee, I love you, and I'll always love you... no matter what. Papa loves you too. He wants what's best for you, so think about what you're doing. Will Jones isn't right for you. He's too old, and his reputation as a rounder makes me suspect you're a passing fancy. He won't offer you much of a future."

When Julia loosened her grip, she stepped back and locked her gaze on me. "You behave now," she instructed in her big sister voice, "and mind Jamie and Bowen for me."

The horn tooted, and she dashed down the steps and into the passenger seat for the long drive to San Antonio. Her trunk was fastened to the automobile's rear, and the backseat held two boxes of her belongings. Papa argued with her about packing things for which she wouldn't have 'any practical use,' but I think in her heart, she knew she wasn't coming back. In the end, he caved to her pleas, like always.

Excitement mixed with guilt covered her face. Julia wouldn't hurt me for the world, but truth to tell, I was relieved she was leaving and taking my secret with her.

As they pulled away, I stood with my arms stiff by my sides, watching her go. I hesitated before lifting my hand in a half-hearted wave. My face burned. Julia was in on my secret.

Once the car was out of sight, I ran into the house, hoping no one noticed my tear-filled eyes. I fled to my room and banged the door closed.

Lost in misery and despair, I threw myself onto the bed and buried my face in the quilt. How long has she known? If she knows, who else knows? Does Papa suspect? Did Jimmy Calvert tell someone what he saw?

I had to tell Will. I stayed in my room the rest of the day, fantasizing about Will and daydreaming about what had grown between us. The evenings we spent at Spanish Bridge formed an unbreakable bond. I talked to Will in a way I never could to anyone else—even my sister.

All summer, I had poured my heart out, sharing all the sadness and anger I had stuffed since Mama died and Papa married Miss Kittinger. When I talked about my stepmother, I got so angry my whole body shook. Those were times when Will pulled me close and let me cry until I didn't have any tears left.

How could Julia expect me to turn my back on the best friend I ever had? How could she ask me to give Will up? What did she know about love? She'd never had a suitor. I wasn't sure I knew much about love either. I thought Will loved me. I hoped Will loved me. But he hadn't said he loved me. Was my sister right? Was I being played for a fool?

CHAPTER 9

WILL

A few days after Julia left, Maizelle told me what Julia had said. We were tucked out of sight under the old bridge. I was lying on my back with my arms folded behind my head for a pillow and had drifted off when a timid voice pierced my consciousness.

"She knew I was sneaking out. And she knew who I was sneaking out to see. I don't know how long she'd known or how she found out, but she knew."

I snapped awake and sat bolt upright. "Who? Who knew?"

"Julia. She whispered it in my ear before she got in Papa's car and rode off."

"Do you think she told anyone? Like Leila?"

"No. I don't think so. She doesn't like Leila any better than I do, and she never confides in her. She just warned me not to bring disgrace on mama's good name."

"Maidee, sweetheart, I would never do anything to put you in that position."

"I know. It's just that she said you're too old for me, and I'm a passing fancy."

"She's wrong. Would it help to know I love you? Because I do more than I thought it was possible to love another person. I've wanted to say it since that night at the river. I just didn't know if I should, on account of your pa and all."

Maidee flung herself at me. "I love you too!" She searched my eyes. "Every time we kissed, I wanted to believe you loved me, but when you never said it…I worried that Julia was right." Her hands were clasped in her lap, and her knuckles were white. "I lie in bed at night and feel guilty like I shouldn't feel this way."

She raised her eyes with guilt and doubt written all over her face. I felt bad I hadn't told her until now.

Her voice dropped to a whisper, and she wiped her nose. "If Papa knew how I felt, I think he'd kill me…or you…or both of us."

She paused and gazed at me with such intensity I thought she was trying to see into my soul. "I hoped you loved me. But I've been so scared all summer, thinking maybe I was wrong. Remember when I pulled away at Tip Toe? I wanted you to touch me. It felt so good I couldn't think about anything else all the rest of the night."

I drew her into my arms and brushed my lips against her hair. I breathed in the scent of fresh lavender and it tickled my nose. When I inhaled, I knew the smell of this night would be with me for a long time. "Every time we kiss, I fight to keep from touching you. Nothing stops me from wanting to. But you mean too much to me to ruin your life because I couldn't control myself."

She hugged me tighter and pressed her body to mine. "Thank you. At Sunday school, the teacher said girls who are too free with their bodies are not pleasing in the eyes of the Lord. Why'd He give us such powerful feelings if that's true?"

I wasn't sure what to say. I was raised Methodist. My grandpa pastored the church here in Utopia. But I admit I never spent much time seeking permission from God for my behavior. My girl was so trusting, like a child willing to accept whatever they're told. I knew she would believe what I said as gospel. I needed to measure my words.

She squeezed closer, looking hopeful she would find an answer. "I can't say about that, Sugar. It does seem strange the Maker would give us these urges if He didn't intend us to act on them."

"That's how I feel! How does He expect us to wait until we're married when we fall in love and have feelings before it's time?"

"We have to be careful. It wouldn't be smart to let our feelings get out in front of our good sense."

"I know."

She reached for my hand and placed it over her breast. Her upturned face held a longing I wouldn't soon forget. I slid my hand down her body and around her waist, pulling her in. "I want to, but I'm too close to the fire to keep my finger on the flame." I released my grip.

She slumped to the ground and laid her head in my lap. If she felt my swollen manhood, she didn't let on, but her warm breath against it didn't do anything to help the situation.

I stroked her hair, smoothed it back, and examined her profile. Her face was a perfect oval. Her green eyes were deep-set with long thick eyelashes both top and bottom. I'd never looked at her like this. I studied every feature.

Her nose was narrow at the bridge and rounded at the end with a slight upward tilt. She had high cheekbones, but her face still had the rosy plumpness of youth. Her generous mouth tilted up at the corners. The strong widow's peak in her hairline pointed to everything I loved about her face. I couldn't imagine a more beautiful woman.

I considered asking her to marry me right then and there. I was pretty sure she'd say yes. She wouldn't try to resist the urges. *She won't be fifteen for two months. Texas thinks fourteen is too young. I'd have to ask her pa for permission, and he'd have to sign. If I thought he liked me, I'd do it, but I am afraid he'd just give me the boot. Seems like there's nothin' to do but wait.*

CHAPTER 10

July 6, 1917
WILL

The first letter arrived on July sixth, three months to the day after we entered the war. I shouldn't have been surprised. I was the kind of man the Army needed for Wilson's war. It wasn't from the Draft Board I'd read about at the post office. It was from A&M. President Ross urged me to do my patriotic duty in "defense of the State of Texas and the United States of America."

My eyes flew across the page "... *honor your commitment to preserve and protect the Constitution...outstanding performance as a Cadet...qualified to enter... Army as an officer.*"

Officer? I don't want to be an officer. Don't want to be in the Army. Don't want to leave my girl. So, what if Ross is proud of the alums who have joined? Bully for them. I have no intention of going to war. My stomach knotted. My face blanched. I stared at the letter quaking in my hands.

I read, "*...we are counting on you to join the dedicated and trained officers needed to win this war,*" and I crumpled the page into a ball. I smoothed it out and patted it flat. I read it twice before realizing this call to action was not an order. They were *encouraging* me to perform my patriotic duty. No one could make me go—yet.

Once the notion sunk in, I put the letter in the desk drawer and out of my mind. I had a business to run, and my recent encounter with Maidee was still fresh. I told myself this was best forgotten. I wouldn't hesitate to protect Texas and my girl if we were invaded. But fight in Europe? Germany? France? That was a horse of a different color.

August rounded the corner, hotter and meaner than any on record. The main staple of my business was in heavy use, salvaging withering crops from the drought. Things were slow at the garage, and I figured the lull would last until after Labor Day. It was easy for me to forget about A&M's plea.

August is always hot in Texas, but not like this. Stifling air hovered over the sidewalk and shimmered with squiggly colored lines like a shattered rainbow. I walked over to pick up the mail. Heat seared through my boots from the wooden walkway.

Compared to the oppressive temperature outside, it was cool in the post office. I lingered a few minutes in the dim light, reading the Army Wanted Poster again and taking another look at the wartime law about conscription. Henry Demeitz, the postmaster, nodded to me and went to the back. When he returned, he poked a bundle in my direction.

I stepped up and took it.

"How's business?" He always asks the same question.

"Fine." I dismissed him with a nod. I never cared much for the German immigrants settling in our valley. They're hard workers and all, just nosey and standoffish. None of them cotton to machinery to do their farm work, which sure doesn't help me any.

I tucked the bundle under my arm and headed for the garage. It was too hot to thumb through the pile. I tossed the mail on my desk and went to the shop. The cement floor was cool. I took off my shirt and slid under a tractor. The shade and concrete cooled my body enough to concentrate on getting something done.

Near closing time, I took a break and sorted the mail. My arms prickled with goosebumps when I spotted the A&M letterhead. I tore the envelope and wrestled the letter out. The weight of the paper told me the words would be urgent and important. I wouldn't be able to ignore this one.

Dear Esteemed Alumna, W. E. Jones,

I am proud to report that over forty percent of Texas Agricultural and Mechanical College alums now serve in the European Theatre. Men like yourself, who distinguished themselves in the AMC Military Corps of Cadets, have answered the call to protect and defend our country. Their actions honor our college, their families, and the nation.

Our records show you are not enlisted. The defense of the United States of America must be your highest priority. The training you received in the Corps of Cadets entitles you to enter the Military as a commissioned officer.

I urge your immediate enlistment.

Yours Truly, President Lawrence Sullivan Ross,

Brigadier General, US Army, Ret.

This was it. The blood drained from my face. I perspired in the heat but felt clammy. I reread the letter to determine if this was a patriotic entreaty or an official action. I pondered the impressive statistic. Over forty percent of AMC alums now serve in the war effort. I felt guilty for ignoring the first plea. Business debt and a budding romance aren't likely to hold up as excuses to avoid service.

The first plea from President Ross was a secret I hadn't shared with Maidee, but I knew we needed to talk when the second one came. Telling Fred Brown, he'd have to wait until the war ended to be repaid, would be easy compared to telling my girl.

CHAPTER 11

MAIZELLE

I skipped along the pathway to my evening rendezvous with Will. The humid, heavy air pressed on me. Papa's mantra, *men sweat, women glow*, played in my head. My thick mane flopped against my back. The blanket of heat it generated made me think of cutting it off in the fashion of the pictures Julia sent from the city. Times were changing. I didn't want to be left behind.

My sister's long locks were shorn within days of her arrival in San Antonio. Julia enclosed a photo of herself sporting the new look with her first letter home. I studied the picture with envy but stopped considering such a dramatic change in my own appearance because of the way Papa reacted. Besides, Will liked to nuzzle my hair and run his fingers through it. The crazy tingling sensation it gave me was one of the most pleasurable things I'd ever experienced.

When I broke out of the trees, I could see a figure on the bridge rail outlined against the sky. A thin spiral of smoke rose. My heart caught, and my stomach pitched.

Will spotted me and snuffed his cigarette under his boot. He jumped off and ran down the bank. We hugged and slipped out of sight beneath the overhang.

"It sure is hot," I moaned.

Will sat on the grass and pulled me down. "Yep, I reckon it's goin' to be sticky like this for the rest of the month."

"I'm thinking 'bout cutting off this blanket of hair," I said, sliding my eyes his direction.

"Cut your hair off?" His eyes went wide, and he stared with his mouth half open.

"Yes'er. Like Julia did when she got to the city, it's stylish now for ladies to have short hair. You can't imagine how hot and uncomfortable this mop is."

His face softened, and his eyebrows pinched together, "Please don't. I love your hair. I can't picture it short. When I picture you, the first thing I see is your beautiful honey-dipped hair." He glanced to see if his words had the desired effect.

I slipped my arms beneath my mane, gathered and twisted it on top of my head. Trying not to laugh and pretending to be coy, I said, "Well? Don't you think I would be comely with short hair?" I held my arms over my head to appear alluring until the laughter I swallowed burst out.

He grabbed me. "Comely-schlumly, come-thee here is more like it."

I shrieked and dropped my arms, rolling away from him and onto my side. He tickled my ribs. He knew how to get me for sure.

Will slid one arm under me and flung the other over. He pulled me close and buried his face in my locks, growling and huffing like a wild animal until he reached my neck. His lips touched my skin, sending trills up and down my spine and the quickening between my legs. My body stiffened.

Will rolled onto his back.

I waited for the sensations to subside and rolled to my side. I lay my head on his chest but kept a distance between our bodies. Will took a deep breath like he wanted to say something.

"What?" I asked.

"There's something we need to talk about."

I propped on an elbow and took him in. He had a strange look in his eyes, kind of sad and scared. "What?" I asked, afraid he would tell me we had to stop seeing each other.

"I got a letter today. The second one about the same thing."

I bolted upright and stared at him, my emotions roiling.

He rolled his eyes toward me, real serious-like. "You know there's a war, don't you?"

I hesitated, trying to figure out what war had to do with us. "Yeah. I heard about it at school. But Papa won't let us listen to the radio when he's not home—and he isn't home much—so I don't know a lot."

Will sat up and wrapped his arms around his knees. His head dropped forward, and his shoulders slumped. "Well, Sugar, it's a big war. We're fighting Germany in Europe. A&M trains men to fight wars to protect Texas and the country. I was an officer in the Corps of Cadets. General Ross has written two letters asking me to enlist."

"Would it mean you have to go back to Brazos County?"

Will stared at me real hard, his jaw twitched, and the cords in his neck stood out. He saw I didn't understand, and his face softened. He said, rather forcefully, "It would mean they'd send me to fight on foreign soil."

My eyes popped open. I held my breath. I had no idea what to say. "I tried to figure a way to keep this from happening, but I don't think I can avoid the call."

I let out my breath and said, "What would happen to your business?"

"I guess I'd close up shop and reopen when the war ends. If I live through it."

It took a moment to sink in. My forehead creased in a worried frown. "You mean you might die?"

"Well, Sugar, that's the result of war. Lots of men die. I hope I wouldn't be one of the unlucky ones, but you never know."

I crumpled. My body trembled. I couldn't stop the tears. The thought of losing Will was unbearable.

He held me in his arms as if he could squeeze me into accepting this awful news.

I pushed away and jumped to my feet.

Will scrambled to stand and reached for me.

I twisted away. "No. I won't let you go! What'll I do if you leave me? First Julia, and now you? I'll die. I'll kill myself if you leave me too."

CHAPTER 12

WILL

Maidee's unexpected outburst threw me. I thought she might be sad I would be gone—maybe shed a tear or two. I didn't realize she'd be so upset. I soothed her, but the storm intensified until she was exhausted and fell against me. She kept saying, "You can't leave me. You can't leave me," and I knew I couldn't. I let her cry until only dry heaves were left.

I pushed her back so I could look her in the eyes. She refused to meet my gaze. "There is one thing I haven't told you."

Her eyes drifted up and met mine with a silent question. *It couldn't get worse, could it?*

"If I register for the draft, I might not get called right away. I've heard they're giving deferments to married men and men with children."

Her voice was flat. "But you aren't married."

"But I could be if someone I loved very much agreed to marry me."

A flicker of comprehension flashed across her face.

I said, "Would you consider such a proposal?"

She gave me a fixed stare, and her mouth hung agape. She snapped it shut and said, "Are you suggesting we get *married*?"

"I guess I am."

Her frown dissolved. Her eyes glowed, and a broad smile swept over cherry-red cheeks. Two arms flew around my neck. "Yes! Yes, yes!" She jumped and wrapped her legs around me, hanging like a joey possum.

My eyes filled. I knew she loved me, and for my part, couldn't imagine any future without her. It wasn't the proposal I practiced over and over, for the past month, but her instant acceptance and enthusiasm pushed any doubts out of my mind.

CHAPTER 13

WILL

I could plead with the Draft Board for a deferment. There were two things to do in short order—the honorable thing, a visit to Doctor Clarke to ask for Maizelle's hand—and writing to my sister to share the news. August twenty-fourth, nineteen-seventeen, a date I wouldn't soon forget, I did the honorable thing. I closed the garage early and put up a sign saying I would be back on Monday. The farmers and ranchers never brought equipment in for repair after noon on Friday, and with only sixteen automobiles in the county, I wouldn't be missed. I took extra time to scrub my hands and nails to make the signs of my profession less obvious. I locked the door and walked home.

"Emma, what would it take to persuade you to iron my linen shirt for me?"

"Why do you need your nice shirt?"

I couldn't keep it inside and burst loose with a full confession. "I proposed to Maidee. I'm going to ask Doc Clarke for her hand."

Emma squealed, clapped, and jumped up and down 'til the whole house shook. I was afraid she'd shake the baby she was carrying right out onto the floor. She bubbled with enthusiasm and said, "That's swell! Does Bobby know?"

"I promised not to tell anyone until we got her pa's permission. I shouldn't have told you. I couldn't keep it inside."

Emma beamed. "It would be my pleasure to iron your shirt. You will look very much a gentleman. Dr. Clarke will be impressed."

My hand was trembling when she handed me the freshly ironed shirt.

"Don't be nervous, Will. I'm sure Doctor Clarke will be happy to see his daughter married and settled with a good husband, same as my daddy."

I put on the cream-colored shirt and a pair of linen trousers the color of seasoned straw. My sister Eula chose the outfit for my graduation from Texas A&M. I'd never had another occasion to wear it.

When I emerged from the bedroom, Emma said, "Come here, Will," and she combed my hair back from my face in the latest style. She took a step back and appraised me. "You cut a handsome figure in those fancy duds."

I was going for serious and respectable as I approached the Clarke residence. The sun sat low in the western sky. My confidence drained with every bead of sweat that ran off my forehead. My stomach churned like a tub of butter. I stepped onto the porch and knocked.

It seemed like I stood there for a month of Sundays until Dr. Clarke answered. I stuck out my hand and said, "Will Jones, Doctor Clarke."

"I know who you are," he said, and not in an unfriendly way. He shook my hand and invited me in.

"Are you ailing?" he asked, his brow puzzled.

"No. Nothing like that," I said. "I'd like to talk to you about a personal matter."

"Oh. Well, in that case, let's sit in the parlor." He motioned me into the room off the foyer.

I stood, hot and uncomfortable. Sweat dripped off my chin. My shirt was damp, and stains formed on the knees of my trousers where my legs met the fabric. Drops of sweat crept down my back. I would have bolted for the door if Doctor Clarke hadn't stationed himself between me and the opening. My head throbbed, and my ears rang.

He said, "Please, have a seat."

The voice sounded distant. I hunted around for someplace to land and sat on the soft cushion of an overstuffed chair. Sinking in, I felt small compared to the doctor.

He loomed over me with his jaw set and his face tensed.

I spoke at the exact moment he offered me a glass of tea. After the word "Sir," I abandoned my speech and accepted his offer. It gave me a few seconds to collect my thoughts before I plunged off the cliff.

Doc Clarke disappeared into the entry hall, and I heard him say, "Prepare tea for our guest."

He returned and sat across the room from me in a small straight-backed chair, which made him appear taller. He looked down at me, sunk into the overstuffed chair, and said, "What did you want to discuss, Mr. Jones?"

My mouth went dry. I pushed against the chair's arms and struggled to my feet. "Sir, Doctor Clarke, sir," I stammered. "It's about your daughter, Maizelle. I have asked Maizelle to be my wife, and I'd be honored if you would give us your blessing."

Dr. Clarke stiffened, then propelled himself to his feet. The veins in his neck bulged, and his face flushed. He shouted, "Your *wife*! Maizelle isn't going to be anybody's *wife*. My daughter isn't fifteen years old. She's still in school. She's not marrying some *mechanic*! I *forbid* this. If you so much as speak to her again, I'll send her away." Spittle foamed at the corners of his mouth, and he stepped up to my face. "Do. You. Understand me. Mr. Jones?"

I stared at him with my mouth open. I was tongue-tied. He looked as though he wanted to strangle me. I needed to get out of there, but I couldn't make my legs work any better than my tongue.

Leila arrived in the doorway with our tea. Her bulk filled most of the opening.

The interruption was a perfect opportunity to escape. I lifted myself out of the chair to leave before I realized I would have to squeeze past her.

The doctor cleared my path for me. "Leila, take the drinks away. Mr. Jones is leaving." The venom in his voice sent chills down my spine.

Leila glared at me and stomped back the way she came.

I bolted for the front door, hoping to escape before the doctor took a fire poker to my head.

As I entered the vestibule, Maizelle appeared on the stairs. I froze and stared up at her. I was sure she'd heard her father's angry voice and come to see what the ruckus was about.

I hadn't spoken a word since Dr. Clarke's outburst. I felt a lump in my throat when I saw her. I loved this beautiful girl wholeheartedly, and it occurred to me that this might be the last time I ever set eyes on her. I held her gaze and shook my head to answer the question in her eyes.

Doctor Clarke exploded into the hall behind me. He bellowed at Maizelle, "Go to your room. If you try to see this man again, I will disown you. Your dead mother would turn in her grave if I let you throw yourself away on this sorry excuse for a man. Go." His hands waved with the fervor of a man caught in a swarm of bees. He nearly clobbered Leila when she returned from the kitchen.

Maizelle's eyes flashed with anger and fear. Tears pooled like lamp oil, ready to spill. She gave her father a defiant glare, her jaw clenched and her head back. Her eyes sought mine, and she said, "I love you, Will Jones," as straight and pure as anything I'd ever heard. "If you wait for me, I'll be yours."

Doc Clarke grabbed my shirt sleeve and propelled me out the door. The shirtsleeve gave way, and I was a tattered and failed suitor by the time he shoved me off the porch.

I wish it had ended there. I glanced back in time to see Leila slap Maidee across the face. She cried out before the door slammed shut.

I jumped onto the porch, but the door was locked against me. It was all I could do to make myself walk out the gate and go home.

CHAPTER 14

WILL

The walk home took forever. Overcome by heat and turbulent emotions, I staggered the mile up the steep incline with my head down. I was drenched with sweat, and my trousers had turned gold around the cuffs where the clay dust clung. My shoes pinched, and my feet burned like hot pokers with every step. The torn sleeve hanging from my shoulder gave me the appearance of a man who had wrestled with a bear. I kept my head tucked into my chest and my eyes downcast, so I jumped when I saw another pair of boots coming down the hill.

I glanced up into my cousin Jimmy's eyes, dancing side to side like a frenzied firefly.

His eyes held a light pink cast. His ghost-like face was so pale he appeared like a dead man walking. Cotton-white hair poked out from under an oversized floppy-brimmed hat, and his face contorted in anger.

I'd dreaded running into him ever since the night he stumbled on Maidee and me at the bridge. I sure as hell didn't need it today. "S'cuse me," I said as I tried to go around him.

Jimmy stood his ground and refused to let me pass. He grimaced at me and gurgled something.

I ignored him and dodged left. Each time I moved he blocked my way. I tried to skirt around, but Jimmy glommed onto my torn shirtsleeve.

"Let go!" I shouted and grabbed his wrist to free the sleeve.

He refused, but something he babbled penetrated my brain fog. "K'l oo, k'l oo," he kept repeating. "H'rt M'zl. h'rt M'zl."

My eyes burned, and my temper flared. I shoved the simpleton with my right hand and stuck my left shoe behind his ankle.

Jimmy's knees buckled, and he crashed to the ground, still holding my sleeve. It tore loose, leaving the cuff still buttoned around my wrist.

I jerked my arm, and the button popped. My arm came free, and the thrust dumped Jimmy backward onto the barbed wire fence. I stared at him, flailing like an upside-down turtle, and fled.

I had to get home, where my broken heart and humiliation would not be displayed. I saw Jimmy wrestling with the barbs tangled in his clothes. His hat was caught on a fence post, exposing his mop of snow-white hair.

Angry as I was, I knew Ma would have my hide if I left him exposed to the heat of the day. I ran back, grabbed him by one arm, and pulled him to his feet. Most of his shirt stayed with the fence. I bolted up the hill.

I pushed the front door open and saw Emma in her rocking chair, red-eyed and wiping her nose. Disheveled and spent, I wanted to escape to my room and a bottle of whiskey, but I couldn't run out on her in this condition.

"What's wrong? Is the baby coming?"

"No. It's something bad, though." And she went to cryin' again.

I knelt next to her. Her chin wobbled, and I could tell she'd had a terrible fright. "What happened?"

Emma wiped her eyes with the corner of her apron and said, "Jimmy came by. He does sometimes, you know. I give him a sweet roll and some tea, and I listen to what he's trying to say."

She looked sheepish like I might disapprove. "Today, he kept saying you hurt Maizelle. I couldn't make sense of his gibberish, so I told him to write on his slate. He wrote WLL HRT MZEL. He said, 'bridge, bridge.' Oh, Will. I'm sorry!"

"Why?"

"I blurted it out without thinking."

"What did you blurt out?"

"I said, 'Jimmy, you have it all wrong. Will loves Maizelle. They're going to be married. He would never hurt her.'"

There was fear in her eyes. "You should have seen his face. He got so angry I thought he was going to strike me!"

"Strike you? Did he raise his hand to you?"

"No," she said, shaking her head as tears fell onto her pregnant belly. "He shook both his fists like he was choking someone. He said he was going to kill you, and he ran out. I don't know where he went or what he will do."

Now I knew why Jimmy was so twisted up when I ran into him. I patted her on the shoulder and said, "Don't worry, I saw him running down the hill, and he seemed fine."

She raised her eyes as if she doubted me, but it stopped her tears.

I wondered whether the fool *would* try to kill me. In my present state of mind, it didn't seem like a bad idea. I said, "Jimmy won't try to kill me. He knows better. I'm sorry he got you upset. You should rest. Do you want me to make you some tea?"

Emma snuffled. "Thanks. I don't need anything. I'm just glad to see you alive."

I fled to my room, thinking I should have left him on the barbs.

The long walk and the run-in with Jimmy exhausted me. My feet and eyes burned. I couldn't get the image of Leila slapping Maidee out of my mind. I took a bottle of whiskey out of my dresser drawer and put it to my lips, gulping the dark liquid like water. It worked in short order. I flopped on the bed and fell into a drunken sleep.

When Emma opened my door and placed a food tray on the bureau, I awoke with a start. I had no idea what time it was or how long I'd been out.

"You okay, Will? Was the news from Doctor Clarke not good?

I nodded, swung my feet off the narrow bed and raised my eyes. "I'm fine." My voice sounded raspy and hollow.

"If you want to talk…" she trailed off when she saw my set jaw.

"No."

"I'm sorry. I only meant to help."

"What time is it?" I asked as she closed the door.

She pushed it open a crack and said, "What time is it? More like, what day is it? You've been in a drunken stupor for goin' on two days." She shut the door. The disgust in her voice hung in the air like a foul odor.

I lifted my bottle off the floor and drained it. It burned. As I insulted it with the last drop, my stomach growled and churned in protest.

On shaky legs, I took the tray and set it on the desk. I noticed a half-written letter to the Browns and wondered when I'd had the presence of mind to write. I attempted to eat but gave up after two bites. I blew my nose and wiped fresh tears off my cheeks.

The constant diet of whiskey wasn't helping. I knew I needed to get the story off my chest, or I might never function again. I took an unsteady step, gripped the back of the chair, and plopped down at the desk. I arranged a stack of paper, uncorked my ink bottle, and settled down to finish my letter to Eula and Fred.

Dear Sis and Fred,

I had hoped this letter would be better news. Sad to say, it didn't work out that way…

…and that's the long and short of it, folks. I asked my girl to marry me, and she said 'Yes.' Her pa refused me, and now I feel deflated and defeated.

I was planning to bring her to San Antonio to meet you, but I'm enclosing this month's payment on the loan instead.

I trust you are well. If the Army doesn't grab me, or I don't drink myself to death, I will come for a visit as soon as I have my feet under me.

   As always, your grateful brother,

      Will

I put down my pen, plugged the ink well, stretched out on the bed, and closed my eyes.

Writing to Eula and Fred was both cathartic and draining. My hand cramped. My eyelids were heavy and scratchy with the remnants of dried tears. I brushed grit from the corners and let my eyes drift shut.

Bobby came in from morning chores, and I heard muted voices as he and Emma discussed what to do about the 'situation'—meaning me.

CHAPTER 15

August 31, 1917
WILL

It's funny how a broken heart feels so much like a physical injury. I'd never been in love, so it was a new experience. I wasn't sure if the pain in my chest was heartburn from the whiskey or an actual break in my heart. When Monday rolled around, I hauled myself out of bed, dressed, and slipped out of the house before Bobby and Emma were up.

Every day that week, I followed the same schedule. I'm not sure why I didn't want to be seen or see anyone, but I had work to do, and I knew it was better to get back to my old routines than stay drunk. Mornings were cooler, and walking to work got my juices flowing.

On Friday, as the sun crept above the horizon, I rolled open the garage bay and pulled on my coveralls like every day. Working was always the best way for me to forget when I didn't have any way to fight back against my pa, and I figured it would work just as well to get over this.

I vaguely recall hearing the town come to life, but I was deep in thought and up to my elbows in grease when I heard a shuffling sound. I rolled out from under the tractor I was greasing and saw Maizelle's friend, Katty O'Brien, standing in the garage bay.

Katherine, as Maidee calls her, is a plain girl, the kind you'd hardly notice if you didn't have a reason. She's two years younger than Maidee and entirely devoted to her. I could see from the determined look in her eyes that she was on a mission.

She gripped a white envelope, and when I looked up, she thrust it toward me. I stood and wiped my hands on my coveralls.

"Hello, Miss Katty," I said, hope clogging my throat. "What brings you to this dirty place so early in the morning? Your tractor need repairin'?"

Katherine said nothing. Not even a smile at my joke.

"Is that for me?"

She nodded and stabbed the air with the envelope.

I took it. "What's this?" My gut churned like an unbroke horse in a small corral.

Katty shrugged her shoulders and shuffled her feet. Before I could open it, she squeaked, "Should I wait?"

The envelope was unmarked, and I had no idea what was inside. I said, "I don't know, Miss Katty. Do you think you should wait?"

She shrugged and shifted her weight from one foot to the other. Then she lifted her eyes and whispered, "Maidee said wait… and see if there was an answer…but I can't wait very long."

When I heard 'Maidee,' I knew the answer. I blurted the first thing that popped into my mind. "Miss Katty, what do you say you let me treat you to a soda for your trouble?"

Her face softened. "Well, Mr. Will, I s'pose I can make time for a soda," she said, staring at her dirty bare feet.

"Why don't you run on up to the pharmacy and get us a couple of stools while I wash my hands and get out of my dirty coveralls? I'll be there quick as a wink. Order me strawberry," I called after her as she turned and fled up the alley.

I didn't want her here when I opened the envelope. I wiped my hands as clean as possible and ripped the flap open. I scanned the note. The words made my heart race even faster than holding Maizelle the first time I kissed her.

Dearest Will,

Papa plans to take me to a girls' school in San Antonio next weekend.

I won't go. I still want to be your wife if you will have me. I'm leaving this house for good tonight. We can elope. It'll be around midnight. I will meet you at the garage if you still want me.

Papa has been called up to the Divide to attend a birthing and probably won't be home before sun-up.

Send a reply with Katherine. One word will do. Please make that word YES.

Yours Always,

MC

My heart hammered and I could barely swallow. I shouted, 'yahoo!' grabbed a matchbook and carpenter's pencil off the bench and scrawled YES in big letters on the inside flap. I thought my head might spin clean off as I struggled to pull my coveralls down.

I stuffed the matchbook into my shirt pocket and ran out. I strode with giant steps up the alley to Upton's Pharmacy. My mind raced. What if Katty doesn't wait for me? What if I scared her and she changed her mind? How will I get the answer to Maidee?

I burst through the door and scanned the fountain. Katty was perched on a stool like she didn't have a care in the world. I sat down and spun to face her. "Did you order?"

Katty nodded just as two strawberry sodas were plunked down in front of us.

Aunt Elizabeth looked disapprovingly at me but held her tongue. I suppose she thought I had no business buying a soda for a twelve-year-old girl. I know she questioned my judgment buying sodas for Maidee Clarke and had mentioned to Bobby that she was "awfully young."

Bobby watched us with unfettered curiosity from the pharmacist's window. I didn't want Bobby, or Aunt Elizabeth, to see me give the matchbook to Katty, so I waited until Bobby engaged a customer and Elizabeth left the fountain to wait on someone.

I put the matchbook under my hand and slid it across the counter to Katty.

She opened her hand, and I put mine on top of it. I placed the matchbook in her palm and squeezed her hand closed.

I leaned over and whispered, "This is for Maidee. Please don't let anyone see it; whatever you do, don't lose it."

Katty stared at me as if she expected more.

I took two quick gulps of the soda and stood. "Sorry to run out on you, Katherine," I said, "but I have work to finish before tonight."

I left a two-bit piece for the sodas and turned to go. "Don't forget what I said." I looked her hard in the eyes.

She blinked and stared at me with a slight nod. Her response didn't inspire much confidence that she could carry out the mission, but I couldn't think of another option.

I gave Bobby a nod and a smile when I passed his window. He raised his eyebrows and gave me a puzzled look.

With one hand on the doorknob, I turned to him and said, "Later." Looking through the plate glass window as I hurried past, I saw Katherine tuck a tightly closed fist into her pinafore pocket.

As I returned to the garage, my emotions rose and fell with each step. I was afraid to believe Maidee would follow through and equally afraid she would get cold feet. The day stretched before me in an endless dream. I could see the image of Maizelle floating in the distance but couldn't quite reach her. Concentrating on work was out of the question.

Hope and despair filled the hours with constant ups and downs. I needed a plan on the off chance she did follow through. I hung the **CLOSED** sign on the front door, locked the rear bay, and taped up a note that said, "Closed for Emergency. Open Monday, 9/3."

I gathered a few things I thought I might need and walked to the First National Bank of Utopia, where I withdrew a hundred dollars. It was all the money I had saved since opening the garage and had earmarked to repay the loan from Fred and Eula. If they tried to cash the check I mailed with my woeful letter, the bank wouldn't make good on it.

The loan repayment would have to wait. Being with Maizelle was the only thing on my mind. I didn't know where we would go or how else to pay for it. Eloping was one thing; having a home to live in when we returned was quite another. I couldn't expect Bobby and Emma to let us live there. I wanted Maizelle to have her own place. I needed to show Doctor Clarke that I could support a wife and provide her with a good life.

There was a new spring in my step when I left the bank and started the walk home. As I passed the pharmacy, I tipped my hat, lifted my hand in a quick wave, and winked at Bobby.

CHAPTER 16

Friday, August 31, 1917
WILL

Emma couldn't contain her excitement when she met Bobby at the door. I could tell from his face he knew something was up. I stood behind her, feeling nervous and guilty.

Bobby kissed Emma and said, "Okay, you two, what's going on?"

Emma's cheeks glowed. She was bursting to spill the news. "Will and Maizelle are eloping tonight! If you'll loan them your automobile. Please, Bobby, you've seen how heartbroken Will has been. You can't say no."

"Well, now, that's a bit of a problem..." he said, real serious like.

Emma's face fell. "Why?" she cried, "we won't need that big 'ol car this weekend. This baby isn't comin' for another month!"

Bobby looked from Emma to me. I had a stupid grin plastered from one ear to the other. "Elope? Are you sure? I just saw Will having a soda with Katty O'Brien, not eight hours ago."

My smile wilted like lettuce in July.

He looked past Emma to me. "Waay-ell," he drawled, "ah might be persuaded for a price."

"I can pay. How much do you want?"

Bobby knit his brows together. When he looked at me again, he broke into a wide grin.

"Aw, shucks, Will. Take 'er. I'm just pullin' yer leg."

My body melted with relief.

"So, what's the plan?" Bobby asked.

"We'll drive to San Antonio tonight. We can make it to Eula and Fred's by sun-up. I know they'll help us. I wrote to them about Maidee. Eula's anxious to meet her. We'll ask them to witness. As soon as the courthouse opens on Monday, we'll get the license, ask the Justice of the Peace to marry us, and head straight back."

"Whoa, Bucko, not so fast. What about Maizelle's reputation? People will talk if you're leaving tonight and won't be married until Monday."

"I'll protect her name. Fred and Eula have a big house. We can stay with them over the weekend. I would never do anything to bring her shame."

Bobby laughed. "Ha! Remember, I know you better than you know yourself."

The flurry of activity we launched must have looked like a colony of gophers preparing for winter. Emma packed food, and Bobby and I prepped the car to make sure it had plenty of petrol and oil and was in proper shape for the journey.

I filled six jugs with water to take in case the car overheated, counted, and recounted my money to be sure I had enough to pay for the marriage license and whatever expenses might crop up.

Emma pressed my clothes and shined my shoes, and Bobby helped me find my birth certificate.

"Do you think Maidee will bring hers?" Bobby asked.

"Of course, she will," Emma said.

"I'm not so sure about that," I put in. "I've been stewing about it all day."

"What if she forgets?" Bobby asked. "What will you do?"

"Don't be so pessimistic," Emma said, "She had a week to get her plan together, and my guess is she has everything packed."

"If she forgets to bring proof of age, we'll abandon our plan and return to Utopia...or not go at all."

"Is she a flutter brain like most girls?" Bobby looked at Emma when he said it and got the expected reaction.

"Like most girls?" Emma pouted, "You think I'm a flutter brain?"

"Of course not," Bobby soothed. "I'd never be fool enough to marry an addle-brained girl."

"Maidee's not scatterbrained," I defended. "She's very practical and sure of herself."

"If she's anything like Julia," Emma said, "she's serious-minded. I know she'll remember."

"Well, there's nothing I can do but wait until tonight and ask her. If she doesn't bring proof, the whole thing is off, and it's all for nothing." My shoulders slumped.

"Oh, pushaa." Emma scoffed.

Her confidence in Maidee lifted my spirits.

At eleven o'clock, I pulled the big car out of the yard and headed toward town. The businesses were dark. I wanted to get to the garage early enough not to miss her but not so early someone might notice I was there and interrupt our plan. I rolled along the quiet street and eased the big car into a spot in the dark shadow of the garage. Inside I lit a small lantern and put it near the front door.

All I could do was wait. Maybe her pa came home earlier than expected. Maybe Maidee changed her mind. Maybe Katherine never gave her the matchbook.

CHAPTER 17

Midnight, August 31, 1917
MAIZELLE

I pressed my hands hard against the stubborn window frame and inched the window open. My shoulders ached after each push. I stopped and listened for any sign Leila had heard.

Silence.

I gave one last heave, and the old wood frame scudded against the sash, reverberating through the still house like a yodel off the red walls of Sabinal Canyon. I froze. *Leila must have heard that.* I listened for footsteps.

Silence.

I stepped away from the window and noticed my heart beating so fast it lifted the thin cotton voile of my dress. I grabbed my pillow and jerked it out of the case. I draped the empty pillowcase over the sill so I wouldn't soil—or worse yet, tear—my dress. My hands trembled as I stuffed the bundle of my belongings out the window and squeezed myself into the opening. Flattened face down on the dirty sill, with one leg outside and the other still in the bedroom, I strained my ears once more.

Silence.

I slipped through and dropped to the ground. A poof of red dust settled on my bare feet. I stumbled, caught my balance, scooped up the bundle, and stretched out in a dead run.

Free.

No sign of Leila. I needed to sprint as far and as fast as I could before someone discovered me missing.

Lucky for me, a full moon lit my way. I raced past the clapboard houses that lined our street, their gas lanterns dark. The O'Brien's dog barked once as I shot toward the south edge of Utopia's business district, where I could see a faint glow from Will's Central Garage.

He'll be there, waiting for me.

WILL

My nerves were as tight as a twisted rubber band. I paced around the back of the garage. Each time I circled near the partly open door, I glanced out.

Nothing.

My mind raced with doubt.

What have I gotten us into?"

I picked a socket wrench off the shop floor and tossed it onto my workbench.

Maybe she won't come.

I went into my small front office, cupped my hands around my eyes, and pressed them against the grimy window. I squinted to see if anyone moved along the street from Maidee's direction.

Maybe Leila caught her.

The explosive scene that had erupted in the Clarke parlor a week ago played in my mind. Dr. Clarke's angry words rang in my ears.

Maybe she changed her mind.

I snatched a chair from the office, carried it to the garage bay, and placed it near the open door. I clenched my jaw so hard my teeth ached. I took deep breaths to slow my heartbeat.

I sat.

I stood.

I paced like a caged animal.

My fingers shook so hard when I tried to roll another smoke I dropped the tobacco onto the floor. I kicked at it and stubbed my toe.

"Shit, shit, shit," I spouted as I danced around on one foot.

I didn't need the smoke anyway. I'd been rolling and lighting one cigarette after another for the past hour. As I waited, I couldn't decide if fear or hope was uppermost in my mind.

What if we get caught? What will her father do to me—or worse yet, to her?"

MAIZELLE

Once I was safely out of earshot and sight of the house, I stopped at a vacant lot and plunked down on a large rock to catch my breath and let my heart still.

Hunched over my knees, I pulled a cotton hanky from my bundle and wiped the dust off my feet. The sweet smell of new leather wafted through the night air as I took out the unworn shoes Papa gave me on my fourteenth birthday. The brown kidskin was delicate and soft.

I caressed the silky-smooth leather as an old rhyme entered my mind...*something new.*

I removed a pair of white cotton hosiery and blue garters from my bundle, resting them in my lap. I unlaced the high-top shoes and slipped a stocking on. I smoothed it over my knee, extended my foot, and threaded the pale blue garter... *something borrowed, something blue.*

Julia would be mighty surprised when she came home to find her good stockings and garters missing from her cedar chest. Good thing I had a big sister who had planned for a wedding.

I rolled the garter into place and slid a shoe on one foot and then the other. The leather felt strange on my rough, calloused feet. I mostly go barefoot during the warm Texas summers. Now that I'm almost fifteen, I'll need to start wearing shoes all the time. I admired my newly shod feet, remembering Papa's voice saying *a lady always wears shoes* when he gave them to me.

Thoughts of Papa made my throat constrict. I swallowed, and a tear slid off my cheek onto the soft kidskin, spreading into a dark spot. I jerked my head up and swiped at my eyes with the back of my hand.

The lump in my throat receded, but my hands trembled as I laced the shoes. A haphazard bow appeared as I hurried to thread the laces through the eye at the top and tied them. Doubt and anticipation roiled through my body in alternating waves. The thought of Bowen waking to find me gone made my chest tight and my stomach churn.

I'm lucky to have a little brother like Bowen. I think he'll forgive me. I hope Papa will.

My new shoes glistened in the moonlight, and I stared at them. I wiggled my toes to see how it felt and squinted through the dark in both directions. I didn't see any movement along the street, so I moved at a fast clip.

I liked the feel of my dress. The soft cornflower-blue cotton flowed around my body like water over smooth rock. It was Mama's dress. I'd never worn it. Papa gave it to me when Leila told him I showed signs of womanhood. I'm not sure why I saved it, only that it was for a special occasion...*something old...*

The rhyme was complete. I slipped along the hard-packed dirt, imagining the feel of Will's arms. Thinking of him gave me a slight shudder.

He's so handsome.

I stifled a giggle remembering Katherine saying, "He has such big ears it looks like he's goin' to fly!"

I gulped back the nervous laughter and came to a complete stop as a more sobering thought occurred.

What if he's not there?

I no more had that terrible thought than I heard a car coming up the main road.

Papa!

Panicked, I ran behind a large live oak tree in Reinhold's front yard. Their dog yapped at me. "Shush, Porky," I whispered into the dark. He stopped when he recognized my voice.

I glanced around the tree toward the main road and watched Papa's car swing wide onto our street. The headlamps swept across the tree and lighted the street I had just come along. The car continued toward our house.

He didn't see me!

I bolted from my cover and ran to Will's garage like the devil was on my tail.

CHAPTER 18

WILL

"Will?"

The soft gasp startled me. I whirled to face the door at the back of the garage. There she stood, a sliver of blue against the moonlit sky. My heart nearly stopped. I had never seen anyone so beautiful. The outline of her figure showed through the silky dress fluttering in the breeze.

She carried a small bundle in her right hand and wore lace-up shoes. I'd never seen her in proper shoes, only at church, and then they were practical shoes with buckles. And I'd never seen her in a dress like this either. She looked fragile, radiant, and womanly all at once.

"Will," she gasped again, and I could tell she was out of breath.

"What's wrong?"

"Papa," she said.

"Is he chasing you?" I thought she was about to faint. I reached for her and pulled her into the safety of the shop.

"No, but he's home. I saw his car make the turn from Central onto our street. We need to leave right now." The urgency in her voice left no room for argument.

"Maidee," I croaked. My mouth had gone dry. I was so full of emotion I couldn't speak. I hurried to the door and closed it.

We stood looking at each other like it was our first time.

I swallowed and whispered, "Are you sure you want to do this?"

She nodded.

I pulled her close and felt her shudder. I stroked her hair.

It always reminded me of seasoned honey. The color wasn't brown, and it wasn't blond; it was more the color of dark amber, shot through with veins of gold.

"Can we go right now?"

"Sure. The car's ready and waiting."

Maidee let me guide her outside to the dark side of the garage where the big Packard was parked. I opened the door, and she slid onto the passenger seat. She looked like royalty in Bobby's blue-black Model '38 Imperial Coupe.

"I'll just be a second. I need to kill the lantern and lock up." I ran to close the door and looked both ways on the empty street. If Doc Clarke was searching, this would be the first place he'd come. I slipped into the shadows and climbed behind the wheel.

The electric start engine caught the spark on the first try. I reversed out of the protective shadow of the building and glanced at the young beauty in the seat beside me, thanking the heavens above for my good fortune. I did not turn on the headlamps.

"If we hurry, we should be able to make San Antonio before sunup. Did you remember to bring your birth certificate? We need to prove you're fourteen to get a marriage license, and I didn't have any way to get the message to you."

She tilted her head and looked askance. "Did you honestly think I'd forget something like that? I've been planning this since you walked off our front porch. I couldn't bring much, but I did bring my birth certificate. Will? What will we do if we can't get a judge to marry us without Papa's consent?"

I reached across the seat and tugged at Maidee's sleeve to pull her close. "I guess we'll have to drive to Arkansas." I put the car in gear, and we rolled off the lot under cover of darkness onto the dusty red clay road to San Antonio. "I didn't think you'd forget, and Emma didn't think you'd forget, but Bobby sure did."

Maidee ducked low in the seat when we approached her street. I could tell from how her eyes shifted that she wanted to take one last look to see if her pa was on the hunt for her yet but thought better of the idea. "I know Leila's going to get hers in the morning for letting me escape."

It was a voice I'd never heard her use before. Full of anger, disappointment, and determination.

"Leila deserves anything she gets."

"I saw her slap you. I came to the door to help, but your pa had locked it against me."

"I know. There wasn't anything you could do. Papa didn't say one single thing to her. If I stayed, it would have just gotten worse. Do you know she laughed at me and said I was 'childish and stupid' for saying I would wait for you? Then she ordered me straight to my room. Papa just stood there and stared, like I was someone he didn't know."

"It sounds like you're trying to convince yourself we're doing the right thing."

Maidee snuggled against my shoulder. When she looked up at me, I knew she was sure. We headed toward San Antonio.

Maidee leaned forward and peered through the Isinglass. "Look," she said, sounding like a little kid seeing them for the first time, "there are billions of stars twinkling and laughing and telling us to follow them." She scooted closer.

I slipped my arm around her, and she rested her head against my chest. We weren't a mile out of Utopia before she fell asleep.

CHAPTER 19

WILL

The car hit a rut and swerved right. The sudden movement propelled Maizelle off my lap and jostled her awake.

She blinked and stretched, looking around, confused about where she was.

Early morning sun crept above the horizon. The sky turned eerie shades of pale gray and orange. Years of use by wagons, buggies, and, more recently, automobiles left the road potholed and rough. The car bounced and joggled along as though it had a mind of its own. I needed both hands and arms to steer. My right leg fell asleep with the weight of Maizelle. It tingled, and I took one hand off the steering wheel to rub it.

When Maidee saw what I was doing, she scooted up next to me and massaged my thigh with her dainty hands. I felt the caress in my groin in a way I hadn't let myself in all these months of our growing love. Her hand was so light on my leg I could barely feel it, but my body knew the touch as pure pleasure. My arm went around her shoulders to draw her close when a jackrabbit scurried out of the ditch and hopped in front of us. I hit the brakes and swerved onto the road's soft shoulder, spraying gravel and dust in an explosive cloud.

Maidee shrieked, covered her eyes, and was tossed like a rag doll onto the floorboards.

I grappled with the steering wheel to get control and wasn't sure I would win the battle. "Sugar!" I bellowed, wrestling the Packard back to the roadway. It was as close as I had ever come to cursing in front of Maizelle.

The car bounced to a rolling stop at the side of the road. I wrapped my arms over the steering wheel and dropped my forehead to the rim. My head shot up when I remembered I wasn't alone. Sometime during that wild ride, Maidee had disappeared.

A tremulous voice said, "Will, are you all right?"

I reared back and reached toward the passenger side. Tears stung my eyes as I searched for her under the dash. She curled on the floor like a kitten. I pulled her back onto the seat and smoothed her hair. I traced the outline of her face with my fingertips for any injury.

"Are you hurt?" I asked, half afraid to hear the answer because I thought she might not be truthful for fear I'd take her back home.

Maidee shook her head and returned my gaze. Something passed between us in that moment. I drew her close and kissed her with the pent-up passion that had burned inside me all summer.

She returned my fervor with an abandon I had wondered if I would ever feel. She'd been so careful to keep space between us and to move my hands if I got too friendly. There was nowhere for her to go this time, no watchful father or hateful stepmother to fear. She clung to me with the reckless abandon of someone with nothing to lose.

I hoped she would always come to me like this. By suggesting we elope, she had chosen me over everyone and everything else in her life. I knew she would give herself to me if I opened this door. I pulled back from her lips and buried my face in her hair.

There was no question about what I felt; I wanted and needed her. She waited for me to take her. The thought *not yet, not like this*, flew through my mind. *It shouldn't be this way, in a car by the side of the road.*

My dream was to carry her across the threshold of our house. She would rest her head against my chest and smile with that delicious mouth that invited my desire. This delicate creature meant more to me than life itself. I could hear her heartbeat, and her body trembled as I held her. She felt so slight in my arms that I feared I might crush her. I'd never held her quite like this.

She pressed close to let me know there would be no space between us again. Her eyes had a deep longing, and I knew she offered me a gift most men only imagine—whatever I wanted, whenever I wanted it. My hands shook, and my fingers were all thumbs as I fumbled with the long row of tiny buttons on her dress.

Not now. Not like this. The unrelenting message repeated itself in my over-excited brain until I stopped and eased her away from my body.

Her eyes quizzed me, but I shook my head and turned toward the car door.

I stepped into the cool night air and reached into my pocket. To settle my mind and body, I spread a row of rich tobacco on a thin tissue inhaling the pungent aroma. Rolling the paper around the tobacco, I held it to my mouth and licked the edge. The cigarette dangled from my lip as I cupped my hands around a match and lit it. Leaning against the car's rear door, I inhaled a long pull of the smoke.

Maidee sat in stunned silence. The shame on her face made me want to weep. Her cheeks flamed, she hung her head with downcast eyes, and the corners of her mouth curled like she was about to cry.

I watched her re-do the few buttons and loops I had managed to loosen. She straightened herself and pushed up against the passenger door, as far from the driver's seat as possible. Her expression, every movement she made, said she was embarrassed by my rejection of her willing offer. Tears crept down her cheeks despite her effort to gulp them back.

She didn't even sneak a glance at me when I opened the door and reached behind the seat for a jar of the lemonade Emma had packed. I climbed into the car and cleared my throat.

"Maidee? It can't be like this. I love you too much to make love to you before it's right. I couldn't live with myself if I caused you any more humiliation and speculation than our elopement will bring."

She turned her face away, but I saw teardrops hitting her dress.

I reached for the gear lever with my left hand and gripped the steering wheel with my right. As my fist closed on the steering knob, a small soft hand closed over it. I turned and met her eyes. Tears left tracks as they rolled down her dusty face. She had a defiant set to her chin but forgiving eyes. Her lips parted, and she whispered, "I love you."

She no longer looked like a young girl to me. She was a fully-grown woman ready to satisfy our mutual desire. I put the car in gear and bumped back onto the roadway.

Once we were rolling again, I took Maidee's hand. I tugged, and she slid across the seat to my side. I slipped my arm around her shoulders and pulled her close. "I love you too," I whispered.

She hiccupped, and I knew she was crying. My shirt felt damp where her face rested.

"It wouldn't have been fair to you in a car. I want you to remember it with pleasure for the rest of your life. Monday, after we're married, in a real bed, in a real house, in a room with a door we can shut behind us." I moved my arm and shifted her more upright while I fished in my back pocket for a handkerchief so she could wipe her nose and tears.

We bounced along the road in silence. Maizelle squeezed and dabbed at her nose, and I wondered if she would ever come to me again after the way I rejected her.

The sun peeked over the eastern horizon behind us as a city emerged in the distance like a mirage. "We're almost there," I said, breaking the long sad silence. "Shall I keep going, or do you want me to take you home? This is your last chance."

Maidee's head whipped around, and her fierce, defiant eyes caught mine. "Keep going," she said, with a determination that left no doubt.

I smiled, and her eyes lit up. She returned my smile, and I thought I might melt. Her face held a sunny countenance, and when our eyes met, I knew she forgave me.

CHAPTER 20

WILL

The outline of the growing city spread before us on the horizon. Early morning shadows crept up the sides of buildings like cat burglars. The macadamed road was smooth under the wheels—a welcome relief from the rutted, bumpy ride we had been on. Maidee pressed closer to me as if the sight of the city frightened her.

I reached down and pressed my hand against her thigh, letting my fingers slide a little way down between her legs. The flesh beneath my hand quivered.

Maidee's face colored, and she placed her hand over mine to hold it in place.

"Shall we go straight to Eula's?" I asked.

"I don't know," she answered, "do you think she'll be happy for us?"

"I hope so. I wrote to her a month ago and told her I was bringing someone special to meet her. I want her to come to our wedding. We'll need somebody to witness for us, and she and Fred are the only ones I feel comfortable asking."

Maidee's forehead wrinkled. "Okay," she said in a hushed tone. "Whatever you think."

Feeling confident and happy, I guided the car through a city that was coming awake. There were more cars on the road, and the sounds of morning rattled in. Tubs of garbage were dragged onto porches. Wastewater was tossed from upstairs windows. Roosters crowed from backyards. Dogs barked raucous warnings as we motored past. Now and then, an *au-oo-ga* horn warned of an approaching vehicle. Stately wood-frame homes, mixed with low square adobe and stone structures, lined the streets.

The car twisted and turned as we wound our way into the neighborhood where my sister and Fred lived. I knew right where it was since I helped them move in. They were a second set of parents to me, in some ways better than my own. For one thing, they were younger and more fun. I had confidence they would accept Maidee and trust that what we were doing was right. I hoped my letter telling them Maidee's pa had declined my offer of marriage hadn't reached them. That might stretch Eula's good nature if she knew.

I pulled the Packard to the curb next to a large white house with a white picket fence and yellow and lavender gingerbread trim. The blooming pansies and lavender-tinted Texas Blue Bells that lined the front walk matched the trim colors perfectly.

Maizelle let out a little "ooh!" when she saw the house. Utopia didn't have anything like it. The struggling farmers of Uvalde County had no time and no money for frivolities. There were a couple of two-story farmhouses, to be sure, but they were utilitarian in form and function, including her father's house. Maidee giggled.

"What's so funny?" I asked, feeling a little defensive.

"Nothing," she said, still giggling. "It's pretty. I was thinking how funny our house would look with yellow and lavender goo gahs all over it."

"Goo-gahs? What's a goo-gah?"

"You know, those little pieces of painted wood they have stuck all over, up by the roof and around the porch and all."

I shook my head, thinking how sheltered she'd been. "Shall we go wake them up?"

Maidee nodded. She let the smile slide off her face and replaced it with a frown.

I walked around the car and opened her door with a grand flourish and a bow.

Maizelle put her feet together and swung them over the door jamb onto the running board. She reached her hand out.

I held it as she stepped to the ground. If anyone was watching, they'd have seen a woman emerge. My chest swelled with pride.

We each took a deep breath and turned toward the house. I offered my arm. She slid her hand through the crook in my elbow and gave me a little squeeze. We paused for a moment, taking it all in, then walked briskly to the front porch.

CHAPTER 21

WILL

Fred and Eula were still in bed when I rapped on their front door. Heavy footfalls hit the floor, and I imagined my brother-in-law, with his short, pudgy legs, bound out of bed in his long johns and standing as though waiting for further instructions to reach his groggy brain. I pounded again.

I pictured Eula clutching her throat and thinking, *who on earth could be knocking at this hour?* I leaned against the door and listened.

"Who stands there?" Fred barked in his most authoritative voice. At five-feet-five-inches tall, he is a round and jolly fellow who wouldn't put a fright into a small child.

I laughed when I heard his attempt to be gruff and protective. "It's Will."

Fred yanked the door open. "Well, I'll be! Come in. Come in. Eula, you'll never guess who has come to trouble you for a hot meal this fine morning," he yelled toward the bed chamber.

She did know because she told us over breakfast my voice had 'wafted through her head like a welcome breeze,' and she'd 'have recognized it anywhere.' My sister raced to the entry hall, saying, "There is no one on earth I would rather disturb my morning than my baby brother." She flew toward me with her nightcap still on and plunged into my arms.

When I released my grip, she stepped back and saw Maidee. "Well, I declare! And who do we have here? Would this be the surprise you wrote about?"

I reached for Maidee's hand and drew her to my side. "Eula and Fred, this here is Maizelle Clarke, my fiancée."

Fred and Eula smiled with curiosity at the woman pressed against me. Eula's eyes roamed up and down Maidee's frame like she was sizing her up for a livestock auction. I half expected her to ask to see Maidee's teeth.

She caught herself and stepped forward with outstretched arms. She clasped Maidee's hands, tugging her away from my protective grip. With a welcoming smile, she pulled my girl toward her. "My dear, how lovely you are. Let's go into the parlor and get acquainted."

She kept Maizelle's hand clasped tightly and stepped through the doorway.

Maidee's face held a desperate plea to be rescued.

Eula walked her into the parlor and guided her to the settee. She dropped Maidee's hand, took her shoulders, and twisted her around before she eased her onto the cushion. The last thing I heard her say before she reached back and pushed the door shut was, "Now, tell me all about yourself."

MAIZELLE

I swallowed. I felt empty in the pit of my stomach. My eyes darted around the room filled with fancy furniture. "There isn't much to tell," I croaked, looking at my white-knuckled fists.

"Oh, honey, we all have a story. I'm sure yours is ever' bit as interesting as anyone else's." Eula smiled and patted me on the knee. Her warmth and genuine interest were hard to resist.

I was working over in my mind what to say when Eula sprang from her chair, scaring me half out of my wits.

"Oh, my," she said, "I'm still in my nightclothes! Please excuse me while I get dressed. I got so caught up in meeting you I forgot my manners. And we have two hungry men in the kitchen waiting for us to put food on the table. Your story can wait. Will you help me? I'll be back quick as a wink."

I nodded, grateful for the opportunity to catch my breath and spend a few minutes alone. Eula closed the door to the parlor. I leaned back against the soft cushion of the oversized chair and closed my eyes. I was almost asleep when the door sprung open again. Startled, I jumped to my feet and blurted, "What would you like me to do?"

We went to the kitchen where Will and Fred were on their third cups of coffee, no doubt wondering if they were ever going to get fed.

I had never cooked a meal for Will. I rarely ever cooked anything. It wasn't in Leila's nature to teach me about cooking, and I avoided the kitchen to stay out of her way. Faced with the reality that I was about to become the matron of my own home, it dawned on me how woefully unprepared I was.

This well-organized kitchen was a wonder. I realized I needed to learn what to buy, how to prepare it, and how to serve it. The weekend turned into a crash course in cooking as we waited for the courthouse to open.

CHAPTER 22

MAIZELLE

Eula moved around with ease getting breakfast on the table as I watched. She took for granted that I knew my way around and asked me to slice the bread, set the table, peel the potatoes, and slice the bacon. The last request presented a problem, as I was not adept at using a carving knife and sliced the bacon too thick and the wrong way of the grain.

When Eula saw what I'd done, she skillfully modified the chunks and offered me a suggestion for peeling potatoes toward the body rather than away. She did it in such a way that I never felt criticized and was only a little embarrassed.

I did know how to set the table, however, and got the knife and spoon on the right and the fork on the left with the napkin. Between us, we managed to put on a real spread. I watched and asked questions, and Eula guided me without ever letting on that she knew I was as lost as a six-year-old.

The four of us sat down to a breakfast of poached eggs, bread fresh from the oven with homemade peach preserves, short, fat pieces of crisp bacon, fried potatoes, and hominy grits.

Eula praised me as if every dish was of my making. "Well, Will, I can see you won't be in danger of starving with this young woman in your kitchen."

My face warmed, and I murmured a polite thank you, knowing full well I had little to do with the meal.

The breakfast conversation was filled with laughter, gentle teasing, and a deepening camaraderie with Will's sister and her husband. I rose from my chair, cleared the dishes, and set a kettle of water on the wood stove.

Eula joined me, and I tried without success to shoo her away. We worked side by side to put things right, laughing and visiting as easily as any two sisters.

"I'll bet my bonnet you're tired to your core, aren't you?" Eula's understanding and sympathy were music to my ears.

"Yes, I am, and I'll bet *my* bonnet Will is, too."

"Then let's get you two tucked into clean beds for a few hours." She pulled Will away from chatty Fred and guided us upstairs and down the hall to separate bedrooms.

WILL

I waited five minutes until I thought Maidee would be out like a light and then tiptoed downstairs to have a private talk with Fred and Eula. They had closed the kitchen door and sat at the table discussing the situation that had dropped into their laps.

When I reached the bottom of the stairs, I heard them, and my curiosity got the best of me. I lingered and eavesdropped.

Fred said, "are you aware these kids aren't going to be able to get a marriage license without her papa's permission?"

"Oh my, does Will know?" Eula sounded shocked.

"Ah'm sure he does."

"Whatever does he plan to do? That poor girl can't go back home after running off."

"Will asked if we'd be willing to vouch for her and witness their wedding."

"We're not her parents. How can we possibly help?"

"Ah'm not sure, but we need to try. We'll go with them first thing Monday and plead their case. If they get turned away, we won't have any choice but to send them home and let her face her daddy."

"Oh, Fred," Eula moaned, "that girl will be devastated if this ends badly."

"Ah know, Eula, and so does Will. He understands her reputation is at stake. He's willing to do almost anything to protect her, including lying about her age."

"What good would that do without proof?"

"Ah guess we'll be finding out soon enough."

I decided against interrupting and tiptoed up the stairs to get some rest.

CHAPTER 23

MAIZELLE

Monday morning dawned with the hope and promise of a bright future. Dressed in the same clothes we had arrived in, we piled into the roomy Packard to go to the courthouse. We were surprised when we found a place to park right in front. We approached the imposing structure and climbed a long flight of white marble stairs.

When we got to the top, Will reached for the handle on the wide double doors and yanked. The doors stayed firmly shut. He pulled again and then tried the other side before he realized the building was locked. He hunted around for some sign or notice that explained why.

Fred slapped his forehead and exclaimed, "It's Labor Day! I completely forgot. I don't know what I was thinking. Well, I guess I wasn't thinking. That's what happened."

Confused, Will and I stared at each other. Labor Day was not a celebration people in Utopia spent much time on, and the two of us forgot there was a holiday in the middle of our escape plan. My eyes went from Will to Fred to Eula. Her brow was furrowed, and her eyes filled with questions. I was near tears.

Eula took my hand. "Oh dear, this sure puts a monkey wrench in things, doesn't it?"

I couldn't hide my disappointment. I dissolved in tears.

"We'll figure something out," Will said, taking my other hand. "I told Bobby I'd have his car back by nightfall, so I guess we'd better head on back to Utopia."

"No! I can't go home. Everyone will think we sneaked off for a weekend of hanky-panky, and if we aren't married when we come back, how will we ever explain? Papa will lock me up. I'll never get away again. We have to get married *before* we go back." I gulped back tears.

"You could telephone Bobby, Will. He has a phone at the pharmacy, doesn't he?" Fred said.

"Yes, he does. But the pharmacy won't be open today because of the holiday. I can't believe I was so stupid as to forget everything would be closed."

"It's my fault," I broke in, talking through tears. "If I hadn't suggested we elope, none of this would have happened."

My face was screwed up like a dried prune trying not to cry. My chin wobbled, and my voice quivered.

Will put his arms around me and pulled me close. "It's not your fault, Sugar. I should have been thinking for both of us. I got so caught up in the excitement of marrying you I put everything else out of my mind."

"Let's go back to the house and talk this through," Eula said.

Fred nodded and started for the car.

Will guided me down the stairway, and we headed back to the Browns in silence.

WILL

Maizelle pressed herself against the door in the seat next to me. I could see she was crying, but since she wasn't making any sound, I decided it would be better not to say anything. Once we were inside the house, we gathered around the table with fresh cups of coffee. A pall hung over the room, and no one knew where to begin.

I drained my coffee cup. "I think we should drive to Uvalde and sleep in the car overnight. We can get our marriage license there as soon as the courthouse opens tomorrow. I'll call Bobby and let him know. We'll get married and be back in Utopia before noon."

Fred cleared his throat. "There may be a little matter of the three-day waiting period. Not to mention the fact that Maizelle is fourteen and requires parental permission."

His statement landed on us like he had announced the end of the world. Big tears welled in Maidee's eyes, and her chin trembled. I stared open-mouthed.

"What three-day waiting period?" My voice croaked. "Did you know about this before we went to the courthouse?"

"Yes. I figured you knew. I guess I thought you'd get the license and get married in three days."

"Fred!" Eula exclaimed. "You knew they were planning to get married today. What would possess you to hold back something as important as this?"

"Well, they could have been planning to stay on here for a few days. I guess I didn't think about it."

Maidee's tears spilled over, and her voice caught. "I thought fourteen was the legal age in Texas. I can't get permission. Papa will never agree." Her eyes implored me. "He already told you no. He isn't going to change his mind. What will we do?"

I was shaken and confused by the notion of a waiting period—I didn't know how to resolve the mess we were in. I don't easily panic, but anxiety welled in my chest.

Eula and Fred were in a stare-down over his withholding of information, however unintentional it might have been.

"This is a fine pickle," I said.

Fred, on the hot seat, broke the stare-down with Eula. "There is one way out of this as I see it. Y'all aren't going to like it much, but what is, is."

We all turned and stared at him.

"There's a clause in the law that says if the woman is under the age of fifteen but has proof of age at fourteen, and has been in a conjugal relationship, or is pregnant, the waiting period and age requirement can both be waived by the county clerk."

The complications of this bombshell struck us like a cannonball.

"What's con-jug-al?" Maidee asked. Three sets of eyes shifted her direction.

I couldn't help smiling. "Well, Sugar, that would be the thing we've been tryin' to avoid all summer. It would be lettin' our feelin's get in front of our good sense."

"Oh!" She looked from one amused face to another. "Oh."

"Fred, are y'all suggesting these two get friendly before they go off to get married?" Eula asked, and I caught the twinkle in her eye.

"Well," Fred dragged the word out, "that could be a solution to the trouble they find themselves in."

Maidee lowered her eyes, and her face turned scarlet as she fidgeted with the handle of her cup. We all fixed our eyes on her.

Fred took a sip of cold coffee and cleared his throat. "Maizelle, Eula and I would like to leave you and Will here this morning and go to town for the parade. If we need to write anything for the clerk in Uvalde, Will can let us know when we get back. Would that be okay with y'all?"

Maidee's long hair fell over her shoulders and hid her face. When she nodded, the motion was barely perceptible.

Fred and Eula stood. Fred put on his Stetson Fedora, and Eula pulled on her white gloves. They glanced at me for affirmation.

I was confused, embarrassed, and very unsure about what would come next.

Together they said, "Good-bye, we'll see y'all shortly," with false cheer.

I moved to where Maizelle sat with her eyes glued to the tabletop. I put my arms around her shoulders and gently tugged her upright. She appeared to be in a trance. "Maidee," I said, "I need to know how you feel about what just happened."

She turned on me with a vengeance. "Feel? How am I *supposed* to feel? You're the one who wanted to wait until we're married. If you'd left it up to me, we wouldn't have to embarrass ourselves in their house."

"You're right. I thought I was protecting you. I didn't want it to be hurried and uncomfortable for you by not being in a proper bed."

"Do you think we should do it?" Her eyes searched mine.

"I don't know. If it's the only way we can get out of the fix we're in, I guess we ought to consider it."

Maidee jumped to her feet and gave me an "I dare you" stare.

I guided her to the stairs with one arm around her waist and the other holding her arm. We climbed in unison, and I lifted her with each step. She pulled away from me, squared her shoulders, and ran up the remaining stairs.

When she reached the bedroom where I slept, she stopped and looked back at me.

I rushed to open the door and led her to the chair.

She sat, dropped her chin, and bit her lip.

I tilted her face to see her eyes. "You don't have to do this, you know. We could tell Eula and Fred we need an affidavit from them without ever doing anything. No one would ever know."

From the apprehension on her face, I could tell she was still thinking about my earlier rejection.

I was about to say something when she stood and said with a sureness I couldn't argue against, "No. I want to do it. I don't care what anyone thinks of me. I want to be your wife." Then she wrapped her arms around my neck and kissed me with a passion I couldn't hope to match.

My heart lurched, and I flushed hot when I realized I was about to become a married man without the benefit of the State of Texas.

Maidee lowered her arms and gave me what could only be described as a seductive smile. She unbuttoned the long row of tiny buttons on her dress with a look that said, "you're not going to stop me again." Her long delicate fingers made faster work of it than my big fumbling ones.

I swallowed hard to cover the discomfort rising in my trousers and turned my back. I removed the cuff links and bow tie I'd borrowed from Fred, opened my shirt, and unbuttoned my fly.

Two hours later, Eula and Fred returned. They rang the doorbell as a courtesy and waited for me to answer. I opened the door, sporting a sheepish grin, and I knew they could tell the plan had been executed. They didn't say anything, and neither did I.

Maizelle hid in the bedroom. When I came for her, she sat fully clothed on the edge of the neatly made bed. I took her hand and eased her to her feet. She met me with questioning eyes.

"What?" I asked.

"What's going to happen now?"

"Well, let's see. I think we'll have some lunch and then hit the road. How does that sound?"

"I doubt I could eat anything, but you should fill your stomach before we head out."

I laughed, pulled her to me, and lifted her off the floor in a bear hug.

She hugged me back and whispered, "I love you so much."

"I love you too, Mrs. Jones—well, almost Mrs. Jones."

"Oh, Will, I hope nothing else goes wrong. It feels so right to be your wife. I'm not sorry it happened. You said, 'in a real house, in a real bed, with a door that closes behind us,' and that's what we got. I'll always cherish the memory."

It amused me that she sounded so comfortable and grown-up.

"It didn't hurt too much?"

"No, only a little pinch, and then it was over. I couldn't imagine what it would feel like," she lowered her eyes and her voice, "but now I can't wait for the next time." She hugged me and nuzzled my chest.

"We better make an appearance downstairs, or Fred is liable to come lookin' for us."

Maidee let out a joyful laugh that brought a smile to my lips. I took her hand and led her downstairs.

Eula and Fred waited for us at the bottom, looking quite satisfied. "Well, what do we have here?" Fred joshed. "The newly minted Mrs. William E. Jones, I presume?"

Maidee blushed and stared at her feet. Her hair fell forward and covered her flushed cheeks.

I reached over and tilted her chin so she was forced to make eye contact. "Sis, Fred, I'd like to introduce my wife."

Eula sounded a little uncomfortable when she spilled the news that Fred had prepared an affidavit for us to take to the clerk in Uvalde County. She said he found someone from his firm to notarize it by promising the guy a bottle of hooch to come downtown on a holiday. I could tell she was nervous by the way she chattered.

"It vouches for your claim you shared the marriage bed. I hope it works. If it doesn't work, you might have to bring this young lady back here to hide out until she turns fifteen!"

"It's only two weeks," Maidee said, to everyone's surprise.

"Only two weeks? Why didn't you just wait two weeks to run off?" Fred asked.

"Because Papa wasn't going to let me go back to school in Utopia. I would have ended up in what he calls a 'proper girls' school' here in San Antonio. Besides, the Army wants Will, and if we're married, he might not have to go."

It was my turn to be embarrassed. An awkward silence settled. This was the first they had heard the war might have played a part in this decision.

They exchanged glances, and then Eula said, "Well, what do you say we fix some lunch."

My voice caught. "That's not the reason we got married...I mean, we're getting married. We love each other. If they conscript me, of course, I'll go."

"Of course," Fred said, and that was the end of it. He handed me an envelope with the affidavit. I tucked it into my breast pocket. We all enjoyed a bowl of Eula's famous corn chowder with fresh bread. We thanked my sister and her husband for all their help and advice, packed our belongings into the car, and headed for Uvalde County.

CHAPTER 24

Monday, September 3, 1917
WILL

The trip to the courthouse in Uvalde was different from the Utopia to San Antonio trip. This time, Maidee snuggled against me with one hand slipped between my thighs as if she'd been doing it all her life. That over-full feeling in my throat was gone when we talked, and Maidee's body relaxed against me. Our wedding would be a formality to allow us to go home again.

"What will happen when you register with the conscription office?"

"I'm guessin' they'll take my information and put it in line with the rest waiting to be called. They probably have a separate list for married and another if you have kids. When my name comes to the top, they'll send me a letter or telegram ordering me to report."

"So, if we were to have a baby, it would make your chances of staying home better?"

I glanced over at her. "Yes'm…I s'pose it would." I drew the words out while I tried to figure out why she asked. I reached over and squeezed her knee. "Are you thinkin' you want to have a baby right away?"

"Not really. I'm just asking. Because, you know, if it happens, it happens. I was just wondering."

"You wouldn't be plottin' to keep me close, would you?"

"Umm, maybe, a little bit." She squeezed my thigh.

"You better be careful," I said, half-serious, "I'm havin' enough trouble keeping this car on the road without you torturin' me to boot."

"Okay, have it your way," she pouted, removing her hand.

I slipped my hand between her legs. "I'll have it any way I can get it, and you're liable to get it sooner than you think if you keep that up!"

She batted at my hand, her pout fighting a smile. My heart swelled, knowing she was mine. The easy banter might have continued to the county seat if I hadn't mentioned my run-in with Jimmy.

"Maidee? There's something I need to tell you before we get home."

"What?"

"I didn't say anything because I didn't want to worry you."

Her eyes widened, and her brow furrowed with curiosity as she waited for me to spit it out. "Jimmy threatened to kill me."

Maidee laughed, but her smile faded when she saw I meant it, and her eyebrows knitted. "He didn't. Why would he threaten to kill *you*?"

"I think he's been nursing some resentment since he caught us under the bridge. He stopped to see Emma the same day I went to see your pa."

"Emma? Why would he go see her?"

"He's Bobby's cousin, too. Emma says he comes by once in a while, and she gives him a sweet and lets him ramble. She's kind-hearted, so she listens. Not many folks around here do. My ma is another one he visits for the same reason. She understands him."

"But why would he threaten to kill *you*? Did he tell Emma that? Maybe she misunderstood. It's awful hard to know what he's saying." Panic rose in her voice.

"He told her I had hurt you on the bridge, and she told him we were getting married. He went off his rocker and made threats. She was real shook up."

"But he didn't say he was going to *kill* you, did he?"

"I ran into him on the hill above the cemetery. He tried to stop me, and we got into a scrap. I was angry and upset over my visit to your pa's. Jimmy grabbed me and babbled, 'k'll 'oo, k'll 'oo. H'rt M'zl, h'rt M'zl... or something like that."

Maidee stared in disbelief. I could see her rapid heartbeat through her dress. "Why didn't you tell me? I could have talked to him. If he thought you hurt me, it would upset him."

"No, Sugar, it's more than that. He was worked up like I've never seen."

"What did you do?"

"Nothing. I shoved him. He fell into the fence and got tangled in the barbed wire."

Maidee's face and voice changed from panic and fear to sympathy and anguish in a single heartbeat.

"Oh, Will. You didn't leave him caught in the fence in the hot sun?"

"No. I pulled him off the barbs. I don't know if he was hurt or not."

"People are so mean to him, Will. I don't think he'd hurt anyone."

"Sugar, you're much too tenderhearted where Jimmy is concerned. You remind me of my ma. She always thinks the best of him and figures ever'body else is at fault for his bad behavior."

"But Will," Maidee pleaded, "you know he's simple. He's like a little boy inside his head."

"I don't think so. He threatened to kill me. Emma thought he was going to hit her. I worried she would have the baby right then and there."

"Jimmy'd never hurt anyone." Maidee sounded like she was trying to convince herself.

"I didn't want to tell you. I knew you'd be upset, but I thought I should let you know so you can steer clear of him. I don't believe he would try to kill me, but we should stay out of his way."

I knew she was thinking about the incident by the way she smoothed her dress over her legs, fidgeted with her buttons, and picked at her fingernails.

We rode in silence for the next hour, and when we approached Uvalde County, I reached over and tickled her.

She squirmed. "Don't!" But she couldn't keep a smile from her face.

I knew I had my girl back. We arrived at sunset to a sky lit up like a circus tent, with huge thunderheads rolling across the horizon. We made a game out of the drive picking out aerialists, animal shapes, clowns, cotton candy—even a Calliope in the clouds.

A small park along the Frio River outside town served as our first home. We made a bed in the backseat of the car, our bodies curled together like the treble clef of a music score.

I ran my hands over Maidee's slender form and pressed against her.

"Will," she said, "I think we should wait until we're officially married, don't you?"

Controlling myself was next to impossible, but I honored her wishes and soon realized she was sound asleep.

As dawn broke, I watched the sun filter through the car's rear window touching Maidee's cheek. The warmth woke her, and she stirred. I'd been awake for about an hour when I felt her shift position and asked, "Are you ready to get up?"

Maidee yawned, stretched, and slipped from her tenuous perch on the seat. I pulled her close and kissed the back of her head. She shifted and tried to turn toward me but slid off and landed on the big picnic basket Emma had packed.

I sat up and ran my fingers through my hair, which flopped over my left eye.

"I've never seen you in the morning before you combed your hair," she giggled as she crawled back onto the seat next to me. "You look like you just took a roll in the hay!"

"I wish," I chuckled as I shifted her out of the way. "I need a smoke." I opened the car door and slithered out.

"And I need a bush!" She scooted out the door and struck out into the woods.

"You better get your fancy shoes on before you go crawlin' around in there with the critters," I called after her, stepping behind the car to relieve myself. I watched her hair glinting in the sun as she zigzagged among the trees.

Once I'd had my smoke and she was ready to face the day, we straightened up our wedding clothes to appear decent for the ceremony.

I walked to the river, dipped my hands into the water, and ran wet fingers through my hair to smooth it back.

Maidee brushed and brushed at her tangles and produced a blue ribbon for me to tie around her gathered locks.

When we were as ready as we would ever be, we took turns checking each other's efforts. There were giggles, and a few snide remarks, before either of us received approval. It was six-thirty, and the courthouse wouldn't open until eight.

Maidee's stomach growled. I reached over and tickled her. "Hungry, are you?"

"Stop it! Yes, I'm hungry. I didn't eat lunch before we left Eula's like you did."

The food Emma packed for us was now entering its fourth day on the road and wasn't very appealing. Maidee set everything out on the checkered cloth, and we each took a piece of stale bread, spread it with honey, and washed it down with warm lemonade.

"I promise to make you a better breakfast when we get home," she said, with her optimistic brightness.

"Ha! And how are you going to do that? We don't have a home *or* a kitchen. We need to figure out where we'll live before you can fix a meal for me."

She slumped. "Oh, I forgot we left a few things out of our plan."

"And what plan would that be? The part where we settle down as husband and wife?"

"Where *are* we going to live?"

"Well, as it happens, I think my parents are moving to Del Rio. Their house was big enough for the two of them and ten young 'uns, so I figure it should be big enough for us until I can build somethin'."

"Isn't it awful far from town? How will you get to work?"

"It's a three-mile walk each way, but I can do it. I figure it'll motivate me to save for a car."

"Is anyone living there now?"

"Sure. Ma and Pa are still there, and the three youngest kids."

"Would they be staying or moving with your folks?"

"The brats? They'll go when Ma and Pa do. Ma's tired, and the arthritis is gettin' her down. Pa's anxious to settle in a smaller place now that he's through with ranching. He told us boys we could carve up the homestead and build our own houses. I didn't think I would be takin' him up on that offer, but now things are lookin' a little different out my window."

"What do you think they'll say about you bringing me home?"

"I've been givin' that some thought. I suppose Pa will hand me a hard time over you bein' young and all, but I'm thinkin' Ma will be happy for extra help around the house."

"Is that where we'll go tonight?"

"No, tonight we should stay in my room at Bobby and Emma's. They were in on our plan, and we have to take the car back. I'll talk to my folks tomorrow. We need to figure out how to tell your pa, too. That'll be a little harder."

"I don't want to think about it. I just want us to get married and *then* tell him so he can't do anything to stop us."

"I don't like how we're doin' this. Getting around the law and all. But I couldn't come up with another way."

"I'm not sorry. I married you yesterday, and that's that," she said with a defiant set of her jaw and a flash of rebellion in her eyes.

"We need to find a phone and call Bobby before we do anything else. I told him we'd be back last night, and he's prob'ly worried sick over his car." I chuckled, thinking about it. "I doubt he's given two thoughts to what happened to *us*. But his *car*, now, that's different!"

We drove up the dirt road from the river onto the highway into Uvalde. I rolled the tires along the street until I came to the pharmacy. I stopped to see if I could use their phone. The woman at the counter asked if she could help, and I explained I needed to call Upton's in Utopia. I said, "Could I pay to use your phone?"

She looked me up and down. "I'll have to ask my husband. Did you mean Upton's Pharmacy in Utopia?"

"Yes, Ma'am," I said, polite as could be. "I live with the Upton's. The name's Will Jones. I'm Robert's nephew."

The woman went into the back and returned with a bespeckled, balding man. "You the one wanting to use the telephone?" He asked in a stern voice.

"Yes."

"So, is this a personal call? Not business?"

"Yes, but Bobby doesn't have a phone at his house, and the only way for me to get a message to him is at the pharmacy. I'd be happy to pay."

"Okay. Two bits will get you a three-minute call."

I thanked him and pulled change from my pants pocket as he opened the pass-through into the work area where the phone hung on the wall.

He promptly returned to mixing ingredients for the prescriptions hanging from clothespins on a string in front of him.

I thought, *great. A three-minute call, but no privacy.*

I lifted the receiver, and the operator said, "Number, please."

"This will be long distance to Upton's Pharmacy in Utopia. The number is four."

"Four," the operator repeated.

"Yes and make it to Bobby Upton."

I heard the operator connect the wires on her switchboard and wait for the phone to ring. When a woman answered, she said, "A call for Bobby Upton, please."

"Bobby's not here yet," the woman on the other end said. "May I ask who's calling?"

"One moment, please. Sir, would you like to give your name?"

"Ask if it's Elizabeth."

"Is this Elizabeth?" the operator asked as if the party on the other end of the line couldn't hear the conversation.

"Yes, it is," Elizabeth said.

"Yes, it is, sir," the operator repeated.

"Yes, I'll talk to her," I said.

"Thank you. I will connect you now. Please go ahead, sir."

"Aunt Elizabeth?" I rushed to get my message out before my time expired. "This is Will. If Bobby's not at work, it's because I borrowed his car Friday, thinking I could have it back last night. I've been delayed and won't be back until after noon today. Can you tell him I'm sorry?"

"Time's up," the bald pharmacist said. "That'll be another two bits."

I searched my pockets for another quarter and plunked it down in front of the stern little man.

"Will, do you have Maizelle Clarke with you?" Elizabeth's somber tone spoke volumes about what we would face when we got home.

I had dreaded this question but felt sure Maidee's father had alerted everyone in town that his daughter was missing.

"Yes. We're married. She is now Mrs. Will Jones. I'm sorry about the car, but we had trouble."

"I doubt if the trouble you had will come close to the trouble y'all will be in when you get back. Her papa is on the warpath... not to mention sick with worry."

"We'll be back by noon if everything goes as planned. Let Bobby know." I hung up before my aunt could say anything, thanked the dour man standing next to me, and left the store.

I bumped into Maidee when I stepped outside and knocked her off balance. She caught my sleeve and said, "Did they let you use the phone?"

I was startled by her voice. "Yeah, for four bits. Bobby wasn't there, but I gave Elizabeth a message. She asked if you were with me."

"She did? What'd you say?"

I don't think she'd counted on this. I could see the wheels spinning, and her eyes darted side to side in fear.

"If Elizabeth knows I'm missing, so does everyone else in town, which means Papa has made an all-out search. What if Kathrine told him where I went? Papa would have looked for me there. Or he might have gone to Elizabeth. Did she say anything else?"

"No. I told the truth. Well, part of the truth. I said you were with me and that we're married. She might have tried to stop us if she knew we weren't married yet."

"Let's get to the courthouse before Papa shows up with a gun!" The frantic look in her eyes said she thought it was a real possibility.

"Right. Let's get a move on."

CHAPTER 25

WILL

I nosed the car into an angled parking place in front of the imposing three-story, granite and stone building in the center of town. Lights were beginning to come on in a few of the windows. Hand in hand, we walked up the long flight of marble steps to the double-door entry. With a grand flourish, I opened the door and stepped aside for Maidee to enter.

She was a vision in her mother's cornflower blue dress. But then, Maidee would have been a vision in a gunnysack.

We scanned the directory and found the county clerk's office on the second floor. I guided her up the sweeping stairway. Holding hands, we climbed to the second floor. I had such a tight grip I half-lifted her up the steps, and muscles and tendons bulged in my rigid arms.

She gave me a curious look. "Are you angry?"

"Angry? No, why would I be angry? I'm happy to be marrying you. Just nervous."

"Okay. I thought you must be angry because you were clenching your teeth. I feel sick to my stomach."

"It's butterflies. Don't upchuck in the clerk's office. Wait 'til we get the license!" A shaky smile tickled her cheeks.

We reached the second-floor landing and faced an opaque glass double door with gold letters. One side read Uvalde County Clerk, the other, Marriage Licenses. Without letting go of her hand, I opened the one marked Marriage Licenses and pulled her inside.

A long, chest-high counter divided the small lobby area from the employee work area. A tall woman in a tailored suit, her hair in a neat bun, came to the counter. "May I assist you?" She eyed us with tightly pinched lips and a scowl. Her stony gaze met mine, eyeball to eyeball. Then she stared at Maizelle like she was a cockroach.

"We need a marriage license," I said.

The woman glared. "I need to see identification that shows proof of age for the young lady, and there is a three-day waiting period in Texas."

I reached into my pocket, pulled out the affidavit from Fred and Eula, and handed it over.

She appraised me disapprovingly, opened the envelope, and removed the paper. Her eyes scanned the page, and her lips pinched even tighter. When she finished, she folded the paper, put it in the envelope, and returned it to me.

"Is there a problem?" I asked.

"No. No problem," she said in a clipped tone. "What identification do you have, and what proof this child is fourteen?"

The frost in her voice chilled the room. Clerks and secretaries at the desks behind her stopped working and stared.

Maidee squeezed my arm in response to the woman's cold disdain. For once, she didn't say anything. It didn't appear the woman intended to stoop low enough to address her directly.

I noticed Maidee lift her chin a little higher. I felt proud that she wasn't letting this holier-than-thou woman shame her when it was me of whom she disapproved. I peeled Maizelle's hand off my upper arm and reached into my jacket pocket for her birth certificate. I handed it to the clerk, along with mine.

The clerk examined everything as if she hoped to find an error, any error that would allow her to deny us a license. When she didn't find anything, she spun on her heel and marched to her desk, where she snatched several forms out of file slots. She put each paper on the counter, one atop the other, and turned the stack toward me. She had a speech all prepared.

"You need to complete each page. Do not skip any lines. Do not fail to answer any question. All answers must be truthful, and both of you need to sign where indicated. There is a two-dollar fee to issue the license. You pay after you complete the papers, and I review them for accuracy. Do you have any questions?"

She sounded like one of my professors' giving instructions for a final exam. A smile tickled my mouth, and I fought to keep it in check. I couldn't help being a hair sarcastic. "No, Ma'am. No questions. If I think of one as I fill out the papers, you'll be the first to know."

Maidee clapped her free hand over her mouth to hide her smile. Her shoulders dropped in relief, and the tension in her jaw faded when she realized we would get the license.

I shuffled through the papers and read each before dipping my pen in the inkwell on the counter and filling in the blanks. If a form required Maidee's signature, I dipped the pen and showed her where to sign. As I finished each sheet, I set it apart to let the ink dry. Twenty minutes later, I stacked each page until the well-ordered pile was ready to return.

I leaned close to Maizelle and whispered, "I hope this meets with the Ice Lady's approval."

Maidee swallowed a giggle and punched me in the arm.

I feigned injury. "Ouch!" I grabbed my arm and rubbed it as a grin I couldn't contain spread across my face. I raised my voice, "I believe we've completed the paperwork, Ma'am. I'll pay the fee at your convenience."

The Ice Lady lifted her well-coifed head and faced me. "I will review the papers when I get time."

I scowled. "We need to find a judge to marry us this morning. We have to be back in Utopia by noon."

The clerk tipped her head back and peered down her nose, lips welded in a tight line. "Right now, I am reviewing someone else's application. Someone who planned with the proper allowance of time."

I glanced at Maizelle, then considered the Ice Lady. "Can you tell us where the judge's office is so we can make an appointment to be married?" I worked to keep my tone civil.

"Third floor. End of the hall. Good luck getting an appointment *today*. I'll finish my review within the hour." She nodded her head once to dismiss us.

I took Maizelle's hand, and we climbed to the third floor. We searched both directions for any indication of which end of the long hallway the clerk meant. A small sign with an arrow, mid-way up the wall, said, Judges Chamber. I tugged Maidee in that direction.

We entered the door marked 'Chambers' and were in a small vestibule outside a narrower door with '*Judge Crandall*' lettered in gold on the glass. I tapped with light fingers, and a man said, "Come in."

We entered a well-appointed office with an enormous desk and a wall of bookcases lined with matching leather-bound volumes. A man with a round face and white hair, spectacles perched on his nose, sat behind the desk. A lighted cigar rested on the rim of a substantial brass ashtray next to a half-empty glass of something that looked suspiciously like whiskey at his right hand.

"Come on in, kids." He motioned with his hand, looking up from a pile of papers. "My secretary's not in today, and we don't have any cases at trial, so I'm holding down the fort. What can I do for you?"

"We want to get married this morning. The clerk downstairs said she would have our license within the hour, and we were hoping we could make an appointment for you to perform the ceremony."

"What's your rush? Last I heard, we have a three-day waiting period in Texas, and if y'all don't even have your license yet, I don't think I can help you."

I produced the affidavit from Fred and Eula.

Judge Crandall read it, his bushy white eyebrows rising and falling. He folded the paper and put it back in the envelope, laying it on his desk. "Take a seat, young man," he directed me, "and ask the little lady to step outside, please."

Maidee's eyes flitted from the Judge to me and back again in panic.

"No need to be upset, young lady. I just need to have a private word with your young man before I agree to perform this ceremony."

I opened the door, and Maizelle stepped into the waiting area and sat in one of the two chairs against the wall. I returned to the Judge's chamber and closed the door.

Judge Crandall nodded toward a chair in front of his desk, and I sat. "Cigar?" he offered.

"No, thank you." I set my jaw in a defiant clinch.

"Whiskey?"

I hesitated. Somehow, drinking whiskey at nine o'clock in the morning didn't seem right. "No, thank you," I said again, although my voice might have hinted at "yes, please."

Judge Crandall turned away, and I saw his attempt to conceal a smile. "You sure about that?"

I nodded.

"Mr. Jones, is it?"

"Yes, Your Honor. Will Jones."

"No need to be so formal, Will. You haven't committed a crime...yet. 'Judge' will do." He smiled. "What's your calling, Mr. Jones?"

"Calling?"

"Yes. How do you make your living?"

"I'm a graduate of Texas A&M with a degree in Mechanical Engineering. I own an automobile and equipment repair garage in Utopia."

"Utopia? What's the population up there now?"

"Around two hundred if everybody's home."

The Judge chuckled. "Doesn't seem like enough of a population to support a garage. How will you provide for the young lady?"

"I do okay. I owe my sister's husband a debt, but it should be paid off in a year."

"You have a place to live?"

"My folks have a 360-acre homestead. I'm going to build a house for us on a piece near the river. We'll live with them 'til I get the house built."

"Your folks aware of this?"

"Not yet. But Ma is in poor health, and Maizelle can help with the house until we get out on our own. They won't mind."

"Young man, I can see why you couldn't resist that young beauty, but I'm reluctant to perform a marriage under these circumstances. If she were pregnant, I wouldn't have any choice because I wouldn't let a young girl live with the embarrassment of having a baby out of wedlock. She isn't pregnant, is she?"

"No, Your Honor."

"So why do you want to marry a fourteen-year-old girl? Why not let me in on your little secret?"

"I love her. That's my only reason."

"Why doesn't she have her father's permission?"

"I asked her to marry me and asked her father for her hand. He refused and threw me out. Her stepmother slapped her for saying she would wait for me. She ran away and came to me for help. We decided to elope. I didn't have the heart to send her back for more abuse."

"I see. And when did this conjugal relationship begin? Before she ran away or after?"

"After. We let our feelings get out in front of our good sense. If she gets pregnant from my foolishness, she'd be shamed, and I won't put her through that. She accepted my proposal before anything happened and says she isn't sorry."

"Well, in that case, I suppose the die is cast. If you're certain this is a love match and not just you feeling guilty for spoiling her, bring back your marriage license in a half hour, and I'll perform your ceremony."

"Thank you, Judge Crandall. May I go now?"

"Yes, unless you've decided you want that glass of whiskey."

"Probably wouldn't be a good idea today." We shook hands.

When I entered the vestibule, Maidee looked up at me with fear written all over her face. "What did he say?"

"He said to bring back our marriage license in a half-hour, and he'll perform our ceremony."

She leaped from the chair and wrapped her arms around my neck. "Really? That's what he said?"

"Yeah. After he told me he wouldn't marry us if I was just feeling guilty for... you know...letting our feelin's get the best of us."

"It's... really... going to happen?" Her voice wavered.

"Yep. I'm afraid it is. Unless you want to change your mind."

"Never."

"Then let's go get our license from the Ice Lady."

We returned to the clerk's office just as the license warden got up from her desk. "Oh!" She sounded surprised to see us. "Were you successful in getting an appointment?"

"Yes, we were. If you have our license, we'll be getting married in just under a half-hour." I felt smug.

I smiled at her, and her voice softened, "I have your license. The paperwork was properly prepared. You have beautiful penmanship. It made my job much easier than usual. If you have the two-dollar fee, I can give it to you now."

I produced the money and laid it on the counter. The thawing Ice Lady wrote out a receipt and handed it to me with an envelope. I opened it, and Maidee stood on her tiptoes to see. A marriage license made out to William Echols Jones and Maizelle Nannie Clarke unfolded before our eyes.

Maidee let out a shriek and hopped up and down.

I swear she was glowing when she threw her arms around my waist and squeezed me. I hugged her with one arm while I refolded the paper with my other hand. We headed to the Judge's chambers and waited in the small entry for our appointment.

Judge Crandall opened the door and invited us in at exactly 10:30 A.M. "Come on in," he said in a jovial tone. "I have a couple of questions before we get started. Stand here."

We stood next to his desk, where he directed, and he said, "What's your religious preference?"

"Methodist," we answered in unison.

"Then you'll be wanting a Christian ceremony, right?"

We nodded, and without delay, he married us with a traditional ceremony, including a prayer for our "happiness, prosperity, and healthy children" through slightly slurred speech.

We didn't have a ring, so the Judge gave us a metal cigar band to use when he pronounced us husband and wife.

When he said, "You may kiss the bride," I gathered Maizelle in my arms and kissed her the way I had at Tip Toe on the Fourth of July. Her knees caved, and I had to hold her up.

When we parted, the Judge reached for my hand and pumped it like a standpipe. He suggested we raise a glass to toast our "happy union" and gave Maidee a peck on the cheek.

I glanced at Maizelle, and she nodded her head just a tad.

I turned back to the Judge and said, "Why not? Seems like as good a reason as any to drink before noon."

We all laughed, and Judge Crandall opened his desk drawer and took out a second tumbler for me. He poured two fingers of whiskey into mine and two more into his. "Sorry, little lady, I only have two."

Judge Crandall and I raised our glasses high and clinked them.

"I raise my glass to celebrate the marriage of William Jones and Maizelle Clarke," the Judge said. "May they live long, be happy, raise successful children, and endure no undue hardship."

We drained our glasses and banged them down on the desktop.

Maidee laughed and clapped her hands. I lifted her off the floor and twirled her.

My head spun from the sudden rush of whiskey. I thought I might keel over. Judge Crandall must have thought so, too, because he shoved a chair up against the backs of my knees. I flopped down, pulled my new wife onto my lap, and kissed her.

The Judge was a little embarrassed because he said, "Okay, kids, party's over. I've got cases to review, testimony to parse, opinions to write, and more trouble to cause, so out you go."

Now, officially, Mr. and Mrs. William E. Jones, we took hands and ran from the Judge's chamber and down three flights of stairs before stopping to take a breath.

I swept the car door open for Maidee, bowed, and said, "Your chariot awaits, Madam."

She giggled and sidled a flirtatious look at me. I felt the rise in my groin and knew I'd better get on the road before I hauled her off to the bushes.

We had one hour to make the forty-four-mile trip from Uvalde to Utopia and keep our promise to return Bobby's car by noon. It didn't look promising.

It took two hours. I drove as fast as I dared on the bumpy road, but I wasn't about to make the same mistake I made on the trip to San Antonio. I needed to return the Packard in one piece.

CHAPTER 26

WILL

Deliriously happy and oblivious to what faced us, I guided the car through Utopia. I glanced at my shuttered garage, looked in at the well-lit pharmacy, trying to spot my cousin, and waved at no one in particular as we rolled by the school before heading to Bobby and Emma's.

Maidee took a long gander toward her old home as we passed her street.

I parked, and my new bride scooted under the steering wheel to jump out on my side.

We joined hands and headed for the front porch.

The door flew open, and Bobby hollered. "Where have y'all been? I've been worried sick something awful happened."

"I called the pharmacy and left a message."

"I couldn't leave Emma. Doc Clarke is on the warpath, and he has her so scared she can't sleep or keep food down. I didn't go to work today."

"Is the baby all right? She's not in labor, is she?"

"No. I was afraid it would start when I didn't have a way to take her to the doctor *or* bring the midwife to the house."

"Sorry. We hit a glitch. But we got married this morning in Uvalde, and we're back."

"You'd better get your things and hotfoot it to the Clarke house. Doc has everybody in town looking for y'all, and he's none too happy she ran off."

"Are you going to work now that we're back?"

"Not until I'm sure the Doctor has settled down. He threatened to have us arrested for 'aiding and abetting' a kidnapping."

"Did you tell him Maidee was with me? Or that we eloped?"

"Not a word. We said we loaned you our car to visit your sister and we expected you back Monday night. He was here on Saturday, last night, and again this morning, demanding to know if Maizelle was with you. He didn't believe us."

Maidee took my arm and said, "I think we should go and put this behind us. There isn't anything he can do now. We have our license and marriage certificate. He'll change his tune when he sees how happy we are."

"I doubt it," Bobby broke in. "I've never seen anyone so angry in all my life. He wouldn't get off the porch until I threatened him with my gun."

"I knew he'd be mad that he couldn't stop us, but I figure when he finds out it's too late, he'll soften," I said.

Maidee dropped my hand and headed for the door. "Just let me tell Emma hi before we go, then let's get this over with."

As soon as she was out of sight, Bobby stepped close and leaned in. "Y'all are in for a scene. He isn't sure if Maizelle was with you, but he suspects it. Once he figures out you're married, we'll hear the eruption clear up here. Want me to get my sidearm and come with you?"

My stomach sank at Bobby's suggestion. "You think he'd do something violent?"

"I doubt it. But I don't know the guy that well. He's always so puffed up when he comes into the pharmacy, like he's above the rest of us because he's a doctor. None of us care for him that much, so we haven't made it a point to know him outside of business. He's Emma's doctor, though, and he has her so upset *I'm* afraid she'll have the baby before it's time, and *she's* afraid he won't attend her like he promised."

"Sorry. We'll take care of this. Would it be okay if we stayed here tonight? I haven't told my folks, and our plan is to move in with them. I don't think they'll mind, but I didn't expect this reaction from her pa either."

"Sure. You can stay as long as you need to—at least until Emma pops. do you think Maidee could help her with the baby for a few days until we're ready to put him in your room?"

"Oh, it's going to be a boy, is it?" I joshed to cover my nerves, "She'd love to help. Let's go!" I hollered to Maidee, who had disappeared into the house.

Bobby said, "Take the car. I'm not going anywhere today."

"Would you object if we went on out to my folk's place after we see Maidee's pa? I'd like them to meet my wife before they get the news from the gossip mill."

"Have fun," Bobby said with a wry smile.

Maizelle appeared to be in a jovial mood for someone about to face her father's wrath. She had a downright smug expression on her face.

"What are you so happy about?"

"We did it. We're married, and Papa can't do anything about it. I hope he accepts you. But if he doesn't, I don't care. I love you. Nothing can change that." She pressed herself against my side and squeezed my arm. "It'll be okay," she said. "Papa doesn't scare me. There's nothing he can do about it now."

"I wish he didn't scare me. I don't think he'd harm you, but I'm not sure he wouldn't shoot me on sight."

I parked the car next to the fence, and we walked to the front door holding hands. Maidee reached for the doorknob, and I put my hand out to stop her. Her eyes questioned me.

"No, Sugar, we need to knock. You don't live here anymore, remember?" I rapped, and we waited.

Leila opened the door. Her contorted face caused Maidee to suck in her breath and step back.

I held firm and said, "Is Dr. Clarke home? We'd like to talk to him."

She peered around me, spied Maidee, and hissed, "You! You have a lot of nerve coming to this door after what you've done. *You* are the most insolent, ungrateful wench I've ever known. How could you do this to me? Running off like that in the middle of the night and leaving me to face the music?"

I thought she might snatch Maidee baldheaded. I stepped between them and tucked my wife behind me. "We need to speak to Dr. Clarke." My voice pitched higher than I intended, and my stomach flipped.

Dr. Clarke appeared behind Leila and approached with loathing in his eyes. He hadn't spotted us yet. If he turned that anger our way, there would be trouble.

When Leila realized he was there, she stepped aside. "It's your precious daughter, Donald. Home safe and sound from her *latest* escapade." Her upper lip curled, and her voice dripped disdain.

She knew Maidee was sneaking out. I didn't have time to wonder if she'd told her husband.

Maidee's pa brushed Leila aside, planted his palms against my chest, and shoved. "I told you *never* to darken my door again."

There was no hug for his missing daughter, no noticeable relief when he saw her. He had one thing on his mind, revenge against me.

I stumbled and scrambled to regain my balance. "I asked for her hand, and you refused. It's too late now. We're married."

My assailant bristled. "That's not possible. You can't marry a fourteen-year-old girl and not face charges. She didn't have permission. I'll have this so-called 'marriage' annulled before the week is out!"

"Papa. Please. Will and I love each other. We wanted to be married, and we are. We have the license and the marriage certificate to prove it."

I produced the two papers tucked in my breast pocket and thrust them at him.

He grabbed and skimmed them before crumpling them into a ball and throwing it into the yard. "How dare you?" His voice was cold and even, with an implied threat that gave me chills.

He turned on Maidee. "I warned you about this sorry excuse for a man. I disown you. I no longer recognize you as my daughter. If you ever set foot on this property again, I will not be held responsible for my actions."

Maidee crumpled to her knees. "Papa, don't. I *love* you. Please don't throw me out of your life because I married someone I love."

"Hear this, Maizelle Nannie Clarke, you are dead to me. Now get off my porch and my property. I never want to see your face again."

"Papa!" She pleaded, "I want to see my brothers and sister... I want to see *you*." The desperation in her voice tore at my heart.

"You should have thought of that before you ran off with this... this... ne're-do-well."

"I love you, Papa. Please don't do this."

Her father glared at her. "You made your bed, now lie in it." He turned his back, went inside, and slammed the door.

I lifted Maidee to her feet and wrapped her in my arms. She dissolved against me, sobbing and staring at the closed door. When it suddenly opened again, her crying stopped, and her head popped up like she thought he had relented—only to discover Leila glaring at us from the doorway.

"I will arrange to send your things if you'll tell me where you're living. Or should I just have them dropped off under the Spanish Bridge?"

We were stunned. She knew. She must have followed Maidee and kept it a secret from him. With that, we both realized there was no repairing this breach. No matter what we said, it wouldn't change anything.

I squared my shoulders and met Leila's gaze. "We'll be at my folks' place on Spring Valley, off River View, three miles out Jones Cemetery Road. You've heard of Jones Cemetery? The one named for my great-grandparents who homesteaded this canyon. But you can have Maidee's things dropped off at my business on Central. Toofy and Sambo can show you. I've been buying them sodas all summer. They know where to find me."

I smiled through the sarcasm, enjoying the tit-for-tat; the diatribe intended to remind Leila that my family has deep roots here and is every bit as important as Doctor Clarke.

The sight of her stepmother dried Maidee's tears. She narrowed her eyes and glared.

I took hold of her arm and turned her toward the steps before she said something we'd regret. Walking fast, I pulled her along. The balled-up papers lay by the gate. I snatched them off the ground and handed them to Maidee as we marched from the yard.

When we were in the car, she unfolded the wad and smoothed it with her hands. "I think I'll have to iron this for it ever to be flat again."

"Can you iron paper?"

She snuffled and swiped at her eyes. "You can if you're careful and don't get the iron too hot."

I reached over and patted her knee, lending her my handkerchief. "I'm sorry, Sugar. I expected him to be mad at me, but I never thought he'd go through with his threat to disown you. You've always been his favorite. Everyone in town knows it."

"How can he just throw me away?"

"He'll change his stand once he's calmed down." I squeezed her hand. "I love you. I'll always be here for you, no matter what. Guess that'll have to do for now. I hope you don't have regrets."

Her youth and insecurity were two factors that wouldn't change for a while. I promised myself to put her first and never let her down.

"Regrets? You think I have regrets? I will spend the rest of my life with the man I love. There is nothing to regret."

"You're still young, Sugar. Sometimes, if we let things set a spell, people come around to a new way of thinkin'. We'll build a house, start a family, and live our lives. This town is as much ours as his. When he watches his grandchildren growing up without him, it might make him think again."

"We can hope, but Papa can be a hard man. I don't expect he's going to soften any time soon." She paused and glanced at me. "Now Julia and I are both gone. I think he's having a real bad time."

My heart swelled with admiration for her tender heart. "You'll be a great mother," I said, squeezing her hand, "you always think of everyone else's feelings first."

CHAPTER 27

WILL

We followed Jones Cemetery Road until it turned into River View, hung a left on Spring Valley, and pulled up in front of my folk's two-story house. I was nervous as a tick in heat. I hadn't been to visit in two months. I wasn't sure what the reception would be and even less confident we would be welcome.

We climbed the steps hand in hand. I didn't knock but opened the door and called, "Ma? It's me, Will. I have someone I want you to meet."

My ma, crippled with arthritis, hobbled into the entry hall, one hand on her cane, one arm spread open in greeting. "Well, Will Jones. I was wonderin' if we was ever goin' to see you again. It's all over town that you run off with the Clarke girl."

Then, she caught sight of Maizelle standing behind me. "Oh, my, I guess it's true then. Is this the young lady in question?"

"Yes. This here's Maizelle, my wife."

"Your wife? You mean you're married?"

"Yes, we are, as of nine-thirty this morning, at the Uvalde County Courthouse."

Ma threw her free arm around my neck and hugged me with all her might. "Congratulations, son. I admit you caught me by surprise."

"Sorry. We didn't intend for you to find out this way, but we sort of jumped the gun."

"I hope it wasn't a shotgun." She raised her eyebrows, reached for Maizelle, and swung her arm around her in a warm hug. "Well, you got a beauty, I'll say that for ya. Welcome to the Jones clan, honey." Ma stepped back and scanned Maidee up and down like she was a prize heifer.

Maidee's face colored, and she said, "Thank you, Ma'am."

Ma patted her flushed cheek. "No need to call me Ma'am, honey. I'm your mama now."

"Ma, we kind of rushed into things without making a plan for where we would live."

"Yep. Elopin' has that side-effect." She shot me a wry look.

"We can stay with Bobby and Emma for a few days, but their baby is due soon, and they will want my room back. I was wonderin…"

"No need wonderin, of course, you can stay here. I sort 'a been expectin' ya with all the hubbub in town. Your pa may even let you drive the Lizzy to work. He don't use it much."

"Thanks, Ma, you're the best. Maidee's willing to help you with the house until you and Pa are ready to move."

"Won't she be in school?"

"We'll see. We aren't sure yet if she's goin' back."

"Well, I can sure do with some help. Maybe I can even teach her a thing or two about your favorite meals and such."

"I'd like that," came a soft voice.

"I can't stand here no more," Ma said, starting toward the kitchen. "Come on in and sit a spell. I want to hear all about this weddin' I wasn't invited to."

We followed her into the kitchen before she said, "Jimmy come by last night. He was awful shook up over the kerfuffle Doc Clarke was makin'. He seemed to think you'd hurt Maizelle."

"He's crazy."

"Will, now don't you be saying things like that 'bout that boy. He's had a troubled life. He's not crazy any more'n you are. He just don't understand things the same."

"He's crazy, Ma. Ever'body but you thinks so."

"I've known that boy since he was born, and I'm tellin' you he ain't crazy. There's just somethin' wrong that makes it so's he can't talk proper."

"I get it, Ma. But the way he stares at me with that goofy grin and gurgling like a babblin' idiot gives me the willies. Besides, I think he has eyes for my bride, and I don't want him near her."

"You may be right about that. He was mighty upset. He'd got it in his head you had eloped with Maizelle, and somehow that meant you'd hurt her. I explained that eloping was just running off to get married, and you wouldn't hurt someone you loved. But he couldn't get ahold of the notion."

"Well, if you couldn't set him straight, no one could. I'll just be sure to keep Maidee out of his way. There's no tellin' what he might decide to do."

Ma sat, rested her elbow on the table, and put her chin in her hand. She looked worried. "Jimmy threatened to kill you. I don't think he knew what he was sayin', but he told me if you married Maizelle Clarke, he would kill you."

"I heard. He told Emma the same."

"I wouldn't take what he said serious if I was you. He gets hisself all worked up over things he don't understand, but he's harmless as a fly."

"Well, he'll have the devil's own time of it if he tries anything with me. And if he ever looks at my wife crossways, I'll make him wish he hadn't."

Ma smiled at my bluster and reached across the table to pat my hand, planted protectively over the top of my wife's.

For her part, Maidee appeared confused. Her eyes darted between Ma and me like she couldn't imagine Jimmy wanting to harm her or anyone else.

"I think Jimmy's gentle as a lamb," she said. "He's kind to everyone, even the kids who tease him and make fun of the way he talks. I've seen him watching me sometimes, but I've never been afraid."

Ma nodded, "He told me you always listen to him and that you scold the others for making fun of him."

"I just treat him like a normal person. I think teasing him for what he can't help is mean." She paused and then said, "Mrs. Jones…"

"Mama, to you, honey."

"Mama." She cocked her head to one side and tried the word as if it sounded strange to her ear. I don't think she'd called anyone mama in the eight years since her mother died. "Thank you for welcoming me. I promise to help out in any way I can."

"I hope you will feel ta home. Havin' company, while the kids are in school will be a nice change. I'm looking forward to it. Now that my girls are gone, I miss their company."

"I don't think I should go back to school if Jimmy is still the janitor. I don't want to do anything that might upset him. If I'm not there every day to remind him, he'll forget about being mad at Will."

"Jimmy's a good boy, honey. I don't think he'd ever do you harm. He's very misunderstood, and your daddy got him awful riled up when you disappeared, but I'd be mighty happy if you stayed here with me."

"It's settled then. Maidee will help you here at the house. I'll feel better if she's safe with you. If Pa lets me take the car to work, I can be back in time for dinner every night. Is he at the barn?"

"I expect so. That's where he spends most of his time."

"I'll go find him and let you two get acquainted."

A moment of panic crossed Maidee's face. I smiled and pinched her cheek before heading out to the barn.

CHAPTER 28

MAIZELLE

As soon as Will left, my new mother-in-law said, "I hope you're okay with an upstairs bedroom. I can't make the climb, and Irv moved us into the room on this floor."

"I don't mind climbing stairs. And besides, I'll be closer to the kids if anyone needs anything, right?"

She smiled with a look that told me I'd just said something kind of stupid. "Right," she said, "but they're old enough to do for themselves. I think the boys are older than you."

I felt the heat rise in my face. "I guess I was thinking of kids the age of Edra and Samuel. They always want someone to come if they aren't well."

"Are they your brothers?"

"Half-sister and brother."

How old are they?"

"Edra is almost six, and Samuel is four."

"Are they your only siblings?"

"No. My sister Julia is eighteen, but she goes to business college in San Antonio."

"I think I remember who she is. A tall, pretty girl, as I recall. Younger than Will. I think she was in school with Will's brother, Sam."

"My brother Jamie is sixteen. I think he's in the same class as your twins."

Ma chuckled.

I should have been embarrassed, but I wasn't. She was so easy to talk to. She reminded me of Eula, asking me questions about how Will and I got to know each other and how we came to elope.

I told her about our visit with Eula and Fred and the misstep at the courthouse in San Antonio. I explained about the affidavit and how we got around the waiting period. If she was shocked— or even surprised— she didn't let on. She took my hand when I got to the part about Papa disowning me.

"That's sad, honey. I'm sure he'll change his mind."

After all my storytelling, we sat in the peace and quiet, sipping our tea. I was tired.

I tried out the word that still sounded funny to my ear. "Mama, do you think Jimmy would hurt Will?"

"I don't know what to think. He's terrible upset over you marryin'. He has it crossways in his head somehow."

I stared at the table. "I know. That's what Emma said, too."

"I figure I understand why he resents Will, but I can't for the life of me figure why he's so protective of you."

"Why? I mean, why does he resent Will?"

"Oh, honey, that's a long story. Too long for today. He's my sister Anna Mae's boy. Most likely, you think of her as the crazy old woman who lives on the Calvert place across the river from here."

"Oh. I never connected Jimmy with her."

"I'm not surprised. She never leaves the house, so you wouldn't have seen them together. Anna Mae's troubled. Givin' birth at her age carried a risk that the baby would be damaged, but she wasn't prepared for a child so fragile lookin' you could almost see through his skin.

"She didn't have normal motherly feelings. She didn't like to hold him. When he cried, she complained it made her skin crawl. On top of it all, she suffered terrible guilt. The kind that only a mother who doesn't love the son she prayed for can feel."

"How is it possible to have a baby and not like to hold it?"

"Oh, it's possible, all right. When the situation isn't real bad, we call it 'baby blues,' but sometimes, like in Anna Mae's case, the blues turn into a real dangerous condition. Sometimes, the family has to take the baby away and give it to the grandmama to raise."

"I hope that never happens to me. I don't have a mother, and my stepmother would probably kill any baby I brought home."

"It isn't a common thing. It's unlikely it will happen. I took on the role of mother to Jimmy *and* my sister. I took him home with me so Anna Mae could rest. I thought of him as my own. His mother was at a loss around him. She cared for her boy in her way, but if she ever had any motherly instincts, they seem to have died long before Jimmy was born." Sarah shifted in her chair and offered me more tea.

"No, thank you," I said.

"Once it was obvious Jimmy wasn't like other children, James arranged for him to be enrolled in a state home for the deaf and dumb down in Galveston. I can only imagine what that did to the little guy. I've tried not to think about it over the years. I guess I felt guilty."

"Why?"

"I didn't try to stop them from sending him away. Things might have been better for him if I'd taken him and raised him myself..." Her voice trailed off, and she blinked like she had just woken up from a bad dream.

"Jimmy was clear growed up when he come home again. They kep' him down there 'til he was twenty-one. He got trained in janitor skills, and they found him the job here." Her face contorted in sorrow.

"I remember when he started at the school," I said. "The kids laughed at him and played tricks to rile him. He knew they were poking fun, but he didn't know what to do about it.

"One day, I went up to those mean boys and said, 'Stop calling Jimmy names. You'll hurt his feelings. He's never done anything to you.'

"Then I took his hand and walked him inside. After that, he always smiled at me and gurgled something when he saw me. He brought me a little wood box for keepsakes right before I graduated eighth grade. It's really nice, and Miss Miller said he made it himself, down in the basement. He made one for her too. I think that's when he got the wrong idea about me."

Sarah scrunched her eyebrows. "How's that?"

"Well, I was so happy with the gift I threw my arms around him and hugged him. He patted me on the head. I never thought anything about it. It was the only way I could think of to show him how much I liked the box."

"I suspect he had a fondness for you long before you ever gave him a hug."

I didn't tell her about when I returned his slate, and he grabbed at me like he wanted to hug me again.

CHAPTER 29

WILL

Pa was trimming the hooves on old Mona. When I approached, he barely glanced up.

"Pa, I need to talk to you about somethin' important."

"I figured."

"How's that?"

"Jimmy come by last night. Your ma says he claimed he was goin' to kill ya."

"Yeah. I heard."

"He's been tryin' to kill ya ever since you was born. Now he thinks he has a reason."

"What's that supposed to mean? I haven't done nothin' to him."

The old man stopped what he was doing and set the mare's foot down, patting her flank as he stood. "The way I heard it, you run off with the doc's kid. He ain't none too happy about it."

"He's not."

"I can't say as I blame him none."

"Well, we're married now, so there's nothing he can do about it. Anyway, what does it have to do with Jimmy? It's none'a his business what I do."

"Accordin' to your ma, he has a fondness for that girl."

"Well, she doesn't have a fondness for him. He's twenty-eight years old. She's way too young for him, and besides, she wouldn't be interested in that idiot."

"Hold your tongue. You're not much younger than he is, and if your ma ever heard you call him an ejit, she'd wash your mouth out. She loves that boy. She don't like seein' him riled. What have you gone and done to get Jimmy and Doc Clarke in a snit?"

"I already told you. I eloped with Maidee."

"Seems like the ejit in town might be you."

"Why? We love each other."

"How old is she?"

"Fourteen, but she'll be fifteen next week."

"That could be why her pa is upset, don't ya think?"

"I asked for her hand. He wouldn't listen. Threw me out."

"You always were bullheaded. If he told you 'no,' he prob'ly meant 'no.' Why were you in such a hurry? Is she pregnant?"

"No, she's not. It's possible, I guess. But she wasn't when we ran off."

"Where'd ya get hitched?"

"Uvalde. Judge Crandall married us."

"How'd you get old Crandall to do it if she didn't have her pa's okay?"

"Fred and Eula swore an affidavit that we'd shared the marriage bed."

"Eula! You involved your sister? You always was pig-headed, but I never thought you'd pull a stunt like this. I ought'a get my strap."

"No, Pa. No more whupping. When I left, I had no intention of returning for another one of your whuppins."

"And you haven't. Fact is you ain't hardly ever been to visit since you got out of that fancy school. We figured you thought you was too good for us. Jimmy spends more time here than you. He's more comfort to your ma than you ever was."

"I didn't come to hear what a disappointment I've been or hear you sing the praises of that dummy. I'm married now, and we need a place to live until I can build us a house."

"So, you're wantin' to bring your little lady here? To my house?"

"Yes. Maidee can be a big help to Ma."

"That's just dandy. How do *you* plan to earn your keep? You still think you're too good to shovel cow manure and milk goats?"

"No, Pa. I have a business to run. I'll be gone most days, but I can do whatever needs doin' around here to help you get ready for the move. You won't be disappointed. I'll put in a solid day's work and then some on my days off."

"I'll believe that when I see it. A leopard don't usually change its spots much, in my experience."

"Maybe if I'd ever had a word of appreciation from you growin' up, it would've made a difference."

"I don't owe you no 'preciation. You're my son. You should'a been grateful to have a roof over your head and food in your belly."

"Yeah. Like Junior was? I notice he didn't stick around to take any more whuppins to show his appreciation."

"Watch your mouth, boy. I ain't too old yet to give ya a strappin'."

"Can we live here or not?"

"I 'spose so, but I 'spect a willin' hand and no back talk."

"You'll have both. And Pa, would you try to make Maidee welcome? Her pa disowned her for marryin' me, and she's feelin' unsure of herself."

"I will. Your ma says she's a pretty little thing. That true? Or is it just Jimmy talkin'?"

"She's a beauty. And she's got a fine character. She'll be a big help to Ma."

"I hope so. Your ma's wore out after birthin' and raisin' ten babies. She's so crippled up with her arth-er-itis she can't hardly do nothin' anymore. I'm hopin' the gulf air at Del Rio will help some. She's a good woman. She deserved better'n me." He walked toward the house, hands stuffed deep into his overall pockets, his shoulders hunched forward by his crippled, round back.

I fell into step beside him. I was now almost a head taller than Pa and had to lean forward to look him in the eye.

"How you plannin' to get back and forth to town? That fancy Packard up there don't belong to you, does it?"

"No. It's Bobby's. I'll either saddle up Mona and ride her or walk."

"That old nag wouldn't get you there and back on a hot day. You'd better take the Lizzy. She don't get much use around here, and it ain't good for 'er to just sit."

"That's right. She needs to be tuned up and kept running if you want her to make it to Del Rio."

"I s'pose you could take care of that?"

"I s'pose I could."

Pa's eyes shifted to mine.

I wondered how things had gone so crossways between us. I met his gaze and thought, *why'd you have to whup us? Didn't you know you would drive us away?*

We walked, lost in thought. When we reached the porch steps, Pa spoke. "Let's go meet this young lady that's causin' so much disturbance."

We stepped inside, where Maidee and Ma sat at the kitchen table.

"Pa, this is my wife, Maizelle. Maizelle, this is Pa."

She moved to stand, but Pa bent forward and gave her a clumsy hug as she half-stood.

"You're a young 'un, for sure," he commented as he straightened.

Our visit was a success, and we drove to Bobby and Emma's, satisfied to have a roof over our heads. Neither of us talked on the trip back to the Upton's, each pondering our reception at the Jones homestead, I suspect. I don't think my girl quite knew how to take Pa. He probably seemed abrupt and awkward compared to Doc Clarke. But Ma was gracious and warm in accepting her new daughter-in-law.

When Maidee broke her silence, she said, "I'm sure lucky to be getting a mother who can teach me the things I need to know to be a good wife. Leila would never have done it."

I was pleased with the welcome from both of my folks since we hadn't been on the best of terms. I hadn't expected much from Pa, so it surprised me when he went to hug Maidee. I ran over my conversation with him in my head, thinking the old boy had mellowed some.

I got to feeling a little wistful and said, "I wonder if Pa thought using the strap on us would make us better men. It sure didn't do much to make us have good feelings for him. All he succeeded in doing was driving us away."

Maidee said, "Didn't your ma try to stop him?"

"Ma and the girls hated it just as much as us boys did, but there wasn't nothin' they could do, 'cept stay out of his way."

"Your ma must have been afraid to say anything."

"She wasn't above takin' a switch to us herself, but she never really hurt us much, and she always hugged and kissed us after."

"I don't think I could ever take a switch to one of my children," Maidee said. It was clear she expected the same from me.

"I'll never raise a hand. I swear."

I rolled the car up the hill to Upton's and stopped in front of the gate. Suddenly I felt exhausted and dropped my forehead to the steering wheel. The stress of the past few days had caught up with me.

Maidee, her face at ease now, reached over and patted my arm. "You okay?"

"Yeah, I'm okay. Just tired. Glad to be someplace where we can relax and get some sleep." I lifted my head and smiled at my new wife; my chest swelled with pride.

She slid across the seat and rested her head against my shoulder. "I hope Emma won't want to stay up late tonight and talk. I think I could fall asleep on a pile of rocks."

"Me too," I said, taking her hand. "Let's get some shut eye before we pack up my things and move to the farm."

"Will? Do you think your folks liked me?"

I put my arm over her shoulders and drew her close. "I think they did, Ma especially. Pa's hard to read, but he seemed to take to you without being ornery. The important thing is they're happy we're going to be living there. They both need help."

CHAPTER 30

MAIZELLE

Will and Bobby drove down the hill to Utopia as Emma and I got busy cleaning up the breakfast mess, chattering like sisters. I noticed how Will downed the meal and wondered if Emma might be persuaded to show me how to make it.

I felt so comfortable with her that I overcame my hesitation and said, "Emma, would you teach me how to make biscuits and gravy like we just had? I could tell how much Will liked it."

"Sure. My grandmamma taught me, and it's the thing I do best. Bobby loves it too." She wrote down the recipe and explained everything.

We practiced making gravy, and I caught on fast. I was eager to surprise Will with my new skill.

I spent the rest of the day packing his things. I held the framed graduation certificate from Texas A&M and wondered what college was like. Did he have a girlfriend? They had female students his last year there. Before then, it was men-only. Would he be happy with me, with only a year of high school?

My heart lurched when I picked up a framed photograph of Will in his military uniform. What would I do if he got called up? My stomach knotted at the thought. I hurriedly packed the picture and covered it with his long johns.

There were three letters from Texas A&M in his dresser drawer. I thought they must be the letters he told me about the night he proposed. I didn't read them. I tucked them under the long johns with his cadet photo. The less I dwelled on the idea of him going away to war, the better.

My head buzzed with thoughts of what lay before me and behind me. I thought about how angry Papa was, and a lump rose in my throat. I thought when he saw how happy we were, he would soften. How could Papa, whom I loved more than anyone except Will, spurn me?

He was always quick to forgive me when I got in trouble with Leila and never acted like he resented or blamed me. I prayed he would change his mind. Thinking about how much he had always loved me gave me hope.

I was glad to have the chance to know Will's folks before they moved. It was a relief that Sarah offered to teach me. I longed to be a good wife, and with Sarah's help, I could learn all the things Mama would have taught me without having to put up with Leila and her snide remarks every time I made a mistake.

The men were home. I was deep in thought when I heard the car. Where had the day gone? It was time to load up and head to the homestead.

I rode in silence as the other three chatted, shared inside jokes, and laughed together about Bobby and Emma's courtship and marriage. I was filled with a case of nerves, unlike anything I'd ever felt. I didn't know what to expect. Moving in with Will's folks might be the best or worst thing that ever happened to me. What if his brothers teased me like they did the girls at school? What if his pa decided to ignore me? I wanted everything to be perfect, but the knot in my stomach said to plan otherwise.

I learned a lot on this short trip by just listening. Bobby's mother, Elizabeth, is Will's pa's sister. That surprised me because they're so different. The cousins grew up as opposite from each other as cows from goats. The stories they told about their raising were nothing alike. Bobby's father is a pharmacist, a college graduate—like my Will—an active Mason, and the way they tell it, gentle as a lamb.

"My mother is very concerned with appearances," Bobby said, and they all laughed.

Emma said, "Bobby's ma is a member of the Eastern Star and the Blue Belles Garden Club. If Utopia has an upper crust, they're it."

Will said, "I appreciate Uncle Robert and Aunt Elizabeth because they encouraged me to go to college when my own pa didn't want any part of it. I couldn't find any reason to want to go home after I left. Who'd want to live with a disturbed rattlesnake? My pa used his strap more often than most men brush their teeth."

"Mother couldn't understand where Uncle Irvin's anger came from," Bobby said. "She just thought he was best avoided."

Emma said Elizabeth told her when the boys were little she and Robert didn't have much contact with Will's folks because she didn't want to expose Bobby to his uncle's behavior. She said their father had been the Methodist minister in Utopia and believed in 'spare the rod, spoil the child,' but Elizabeth remembered him as a "kindly father who treated all his children well."

Will said his pa would "never guess Ma encouraged us kids to leave the farm. She got Irvin Jr. to head for the Oregon Territory when an opportunity for land grants came up, and Elizabeth helped her arrange marriages for my two oldest sisters with college friends of Robert's. That's how they ended up in San Antonio." He said, "Ma suggested Thomas return to Tennessee and reestablish the right of ownership on the plantation lands her father abandoned after the war."

It sounded like Sarah protected herself from his abuse by never interfering with Irvin's discipline. It was easy to see she had done everything in her power to help her children escape from him as soon as possible. Seven were launched, and she still had three to go when we dropped into the family. The conversation in the car hadn't done much to make me feel at ease living under their roof.

CHAPTER 31

MAIZELLE

Will and I were in the big house barely a month when I guessed I was with child. At first, I didn't say anything to Will or Mama Sarah, thinking that perhaps all the new activities in my life had caused me to skip my period. My monthly was so regular you could set the calendar by it. Julia and I got it the same year—only she was fifteen, and I was eleven.

Secretly, I was elated. If we had a baby on the way, maybe Will wouldn't have to go to war. I felt fine and spent my days in Mama Sarah's company. I learned to read recipes, prepare fruits and vegetables for canning, make preserves from the apples and pears that grew in the small orchard, and absorb everything she had to offer.

When month two arrived without my visitor, I was certain and thrilled. This meant Will might not get called, and that was all that mattered to me. One night, after we made love, I rolled toward him and whispered, "I have a secret."

"What?" He propped himself up and looked at me with puzzled eyes.

"We're going to have a baby."

He sat bolt upright. "Say what?"

"I said, we're going to have a baby. I've missed my period two months in a row, so I think we'll have a new addition sometime in May."

Will grabbed me and pulled me to him. "Maidee, Maidee, Maidee," he said, "that's about the best news I've ever heard."

He nuzzled my hair and traced the outline of my face with his fingertips, giving me chills up and down my spine.

"I hope it's a girl, and she's as beautiful as her mother." He pushed me back a little and stared into my eyes. "Does Ma know?"

"Of course not, silly. Why would I tell your ma before I told you?"

He buried his face in my hair again. "Let's not tell them. If we wait another month—to be sure—it will be our secret."

My body slumped with relief. I wasn't certain Will would be happy to have additional responsibilities so soon. "Thank you," I whispered. "I was afraid you might not welcome this news."

"Not welcome the news? Are you kidding me? I can't think of anything I want more than having a family with you. I just want to keep it between us...for a while. Just us. Okay?"

My eyes brimmed. "Of course," I choked out, "I'm so relieved you're happy. Maybe we can breathe a little easier about you getting called up."

Will looked me in the face and blotted my tears with a corner of the pillow-case, his face set in that determined way he sometimes gets. "Maidee, my love, the president himself can order me to report now, and I'll find a way not to go—if I have to break my own leg. I promise I won't leave you to go through this alone." He flopped back onto the bed and pulled me close.

"We don't need to wait to be sure," I murmured, "I knew a baby was coming after our first time." We fell asleep wrapped in each other's arms.

A rooster crowed a rousing welcome when dawn cracked through the darkness into the upstairs bedroom. Will and I lay welded together under the thin quilt. He stretched and drew me to him for one last hug before he rolled out and scrambled into his clothes.

I tossed the covers back to get up from the other side, and he stopped me.

"No reason for you to be up yet, Sugar. It's still early, and Ma won't be up for at least another hour."

"But I should be fixing your breakfast."

"I can fix something for myself. You need your rest now that we have a baby coming."

"Will, if you start coddling me this soon, it won't be a secret for long. Don't forget, your ma and pa have been through this a few times."

"I know. Pa never gave her any rest from her chores when she was carryin' even one of the ten of us. Now, look at her. She's broken down and crippled up and can hardly do for herself anymore. I won't let that happen to you."

Touched by his concern, I felt like the luckiest girl alive. I reached for my dressing gown and went to where Will stood, buttoning his shirt. I pressed my body against him and laid my head on his chest. "You are the kindest, most thoughtful man I've ever known."

"I better be the only man you've ever known." He kissed my forehead and carried me to the bed. "Now, you stay put until you hear someone else rustlin' downstairs."

I snuggled into the warm covers and dozed off. When I woke again, the sun was up and warming the room. I threw back the quilt, hurried to dress, and made my way down.

My mother-in-law was already in the kitchen, cane in hand, hobbling from sink to stove to table and back again. Papa Irvin, the twins, and ten-year-old Minerva sat there, letting her serve them without lifting a finger to help.

"Well, look who we have here," Papa Irvin said. "If it isn't the princess royal herself."

I wondered if this was his way of chastising me for sleeping in and leaving all the work to Sarah. "I'm so sorry. I overslept. I think I fell back to sleep after Will left."

"No worries," Sarah said. "I expect you'll be findin' sleep wantin' to overtake you a lot more often now."

"Why?" Papa Irvin asked, "Is there somethin' wrong with her?"

"Might be," Sarah said, with a smug look, "or maybe somethin's right with her."

Our eyes met, and heat rose in my cheeks. I hurried to take plates of food to the hungry group at the table. I don't know how my mother-in-law knew, but it was obvious she thought she knew something. I felt like a fly caught in a spider web.

Will's pa lost interest in the discussion as soon as his breakfast was in front of him. That would have been the end of it, except Minerva piped up, "What's the matter with her?"

"Nothing. Nothing at all. I just overslept. Now eat your porridge so you can ride to school with Will."

"Mama? What's wrong with Maidee?"

"That's for her to say."

"Maidee, what's wrong? Why won't you say?"

I looked at Minerva, then Mama Sarah, burst into tears, and fled back up the stairs.

"Now look what you've done." Papa Irvin scolded, "You've gone and upset the girl. Best you go apologize before you take another bite." His stern voice never missed on his children.

Her feet hit the floor. "Maidee, I'm sorry," Minerva called as she pounded up the stairs after me.

I made it to our room and closed the door.

Minerva banged on it. "I'm sorry. Please come back." Apology delivered. She rushed back down to finish her breakfast.

I heard Will come through the back door from morning chores and muffled voices as everyone got ready to leave.

WILL

I was feeling jovial when I came in from the barn. "Are y'all ready for school?" I asked as Minerva scooted past me and slipped into her chair.

"Not quite. I had to 'pologize to Maidee for making her cry. I have to eat my porridge."

"Apologize? What did you do?"

"I asked her what was wrong with her, 'cuz Mama said there was somethin' wrong with her, but she wouldn't say what."

I looked at Ma. The question in my eyes and her knowing look collided in midair. If I asked, the cat would be out of the bag.

Ma appeared to revel in the fact that she had hit a nerve. A self-satisfied smile played dangerously close to the surface. She arched her eyebrows and gave me a look that told me she knew.

The thought *she suspects Maidee's pregnant* raced through my mind. I turned to my three passengers and said, "Y'all'd better hurry up and get yourselves to the car, or else you'll be riding Mona to school."

I said to Ma, "Maidee didn't sleep well last night. I told her to stay in bed until she heard you. I'm going to run up and see if she's okay."

"She's fine, Will. Let her be. She's just fightin' the changes in her body right now. Another month and this will all be forgotten. When she comes down, I'll talk to her. I've been meanin' to anyway. There's a lot she doesn't know yet about what to expect."

"How'd you know?"

"Let's just say after ten of my own, I know the signs."

"She wanted to tell you. I wanted to keep it secret."

"What are you two jawbonin' about?" Pa asked.

"Will and Maidee's expectin' a baby."

"Well, I'll be! That was fast. Jones men don't waste no time."

"Please don't tease Maidee about this. She isn't quite sure how to take your joshin.'"

"You better get these kids to school. Go on. I'm not gonna say anything to your gal." Pa grabbed his hat off the peg and headed to the barn.

The uneasy truce between us held.

MAIZELLE

Not wanting to raise a further alarm by blowing my nose, I took a fresh handkerchief and blotted the drips, always mindful of Papa's guidance that a *lady always wipes her nose*. I cringed over my emotional breakdown and dipped a corner of the hanky in the washbowl to dab at the tearstains on my cheeks before I made my way down the stairs.

Mama Sarah was washing dishes when I approached with my chin tucked. "I'm sorry. I should have stayed and helped you. I don't know what came over me."

"I know what came over you. You're carrying another Jones boy inside that little body. They have a way of bringing out these little fits of emotion, so you might as well get used to it." Her voice was kind but matter of fact and not especially soothing.

I tried to read her expression for reassurance that my mother-in-law wasn't angry or upset. A knowing smile and arms open for an embrace greeted me. When she hugged me, I felt tears start. I swallowed and blinked to hold them back to stave off another bout of crying.

She released me and stepped back, still holding me by the shoulders. The sympathy in her eyes went deeper than just forgiveness for a momentary lapse of self-control. "You poor unsuspecting child. If I could have done anything to help you prevent pregnancy at such an age, I surely would have. I just hope this isn't the first in a long line of Jones boys to wear you down, break your back, and smother your spirit. If my son proves as good at sowing seed as his pa, you'll have a long row to hoe."

I was crushed, and my eyes brimmed. "So, you're not happy for us?"

She shook her head and looked at me with a doleful expression. "It's not that I'm not happy for you. It's just—you're so young and have much to learn about havin' babies." Then she pasted on a broad smile and squared her shoulders. "I'm probably just the person to teach you," she said with false cheerfulness. "When you've been pregnant nine times and produced ten babies, you learn a good bit. Unexpected crying jags are more common than you think. I've had six boys and four girls, and I never had the crying when I carried the girls, only the boys, so I think you're expectin' a boy."

I stared open-mouthed. "You really think it's a boy?" My voice quivered, and my chin trembled as a hopeful grin spread.

"I'd bet the crops on it."

"Oh, Mama Sarah, that makes me so happy! But Will wants a girl. I hope he won't be disappointed."

"He won't be. Once he figures out that boys are a lot more help around the farm, he'll be durned glad he got one. It's you should be wishin' for a girl, not him. Daughters relieve the burden of running the house, and that's the only help you'll get from here on out."

"Will told me he'd always find a way to help me with household chores. He doesn't want me to have to work as hard as you. He doesn't think his pa has been fair to you that way."

"Irv give me four girls. To his way of thinkin', that's more than any woman needed or deserved." Mama Sarah let go of my shoulders and turned away to hide her pained expression.

"My papa always hired someone to help mama with the house, but he never hired anyone to help after Leila came. I guess because she was the one to take care of the house and us kids before mama died, he thought she should just keep doing what she was."

Mama Sarah dried her hands on the dishtowel and picked up a teacup. "Didn't you and Julia help with the house and the children?"

"Not much," I said, taking the cup from Mama Sarah and filling it from the kettle on the woodstove. "I looked after Edra and Samuel quite a bit, but she never wanted Julia or me in the kitchen. Julia learned some from mama before she died, but I was too young. All I ever learned was from my sister. She showed me how to make a bed, set the table properly, and iron. That's about all. I wouldn't have known how to cook anything if it hadn't been for Will's sister and Emma."

I followed Mama Sarah to the table. She smiled. "A weekend with Eula was probably worth a month with anybody else. She was always the best cook of my girls. The younger ones all learned from her before they left the nest."

"But you taught her, so you must be the best."

"Not really. She could turn a basic recipe into something much more interesting than I ever could."

Warming her hands against the cup, she cast her eyes down and took a sip of tea. "She also taught Eloise, and the two of them cooked every day for my sister and her husband after Jimmy was born."

"Why don't Eula and Fred have children?" I ventured the question that had been on my mind.

"I'm not sure. For some reason, God hasn't blessed them. Sometimes I wonder if she got enough of parenting with her younger brothers and sisters and took extra care not to get pregnant."

"She was so kind to me," I said, and my face warmed. "She must have realized straight away that I didn't know much about cooking or being in a kitchen, but she showed me without making me feel stupid." I glanced at Mama Sarah. "And then, she made out like I'd done it all myself. I think she would make a great mother."

"I'm sure she would, honey, but sometimes God has a different plan than the one we think He should have." She paused and stared off into the distance. "Like sending a little soul like Jimmy Calvert to an old woman who didn't have other children and didn't know the first thing about raising a damaged child. I've never been able to figure that one out." She shook her head and shifted her eyes away.

"Did he really threaten to kill Will if we got married?"

"He sure did, honey. He was all riled up by your papa runnin' all over town huntin' for you. He took it on himself to be your protector."

"Have you seen him lately?"

"I went across the river to see him once and explained that it wouldn't be a good idea for him to visit us while you and Will are livin' here."

"How'd he take it?"

"He was upset. He's in love with you, and he's always harbored bad feelings for Will. He doesn't understand why, and explaining to him is too hard." Mama Sarah drained her cup and set it down so hard the cup rattled in the saucer. Her voice took a defensive tone. "In Jimmy's mind, *he* was my baby. Will was a newborn, and Jimmy was jealous. It wasn't his fault he hurt Will. He don't think like reg'lar children."

"How'd he hurt Will?"

"Hit him in the head with a Pound-a-Peg hammer when Will wasn't two weeks old. A big ol' knot raised up, and Will bawled like a calf that lost its mama. I told his folks I couldn't let him come visit anymore. His child mind blamed it on the arrival of Will. Now his grown-up mind can't work out why he's so angry."

She had that distant look again as if she could see the past and the future at the same time. "I don't think Jimmy would hurt Will now, but it's best to keep them separated."

I carried her cup to the stove. "What makes you think Jimmy's in love with me?"

"Oh, honey, that boy has had eyes for you ever since he come back to Utopia. The first day he started work at the school, he stopped to see me and babbled about M'zl. He had somethin' to say about you ever' time I saw him. 'M'zl pretty. M'zl nice. M'zl talk.' Whatever happened in his day, the thing that mattered was whether the pretty Maizelle was nice to him or talked to him. It wasn't hard to figure out he had a crush on you. I never give it much thought 'cause you was so much younger. But his actual age and his thinkin' age are two different things."

I poured hot water over a tea ball and carried Mama Sarah's cup to her. "I never did anything to give him the wrong idea."

My mother-in-law searched my face. "I'm sure you didn't. How could you? It probably never occurred to you that a simple man would have feelin's like that. But there's the problem. People think he doesn't have feelings 'cause he can't express hisself." She patted my hand. "It's not your fault he fell in love with you. I appreciate that you were kind to him. So many taunt him that he comes around in tears half the time."

"Will told me if he comes here, I should stay upstairs until he leaves. I don't want to be rude, but Will doesn't want me to have any contact with him."

"Will's right." Mama Sarah set her jaw and pursed her lips. "The best way for Jimmy to get over his feelin's for you is not to see you. Now that you're expectin', it's even more important. I'll see my sister from time to time and check in on him. That way, he can visit with me, and he doesn't need remindin' of what he can't have ..." She closed her eyes and heaved a big sigh, letting her voice trail off.

It left me wondering where she went when she was like this. I had noticed that she often faded out this way and assumed the pain from her arthritis was too intense to allow her to continue. This time, though, there seemed to be more in her silence.

When her eyes opened, she looked sadder than anyone I'd ever seen. "How can I forgive myself for turning my back on that poor child? How can I explain that he can't have the girl he loves? If I'd been a better person, or stronger against Irv, I might have made a difference in Jimmy's life." Anguish was written in every line of her wrinkled face. "After Jimmy left for Galveston, not a day passed that I didn't think about him, worry about him, and miss him like one of my own—maybe even more than I missed my own."

CHAPTER 32

May 30, 1918
MAIZELLE

When the first pain hit, I was peeling potatoes at the kitchen sink. I cried out and doubled over, holding onto my pregnant belly.

Mama Sarah was sitting at the table stringing beans. She looked up. "Is it time?"

"I don't know. It felt like somebody grabbed me from behind and squeezed me real hard."

"You'd better sit."

There was no one to go for the midwife. Will was still at work, and he had Pa's car. We didn't have a telephone. There was nothing I could do but wait and hope Will came home.

When I was six months along, I wrote a letter to Papa, begging his forgiveness and telling him I was pregnant. I told him how much I missed everyone and how happy I was married to Will. I asked him to attend me and deliver his first grandchild.

He didn't answer for two months. When his answer finally came, I wept. The refusal was abrupt and cold; a single sentence said, "I have no interest in attending to your pregnancy or the birth of your child." I was heartbroken, and Will held me that night until I cried myself to sleep.

Now, I wanted Papa. If it was time, and the baby was coming, I couldn't think of anyone else I wanted more than Papa.

"Sit in the rocking chair," Mama Sarah said, bringing a clock so I could time the pains. "These things usually take several hours. I think we have plenty of time."

It was four-thirty in the afternoon. When a pain took me, I rocked. I let out a long moan, and Mama Sarah pulled me to my feet and told me to walk around the room. She said it would ease the discomfort but didn't help much. At five o'clock, my water broke, and I was drenched. I cried because I didn't think I could clean up the puddle, and I didn't want her to have to do it. I prayed for Will to come home.

By five forty-five, I was having contractions every minute and a half. Mama Sarah put me in her bed because she couldn't climb the stairs. Writhing in agony, I cried out, first for Papa and then for Will.

Mama Sarah lifted the sheet and told me to spread my legs so she could see how things were progressing. Her eyes grew big and round, and she said, "Oh, my."

"What? Is something wrong?"

"No, honey, nothin's wrong. We're just goin' to have us a little one a bit sooner than expected. I'd suggest you not push too hard. If we can slow you down, maybe Will will get here in time to go for the midwife."

At six o'clock, Will walked in the back door and found the kitchen empty. "Maidee?" he called.

I screamed, "Get the midwife."

He poked his head into the bedroom. "You'd better hurry, or I'm goin' to be deliverin' a baby by myself," his ma said.

Minerva stuck her head in to see what was happening.

"Minnie, I want you to boil water and bring me clean rags. We're about to have a new baby here," Mama Sarah said.

Will spun around and raced out.

I screamed, hollered, and cried for Papa until my throat was sore. I knew he wouldn't come, but I couldn't stop myself.

At six-thirty, Will exploded into the house and shouted, "In there."

The midwife rushed in. "Breathe," she instructed, "just take deep breaths and let them out real slow." She lifted the sheet and reached for me. "Well, I'll be," she exclaimed, "I do believe we're havin' a baby. Push hard, and we'll be done here before you know it."

A huge contraction gripped me, and I pushed, then screamed, and Will burst into the room. "What's wrong?" He rushed toward the bed.

"Will, you get on out'a here, NOW," Mama Sarah said, "the baby's arrivin,' and you're in the way."

"Push," the midwife said, "push once more, and you'll be done." I took a big breath, gritted my teeth, and pushed with everything I had. "Well, look at that. We have us a new Jones boy."

I collapsed against the mattress and said, "Mama Sarah, could you get Will?"

She smiled, and I noticed tears in her eyes. "Sure thing, honey. You dropped this baby easy as a rabbit drops a litter. I wish I'd had even one of my ten labors start and finish in two hours and fifteen minutes."

Minerva came with warm wet cloths to wash my new son, and the midwife cut the cord and tied it off neat as a pin. They laid my new son on a towel on the bed and cleaned him before they put him on my chest.

I was too exhausted, sore, and run over by the flood of emotions to complain. My heart swelled, and I got a funny happy sensation that made me feel almost giddy.

Will stood by, looking at me with the proudest look I'd ever seen. I reached for his hand and announced that our son's name would be Charles Hunter, after Will's pa's middle name and my pa's middle name. No one uttered a word of disapproval. If Will, or his parents, thought it odd or sad that I clung to the hope of reconciliation with the papa I adored, they never let on.

My firstborn, Charles Hunter Jones, arrived precisely two hundred thirty-eight days after Will and I first made love. According to a book Mama Sarah gave me to read on birthing, that is the exact average gestation period for human birth.

"He looks small for a full-term baby," the midwife said.

He was fair, with light blond hair and pale blue eyes. To me, he was the most beautiful baby ever born. My milk turned out to not be as hearty as it should have been, and that, coupled with the fact that he was not a strong suckler, kept him thin and fragile looking.

I was thrilled with our new son and devoted to his care. I sought Mama Sarah's guidance and gradually gained enough confidence to feed, bathe and change him on my own. Minerva adored her nephew and helped with him every chance she got. She hadn't practiced infant care of a younger sibling and was eager to take over for me whenever I let her. This freed me to do the household chores, a godsend to my arthritis-crippled Mama Sarah.

The arrangement worked out splendidly for all three ladies in the Jones house. Will's ma got the help she needed, I got a break from the demands of caring for a newborn, and Minerva got relief from chores.

Mama Sarah and I competed to hold or play with Charles. She adored him. I think she was particularly attentive because she wouldn't be having more of her own. It helped that someone else changed his nappies and fed him.

He rarely cried, and when Will came home from work, he rushed to see his boy, snatched him out of the arms of whichever of us happened to be holding him, and tossed him into the air, nearly giving me heart failure.

"Yer scarin' the girl," my stern, abrupt father-in-law, said, and Will laughed and tossed Charles again.

"Give 'em to me," Will's pa would say, and the two of them pretended like they were going to toss my baby between them until my cries of protest penetrated.

"Ain't he just a spittin' image of his grampa," Pa Jones declared, and Will countered, "no, he looks like me."

I loved the games they played with Charles as the object of their affection. I think it was the thing that helped them stay civil to each other during our time at the homestead.

CHAPTER 33

MAIZELLE

Since our hasty marriage, I had rarely left the security and privacy of the big ranch house on the Jones Homestead. Will and I visited Bobby and Emma a few times before Charles arrived, and she clued me in on what to expect. After Charles was born, we compared our babies' achievements. The boys were less than a year apart, which helped me to know what was normal and what might be cause for concern.

The one place I never went was Papa's home. I respected his decision to cut me out of his life, even though my heart ached with longing to show him my infant son and introduce Charles to my brothers and Edra.

We visited Elizabeth and Robert when Charles was a month old. I liked to visit them because Elizabeth was elegant in the way she dressed and her manner. I enjoyed listening to her talk as she spoke in such a refined way, unlike Mama Sarah and Papa Irvin. Will's aunt had been my mother's closest friend, and I felt a special bond with her.

When we arrived to show off our new son, Uncle Robert took Will by the elbow and guided him into the study. Elizabeth steered me toward the kitchen with the baby.

WILL

Uncle Robert handed me a cigar. "Take a seat, Will." He reached for his pipe, settled back in his oversized leather chair, and put his lighter to the tobacco in his bowl. I sat opposite him and worked at lighting the cigar.

"That's a good-looking boy you've got there," he said, pulling on the pipe stem. "Tarnation, I need to repack my bowl." He ran a cleaner through the stem of his walnut-burled pipe and tapped it over a large crystal ashtray to empty. With a serious look, he said, "Will, my good man, you do realize how important affiliations are for business, don't you?"

Puzzled by the sudden change of subject, I said, "I sure do."

He tapped the pipe once more and reached for a pouch of tobacco. "I know how busy you are, starting a new business, building a place for your family, and helping your folks, but I'd like to nominate you for membership in the Masonic Lodge. Bobby is working to earn the rank of Master Mason. It would be terrific if you boys achieved the honor together.

"You're a fine young man, Will. I've been impressed with your dedication to providing for your wife and child. You have a good education, and you're a solid Christian." He put his lighter to the bowl and drew through the stem three times before he exhaled the sweet-smelling smoke.

"I don't think I'd have time to go to meetings and study. Like you said, I've got a lot going on."

"Your business is growing. Your standing in the community would be strengthened by affiliation. Think about it. It won't be long before Maizelle is eighteen. She'll be eligible to join Eastern Star if you're a Mason. Her father can hardly hold to his position if you establish yourself as a person of standing." He fixed his gaze on me and reached for his lighter again.

I broke the stare and pondered Robert's suggestion as the sweet smell of tobacco filtered around me. I could see his point, but leaving Maidee alone in the evenings didn't appeal to me. I could hear her and Elizabeth cooing and admiring Charles.

"I'll give it some thought, Uncle Robert. Being newly married and all, I can't say the idea excites me much."

"It takes about three years to master everything and promote through the degrees. You've got time to accomplish what you need to set Maizelle up for Eastern Star. Your aunt's heart is set on seeing that Maizelle has this opportunity."

That's when I knew arguing was pointless. This wasn't about me and my prospects. It was about Elizabeth's desire to put Maidee on a proper path. Going up against Aunt Elizabeth when she sets her mind to something is a fool's errand. I took a puff of the cigar and blew smoke into the air.

MAIZELLE

Elizabeth smiled at her new grandnephew and me as she prepared tea. "Maidee, darlin', bless your heart. I just know your mama would be so proud of the fine mother you are to this beautiful boy. It's sad Ellie didn't live to see you married." The Tupelo honey that dripped from her lips was music to my ears.

I laid Charles on a bed of soft towels in the makeshift bassinette we'd fashioned from an old wicker laundry basket. "Thank you, Aunt Elizabeth. It means a lot to me that you think mama would be proud. I wish Papa would see me the way you and Uncle Robert do. I never meant to hurt him. I miss my family so much." I pulled the basket close and peeked over the edge at my son. My heart swelled. "He's never going to have a grandmother on my side, so I hope he grows up thinking of you that way."

Elizabeth set a plate of fresh peanut butter cookies on the table, and her expression warmed as she looked at Charles and then at me. "Maidee, I wouldn't be a friend to your mama if I didn't look out for you and see to it you enjoy a position of prominence in the community." A cup of tea appeared in front of me. "If Will joined the Masons, you could become an Eastern Star." Offering the cookies, she said, "It's the best way I have to help you get established."

I bit into the soft, fragrant cookie. "What are Masons?" The look of pity on Elizabeth's face made me wonder if it was a really dumb question. Embarrassed, I looked down. When I glanced up, Elizabeth held my eyes.

"Robert is a Master Mason. He's a member of the Texas Grand Lodge and a founding father of the lodge in Utopia. I helped him organize the women's branch, known as Eastern Star. I serve as Worthy Matron."

"What's a worthy matron?"

"It's like being the president of the organization. Women can't join until they are at least eighteen."

Since I was only fifteen, I wasn't sure how it related to me until Elizabeth explained that Robert would invite Will to join the Masons, setting up a pathway for me to join Eastern Star.

Elizabeth said, "Masons are a group of men banded together in a fraternity of believers to do good works in the community. Women in Eastern Star are related by blood or marriage to a Master Mason. The sisterhood is established for the same purpose as the fraternity. Joining would be an opportunity for you to make your mark on the town, just like your mama did with the Blue Belles."

"Mama loved the Blue Belles." I scowled. "I could never join, though, because Leila's a member, and she hates me."

Elizabeth placed her hand over mine. "Oh, child, I don't think she hates *you* in particular. She is simply a very unhappy woman, married to a strong-willed man who doesn't love her." She let go of my hand and leaned back with a vague look in her eyes. "She seems to have a sour ball between her lips these days. I remember she was always beaming when she was getting ready to marry the doctor."

"Well, she sure stopped that in a hurry."

"She was young. She had no idea what it would be like to be married to someone who would never get over loving the devoted wife he lost. Leila's not a bad person, just a very disappointed one."

"I suppose so. But, if you think she's sour now, you should have tried living with her. She was born with a sour ball in her mouth." I leaned forward, "Do you know she slapped me across the face, right in front of Will? And it wasn't the first time, either."

Elizabeth put a hand over her mouth, and her warm smile faded. "No, I didn't know. I'm sorry to hear that." Her lips pinched shut, and her eyebrows squeezed together.

"It's okay. I put it behind me after Will and I got married. Papa saw her do it and never said a word. That hurt worse than the slap."

Elizabeth reached for my hands and held them. "It is unfortunate your papa felt it was necessary to marry so soon after Ellie died. I tried to persuade him against the idea, but he was set on having a mother in the home for you children. He was not to be reasoned with."

I allowed myself to wallow in her sympathy. "I love you, Aunt Elizabeth. I don't know what we would have done if you hadn't been there for Julia and me after mama died."

"After you and Will married, I wanted to invite you to join the Blue Belles. But with Leila being a member, I thought better of it. It only takes one black ball to kill an invitation, and I couldn't risk it. Being asked to join the Blue Belles was Leila's most fervent desire. It gave her the acceptance she needed when she married your Papa so soon after your mama died. I arranged her invitation, you know, at her mother's request. Edra is an old friend who was worried about unseemly gossip if her daughter married Donald before Ellie was gone a year."

"It's okay, Aunt Elizabeth. I know it would have pleased Mama for me to be a member, but I have too much to do helping Will's ma and taking care of Charles to spend any time going to meetings."

"Oh, honey, Eastern Star is so much more than going to meetings. It's a sister-hood of like-minded women who are there in times of need to help others who are less fortunate. If something goes wrong for one of our members, we're there to make it right."

"I'm sure it's very worthwhile, but I'm fine, really. I have a lot to do, and it isn't easy for me to get to town anyway."

"I can't offer you Eastern Star until you're eighteen, and only then if Will is a Mason. It would help Will's business to have you involved."

Charles stirred and let out a whimper. I plucked him out of the basket. "What's the matter with my boy," I cooed, "are you hungry again?" He squirmed and stretched in my arms, opening his light blue eyes wide. "Oh, look," I exclaimed, "he smiled at me."

Elizabeth cocked her head and said, "It was probably a gas pain. It does look like a smile. All new mothers think it is, but I'm afraid it's still a bit early for a real smile."

I knew Charles smiled at me, but I didn't argue. I rocked him in my arms and made goo-goo eyes at him.

"Maidee, darlin'," she said, "that boy's a spitting image of his daddy, except for the ears. The Lord blessed him with your ears."

I giggled. "I know, and I thank Him every day for that little gift."

Charles squirmed and let out a warning squawk.

"We'll need to be going soon, or I'll have to find a place to nurse him."

"I'll tell Will. Think about the advantages of his joining the lodge. I'm going to need you in Eastern Star."

CHAPTER 34

MAIZELLE

When Charles was three months old, Will said, "Leave him with Ma and Pa tonight. I want to show you something. Let's take a walk." I didn't have a clue what he had up his sleeve, but I reluctantly turned my baby over to Will's folks and went with him.

We went up a small hill toward the river. Over the crest was a horseshoe bend around a piece of flat land extending uphill from the river to a picturesque spot with a large live oak tree. We waded through a shallow and walked across the flat over a carpet of fragrant wildflowers.

When we reached the tree, Will stopped and looked toward the river. "Here's where I'm building us a house," he said. He took me in his arms and tenderly kissed me. "I hope you like it."

It was a beautiful spot. We could see the tree line from where we stood, and it provided a solid protective barrier. The hill we had descended made a natural obstacle along that side of the property. It felt very private. The tree offered ample shade, and a big barn was already on the property. Will's pa stored hay there for cattle he pastured on this piece of ground. The site pleased us both, although there was no easy access to the town and no neighbors nearby.

"How will we get back and forth?" I asked, feeling like I might be isolated with the river making a full bend around the land.

Will wrapped me in his arms. "I promise I'll have a bridge across before the end of our first winter. Besides, you won't be that far from Ma and Pa. If you need anything, you can always walk up to the house."

Showing me this spot excited Will. I didn't argue—or bother to point out that borrowing a cup of flour from someone who lived a mile away and across a river might stretch my tolerance with a toddler in tow. I knew better than to show any dissatisfaction that might hurt his feelings. I would make do. He was the one I chose, and this spot was the one he chose. I thought it best to keep my tongue in my head.

News of the war in Europe in the summer of 1918 was not good. I rarely heard any news at all, but I inquired about the war whenever I visited someone with a radio set. I had my baby as insurance against Will being called up, yet I still lived on pins and needles. Each tidbit I heard was worse than the one before.

Will, Papa Irvin, and the twins spent every evening and weekend preparing the ground and working on our new house, something I truly appreciated. The day after Charles turned five months old, I prepared a mid-day meal for the men and walked to the building site to deliver it.

When I arrived, they were deep in discussion with Al Foster, a neighboring rancher with an unreliable radio set that Will frequently repaired. I thought nothing of it, assuming he sought Will out to work on his radio.

They were so engrossed in their conversation that they didn't notice me. When I came close, I overheard Mr. Foster say, "... over twenty-thousand troops dead this week, and they're jes gettin' started."

My ears pricked right up. Mr. Foster said his radio had crackled to life early this morning with a report on the devastating loss of troops. "The news upset me plenty," he said, "and when I saw y'all across the river, it gave me a good reason to get away from the women and talk about it."

Mr. Foster referred to a joint offensive between the U.S. 1st Army and the French 4th Army to clear a strongly defended corridor between the Meuse River and the Argonne Forest.

My heart lurched, and I froze, holding my basket of lunch at arm's length. I uttered a little wail and swooned when I heard what he said.

Will turned at the sound and caught me as I slumped to the ground. My basket crashed to the hard-packed earth, scattering food, jars, and dishes at the men's feet. Will knelt and gathered me to him.

My eyes were awash with tears when they met his. "Maidee," he said, cradling my head against his chest, "don't fret about this. I'm here, you're here, Charles is safe, and nobody has ordered me to report for duty. You have to stop worrying so much about this war."

I searched his eyes for any hint he was sugarcoating. "But if twenty-thousand men died in a week, won't they need replacements?"

"Of course, Sugar, they always need replacements. But I'm not goin' anywhere anytime soon, so you need to quit worryin'. It won't do any good, and I'll be among the last to be called now that Charles is here." Lifting me to my feet, he said, "Let's see if we can salvage any of this dinner."

His reassurances did little to calm my jitters. When I tried to question Mr. Foster about the news, Will shushed me and changed the subject. The dinner I worked so hard on and walked so far in the hot sun to deliver looked like a complete loss to me. But the men brushed the dirt off the fried chicken pieces and ate as if they were being presented on porcelain plates with fine linen napkins.

WILL

The joint offensive reported on that day ended six weeks later with over seventy-five thousand Americans injured or dead. Maidee was right to worry, and I received a letter from the Army on November 8th, one day after the offensive ended.

It read:

```
Dear Cadet William E. Jones,

Your deferment request pending the birth of your first
child is conditionally approved. You are hereby granted a
six-month deferment from the date of your request. If an
Armistice has not been signed before that date, you will
report for duty at the assigned recruiting center in your
registration papers on or before November 30th, 1919.
```

After work on that dark Friday, I shared the letter with Maidee. She broke out sobbing and fled to the bedroom. In her mind, it meant I would leave before Charles' first birthday. She remained inconsolable no matter how I tried to stem the tide of her premature grieving over my departure. Weeping and gulping, she beat her fists against the bed like a child having a tantrum. Spent from the pent-up emotion breaking through the dam of her resolve to be strong, she fell into a deep sleep.

I could not rouse her when it was time for the baby's next feeding. Minerva brought Charles to the bed and helped him latch on while Maidee slept. I sat by her bedside until she woke eleven hours later.

She held her head in her hands and complained of a 'splitting headache.' Her eyes were swollen, and her body was weak with exhaustion. When she tried to stand, her legs gave out. "What time is it?" she asked timidly, "Where's Charles?"

"Charles is fed and resting in Minerva's tender care."

"How did Minerva feed him?" She popped upright, "He needs me to feed him."

"You did feed him, Sugar. When he was hungry, Minerva brought him, and she hooked him right up to you."

I lifted Maidee to her feet and helped her downstairs. Ma tried to get her to eat something without success.

Maidee moved through the weekend in a trance. She cooked, cleaned, changed Charles' nappies, and nursed him without showing any emotion. There was a distant look in her eyes. Nothing Ma or I said or did brought her back to us.

I worried. I knew I couldn't leave her in this condition. Maidee was a strong woman, but the one thing she couldn't cope with was the thought of being left behind if I was called off to war. Even though the reporting date was still a month away, to her, it might as well have been tomorrow.

She resisted my attempts at conversation, and when we climbed into bed that night, she turned away from me for the first time in our married life.

The Armistice was signed on Monday, November 11th, 1918, on the eleventh hour of the eleventh day of the eleventh month—ending 'the war to end all wars.' When I heard the news crackle over my crystal radio, I jumped, clicked my heels together, and shouted, "Yippee!" I hung the CLOSED sign early for the second time since opening the garage and rushed home to share the news with my wife.

I barely turned the engine off before my feet hit the ground. I ran for the house, letting the screen door clatter shut without thinking about the baby's naptime. "Maidee," I hollered at the top of my lungs. "The war's over! President Wilson signed the Armistice!"

I was sadly mistaken if I thought my announcement would bring gales of laughter and wild dancing around the parlor.

Maidee sat in the rocker with a blank look in her eyes, staring into the empty room.

I rushed to her side, lifted her from the chair, and swung her in circles. "The war is over Sugar. It's over. I won't have to leave you and Charles. We'll move into our place before Charles's first birthday and celebrate it as a family."

When I set her down, she looked around in confusion. Then the dam burst. This time, they were tears of joy and flowed like a spring thaw on the Sabinal River. "Over? It's over?" she repeated between gulps of air and great sobs of relief. "How? When? What happened?"

"The Krauts gave up! They lost the war."

The wife I feared I'd lost collapsed against my chest and wept until she went dry.

Charles, awakened by all the commotion and loud voices, whimpered, and his urgings pulled her out of her confused state.

"I need to feed the baby," she said, pulling herself out of my arms and making her way toward the cradle.

She never mentioned the war again, and neither did I. I understood that her dependence on me was total and complete. I swore to shield her from anything in our lives that could cause such anguish.

MAIZELLE

A hearty toddler had replaced our frail infant in the six months since the end of the war. Charles took his first halting steps at eleven months. It was a great source of pride for me and a reason to celebrate.

When he let go of my hand, reached for Mama Sarah, and took a tentative step in her direction, everyone held their breath. After the first step, pandemonium broke out as Minerva clapped her hands, and the twins cheered. Our little boy looked from one grinning face to the other, moved his other foot forward, then sank to the floor in tears. I scooped him up and turned his face away from the laughing adults. The look would have frightened anyone.

When the room quieted, I placed him down once more and scooted back with my arms out to him. Charles stepped once... twice... as I eased further back. He took another unsure pair of steps and fell, laughing into my outstretched arms.

Everyone cheered and clapped. From that moment on, Charles was unstoppable. His towhead could be seen climbing onto chairs, furniture, countertops—anything to give me a fright. When I lifted him from some precarious perch, he laughed and squirmed to get free. As soon as he escaped, he would dart in a different direction to ascend some new obstacle. Will and I were delighted with his curious and fearless nature.

Within a month of walking, Charles weaned himself from the breast, and I suspected I was pregnant again. I hadn't been this tired since the early days of my first pregnancy.

Mama Sarah said, "Me and Pa enjoy havin' our grandson in the house more than we ever enjoyed any one of our own." So, they were taken aback when Will announced his plan to move us into the little two-bedroom house near the river.

Mama Sarah could no longer do much around the house and relied on me for most of the housework and cooking. Pa Jones had grown used to Will's help with the animals and the heavy farm work and spent more time in the house playing with Charles.

One morning as I was coming down the stairs to start breakfast, I heard them talking. I stopped and listened.

"Ma," Irvin said, "I think it's time for us to make good on our threat to move to Del Rio."

"I suppose so," she said, resigned and unenthusiastic.

"If we go now," Pa Jones continued, "we'll have Will and Maidee to help with the packin', and it won't be as hard to leave the boy if we make the break before he starts talkin'."

Mama Sarah said, "That's true."

I could see from where I stood that she had that faraway look in her eyes. "Are we sure this is the right thing?" She sounded wistful as she ran her gnarled finger around the rim of her coffee cup. "We won't have any help gettin' settled on the other end."

"That's right. But the weather will be better for your arther-i-tis, and I won't have nothin' else to do but get us settled."

Mama Sarah's shoulders slumped. I saw tears seep out of her wrinkled eyelids, wend their way through the creases on her cheeks, and fall into her lap.

"Now don't ya' go to cryin' on me, now. We talked about this before the kids come back and agreed that when they moved, so would we."

"I know, Irv. I know. Just thinkin' about leavin' that little towheaded boy brings back the sadness of Jimmy's leavin' is all."

Papa Irvin stood and grabbed his hat off the peg. "You have to put that behind you." His voice took a stern and forceful tone. "We've talked it blue in the face. You done what you had to do. It ain't your fault his ma and pa decided to send him away."

Mama Sarah turned her face up to meet his. "I know. What will Anna Mae do without us?" She searched his eyes. "I'm not sure Jimmy will be any help to her, and she doesn't have anybody else."

"That's none of our concern. You've helped all you can, and as crippled up as you are, you ain't much help to her anyway." He held his hat close to his chest as if it could protect him from her sorrow.

"Yes, but Minerva goes to her every day after school and sees she has a meal started. Maybe we should take her with us."

"No." Pa Jones was firm in his response, and I think Mama Sarah knew better than to argue the point. "You can talk to the ladies at the Eastern Star and set it up so someone checks in on her. You've put in your time. It's somebody else's turn. Besides, she has Jimmy. If she falls, he knows enough to get help." He put his hand on the doorknob.

"Irv," she said, "I need to talk to Jimmy. I need you to take me across the river and make sure he understands what to do for his ma."

"I'll take you to talk to Jimmy after we get our plans in place."

"Thank you," she called after him. "I'll ask your sister about lookin' in on Anna Mae," she said to a closed door.

As soon as Pa Jones was gone, I continued down the stairs. Mama Sarah looked at me with a pained expression.

"Is everything okay?" I asked, trying to sound innocent of my eavesdropping.

"Fine, honey. Just fine," she said.

That evening they told us their plan to move to Del Rio. I let Will do the talking and sat quietly with my secret.

Will's folks said they had divided the homestead five ways for their five sons, and the big house was on Irvin Jr.'s portion. The fact that he moved to Oregon with his new wife, Beulah, and was planted there on his own land, didn't make any difference in his inheritance. He owned the house and the land it stood on.

We needed to make do with the spot Will picked for us or pay rent to Irvin, Jr.—even if it meant the big house stood empty. I noticed there was no mention of any inheritance for their daughters.

CHAPTER 35

WILL

A voice startled me when I was under a car on my mechanics' creeper.

"I was just wondering how my sister is?"

"Say what?" I said, rolling out from under the car.

"My sister, Maidee. How is she?"

"Fine. She's fine. You Jamie?"

"Yeah." The boy blushed, stared at his feet, and shuffled from one leg to the other. "Well, thanks. I was just wondering because we aren't allowed to talk about her at home, and I haven't seen her since she ran off. Guess I'd better be going then."

I scrambled to my feet, wiped my dirty hands on a shop rag, and extended one toward him. "Good to see you. Maidee will be glad to know you stopped to ask after her."

It had been two years since I had set eyes on any of my wife's family. Jamie had taken a growth spurt and filled out through the chest and shoulders, so I hardly recognized him. His face was broad and solid-looking with evidence of dark whiskers. It occurred to me that he looked a lot like Doc Clarke. I took in every detail of his appearance to report to Maidee.

"Did you know we have a son? Charles Hunter?" I was sure to get the doctor's middle name out there, so Jamie would know his sister had tried to stay connected.

"Yeah, I heard. How's he doing?"

"Great. Just fine. He started to walk a few weeks ago, and Maidee has the devil's own time tryin' to keep up with him. You'd be welcome to come out to the place and meet him sometime if you'd like."

"Nah. That's okay. Just wanted to see how my sister was getting along."

"She's expecting another baby in December." I searched Jamie's face. "I know your sister would be happy to see you and Bowen if you ever get out our way. She'd love to introduce you boys to your nephew."

Jamie's face relaxed, and he offered a half-smile. "Yeah, I'd like that, but Papa wouldn't let Bowen come, and he's not eighteen, so he can't decide for himself. Papa told us if we wanted to see Maidee after we turned eighteen, it was our decision, but not a day sooner."

"That's swell, Jamie! Maidee will be glad to know you want to see her. If Bowen feels the same, it will make her the happiest woman alive. She misses you boys." I clapped Jamie on the shoulder. "You out of school yet?"

"Not yet. I graduate at the end of the month. If I can earn enough money, I want to get a mining engineering degree. Papa will help some, but the more I take from him, the worse it will be. Leila is mean and nasty to him whenever he has to put money toward Bowen or me."

An idea took hold of me. "I could sure use some help around here. How would Doc Clarke take to you workin' for me?"

Jamie stared open-mouthed. "I don't know, Will. It might cause more trouble than it's worth."

"Think about it. Can't afford to pay much, but if you can work for two bits an hour, I can give you twenty hours a week."

Jamie glanced around the shop, admiring my tools. The idea of learning to mechanic was taking hold. When he started talking, it was more like he was thinking out loud.

"I'm eighteen. Papa told us we were free to make our own decisions when we turned eighteen. If I get a job, he should appreciate it." The words tumbled out rapid-fire. He paused. "He'd a lot rather my job was working for someone else, though..." His voice trailed off, and when our eyes met, he blushed beet red.

I stuck my hand out, and we shook. "It would be swell if you worked here for the summer. I'm gettin' behind with all the new cars in town, and I'm tryin' hard to finish our house so we can settle in before the next baby comes."

Jamie pumped my hand. "When can I start?"

"How about tomorrow? Come first thing in the morning. Say eight o'clock. That way, I can show you how to set up the shop for the day."

"I'll be here," Jamie said, beaming. "Tell Maidee I said 'hey.' I'd better be going now. Leila will have dinner on soon, and if I'm not there, she'll raise holy Ned. I'd as soon miss that show," he added under his breath.

"See you tomorrow, Will. And thanks, a whole lot!"

Central Garage had prospered beyond expectations. My debt to Eula's husband was retired, and I had begun saving to buy a used Model T. The end of The Great War ushered in a new era of prosperity and optimism. More families had the means to own an automobile. I wasn't able to keep up. I needed to find a young man to help me, and one just dropped into my lap.

The rest of the day swept past as I hummed and whistled with renewed vigor, sure Jamie's visit would make Maidee glow. I rushed home to share the news. When I pulled up, she came to greet me with Charles perched on her hip. I lifted the pair of them off the ground and gave her a smooch.

She squirmed and turned her head away, laughing at my exuberance.

"Sugar, wait 'til you hear what happened," I said as I set her down to see her eyes.

"What happened?" Her voice teased as if whatever it was couldn't possibly warrant such an obvious show of affection.

"Jamie came to the shop and asked after you."

"Jamie? My Jamie?"

"One and the same."

Maidee's eyes grew wide. "What did he say?" Her voice was a whisper as if the answer would be too much to bear. I could see her heart thumping. She searched my face for a hint of bad news.

"He said to tell you 'hey.'" I couldn't keep a straight face, and she could tell I was teasing.

"That's all? Just, hey? Will, don't you hold out on me! Has something happened at home? How is Bowen? Does Papa know he came to see you?" The dam burst with all the questions she had shoved into her dark place for the past two years.

"Whoa. Hold your horses, Maidee. Jamie just stopped by to ask how you're doing. We talked a bit, and I ended up hiring him. He's eighteen now, and he says your pa told Bowen and him that they could make up their own minds if they wanted to see you when they turned eighteen. Jamie decided he wants to see you and meet his nephew."

"You told him about Charles?"

"Yes, but he already knew, and now he knows about the new baby we're expectin', too."

"You told him? How did he seem? Is he healthy? What did he say about Bowen and the kids?"

"He's fine, Sugar. He seemed happy about the new baby. He didn't say much about anyone else except that Leila is still up to her old tricks, making life miserable for them." I lifted Charles off her hip, put my arm around her, and walked her toward the back porch. "He's filled out a lot. I didn't recognize him at first. He has dark whiskers now."

"No. He does not," Maidee said, her eyes askance.

"Oh, but he does," I said. "He looks a lot like your pa." I gave her a squeeze and a smile. "He needs money for college. I hired him half-time for the summer. He starts tomorrow."

Maidee pulled away. "Can you afford a hired hand? Jamie shouldn't need money for school. Papa will pay for him."

"I need help in the shop to keep up with all the new work since the war ended. I spend so much time helpin' Pa around here and workin' on our house, I'm falling behind."

She flung her arms around my neck and gave me a mighty hug. "That's so kind of you to hire Jamie. I can't wait to see him. When will he come see Charles?"

"Don't know yet, but I'll bring you every scrap of information I get from him. Promise."

She absorbed everything as if I quoted from the Bible. Without warning, her eyes brimmed. She collapsed against my chest and cried like the world was comin' to an end.

Charles reacted like any frightened child and began wailing along with his mama.

I hadn't expected this. It never occurred to me that my wife still grieved for her family, surrounded as I was by my folks. I was happy and assumed that Maidee had gone from one to the other without a hitch.

I held her and let her cry as I stroked her hair and tried to still her trembling while I jiggled Charles up and down in my other arm to quell his crying. The joy I expected my news to bring turned out to be the key that unlocked two years of pent-up sorrow and feelings of loss.

CHAPTER 36

MAIZELLE

Will's ma and pa sold their car to Will. The price was fair, and he could make payments. After many conversations, it was decided that the horse was too old to haul a wagon to Del Rio, so they would ship their belongings by rail.

I knew Will would take the car to work each morning, and we wouldn't have a horse unless Irvin and Sarah decided to give us Mona. She wasn't of much value, but neither could we afford to buy her for any price. Although they had mentioned it, no decision had been made. I didn't relish being isolated in our new place, pregnant, and with no means of transportation to go for help if I needed it. I experienced a little emotional breakdown as moving day approached.

Charles was eighteen months old and into everything. One day I found him in a nest of kittens under the front steps, giving them 'uggs.' The kittens squealed and mewed at such a pitch that anyone walking by would have been alerted. The mama cat returned to the distressed cries just as I figured out where Charles had disappeared.

He grabbed a handful of the mama cat's fur and tried to pull her to him for an "ugg." She squalled in protest and took a swipe at his face, catching him squarely on his plump cheeks. I think he screamed more in surprise than pain, and three deep scratches oozed blood.

My protruding belly stopped me from reaching him with both arms, so I turned sideways, grabbed him with one hand, and dragged him out from under the porch. The cat hissed at us like she would scratch our eyes out before settling down to nurse her upset kits.

Charles was covered with blood and dirt. I took him onto the back porch to wash him, and the ordeal exhausted me. My huge pregnant belly stuck out so far I couldn't see my feet. The incident with the kittens was typical of what Charles put me through every day.

I felt myself buckle under the stress of getting everything ready for the move... thinking about being on my own for the first time in my life...losing another mother just when I needed her the most... I collapsed on the porch in tears, clutching my boy to my breast. I sat there and cried, saying, "I can't do this anymore."

Bless his little heart, Charles patted my cheeks to comfort me while he squirmed to get free and into more mischief. I was so frustrated and upset with him that I spoke harshly for the first time in his life. "Stop!" I said. "Stop wiggling and let me be." It wasn't the words so much that upset him. I think it was a tone of voice he had never heard me use, and he howled like a stuck pig.

His loud wails brought Mama Sarah to the porch to see what was wrong. "Whatever has happened here?" She balanced with her cane and reached for Charles with her free hand.

He pitched himself backward in my arms and reached for her. His little face was red as an apple and twisted up like a walnut shell.

I lost my grip and fell. Charles lurched out of my arms and banged his head on the porch.

Mama Sarah tried to catch him but missed, lost her balance, and tumbled down beside him. That made three of us piled together in a messy knot.

I sobbed, Charles wailed and gulped air, and my poor mother-in-law sat motionless, unable to get up. I'm still unsure how we got untangled and upright again. Charles crawled away from me and clung to his grandmother, looking at me with something I'd never seen in his eyes. Fear.

Mama Sarah cradled and soothed him, stroking his blond hair and dabbing his tears with her apron.

I rolled onto my hands and knees and lifted my backside like a pregnant cow. When I was on my feet, I took Charles from her.

He pummeled me with doubled-up fists and kicked like a donkey.

His granmama looked at me with a question that asked *what did you do to this baby?*

I turned away, took my toddler inside, and put him in his highchair. He continued to howl like he had his foot caught in a coyote trap. I left him there and went to help Mama Sarah to her feet. We went into the kitchen with arms wrapped around each other like we didn't want to let go.

And we *didn't* want to let go. Mama Sarah and I loved each other. The prospect of a permanent separation was difficult for both of us.

When Will got home, I fled into his arms. "I can't do this anymore," I said, breaking down in tears for the second time that day.

"Calm down, Maidee," he said, "what can't you do anymore?"

"I can't be pregnant and manage Charles at the same time. He's into everything. Look at his face. I need to help Mama Sarah, and I'm afraid to turn my eyes away from him for even a minute."

"What's wrong with his face?"

"Look," I said, "just look at what the cat did to him when he tried to take her kittens."

Will turned to Charles, sitting in his highchair, calm as a summer breeze, and saw for himself the damage the cat had inflicted. He said, "I'll hire someone to help you out until after the new baby comes."

The kitten scratches had little or nothing to do with my state of mind, but I never told him.

The 'someone' he hired was my dear friend, Katherine O'Brien. She had turned fourteen in November and asked around for a placement. When she saw Will's notice on the bulletin board at the post office, she went straight to the garage and presented herself. Will told me they had a good laugh over the last visit she'd made with a note from me.

For my part, it was like having a sister again. Katherine wasn't ready to leave home yet, but with too many hungry mouths to feed, her parents would have married her off if she'd had a suitor. It was our good fortune that Katherine entertained no such plan.

Will spoke to his pa and Mama Sarah, and they agreed to let her share a room with Minerva until moving day.

Our new helper was slender as a reed and didn't appear much older than twelve. Her boyish figure was quite a contrast next to my plump arms and pregnant belly. Her thin brown hair wasn't quite shoulder length; mine reached my waist when left loose. I've heard unkind people refer to Katherine's appearance as mousey but make no mistake—she bubbles with confidence and independence.

Katty, as most folks call her, has soft gray-blue eyes and displays a gentle manner with children. I've always admired how patient and kind she is with her brothers and sisters and how sweet she is to Toofy and Sambo. She's a tomboy at heart, a good counterbalance to my more womanly bent. I knew she'd be a perfect fit.

I flung my arms around Will's neck and kissed him on the lips.

She was a perfect choice. Straight away, she took on the more labor-intensive tasks and outside work, leaving the easier household responsibilities to me. Her presence freed Mama Sarah to spend more time with Charles, and the idea of the move no longer hung over us like a wet quilt.

Katherine and I are like family in our fondness for one another. Since childhood, we have confided everything. I was so happy to have her back in my life that the tearful breakdowns stopped during the last two months of my pregnancy.

Katherine could keep up with the curious and ever-exploring toddler we placed under her watchful eye. She easily blended into our family, and the move went forward without a hitch.

One day she said, "Maidee, do you know how to saddle a horse?"

"No," I said, "why?"

"'Cuz I think we should be usin' that old nag, Mona, to haul stuff between this house and the new one."

"That's a great idea," I said. "I'll ask Pa Jones if he can show us."

I waddled out to the barn and found my father-in-law sitting on a hay bale, sucking on a piece of straw. To say he wasn't 'busy' would be an understatement.

"Pa Jones, could you teach Katherine how to saddle Mona so we can use her to help us haul things to the little house?"

"That old nag ain't goin' ta be much use to ya." He drawled, not changing his position one bit.

"We won't put too big a load on her," I said, "but we could sure do with some help carrying the heavier things."

"I'll see what I can do," he said, still not moving.

I waited. We stared at each other. Me with my pregnant belly and him chewing on a piece of straw. I decided not to leave because he might forget all about teaching us. I shifted my weight, looking as miserable as possible.

After some time, he pulled the straw from his mouth, spit, and hauled himself upright. "Let's go then," he said. "Seems like you're in a real hurry."

"We just have a lot of stuff to move today, and I'd like to get started if you're going to let us use the horse."

"Can't see why not."

Katherine caught on immediately and was strong enough to pull the straps under the horse's belly nice and tight. Pa Jones said, "She's mighty strong for a girl. You'd never know by lookin' at 'er."

We loaded old Mona the way he showed us. When it was time to take the first load, Katherine pulled Charles up by one arm and swung him onto the saddle in front of her. She wrapped an apron sash around her waist and tied him to her as we moved between the two places. I trundled along beside them, feeling like an overripe pumpkin.

CHAPTER 37

MAIZELLE

When the time came for Pa Jones and Mama Sarah to move to Del Rio, he made good on his promise to take her across the river for a conversation with Jimmy.

I asked Mama Sarah to fill me in on how the visit went. She said, "Irv helped me into the cabin and waited in the Lizzy. Jimmy sat on the bed, and I took the chair. I said, 'Jimmy, I need to talk to you. Irvin and me are movin' to Del Rio. It will be too far for me to visit you." A flicker of panic crossed his eyes, and she knew he understood at least some of what she told him.

After that first flash of fear, his face brightened. He smiled at her with the hopeful innocence of a small child and said, 'I c'm.'

Mama Sarah said, "No. You need to stay here to look after your ma. She needs your help."

His eyes darted away like he didn't want to hear. "I c'm," he said.

Mama Sarah said, "I struggled out of that chair and wrapped him in my arms. I told him I loved him and that I was proud of the job he does at the school. But now he's needed to help his ma. I said, 'you need to cut her firewood and carry her supplies. Can you do that?'

"He pulled away and stuck out his lip. He said, 'No. C'm wif oo.'

"Oh, Maidee, his eyes were so sad, and the set of his jaw said this wasn't going to be easy. I said, 'I wish I could take you, but I can't. You need to take care of Anna Mae. I'm sorry.'"

She said tears welled in his eyes, and she had to turn away to hide her own. When she regained control, she reached for his hand and squeezed it. That's when he said, "M'zl go?"

Mama Sarah said she dropped his hand and asked, "What did you say?"

"M'zl go?" he repeated, his voice little more than a childish whine.

Mama Sarah said, "No, Maizelle isn't coming. She lives with Will now in their house. You understand that she's married to Will, don't you?"

She said, "he nodded his head like he understood, but I saw something in his eyes that I didn't like. I said, 'Jimmy, you can't see Maizelle anymore. She's Will's wife. She loves Will. She doesn't love you. Do you understand?'"

He stared at her with a very odd expression. After a time, he said, "I se." She said his voice sounded 'strange,' and she wasn't sure he understood.

She left the bag of cookies she brought on his bedside table and stood to go. She said, "Irvin's waitin', and I need to get home. When we walked to the car, I put my hand over his and said, 'I hope you will think of me kindly.'

"He took my hand, but I saw a smile flicker without landing. I sensed that he was not all that sorry to see me go. You stay away from him, Maidee. He's a grown man now, and I'm not sure I can trust him anymore."

Her words gave me a chill.

CHAPTER 38

MAIZELLE

Katherine and I outfitted the kitchen cupboards with all the implements Mama Sarah had provided, and we put the braided rug in the middle of the front room floor. Mama Sarah's grandmother made the rug, and she and Pa Jones hauled it from the family plantation in Tennessee.

The hand-me-down rocking chair was given a place of prominence at the far end of the room near the wood stove. We hung a large, framed mirror on the wall opposite the rocker. I was uncomfortable with that as I didn't like looking at myself, but Katherine pointed out that it made the room appear larger. We positioned an overstuffed mohair chair from my in-law's parlor with a small needlepoint-covered footstool facing the rocker. With this arrangement, Will could relax in the plump chair and visit me while I nursed the new baby.

Will prepared Katherine a room in the barn, so she could have privacy and a place to get away from the family for a few hours. He also made a pallet on the floor in the living room near the wood stove, where she could sleep once the new baby arrived and help me at night. The weather stayed warm and mild throughout October and November, but the nights grew cool when December came, and Katherine preferred her pallet in the house.

"Maidee, when do you think this little one will make his appearance?" Katherine asked one afternoon in early December.

"I'm not sure, but I hope it's soon. I'm so tired of carrying this load."

"Do you think it's another boy?"

"I don't know, but Mama Sarah sure did, and she was right about Charles."

"Wouldn't you like to have a little girl?"

"It doesn't make any difference to me. I'd just like to have it, whatever it is!"

We readied the cradle I used for Charles with a new liner and clean pad covered with soft cotton sheeting. We chose yellow as the welcome color for the new infant and busied ourselves hemming diaper cloths and receiving blankets, sleep sacks, and soakers.

We cleaned the blankets and clothing I'd used for Charles, repaired worn spots, and readied them for the new baby. Once the house was in order and the layette prepared, we spent our days conversing, surrounded by the peace and quiet of the isolated spot Will chose for our family.

CHAPTER 39

MAIZELLE

My water broke less than an hour after I crawled out of bed to wake Katherine. William Echols Jones, Jr. appeared in the early morning of December 15, 1919.

Mama Sarah had warned Katherine that I dropped that first one like a nut from a tree and said she'd better keep a close eye out for signs I was in labor. I'm glad she did because there wasn't much warning and no time to go for the midwife.

Will was asleep, and I wasn't sure what I should do. Katherine told me to sit in the rocking chair and spread my legs so she could see. She lit a lantern, and when I lifted my nightgown, she shrieked and fumbled the lantern, muttering, "Oh no, oh no."

"What," I said, "what's wrong?"

"We need to get you back to bed real fast. The baby has crowned!" She set the lantern on the woodstove and reached for me just as I had a huge contraction. My whole body stiffened.

"Oh no, oh no," she kept repeating. "We have to get you back to bed."

When the pain passed, she helped me stand, and we shuffled toward the bedroom. "Will," I called out, trying not to wake Charles, 'It's time. I need the bed."

I never did see a man scramble into his drawers as fast as Will. He was on his feet, stumbling around in the dark while Katherine settled me.

"She okay?" he asked. "What's happenin'?"

"You're about to be a papa again, is what's happenin'," Katherine said. "This young'un done crowned. Boil water and bring me clean rags. NOW."

Another contraction gripped me, and I cried out.

Will did what he could to help. He boiled water, brought her rags, held my hand, and wiped the perspiration off my forehead. He suffered every push and pain with me as if we were welded together. I could tell from his face he hated to see me suffer. He apologized over and over like he had caused it. He stayed by my side as much as he could stand. When he got up to leave the room, I reached for him with my hands and eyes.

He said, "I need a smoke."

"Please don't go," I said through gritted teeth, trying to keep from crying out and scaring Charles. Will sat in the chair by our bed and clutched my hand to his chest.

"Push!" Katherine ordered from the foot of the bed. "I see 'is little head. Push Maidee. It's almost over."

I pushed and squeezed Will's hand so hard I thought his fingers might pop. I took a deep breath and shoved again.

Katherine said, "One more. Push, Maidee, and we should have us a young'un. Will, I need your help here!"

He pulled himself upright and blinked to clear the tears from his eyes. "What do you want me to do?" he said.

"Hand me those shears and that piece of twine on the dressing table."

He did as he was told, and Katherine handed him the gooey, naked little mass with the red face. She tied twine around the umbilical cord and cut the baby free. Then she snatched his little ankles, and he slipped from Will's hands like a greased pig. He hung upside down in her firm, one-handed grip. With one resounding swat on his wrinkled bottom, she got the yelp she was waiting for. "Sarah was right," she said, "it's a boy."

"Let me see him," I said from the bed where I lay exhausted and spent.

She laid the wriggling baby on my stomach and touched his head with a tenderness that choked Will up. He watched as our new son crawled up my body and nuzzled my breast. "Did you see that?" he asked, sounding like he couldn't believe his eyes.

"He's ready to eat," Katherine announced, covering his nakedness with a soft cotton blanket and helping him nestle onto my chest.

Will couldn't stay. He needed to be somewhere we women wouldn't see his tears and left us to manage the feeding and bathing of his baby boy. Later, as we sat recalling the early morning events, he told me the flood of feelings caught him by surprise.

He said, "I haven't ever felt anything like it before. Sorry I ran out on you like that. I went outside and rolled a smoke or tried to. The paper kept getting wet from my dripping eyes."

After it was over and we had finished cleaning up, Will told us his ma had chased him from the room when Charles was born, so this was his first experience watching a human birth. "When Katherine slipped that squirming, slithering, little blob into my hands, I almost lost last night's dinner," he said.

His story made Katherine emotional. "I've never been around a man sharing feelin's," she said. It made her throat tight, so she sounded funny when she talked.

"How'd you know what to do?" Will asked.

Katherine snuffled and wiped her tears away. "I watched my ma deliver my brother and sister. The midwife explained everything to me as it went along. I watched her cut and tie the cord, but I wasn't doing the cuttin' and tyin' off. I never expected to be put to the test so soon," she said. "I'm glad it was your baby, Maidee, not mine."

We gave our new son Will's name, and he puffed with pride. You'd have thought he delivered him himself if you didn't know.

This hefty, healthy infant was very different from my firstborn. He showed the same towhead his brother sported and the same light blue eyes, but I soon realized his temperament was more forceful. He wailed when Katherine whopped him at birth, and he continued his loud wails to announce wet diapers, hunger pangs, lack of attention, and frustration when my breast milk didn't drop fast enough to suit him.

She took to calling him 'Little Dubbya'E,' and it stuck.

Charles slipped backward to a demanding toddler, jealous for my affection, and Katherine spent most of her time walking or rocking the new baby to quiet his crying while I coddled Charles.

One day Katherine said, "You sure did get one with good lungs this time."

"Yes, I did, and I'm glad for it," I said.

"Why's that?" she asked. The edge in her voice told me she would have been happy to be caring for a less demanding infant.

"Because, when Charles was born, he hardly cried at all, and I worried myself sick that there was something wrong. The more I worried, the less milk I had and the skinnier he got. With Little Dubbya'E, every time he sets to wailing, I feel my breasts swell, and when I feed him, I know he's getting full."

"Oh," was all she could muster.

Little Dubbya'E grew like a bad weed until he was as roly-poly as a fat puppy. I was correct about the signals that made my body respond to milk production. The butterfat this time must have been very high because Little Dubbya'E didn't stay little for long. He was a hearty eater who enjoyed the experience of nestling into my breast. I relished the way he looked into my eyes with pure devotion. I hadn't experienced this connection with Charles and treasured the bond I felt.

I told Katherine, "I don't care if I ever have another baby. This one is perfect."

Of course, I wasn't the one walking the floor with him at night while he grumbled about his wet diaper or his bellyache because he overate—that was Katherine.

CHAPTER 40

WILL

Maidee turned eighteen three months before Little Dubbya'E's first birthday, and I thought the time had come for her to have more freedom. I harbored some guilt for deciding she shouldn't return to school after we ran off and got married. She read everything she could get her hands on, and I knew she felt isolated and cut off from things.

She was now old enough to join the Eastern Star and would need to study with Elizabeth and Emma in town. I sat opposite her in my easy chair as she nursed the baby. "Maidee, it's time you learned to drive."

"Oh, pushaa," she said. "Why would I want to do that?"

"Because it would be good for you to get off the place once in a while under your own steam."

"Not now, Will. I'm happy the way things are."

"I'm teachin' you to drive, girl, so you'd better get ready."

"Maybe after Dubbya'E's not nursing anymore."

She ran her fingers over the baby's cheek and gazed at him in a way that made my heart clutch. Dubbya'E let go of her nipple and smiled, with milk drooling out of his mouth.

Maidee looked at me and said, "There's plenty of time. Let's wait until you get the bridge finished."

Her challenge spurred me to work harder to complete the bridge by Dubbya'E's first birthday. It would open a whole new world for my wife. She never complained about being isolated, but it had to chafe. She was such a spirited and inquisitive girl when I met her, and now she didn't even know what was happening in town, let alone the world. If I taught her to drive, I figured she might see some of her family occasionally and visit more with Emma and Elizabeth.

I worked diligently on the bridge across a slow-moving shallow. Most evenings, Maidee would leave the boys with Katherine and join me on the riverbank. She sometimes sat on the structure laughing and chatting, her skirt hiked up and her legs dangling over the side. Her presence made me happy to be working so hard, but the sight of her bare skin caused stirrings in my groin.

After a long night of work on a sweltering day, Maidee and I took a dip in the river. We shed our clothes and undergarments holding hands as we stepped into the water. We splashed each other like a couple of kids. I ducked beneath the surface to avoid her next volley and wash off the sweat before grabbing and pulling her under. The shallow was only thigh deep.

After I finished rubbing my hands over Maidee's body to bathe off her perspiration, we stood naked in the moonlight, our bodies pressed together.

CHAPTER 41

JIMMY CALVERT

I watch them work on that bridge long time. Hide in bushes. Spy on W'll and M'zl. I see her. She act like he only one who see her. She he'p him. I see ever'thin'. They don't know.

As Jimmy watched Maizelle and Will, his body responded in a new and uncomfortable way. His privates engorged and pressed against his coveralls. The sensation excited him when he rubbed it to make it shrink until it erupted with a sticky fluid that made an awful mess on his clothing.

He was reminded of the time at the boarding school when it happened at night. The attendant called it "wet dreams" and told him it was common for boys his age and not to worry. He had also warned him to "never put your privates near a girl. If you do, you could get in big trouble."

Jimmy took the warning to heart and was careful never to get close to a girl. The time Maizelle hugged him when he gave her the box was the only time, and it made him feel good inside. After that, he got the same feeling whenever he looked at her.

Now, watching Will touch Maizelle and rub his hands over her body gave him the same feeling, except now it made his privates swell. It swelled when he closed his eyes and pictured her sitting on the bridge with her skirt pulled up.

He could see them hugging in the moonlight tonight as Will and Maizelle worked late. Will removed Maizelle's blouse and exposed her naked breasts. Jimmy's privates swelled and ached.

Will pulled her skirt down, exposing her bloomers, and Jimmy sucked in his breath so suddenly it made a slight noise, and Will looked his way.

Jimmy flattened himself on the ground and held his breath.

Will continued removing his clothing. When he and Maizelle were naked, they hugged with their bare skin touching, and Jimmy's erection exploded.

They go in water and splash. They laugh. Splash more. My eyes bug out. W'll hug M'zl close. Smash her neckid top parts. He kiss her. He hold her top parts. Put mouth on one. My pecker squirts. I press on ground. Quiet. Make no sound.

W'll's pecker swolled. Cloud cover moon. It dark. Pinch eyes to see. He puts it in M'zl's legs. Hold her bottom. Push on her. She look happy. I want to do it.

Jimmy watched the lovers with a growing fascination and interest. When Maizelle cried out in pleasure, he thought Will had hurt her, making him angry. His first instinct was to go help her. Get her away from Will.

He watched Will remove her hairpins and her long hair fall free. Will washed her body as they knelt in the water. When they dipped beneath the surface, her hair floated.

For a moment, Jimmy lost sight of them and crawled closer. When he saw her again, he thought *she look like the angel pi'ture in church.*

Maizelle floated, her hair spread in an aureole.

She stood and lifted her arms above her head to gather and wring her wet hair. Her naked body glistened in the moonlight, and Jimmy felt his body respond as before. He watched her leave the river and bend over for her bloomers. His privates erupted again, and he let out a groan.

Maizelle turned and looked directly at the spot where he lay hidden. "What was that?"

"What?" Will asked.

"I heard something."

"I thought I heard rustling up there earlier. Do you see anything?"

Jimmy lay still, held his breath, and kept his head down. His heart beat a tattoo against the ground.

"No. Nothing. Maybe it was just a bird in the bushes, or a racoon."

"I don't hear anything," Will said, "we're probably imagining things."

The pictures of Maizelle Jimmy held in his mind now formed the foundation for his excitement and lust. Feelings he called 'love.' He wanted to hold her naked breasts and touch her round bottom. He pretended to put his lips on her, taste her neck, and planned new ways to hide on their side of the river, ways that would allow him to see her more often. Ways that allowed a fantasy to become an obsession.

CHAPTER 42

MAIZELLE

Will began my lessons when Little Dubbya'E was fifteen months. One evening he said, "Maidee, get yourself together, we're going for a ride tonight, and you're driving."

"Oh, Will, not now," I protested, "I've still got to feed the baby and get him ready for bed."

"Let Katherine do it. He drinks from a cup during the day. There's no reason he can't drink milk from a cup at night."

"Yes, there is," I said, my voice sounding whiney, even to me. "He needs the comfort of the breast to put himself to sleep. He isn't like Charles was. He enjoys nursing."

"Well, tonight, he's going to need to find a new way to put himself to sleep. We have to get underway while there's still daylight. Take him to Katherine, and I'll pull the car up out front." His tone didn't leave me any room to argue.

In my heart, I knew it was time to wean Dubbya'E. It was clear another baby would arrive in six months, although I hadn't shared the news with Will or Katherine. I picked Dubbya'E up and carried him to where she cleaned the dinner dishes. I was envious of her slender figure, knowing I would be big as a house in short order. "Where's Charles?"

"I sent him to fetch the eggs. He likes to do that."

"You think he's old enough to do that by himself?"

"He is. Once in a while, he breaks one, but he feels so grown-up and important when I let him go on his own. We have lots of eggs now that Spring has sprung. Losin' one or two won't hurt none."

I pondered her decision and watched her for a minute before saying, "Katherine, Will's going to teach me to drive tonight. Heat milk for Little Dubbya'E and feed him from the cup before he goes down."

She scowled. I ignored the question in her eyes.

"Make a sugar tit for him to take to bed. You might try dipping it in warm milk before you give it to him. He'll probably fuss for a while, but it's time he came off the breast."

She tried to say something, but I rushed on, "If I stay in the house and hear him cry for me, my milk will drop, and I'll never wean him. This is a good time to get started."

Katherine, who adored Dubbya'E, was taken aback. The panic on her face and her wide eyes let me know she did not relish the task. When she found her voice again, she said, "Are you sure? It's so sudden, and you know how he likes to be nursed to sleep."

"Yes, I'm sure. He will have a new brother or sister in a few months, and my body needs a rest. I can't have two of them on the breast at once. Dubbya'E doesn't show signs of wanting to wean himself, so I have to do it."

"Another one?" Katherine's voice wavered, and she stared at me in shock before she broke into a broad smile. She threw her arms around me in a bear hug. "I had no idea! How long have you known? Why didn't you tell me?"

"Probably because I didn't want to believe it myself. I've suspected for two months, and as of this week, I'm sure. Will doesn't know, so don't make a ruckus until I have a chance to get him alone, okay?"

Katherine grabbed onto me as she squealed and danced up and down.

So much for not making a ruckus, I thought, trying to pry her hands off my arms.

"Okay. I'll start weaning Little Dubbya'E tonight. Now you go learn to drive that big 'ol car so's we can take a spin into town together."

We laughed and hugged as we danced in a circle on the kitchen floor. My toddler dangled on my hip, and Katherine encircled the pair of us with both arms.

Little Dubbya'E was delighted by the cheerful exuberance his two mamas showed and burst forth with a volley of laughter as he bounced up and down on my hip. I broke free on the third circle around the floor and handed him to Katherine.

As Will came in the door, I said, "Let's go. Let's get out of here before he discovers I'm gone...and Katherine, you'd better check on Charles."

We stepped out the seldom-used front door onto the small porch facing the river. The slope downhill was gradual, but you couldn't see the bridge in the tree line even from this height. Will took my hand and helped me down the three steps to where the car waited.

With a dramatic flourish, he opened the driver's door the way he had on our wedding day and assisted me as I stepped onto the running board. After all this time, I still felt a small electric rush through my body from the touch of his hand. Playing the part of the helpless maiden to his gallant prince, I smiled coyly.

Practicing all my manners about how a lady modestly enters an automobile, I seated myself and gathered my skirt beside me.

Will closed the door, leaned in the open window, and gave me a peck on the cheek. "Ready to learn to drive, pretty lady?"

"Oh, Will. Do you really think I can learn to drive a big 'ol car all by myself?" I teased with my voice as I fluttered my eyelids and smiled demurely.

Will reached through the window and tickled me under my outstretched arm, braced against the steering wheel.

I giggled and twisted away from him. His tickles always made me laugh.

He walked around and climbed in. Our eyes met and held when he looked at me to start his instructions, just like they had that day in Papa's car. His face flushed, and he opened his mouth to speak, but not a syllable ushered forth.

The intimacy of the moment made me pause. My face warmed, seeing the desire in Will's eyes. I lowered my eyelids, then raised them, and without thinking, I blurted out, "We're expecting another baby in September if my calculations are right."

Will was dumbstruck. His mouth dropped open. I could almost hear him thinking, *another one? It isn't possible.*

We had been careful, planning our lovemaking around my cycle and counting on the enthusiastic nursing skills of Little Dubbya'E to provide an additional layer of protection.

"How...? When...?" was all he could muster.

"Probably that night at the river. All our babies seem to be conceived at the beginning or end of something wonderful. First, our wedding night—or afternoon, I guess it was—then the news of the war ending, and now the bridge. We better be more careful about how we celebrate if we don't want this to keep happening."

"Maidee, I don't want this to quit happening. I worry about you, though. You're young to already have two, and now another one? I need to learn to resist you, is all. You are the most beautiful woman I've ever known. When I see you and know you're my wife, my urges get the best of me."

"No need to be sorry—or apologize. Women aren't supposed to enjoy it like men do, but I look forward to it. Promise me you will never stop, no matter how many young 'uns God decides to give us."

Will reached over and patted me on the knee. "I promise. And that will be an easy promise to keep. Anyway, who says women aren't supposed to enjoy it? Now, let's teach you how to drive before your belly is too big to fit under the steering column."

Will was a patient instructor as the Lizzy bounced across the field toward the river. I turned the wheel this way and that. He had me stop over and over to practice starting the car with the hand crank. He taught me how to back up. I turned the wheel hard to the right, then hard to the left. I set the parking brake, shifted the gears, and learned to steer around obstacles Will had set up in the pasture.

We stopped short of the bridge on this first lesson, but he promised me I would drive across the river and into town next time. Imagine me driving up Central Street with everyone gawking in surprise. I could hardly wait.

CHAPTER 43

MAIZELLE

After Will finished the bridge, we agreed the time was right to accept Uncle Robert's challenge and begin his studies to become a Master Mason. Bobby was in pursuit of the same goal.

I was now the proud owner of a driving license, and although Will took the car to work during the day and was often gone with it in the evenings, the sense of freedom it brought was exhilarating. I took the car whenever I could, negotiated the narrow bridge across the river, and called on Emma or Aunt Elizabeth. Both women were very keen on the Eastern Star. Each encouraged me to pursue membership by supporting Will in becoming a Master Mason.

By our third baby's due date, Will had achieved his Second-Degree status and actively pursued the Third-Degree designation. Life in the Jones household took on an entirely new rhythm after Aaron's birth. Some days I drove Will to work in the morning. Then I'd run errands, buy supplies, take Katherine to visit her family, and meet with Elizabeth to prepare for initiation into the sisterhood.

One day, when Aaron was a month old, I dropped Katherine and all three boys off at the O'Brien's so I could take care of a couple of things before the next feeding. I motored down the lane past Papa's house, hoping to glimpse the little ones or Bowen. I felt important driving the car, and a part of me wanted someone in my family to see.

After Will hired Jamie, I saw him twice before he left for school. Our reunions were bittersweet. I was always closer to Bowen than Jamie, and we didn't seem to know what to say to each other. He was not forthcoming with news about the family and acted like he didn't know how to talk to me now that I was a mother. The only satisfying result was his repeated statement that as soon as Bowen turned eighteen, he would make it a point to see me. It was hard to wait. It was him I secretly hoped to see this morning. My heart pounded, and my throat was dry. It reminded me how I felt the night I ran away with Will. But luck was not on my side. The only sign of life at the house was a patient of Papa's, standing on the stoop waiting to be let in.

I turned around at the end of the street, swallowed the lump, and headed to town. I don't know which was worse, not seeing anyone or worrying that I might.

The day held a pleasant surprise, however. When I stopped at the post office to pick up the mail, there was a fat letter from Julia.

I pulled into the parking lot next to Will's garage and tore open the envelope. Several news clippings fell into my lap. The San Antonio Chamber of Commerce, and the Y.W.C.A, had chosen Julia, Miss 1921 All-Around American Girl.

The San Antonio Express ran a full story and photo spread, with pictures of Julia dressed in her professional clothes, a bathing dress, and sporting clothes that highlighted her athletic skills. She was pictured as a horsewoman, a golfer, a basketball player, and finally, dressed in the latest flapper fashion for a social night on the town. She was described as a "young beauty of serious purpose," credited with a "keen mind, equal to many young men of her age."

The article said, "The ideal girl must have high standards and ideals, depth of purpose, and an outstanding ambition in life, whether it be within the home or that much-discussed thing, a career." It concluded with, "Miss Clarke is a business girl."

I loved the stories, but I liked the photos best. My favorite portrayed Julia sitting on the ground, legs bent at the knee, with her stocking-covered ankles and calves exposed. She wore a slim skirt and a high-necked white blouse with openwork across the front yoke. Her hair was fashioned in a bob with a cloche pulled down across a fringe of bangs. A lovely smile radiated from her face, and she looked genuinely happy.

I was more than a little surprised to see my sister astride a Thoroughbred horse, swinging a golf club and holding a basketball. To my knowledge, Julia had never been on a horse of any kind, wouldn't have known a golf club if she tripped over it, and a basketball? Well, that really stretched my imagination.

My eyes grew blurry as I stared at the newsprint photos, and tears plopped onto the paper. I missed my sister and realized how little I knew of Julia's new life.

The letter accompanying the news clippings announced that she was coming home for a month-long visit. This news burst the dam of emotion I'd been shoving down for so long. I wiped my eyes and gathered up Will's mail.

When I stepped into the shop, Will took one look at me and dropped what he was doing. "Sugar, what's wrong? What happened? Are the boys alright?" He wrapped his arms around my shoulders as I shook and dissolved in tears. He held me close while I tried to explain.

"Fine. Fine," I choked out. "Boys, fine. Julia..." I hiccupped. "...Julia," and the flood started anew.

"Something happened to your sister?"

That made me giggle. I shook my head. Laughed and cried at the same time. Talking was out of the question. Will offered me his handkerchief, and I wiped my nose and eyes.

He led me into his office and sat me on the lone chair. Gripping my shoulders, he leaned in toward my face. "You need to get control of yourself. Now stop this and tell me what happened."

"I'm sorry," I managed to spit out, breaking the hysteria. "It's nothing. Julia's coming for a visit. That's all." I leaned back and stared into his eyes, which were as puzzled as I was confused. "She sent a letter. I don't know why, but it all seemed to pile up at once, how much I miss her, how long it's been since I've seen her, how different our lives are..." my voice trailed off. "I guess I just had a little breakdown, like when you told me Jamie came to see you."

Will pulled me upright and wrapped his arms around me. He held me so close I couldn't catch my breath. "Maidee," he said, "I'm so sorry. I tore you from your family like pulling a turnip out of the ground. I know you miss them. I know how much you miss Julia."

I pushed against his chest to get room to breathe.

He said, "I know it's been hard for you not to see your papa and the kids. If I could change the way we did this, I would. But I don't regret marrying you or having our boys."

Pushing back, I realized he was crying almost as hard as I was. I handed him the rumpled handkerchief. "I love you, Will. I love our boys. It's enough. It will be wonderful to see Julia. And when it's time, I'll be happy to see Bowen and the others. But I wouldn't trade my life for anything in the world."

Will blew his nose. "I love you too, Sugar. Always have, always will. Can't imagine life without you...you and the boys, I mean."

"I know what you mean. There isn't any *me* without those three little ragamuffins."

He stuffed the handkerchief in his overall pocket and reached for me, giving me a quick hug.

"I should head back. It's almost time for Aaron's next feeding. That's one thing Katherine can't do for me. Besides, they've been with her half the afternoon already."

"We were lucky to find her. I can't think of anyone who would have been better for you or the boys."

"I know. She's the best. But we need to remember that she's a young woman with desires and hopes of her own. We can't keep her prisoner at our place forever, no matter how much she feels like a part of our family. Someday, someone will come along and steal her heart."

"You're right. Don't encourage her, okay?"

We laughed and hugged before I bounced out the door and climbed into the car. Will followed to crank it for me. He patted the hood and stepped back as I engaged the gears and rolled toward the street.

"Katherine! Katherine!" I called from the front walk, my excitement oozing from every pore. "Julia's coming!"

"What? What are you hollerin' about, fit to wake the dead?" Katherine said as she fumbled with the hook on the latched screen door.

"Julia's coming home for a whole month! She sent me a letter and pictures, too. She won a special honor and is in all the papers." The words tumbled out and stumbled over each other.

Katherine stared open-mouthed. She'd never seen me this excited.

I hadn't seen Julia since before Will and I eloped, and she knew from our long talks how deeply I felt the loss of my sister. It was the hardest part of leaving my family. My brothers were within arm's reach. I had even seen Jamie. But my sister's absence left a hole in my heart that even dear Katherine couldn't fill.

I pulled open the screen door, and she stepped aside. "Oh, Katty, just think! Julia's coming. She'll be staying with Papa and Leila but will visit us every chance she gets. She wants to meet the boys and have them know their Aunt Julia!"

My eyes brimmed with tears of joy. Katherine threw her arms around me and swung me in circles. I had grown three inches and added a good twenty pounds since the babies. It surprised me she could get me off the floor.

When she set me down, her face held a puzzled expression.

"What's wrong?" I asked.

"Katty?" she said. "You've never called me Katty. Are you possessed?"

CHAPTER 44

WILL

I had finished cleaning the shop and stepped out front to put used oil in the barrel when a flash of bright yellow caught my eye.

I looked up to see the most beautiful and unusual car I'd ever laid eyes on coming over the rise.

The automobile was golden-rod yellow with metallic gold fenders. I'd never seen a car like this up close. I'd seen photographs and heard people describe it, but it was something else to see one in Utopia. The car crept along the main street like it was in a parade. I was puzzled about the model until it got close enough for me to see it was a Handley-Knight five-passenger touring car.

A very citified couple was in it. The driver was an older gentleman with a small, tightly trimmed mustache, sporting a light grey Fedora. The woman was away from my line of sight, but I saw her waving to everyone they passed along the street.

I stared open-mouthed as the car slowly motored past. The man gave me a nod as they went by. I wanted to holler at him to stop, so I could get a good look at that car. Embarrassed that he caught me gawking, I looked away and went inside to watch through the window.

The car motored the length of Central Street and pulled into the schoolyard to turn around. When it came back my way, I could make out a woman wearing one of those cap-style hats pulled down over short hair, like the picture of her sister Maidee had on our dresser. She smiled and waved to everyone they passed as if she knew them. She looked like the Queen of England riding in that elegant car, tipping her hand at folks.

When the big car reached the edge of my parking lot, it turned in and pulled to a stop. I watched the driver move swiftly to the lady's side to open her door. She put out a gloved hand, and he steadied her as she stepped onto the running board and then the ground.

He offered his arm, and she took it as they started toward my door. She wore something so filmy that it almost looked like she had nothing on. Her knee-length dress showed slim legs and well-turned ankles. The material sparkled in the sun and moved like slow water over smooth rocks when she walked.

I didn't want to get caught watching them, so I ran into the shop, flattened myself on my creeper, and rolled under a car. I heard the bell on the door tinkle when they came inside but ignored it so they wouldn't know I'd been staring.

After a few minutes, they opened the door to make the bell tinkle again. "Ahem." A man's voice echoed through the shop. He cleared his throat and said, "Could we get some assistance, please?"

I scrambled from under the car and bumped my head on the undercarriage. "Sugar tit!" I cursed, rubbing my forehead to see if there was blood.

"Sorry," the man said, "Are you okay?"

"I didn't hear the bell," I fibbed, "how can I help?" I stood and looked at the well-dressed gentleman for any hint of recognition. "Will Jones," I said. "I'd offer my hand, but it's dirty. What can I do for you?"

"I'm Sam. Sam McGavern," the man said. "I brought someone who would like to talk to you. She's in your office."

I leaned around the man and saw a tall, attractive woman dressed in sharp contrast to the cotton skirts and blouses worn by the womenfolk around here.

Her loose-fitting dress offered a clear view of the slip she wore underneath. The citified style of her appearance was not lost on me.

She smiled and offered a little wave of her hand from the doorway. Her face was familiar, but I had no idea where I might have seen her. I nodded to her, and it clicked. The picture on our dresser. My eyes returned to the man standing in front of me.

"Julia?" I asked with a fair bit of doubt.

"Yes," the man replied, "my fiancé, Miss Julia Clarke, would like a word."

"Of course," I said, "give me a minute to wash my hands. I'll be right there." I hurried to the washbasin at the rear of the garage. Mr. McGavern returned to the office.

When I walked inside, I saw the bright yellow Handley-Knight parked in front of the building. My attention was torn between Julia and the stunning automobile.

Good manners prevailed, and I turned to the fancy-dressed woman. "Julia, I presume?" I offered my hand, and she put the tips of her gloved fingers in it for a brief moment.

"Yes, Will, I'm Julia. Are you surprised to see me?"

"That would be the case. I barely recognized you. Are you looking for Maidee?"

"Yes. I want to see her before I go to my father's house. I need to hear from her how things stand."

"There's not much to tell. He disowned her, and she hasn't set eyes on him since the day we got married. She'll be happy to see *you,* though. She's at our place across the river. Up the road past the school, take the first left. We built a new bridge across. The road goes up to the house. Are you going now?"

"Yes, I think so. Is that all right, Sam?"

"Yes, darling, whatever you want."

"Oh, Will, this is my fiancé, Sam McGavern."

"We met. It's awful dusty and dirty up at our place. Are you sure you want to go in these fancy clothes?"

Julia's dismissive laughter filled my small office. "Of course, Will. Where isn't it dusty and dirty around here, anyway? I'm sure Sam and I will be fine."

Julia probably didn't mean to disparage Utopia, but her flippant tone offended me. It was as though she felt she would be slumming anywhere in Utopia, so why should our house be any different?

I bristled, "Maizelle does a great job keeping our house clean. I just thought maybe you would be more comfortable in less dressy clothes for a visit to the homestead."

Julia flashed a sweet smile. "No worries, Will. I want to see my little sister, and I wouldn't care if she lived in a garbage heap. We aren't concerned about our clothes, are we, Sam?"

"I'm not if you're not." Sam wrapped his arm around Julia's waist and turned her toward the door.

Julia, still smiling, looked over her shoulder at me as Sam guided her out. She raised her hand in a little wave when Sam assisted her into the Handley.

He pulled the big car onto the street and turned toward the school.

Julia smiled and waved at people as if she recognized and knew them all.

I watched until they turned onto the narrow road leading to our new bridge. The bridge wasn't built for such a heavy car. I bet it bows when they drive across.

MAIZELLE

I was sitting on the front porch in the rocking chair with baby Aaron in my arms when Dubbya'E said, "What's that, Mama?"

Curious, I watched as a cloud of dust rose on our narrow road, billowing around a bright yellow car as it made its way toward the house. All the windows were rolled up to keep the occupants from being covered in a veil of red Sabinal Canyon dust, preventing me from seeing who it was.

"Katherine, come see this. Hurry!"

Katherine appeared behind me, shielding her eyes from the sun.

Charles and Dubbya'E stopped playing and stared. Charles abandoned his younger brother and ran up the steps to hide behind my skirt.

Dubbya'E, realizing he alone faced the yellow monster, cried, and reached for me, hoping I would carry him to safety.

Katherine squeezed past and jumped off the porch to scoop Dubbya'E out of the path of the approaching automobile.

The big car stopped in front of the stoop. As the dust settled, a door opened, and a man dressed in a business suit stepped out.

All of us gaped, and no one spoke.

The man opened the passenger door, and a tall, elegant woman emerged. She smiled broadly at me.

"Maidee? It's me, Julia."

"Julia? How...what...I didn't know you were coming today." I stood and shifted Aaron to my hip as I peered out from my big sunbonnet at the lady in my front yard.

Julia took three quick strides and mounted the short stairway. She wrapped her arms around me and nearly lifted me off the porch.

We hugged until the baby on my hip began squirming and crying at a fevered pitch.

Julia let go of me and bent over Aaron, cooing, "Well, who do we have here? I'm your Auntie Julia. This isn't a very nice way to welcome me when I've come so far to meet you."

I shifted the baby back into my arms and rocked him, patting his tiny back and shushing into his ear. "This is Aaron," I said, "and back here, hiding, is Charles. Katherine has Little Dubbya'E down there by the car."

"Katherine O'Brien? Oh my, everybody has changed so much. I didn't recognize her at all." She turned toward Katherine and called out, "Katty O'Brien. The last time I saw you, you were still in pigtails!"

Katherine smiled and moved toward the porch. "Dubbya'E, this here's your Aunt Julia. Now stop your whimperin' and say hello."

My toddler turned his face away and buried it in Katherine's shoulder.

"He's at the shy stage right now," Katherine offered by way of apology. "Dubbya'E," she coaxed, "show your Aunt Julia what a big boy you are."

He burrowed deeper into her shoulder and wrapped his chubby legs tight around her waist.

Julia's lilting laughter floated like fairy dust around our little gathering. She looked at me with a self-satisfied expression and said, "Maidee, there's someone I want you to meet. Someone very special to me." She motioned for the man in the suit to join her, took his arm, and walked him to where I stood holding Aaron, with Charles leaning against my side. "Maidee, this is my fiancé, Sam McGavern. Sam, this is my baby sister, Maizelle Jones."

You could have knocked me over with a feather. I didn't know what to say, so I nodded to the man who could barely see my face beneath my bonnet. I hoped he missed my look of complete shock before I said, "Pleased to meet you." I gave a little curtsy and then felt like a complete fool.

"Likewise," Sam said. "I've heard many fine things about you." He was polite— like he hadn't noticed my knee dip and bobbing head.

With no free hand to offer, I blurted, "Why don't we all get inside out of this heat? Katherine, will you prepare sweet tea for our guests?" I sounded overly proper and formal, even to my ear, and Katherine stared at me with a scowl and a question. I was thankful the house was clean and the dishes were done.

Julia, Mr. McGavern, and I entered the living room, followed by Katherine, Dubbya'E, and Charles. The room held the two chairs Will's parents handed down as they left for the gulf. I directed Julia to the rocker and the well-dressed Mr. McGavern to Will's easy chair. I looked around for Katherine, who had disappeared to the kitchen for the tea.

"Excuse me, please, I need to get more chairs," I said, hurrying into the kitchen and tearing off the big sunbonnet. I tossed it at the hook near the back door and grabbed a chair from the end of the table. It was the only chair in the kitchen, as

Will had fashioned benches for seating, and we had inherited his old highchair for the baby. I lifted it with one hand, and half carried, half dragged, it into the other room, holding Aaron in the crook of my other arm.

Mr. McGavern rose and took the chair as Aaron was about to slip out of my grasp. I hoisted the baby back to my hip and followed.

Sam placed the chair in the middle of the floor.

"Oh, Maidee, I'm sorry. Let me take the baby," Julia said without rising. "I'm dying to get a good look at him."

I handed Aaron to my sister. He took one look at her and began to wail, kicking his tiny legs in protest. "He must be hungry," I said, snatching him back, to Julia's relief.

Katherine appeared with a tray holding three glasses of cold tea. She served Julia first, Sam next, and me last. She raised her eyebrows when she reached my chair and looked directly at me. "Will there be anything else, *Ma'am*?" Her intense gaze backed up the sarcasm.

I was stunned. "No, nothing," I said, feeling chagrined and embarrassed. I redirected my eyes to Julia. "I need to excuse myself for a few minutes while you drink your tea. I have to finish feeding the baby. He wasn't done when you came driving up." I started toward the bedroom, saying, "Katherine, take my chair and fill Julia in on the goings-on in town."

I spoke lightly, and in my heart, I hoped it might make up for the officious way in which I had treated my dearest friend and companion. When I returned with a satisfied and sleeping infant, I handed him to Katherine and said, "What did I miss?"

Katherine stood and said, "Not much. I'll put Aaron in the cradle and finish what I was doin'. Y'all go ahead and visit. I'll try to keep the boys out 'a yer hair for a whil."

I stared at Julia. I wasn't expecting her and didn't know why she was here instead of at Papa's. I couldn't think of a single word to say. I hoped she would fill the silence, and I wasn't disappointed.

"Maidee, I'm getting married at Christmas in San Antonio. I want Papa to give me away and you to be my Matron of Honor. Sam brought me home so he could ask Papa for my hand. I'll stay until Thanksgiving to plan the wedding, and then Sam will come for me. What do you say?"

"Papa will never give you away with me standing by your side. He disowned me."

"Don't you think he'll change his mind if *I* ask? Having you there is important, and I need papa to walk me up the aisle."

"You can ask him. But don't count on him saying yes. He'll tell you it's one or the other. You can't have both."

"Have you forgotten, Honeybee, about my special powers of persuasion?" She laughed and placed her hand on my knee.

"No, I haven't forgotten. But you don't know how mad he is at me for getting married. He told me never to come back—that I was dead to him." My voice cracked as I choked back the tears that always threatened when I spoke of Papa.

Julia stood with her arms outstretched for an embrace. "Honeybee, I'm so sorry. I didn't mean to open old wounds."

We hugged until my arms ached. My resolve collapsed with the feel of Julia's arms around me, and I let go of the deep hurt in a flood of tears.

Julia rocked me back and forth in her arms, much as she had done every night for a year after Mama died. Once again, I was the inconsolable baby sister, and Julia was the mother.

Sam had the good grace to remove himself from the room and go to his car while we worked through this grief-filled chapter. I had no idea how much I'd missed my sister, and I don't think Julia realized how much she missed me.

When the tears were spent, we were both weak from emotion.

I stepped back and looked Julia in the eye. "You need Papa to give you away, Julia. He'll be heartbroken if you get married without him. I can be there in spirit, but I can't be by your side. I'm sorry."

I lifted a handkerchief from my skirt pocket and handed it to Julia, who wiped her nose, blotted the tearstains on her face and neck, and then dabbed at my eyes and nose, just as she had when I was a child.

"Will you come to the wedding and sit with the guests then? I can't imagine getting married without you."

"I'll talk to Will and see what he says. If he agrees to come with me, I'll come. Maybe if Papa doesn't know we're invited, he won't notice until it's too late."

"Oh, Maidee, you're the cat's pajamas! And I want you to bring the boys, too. Has Papa seen any of them?"

I stared. *Cat's pajamas?* "No. I've seen Jamie, and he says Papa won't allow the mention of my name, so unless he read the birth announcements in the Sabinal Graphic, he doesn't even know I have them, and he's never come around to see them." I couldn't keep the tremor out of my voice.

"That's so sad. His own grandsons. Maybe the wedding will be a good opportunity for them to meet." Julia sounded so positive and hopeful I hated to do anything to dampen her spirits.

"You're barking up a hollow tree, Julia. He doesn't want to meet them. He doesn't want to admit they exist because then he would have to admit I exist. I'm one of the only women in Utopia, or Uvalde County, who had to deliver my babies without help from a doctor—and he's my *father*! You can have your dream, but I've given up on fanciful notions."

Julia tilted her head and looked at me with pity.

"Don't pity me, Julia. I made my choice knowing Papa had forbidden me to see Will." I twisted away and plopped down on the rocker. "Papa wanted something for my life that I didn't want. I couldn't stand living with Leila after you left. She was worse than ever." I wadded the handkerchief and stuffed it back into my skirt pocket. "I loved Will, and he loved me. I knew if we didn't get married, Papa would send me to a boarding school, and Will would get called up for the war. I'd already lost you. I couldn't stand the thought of losing him, too."

Julia sat on the edge of the easy chair. "I didn't mean to pity you, Honeybee. I can see you're content here."

"I'm not content, Julia; I'm happy. Will is good to me. He shows me he loves me every day in ways you would never understand."

Julia furrowed her brow like she didn't know whether to be insulted or happy for me.

"When I felt overwhelmed with a toddler underfoot and another baby on the way so soon after, he hired Katherine as a live-in to help me." I leaned forward and said as kindly as I could, "I'm not like you. I never wanted a fancy house or a big car, and I never wanted to be a career girl. I wanted Will. I wanted to be his wife and the mother of his children." I smiled. "I hope when you marry Sam, you find half the joy and happiness I've been blessed with. Then I'll know you're not only content but truly happy."

Julia straightened her back, raised her chin, and pursed her lips. "Sam and I have a very special relationship. He treats me like a queen. If we can afford it, I don't see what's wrong with a nice house and a fine automobile." She looked away and reached for the glass Sam had left sitting on the side table. She ran her finger around the rim, causing drops of moisture to run down the side. "Sam is a successful businessman, and I admire his accomplishments. I'm sure we will be quite happy."

The clipped tone of voice told me my sister was offended. The four-plus years we'd spent apart had changed us both. Julia's defensiveness held a note of doubt. As if what she said was more to convince herself than me. "I'm sorry, Julia," I said. "I didn't mean you wouldn't be happy or weren't as much in love with Sam as I am with Will. You want different things for your life than I do." I leaned forward and met her eyes. "I never wanted to leave Utopia, and now I don't have to. I've found what I was looking for with Will." I waited for Julia to say something, but she stared at me in a daze. I broke the stare-down and said, "I hope you find the same with Sam."

I watched as Julia lifted the glass and brushed the condensation off the table with her finger, eyes cast at the floor. "I wouldn't trade a single one of my boys for the latest fashions and all the finery in the world. But I'm glad for you that you're able to live your dream. Maybe after you have your first child, you'll understand what I am talking about."

Julia's eyes brimmed. "That's *if* we have a child." Her voice pitched higher, and she squeaked out, "Sam is twenty years older than I am, and we aren't certain we should have children." With a quivering smile, she dabbed the corners of her eyes and said, "I may just spend my time this month getting to know your little ones and satisfy my maternal longings by being the best auntie in recorded history."

For once, I felt older and wiser and like the mother. "Oh, Julia, there's nothing like having one of your own. I feel so sorry for Will's sister, Eula, because Fred's older, and she's never had a child. Don't miss this opportunity if you can help it." I placed my hands on Julia's shoulders like she gripped me on the day she left Utopia. "I realize sometimes God doesn't send children to every couple who wants them. I guess the mystery of how He decides who to bless and who to burden is one we can't answer." I let my arms drop. "I hope he blesses you the way he blessed me—that is... I mean... if you want babies."

I saw the look of confusion and fear in Julia's eyes. I put my arms around her once more and whispered. "I love your beautiful dress and your short hair. You look so sophisticated. Having babies ruins your figure, so you might not want to have one while you're still working."

"Thanks, Maidee. I might not. Sam likes me to dress in the latest styles, and we enjoy going to speakeasies and dancing the night away. It would be hard to do the Charleston with a big pregnant belly!" She pushed away. "I guess we'll have to wait and see what happens."

With a false, light laugh, she picked up her gloves from the arm of the chair. "I should be going now. Poor Sam. Sitting out there in the car in this heat. At this rate, he'll be all smelly and melted by the time we get to Papa's." She threaded her fingers into the gloves. "Thanks for the tea. Tell Katty and the little boys I'll be back for another visit in a few days."

She glided across the floor and out the door, looking like a will-'o-the-wisp.

CHAPTER 45

MAIZELLE

As soon as Julia and her fiancé were out of sight, I ran to find Katherine. I felt awful for treating her like a servant. Katherine was important to me, and so much more than hired help. I found her in the kitchen up to her elbows in dishwater.

"I'm sorry," I said, "I thought we finished the dishes before they arrived."

"We did."

"What's this then?

"Jus' puttin' some pans to soak to make 'em easier to wash later."

"Katherine, I'm sorry for treating you like I did. I don't know what got into me. I don't ever think of you as 'help' so why did I treat you like my servant? I am so, so sorry."

Katherine looked into the sudsy water and refused to turn her face. I put my hand on her shoulder. Her body stiffened under my touch and knew it was going to take more than a quick apology to fix what was broken.

"I swear it will never happen again. I'm not making excuses, but I think I was so thrown off balance by Julia's arrival, her outlandish outfit, and meeting her fiancé that I forgot for a minute who I was, and the wonderful friend you are to me." Her shoulder relaxed. I turned her toward me and wrapped her in a bear hug. Before either of us could say anything, Little Dubbya'E and Charles slammed open the screen door and burst into the room.

"Mama. Kath'ern." They shouted, "Ginger's having babies in the laundry basket."

"Oh, my," Katherine muttered, "I was taking Aaron's diapers off the line when you called me inside to see what was comin'."

"Who's Ginger?" I asked.

"That mangy old yella cat that lives with me in the barn. I thought she was too old to have kits, but I guess I was wrong." The screen banged shut behind her.

"Mama, Papa won't drown the kittens like he did the baby mice, will he?" The plaintive voice of my tenderhearted Charles penetrated deep into my heart. That had been such a traumatic experience for my toddler. He was so young I assumed it was long forgotten.

"No, baby. I won't let Papa drown the little kittens. We'll help Ginger hide her babies until they're too big to drown." I took Charles and Dubbya'E by the hands and went to see how Kathrine was solving the problem.

"Look here," she said when we stepped up to the basket full of clean diapers with a long-haired orange cat and three squirming kittens settling in.

"Is she finished?" I asked.

"I'm not sure. I don't think so. Number three was comin' out when I got here. I couldn't disturb her, Maidee. I'll soak the diapers and get everything cleaned up as soon as I'm sure she's got 'em all out."

Ginger hissed as Dubbya'E reached into the box to touch a new kitten. I grabbed his wrist and pulled him away. "No, Dubbya'E, the mama cat doesn't want anyone to touch her babies." I looked back as another slimy little head emerged.

"Look, another one," Kathrine said. "I hope this is the last."

Her wish was granted. The barn cat, Ginger, with whom I was barely acquainted, delivered her four kittens to us on that day of already unusual and disturbing events.

Katherine announced that she would prepare a place for the mother cat and her kits in the room Will had fixed up for her in the barn. She said, "I'll enjoy watching the kittens grow. They'll be good company." With that, she lifted the laundry basket and hiked off toward the barn.

I thought that was a great place to hide the babies and avoid a confrontation with Will. He never went into Katherine's private space so we could avoid him knowing so long as the boys could be quiet. That would be a tall order, for sure, asking a three-year-old and a two-year-old to keep a secret like this.

I took the boys into the house and changed the subject to the visit from their Aunt Julia. I meant to keep the conversation lively when Will got home and avoid any mention of new kittens.

All Will could talk about was the Handley-Knight automobile that had parked in his lot to the great admiration of everyone in town. I was on pins and needles waiting for Julia's next visit when I was sure to get the first real news about my family since Will and I eloped. Will laughed about the "get-up" Julia was wearing and the stiff, formal man she dragged home to Utopia.

After dinner Katherine took the boys to get ready for bed. I was exhausted from the cascade of events, seeing my sister again, and fear the boys would spill the beans about what was hidden in a dark corner of the barn.

I talked Will into taking a stroll down to the river before we turned in. He protested that he wanted to tell the boys goodnight and I glued myself to his side so I could fend off any conversation about the kittens.

He held my hand as we walked the short distance to our little bridge. We both had happy memories of building it. Will said, "I worried all afternoon that Sam's big heavy car might take the bridge downriver." He chuckled, telling me about Julia and Sam's arrival, and showed me the goose egg he got trying to scramble to his feet to greet them.

We laughed about Julia's fancy clothes and the funny little cap she called a "cloche." I thought she looked dazzling, but Will thought she was putting on airs. Then he asked me the strangest question. He said, "Maidee, do you ever wish you'd waited until you were older to marry? You might have married a gentleman, like Julia, if you'd gone to that girl's school your pa wanted."

I stopped and faced him square. "Will Jones, that is about the stupidest thing I've ever heard you say. If you don't know after three boys how much I love you, I don't know what it will take. I wouldn't trade my life with you for anything Julia's has to offer. As for marrying a gentleman—there is no other man on the face of this earth I would want to be married to—least of all some fancy man like Mr. Sam McGavern."

Will gathered me into his arms and almost squeezed the air out of me. Then he kissed me in that way that makes my knees weak. He said, "I love you," and I knew he did.

I chose this moment to bring up the kittens. "Will, something else happened today that needs discussing."

He stroked my hair and said, "What might that be, pretty lady?"

"The barn cat, Ginger, had kittens. There are four of them and I promised Charles you wouldn't drown them."

"Why'd you go and do that?" He scowled and the moment of tenderness was over.

"I did it because he has never gotten over you drowning the baby mice he found in that nest in the chicken coup."

"Aw, Maidee, I wasn't about to let a batch of mice grow up eating the chicken scratch. We have enough mice around here to start our own mouse farm."

"I know. But he was so little, and it stuck with him like nothing else ever has. When he saw the kittens the first thing he said was, 'Mama, Daddy isn't going to drown them like the baby mice, is he?' If you could have heard his voice, I think you'd agree with me."

"Where are they?"

"Katherine has hidden them away where the mama cat can have some privacy until she gets them raised."

"You sure about this? Do we want four more cats marauding around the place?"

"They won't hurt anything, and they'll grow up to be good mousers if we leave them on their own. It's important to me, Will. I have a tenderhearted boy and I don't want him to worry about this."

Will put his arm around my shoulders and steered me up the hill. "You have my word, but I may have to spend a little time toughening up that son of mine." He gave me a squeeze.

We were almost back to the house when Will took my hand and said, "Why don't you tell Charles to pick his favorite from the litter, and when it's old enough he can bring it to the house and make a pet of it."

I was taken aback by his offer and stopped cold to look at him. I was certain I hadn't heard right. "You sure about that? I didn't think you wanted a cat in the house."

"It'd be good for Charles to have something to take care of on his own. I know he's tender-hearted, Maidee. He's just like you."

CHAPTER 46

MAIZELLE

Julia's next visit came two days later. Sam dropped her at the porch and drove off. That meant Julia and I would have some real sister time. I was anxious to hear her news about the visit with Papa and Leila. I knew it was unrealistic to hope Papa had relented and I would be a bridesmaid, but I couldn't help myself.

Katherine, bless her soul, asked me if I'd like her to take the boys up to the barn to explore—and see the kittens—something they loved but weren't allowed to do on their own. I told her about Will's offer to let Charles have a kitten and she said she'd help him choose one.

Julia was dressed more comfortably this time in a plain cotton dress of light blue. It was shorter than anything any woman in Utopia wore but it looked more serviceable than the frock she arrived in the first day, and it didn't make me uncomfortable. I poured tea and we sat at the kitchen table.

I put a lump of sugar in my tea and stirred. When I made eye contact with my sister, she could hear the questions without me speaking, the way sisters do. She looked into her tea, then lifted her chin and said, "Sam and I got to Papa's house a little after three. Sam parked our car in front where everyone could see."

Up to that point, her tone was imperious. I raised my eyebrows and gave her a look. She smiled, and her shoulders dropped.

She continued in a more normal tone. "I saw Leila staring at us from the kitchen window. She looked quite impressed with the car and the man helping me from the front seat. When we started up the walk, it must have dawned on her who it was because we heard her shout, 'Donald, Donald, come quickly. Julia's here!' She disappeared from the window, and I could imagine her lumbering down the hall toward Papa's office shaking the whole house."

We both laughed.

"When I heard her shouting I knew he wasn't with a patient, and she would soon pound on the door he keeps shut against her. When we got to the porch, I opened the door a crack.

"I heard Papa say, 'What are you hollering about? Can't you see I'm busy?'

"Leila said, 'Julia's here, and she has a man with her.'

"Sam kept rapping. Leila's words barely had time to register before Papa heard us. I stepped inside as he burst into the foyer. He stopped still and stared. I shrieked, 'Papa', and rushed to give him a hug."

Julia stopped talking and looked at me with a funny little crooked smile. "I'm taller than Papa now," she said. "He has a bald spot that wasn't there before. I leaned down and kissed him and left a bright red lip rouge print on it.

"He looked past me and saw Sam. The two most important men in my life took quick measure of each other and shook hands when I introduced them."

"Do you think he was happy to see you?" I was half afraid to hear the answer.

"Oh, yes, of course, he was. Just terribly surprised that I had a fellow with me.

"We were still standing in the foyer when Leila reappeared. She said, 'Julia. How nice to have you home again—even if you have taken us by surprise.'

"You could have sharpened a knife on the edge in her voice." Julia swirled her tea. "I felt bile rise and my throat tightened in the old way."

I knew what she meant. That's the thing about being sisters, you know things about each other in a way a friend never will.

Julia laughed and shook her head. "Sam dropped Papa's hand and turned to Leila. He said, 'You must be Leila. Julia's shared many complimentary things about you.'"

Julia rolled her eyes. "The shocked look on Leila's face was priceless. She forced a smile, stepped forward and shook Sam's hand. She said, 'How very kind of you. Please, join us in the parlor where we can find out all of Julia's news. There must be a great deal to share judging from the unexpected visit and that handsome automobile.' She sounded so phony I could hardly keep a straight face."

"What happened then? Did Sam ask Papa for your hand?"

"Sam followed Leila into the parlor. Papa and I were close behind. After everyone sat down, Sam cleared his throat and said in a very official-sounding voice, 'Dr. Clarke, I was wondering if I might have a word in private?'" Julia's imitation was priceless.

"Papa stood, pulled out his pocket watch, looked at it, tucked it back into his vest and nodded his head once. He said, 'Come to my office. We can talk there.'" Julia dropped her voice an octave imitating Papa too.

I couldn't help giggling as she told the story.

"The whole thing was so artificial. Leila putting on airs like she was used to hosting important guests, Papa pretending he didn't have much time...even Sam sounded like he was conducting business with one of the bank's important customers. I wanted to sink through the floor. My heart was in my throat. I sure didn't want Sam to go through what you told me Will endured."

"What did you and Leila talk about while they were gone?"

"Honestly, I can't remember. Toofy and Sambo came in to see me and I spent most of the time hugging and talking to them."

"Did Leila bring me up?"

"No." Julia glanced at me with a sheepish look on her face. "I didn't either. I didn't tell her we had already seen you. I was a nervous wreck waiting for Sam and

Papa to return. I hoped that Sam had Papa's blessing, but my heart hammered so hard I could barely hear.

"When they came into the parlor, Sam smiled at me and gave a slight nod. I suspected the private conversation I would have with Papa, would not be so easy, nor end so well."

"Did Sam tell you what happened?"

"Some of it. You know how men are. They never give details. Sam said Papa told him he seemed like a 'nice enough chap,' and that he had 'confidence in my judgment.' But the age difference concerned him.

"Sam says he explained that we are twenty years apart in age but that he's never been married. He told Papa he's president of the First National Bank of Texas."

"Is that true? That Sam is the president of a bank?"

"Yes. Sam is my employer as well as my fiancé. He told Papa I would never want for material comforts, and that he would introduce me into San Antonio society at the highest level.

"You know, Papa is not accustomed to being on the receiving end of a conversation in which the decision has already been made. Sam said he got real quiet but finally said, 'I can see you offer her a comfortable life. I'm sure she will be well provided. You have my blessing, and I will walk her down the aisle if she asks.' Then Papa reached across the desk, and they shook hands."

"Will you keep working after you're married?"

"We haven't decided. I suppose for a while, at least. Unless I get pregnant. Pregnant girls aren't allowed to work at the bank."

"Then it's a good thing I didn't want a career. Seems like I'm pregnant all the time."

"You aren't sorry, are you? About marrying so young?"

"Heavens no. I wouldn't trade Will, or any of these boys, for anything else in the world."

I drained my teacup as the door burst open and Charles exploded into the room. "Mama! Mama!" he hollered, "Kath'ern says I can have a kitten soon as Ginger kicks them out of the nest." His eyes were lit up like a Christmas candle and he launched himself onto my lap. "Kath'ern says Daddy said I can bring it in the house when it's big."

"That's wonderful, Charles. Now, give your Aunt Julia a hug, please. She's come a long way to see you."

Charles scrambled down and climbed Julia like a backyard tree. His skinny little arms wrapped themselves around her neck and he nestled his face into her. She hugged him with genuine affection, and I knew the two of them would be fast friends.

CHAPTER 47

MAIZELLE

Julia and Sam spent Thanksgiving week at Papa and Leila's. Julia had not spoken to Papa about the situation between us or my participation in the wedding party. She told me she approached the subject with Leila and was promptly told not to mention my name in "this household." That verified what Jamie told me, and Julia knew better than to rock the boat before Papa was thoroughly softened up.

Sam brought Julia to visit me every day, and we laughed, teased, and shared stories like we had growing up. Julia thought Charles was 'precocious and precious' and the two of them developed a very strong bond. Charles took her by the hand and led her out to the barn to see his kittens. She was unable to resist his big blue eyes and the tenderness in his manner.

"He's angelic, Maidee. If all children were like Charles, I wouldn't mind having one or two. But then, there's Dubbya'E, who is a regular little hellion. He torments Charles for no reason I can see, and when Sam dropped me off today, Dubbya'E came down and kicked Sam in the shins when he opened my door. The thought of having a child like that one overrules any maternal instincts I may have entertained."

I nodded but didn't add any fuel to her fire. Little Dubbya'E was more spirited than Charles, but I loved him just as much.

Aaron was too young to interact with my sister. She left him to Katherine and me. She said, "I've personally changed enough diapers to know it's something I can easily do without." And since he was on the breast, she couldn't feed him. When she did hold him, he always cried. It made her uncomfortable, but there wasn't anything I could do to change his reaction to her.

"Maidee," Julia said one day, "I always thought you'd be the adventurous one in the family, and here you are—married, a mother, and completely contented."

"One could argue that running off and getting married at fourteen was adventuresome," I said, "but that seemed to be the end of my wanderlust, and you're right, I am content."

Julia shared that her week at Papa's had passed uneventfully, until one evening at the dinner table she said, "Are Maidee and Will, and the boys, joining us for Thanksgiving Dinner?" Laughing when she told me, she said everyone stopped chewing mid-bite, and all eyes turned her direction. She said the silence was 'palpable,' and she knew she had crossed the line.

She said, "When Papa finally swallowed what was in his mouth, he said, 'Who? I don't know anyone by that name.' Needless to say, I let the matter drop. Everyone looked at their plates and we continued the meal in silence."

After Thanksgiving, Sam returned to San Antonio and his duties as bank President. Julia stayed in Utopia to plan the wedding, now set for December 19, 1920.

In order for us to continue our visits, I left Aaron with Katherine, drove Will to work, and picked my sister up in front of O'Brien's house.

Julia was not keen on the idea of spending time with Leila, any more than I would have been. We planned the wedding with the help of our mother's best friend, Elizabeth, and our friend, Emma.

On days when I stayed in town to meet with the others, I put Aaron in a basket and brought him along, leaving Charles and Dubbya'E in Katherine's care.

Julia was a regular at the Western Union window in the post office, wiring instructions to the florist, the dressmaker, the reception hall, and Sam. Somehow, we four women managed to plan and execute a flawless event for Julia and Sam from sixty miles away. Telephones were present in Utopia, but not readily available. The Upton's, where we usually gathered, had a phone at the pharmacy, but not the house.

Julia relied on the convenience of Papa's office to make arrangements that could not be handled by wire. She took advantage of his telephone to speak to Sam every evening. She says they kept the calls brief because they were costly, and avoided conversations of a personal nature out of fear Papa or Leila would disapprove, and the fact it was a party line. It appeared to Emma and me that Julia's was an engagement of serious purpose, unencumbered by frivolous sentiment. She was, after all, a secretary of 'exceptional skill,' according to Sam. Their concession to propriety was to have her return home following their engagement, to prevent any chin-wagging within the bank or San Antonio society.

She asked our dear papa to escort her down the aisle and give her away, but she never mustered the courage to suggest he pay for a wedding that would include me as the Matron of Honor.

Julia was relieved when Will agreed that we would attend the wedding. Her fantasy that Papa would be delighted to meet his grandsons was just that, a fantasy. Aaron was the only one of the boys who would join us, and only because he was still on the breast.

Julia told me that baby bottles with rubber nipples were all the fashion in San Antonio, but I wouldn't have it. I take motherhood very seriously, and nursing my babies is part of that. I explained to Julia that nursing also offered some protection from another pregnancy, which I was anxious to avoid.

"Papa could hardly bear to see me go," she said, "but he promised to join Sam and me to host the rehearsal dinner. Oh, Maidee, it's going to be grand. Sam selected San Antonio's most exclusive restaurant and made reservations for Friday the seventeenth of December. I do so wish you and Will could be there."

Will and I arrived on the seventeenth and spent the evening of the rehearsal dinner with Eula and Fred, who we hadn't seen since we eloped. I was excited to have Eula meet at least one of our boys, and she was thrilled to hold Aaron, cooing, and making eyes at him like she was his grandmother. She said, "Maidee,

I'd love to keep him here while you attend the wedding. I don't think he'd be any trouble at all."

I considered her offer but worried that Aaron would be frightened in a strange home with someone he'd only just met. And if he needed to nurse, she wouldn't have any way to satisfy his demands.

"I appreciate it, Eula, really, I do. It's just that he's never been away from me, and I don't know how he would react when he discovered me missing."

We planned to arrive at the church just before the ceremony. We would be escorted to our seats and remain inconspicuous until after Papa walked Julia down the aisle. If I could keep Aaron from crying or fussing, we would avoid alerting Papa to our presence before the reception.

We were shown to our seats by a handsome young man who asked, "Which side, the bride's, or the groom's?"

I stammered, "I...I...which side will the bride be walking on?"

"Part of the bride's family, then, are you?"

"Yes," Will said, "but we don't want to sit too close to the front in case we need to take the baby out."

The young man stopped five rows from the front and said, "Will this be okay?"

"Yes," Will and I said in unison, as we slid into the pew and lowered our heads.

Julia walked down the aisle on Papa's arm, behind Edra and Samuel, as flower girl and ring bearer. My heart lurched when I saw them. I missed them more than I realized. They looked so grown-up all dolled-up in their finery, and I'm sure Leila's chest swelled with pride.

As Julia traversed the long aisle her eyes scanned the pews for us. We had agreed that we would look away or keep our faces down during her entrance to avoid Papa spotting us. I glanced up briefly and caught her eye, before turning my head so my hat concealed my face. Julia and Papa passed without incident.

Once they reached the front of the church Julia relaxed and looked at Papa with a big smile. He squeezed her arm against his side before lifting her hand from the crook in his elbow and placing it in Sam's.

She wrote to us later that when she looked at him, he had tears in his eyes. Tears! Neither of us had ever seen Papa cry. She said her own eyes brimmed, and she swallowed hard and blinked to keep them from overflowing and spotting her silk gown.

Everything went according to plan. Papa took his seat in the front pew next to Leila and the rest of their family. When the ceremony concluded, the minister introduced Mr. and Mrs. Sam McGavern and told Sam he could kiss the bride. He lifted Julia's veil and gave her a chaste peck on the lips. It wasn't the most romantic kiss I'd ever seen, but Julia had told me neither of them was big on public displays of affection, and they'd agreed in advance.

The first row of guests, including Papa, with Leila on his arm, began filing out of the church behind the wedding party. My eye caught Bowen as they went by. He looked shocked to see me and hurriedly looked away. As they moved toward the fifth row of pews where we were seated, Aaron let out a wail of impatience, and Papa's eyes instinctively went toward the sound.

My face burned and my eyes glistened.

Papa's face colored like a Texas sunset and his jaw trembled. "You," he mouthed.

I made direct eye contact with him, then lowered my eyes to tend to Aaron. No one in the church missed the look on Papa's face. All eyes turned to see what caused his dismay.

Will and I sat with heads bowed. But we were the only ones *not* craning our necks to see what the bride's father saw, and soon were the focus of everyone's attention. As the church emptied, row-by-row, all eyes remained on us. When we reached the outer foyer the scene playing out at the bottom of the steps made it clear we wouldn't be attending the reception.

Papa stomped out of the church and went right up to Julia's face. He glowered at her and sputtered. "Her. You invited *her*."

Bowen ran after him and tried to pull him back.

His face was so inflamed we thought he might be having a heart event. His eyes bulged and his temples throbbed. He shook Bowen off his arm and shoved him away.

It scared Julia half to death. She put her hand on his arm and said, "Papa. Please, she's my sister. I couldn't leave her out."

He pulled Julia's hand away and spat, "You have one sister. Toofy. And don't you ever forget it."

I was mortified. Being disowned was one thing, but being denied existence wasn't something I'd ever imagined.

Bowen looked longingly in my direction. I shook my head 'no' so he wouldn't approach me.

Sam stepped in and said, "Donald. This is our wedding day. We invited Will and Maizelle because they are part of our family. I'm asking you not to spoil this for Julia."

The two men faced off and Papa gave Sam a stone-cold glare, but he didn't say any more. His body was rigid, and his hands shook.

Will told me later he thought Papa was going to strike Sam.

I clutched Will's arm and said, "I think we'd better go. Aarons fussy. He would just be a distraction at the reception."

When Julia saw me standing there trembling, and realized I'd heard the exchange, she rushed to me and wrapped me in her arms. "Maidee, I'm so sorry. I wanted this to be a chance for him to see how beautiful and happy you are. I realize how wrong I was to ask you to come. Please say you forgive me. I promise I'll come to see you and the boys again soon. I love you, Honeybee. Always know that I'm here if you ever need anything."

Will put his hands on my shoulders and turned me. "It's okay Julia," he said, as my tears began dropping, "we need to get on the road anyway—we've left Charles and Dubbya'E with Katty long enough." His voice carried to where Papa and Sam stood.

I looked back and saw Papa step away. He no longer looked threatening.

Julia had put a practiced smile on her face and moved into the crowd pressing to get a glimpse of the new Mrs. Sam McGavern.

Will and I drove straight back to Utopia, our utopia, a plain little house, on a plain little knoll, in a plain little town, where two loving children waited for our return.

The husband I loved with my whole heart patted my knee and said, "If you want to talk about it this would be a good time. There's no one to hear but me."

I couldn't talk about it. I rode in silence. We never spoke of Papa again.

CHAPTER 48

MAIZELLE

Will kissed me hard on the lips and pulled my body close. I protested with a giggle, pushed against his chest, and turned my face away. "Go to your stupid old roosters," I pouted. "They make you happier than I do anyway."

Will laughed and tickled me.

I twisted away and cast him a look that both invited and scorned. I might have made good on the invitation part if we hadn't been in the kitchen.

Tonight, Will would play host to one of his favorite pastimes, rooster fighting with betting and drinking whiskey. He loved the excitement. Even the cruelty slipped off him like a whiff of sour breath. Will liked the gambling, the camaraderie with other ranchers and businessmen, the moonshine that always found its way to the cock barn, and the brief respite from work and family it gave.

I detested the cruel sport. Having the event on our property went down like a gulp of spoiled milk. We'd had quite a serious row when he told me his plan. I didn't like the idea of the children hearing the merriment from their bedroom window and trying to explain why people were having so much fun doing something so disgusting. Tonight, I would leave that chore to Katherine. The memory it dredged up, from the only time I watched the roosters fighting, sickened me.

It was five months since Julia's wedding, and this was her first visit home as Julia McGavern. Since Papa forbade me to enter his home, we arranged to meet at Robert and Elizabeth's for an evening of girl talk. I would escape to town to visit my sister one last time before she returned to San Antonio, Sam, and her career.

It seemed Robert, the respectable pharmacist, and gentleman rancher, would attend the cockfight along with Bobby, and nearly every man in the Utopia Masonic Lodge.

Emma would join Julia and me at the Upton's.

After our tussle, Will, grinning like a four-year-old with his hand in a fresh cow pie, grabbed his Fedora off the peg. He stuffed it on his head until his jug ears stopped its descent and dashed out of the kitchen. His boots clopped on the wooden planks of the long, covered porch.

I listened until the clopping stopped, and I knew he was bolting across the yard toward the chicken coop. Katherine had the boys well enthralled with her storytelling, so they didn't ask where their pa was going.

Katherine sat in the rocking chair with all three of my precious boys gathered around her knees, reading them *How the Camel Got His Hump*. The way Katherine read stories was magical.

I paused, drinking in the scene. It made my heart swell with pride to look at those three rambunctious youngsters gazing up at Katherine with wide eyes and open mouths. When I crossed the room, they closed their mouths as one and looked at me.

I bent to kiss Charles on the top of his head, then little Dubbya'E, and finally Aaron, planted between Charles's legs. My boys were handsome like their father, but without his big ears, and blessed with my more oval face. I knew their blond locks would turn dark as they got older, but none of the three had inherited my wavy hair.

"Take care 'a yaself," Katherine said, "and tell Julia I said howdy."

"I will. Julia was sorry she didn't get to see more of you and the boys this trip, but Papa is selfish with her time."

"I know." Katherine let the subject drop. She looked back to the storybook and began to read. Three blonde heads turned away from me and back to her voice, eyes upturned in rapt attention. This was my chance to slip from the room and out the backdoor.

Will had parked the car just outside the fence. I opened the door and reached for the crank. It only took two hard turns before the little Model T began to rumble, settling into a determined hum. I climbed in, set the floor lever on the driver's side to the center position, and pressed the left foot pedal to the floor, engaging low gear. One thing about having an auto mechanic for a husband was that he kept the car in perfect running order. Will spent many hours teaching me how to use the three foot pedals and the floor lever. I knew it was a source of pride for him when I came tooling up to his business with his little boys spilling out of the open windows.

Most of the women in town—even Emma—were reluctant to drive their husband's cars, but not me. Using the throttle lever on the steering column, I accelerated slowly down the long stretch of lane between the house and the new bridge across the Sabinal River—the one responsible for Aaron's birth. The land sloped away from the house, and by the time I neared the tree line, I was out of sight of the homestead.

I saw someone walking toward me and slowed. *Someone going to the cockfight,* I thought. When I drew close, he raised his hand in greeting. I knew him. It was Jimmy Calvert. My heart lurched. I recognized my fear and scolded myself for being such a boob. Jimmy had never threatened me or given me any reason to be afraid of him, but Mama Sarah's and Will's warnings had planted caution. I assumed he was on his way to the cockfight, though it seemed odd because I knew Will wouldn't have invited him.

Jimmy stepped to the side of the road. The look on his face struck me as off-beat. He had an odd grin and he raised his eyebrows almost like a greeting. He appeared to be holding something behind his back. I wondered what he was up to as I motored past and off the bridge on the town side of the river. He wouldn't be planning to confront Will tonight, would he? I wondered if I should turn around and go back to see if he had continued toward the house, but I pushed the suspicious thoughts out of my mind in my hurry to meet Julia.

It made me uncomfortable to think Jimmy had a crush on me. I'd always treated him kindly, and I guess that's what caused the trouble. I thought, it doesn't seem fair. It's a shame I can't be friendly to a person without giving the wrong idea. I was pleased when he made me the beautiful wooden box I now use to hold mementos of the babies 'firsts.' I probably shouldn't have given him a hug when he offered the box to me, but it was pretty, and he was so proud of it.

He made one for my teacher, Miss Miller, too, so I didn't think it was special just for me. It's still hard for me to believe Jimmy threatened Will. I wouldn't have considered it serious if Mama Sarah hadn't been so strong with her warning. I took Will's order to heart and stayed away from him.

That was over four years ago. I hadn't seen much of Jimmy since. I avoided him when I was in town, and to my knowledge, he never came near the homestead. He was a nice-looking man, but his ghostlike appearance and twitching eyes made it difficult see him as normal. Honestly, I felt a little flattered that he had feelings for me.

I was lost in thought as I approached the Upton house. I stopped at the front gate and turned off the motor. Julia erupted through the front door and bounded down the steps to greet me.

We walked to the porch arm-in-arm, heads together like Siamese twins. I was wearing one of the new slimmer fitting dresses she had sent me, and she gushed, "Maidee, Maidee, Maidee. You look great, little one."

"Not so little anymore, after birthing three big boys."

"Oh, pshaw. You'll always be my little one. Speaking of little ones, you don't have any news for me this trip, do you?"

"Nooo," I drew the word out for effect. "I don't think we'll be bringing any more mouths into this world for a while. Will still wants his girl, of course, but for now, I'll just have to be enough girl for him."

Julia giggled the tinkling-bell laugh I so loved and squeezed me even more tightly. "Well, I have to live vicariously through your fertile little body since my own won't cooperate."

"Doesn't the doctor give you any hope?"

"No. Sam is older, and there might be something wrong with the way I'm put together. They just don't know. It doesn't really matter. Neither Sam nor I are overly eager to have children. I pray. I hope. and I love your babies from afar."

"I keep you in *my* prayers, too. Only I pray the next one is yours and not mine!"

She gave me a shove and we laughed.

Elizabeth chuckled when she saw us. "You two! It's always the same with you, laughin' and gigglin' and huggin'. You sound just like your mama and me when we were young. Goodness, I miss her."

The mention of Mama brought a quick end to our merriment and Elizabeth hastened to offer sweet tea and shortbread to fill the vacuum. The moment passed, and when she and Emma brought refreshments, we were chattering like chipmunks.

Our visit was wonderful. Julia filled us in on her life as a 'socialite' in San Antonio and I rolled my eyes in disbelief at all the stories. She brought newspaper clippings of Sam and her out on the town, dancing like a pair of young kids. Julia wore the latest flapper outfits, and silk stockings over her bare legs! It would have been quite shocking to Papa, I'm sure, but somehow for Julia and Sam, it seemed fine. Emma and I oohed and awed at the pictures, the daring outfits, and the tales she told, exchanging glances to let each other know it wasn't a life either of us would want.

As dusk fell, the air calmed bringing the humidity down on us. I fanned myself with one of Julia's fancy magazines and allowed as how I should probably be heading back home.

The corners of Julia's mouth turned down and her shoulders slumped, but she nodded her head in reluctant agreement.

We rose, thanked Elizabeth for letting us have our sister time in her home, hugged Emma, and walked to the car. I climbed into the driver's seat and Julia got in the passenger side. We drove to within a half-block of Papa's house and stopped.

I let the car idle as Julia got out and came around to my side. She leaned in and gave me a quick kiss on the cheek. "Take care of yourself," she said before turning to walk the short distance to the house.

I watched her go with a lump in my throat and a deep longing in my heart. I turned the car around and started home.

CHAPTER 49

MAIZELLE

When I reached the access road to the bridge, it took all my strength to turn the big steering wheel for the hard left. As I crossed the bridge, I saw Jimmy standing at the other end, waving for me to stop.

What now? I thought. I pulled over, getting my tires a little too far off the roadway, and causing the car to tilt.

Jimmy ran toward me waving his arms.

Will's warning, *you stay away from him,* flashed through my mind as I opened the car door. "What's wrong? Are you okay?"

Jimmy motioned for me to get out of the car. The only word I could understand in his excitement was "see, see," repeated over and over.

"You want to show me something?"

"Y's, y's," he gurgled and nodded. His eyes danced wildly from side to side.

I cut the motor and reached for the floor brake, to set the car in place. Jimmy ran around and pulled open the passenger door as I stepped out on the driver's side.

Is he trying to get in? I wondered what I should do. I pushed my door shut, but it didn't latch.

Jimmy backed away from the car.

Curious, I went around behind the vehicle. "What did you want me to see, Jimmy?" My eyes scanned the embankment for something unusual. I didn't see anything. The prickly mesquite looked undisturbed. There was no car pointing nose down toward the river. I glanced up in search of Jimmy.

He stood beside the open passenger door with a hunger in his eyes that sent an icy chill to my core. Our eyes met and I felt the blood drain from my face.

I turned to run. My knees buckled.

He lunged and grabbed my arm.

I shrieked and lost my balance on the loose shoulder gravel.

Jimmy grabbed me around the waist and pulled me to him with one arm. He groped at my breasts. My whole body ran cold with fear.

I pushed against his chest and pummeled him with my fists. "What are you doing? Let me go! Let me go!" I twisted and turned and kicked without success.

Jimmy tried to kiss me. When he failed, due to my head whipping back and forth, he slid his right hand inside the front of my blouse and squeezed my breast. Milk spurted and ran down my body. Jimmy eased his grip and returned his focus to the kiss.

I pitched my head from side to side and pulled down on his forearm to dislodge his grip.

With one hand on my breast, he pushed me backward until I was wedged between the edge of the passenger seat and his body.

"Help! Somebody, help me!"

He shoved me onto the car seat, flattened my body under his, and held me down with one arm. He took his hand out of my blouse, slipped the straps off his coveralls, and pulled them clear of his engorged member.

I screamed. The sight of him disgusted me. His penis looked almost blue against his white body. I gagged and kicked. "Get off me! Stop! You're *hurting* me."

"Don' scrm," he warned in a guttural tone, as he pulled my skirt above my thighs. "Wuv oo, wuv oo."

What? I twisted and bit his arm.

He yanked my bloomers down, clapped his hand over my mouth, and pressed my head against the car seat. "Don' scrm," he warned again. The hand over my mouth lifted and he used it to grab his member, shoving himself into me.

I felt a sharp pain. Tears of fury filled my eyes. I let out a yelp. A scream rose in my throat but died there as he again pressed his hand over my mouth. The musty smell of his penis and the perspiration from his palms stung my nostrils.

I gagged as I tried to think of a way to get the brute off. His body slammed against me like a horse fighting a bit. Bile rose into my throat, and I vomited. The foul mess oozed past his hand and dripped into my hair. I felt it run down my neck onto my back. My chest heaved and I knew another blast was coming. I struggled to hold it back, but Jimmy slammed into me, and it burst into my throat.

He didn't move his hand and I thought I might drown. I fought for breath. Every time I turned my head the sour smell assaulted me. I squirmed and twisted, fighting as hard as I could in the confinement of the car. I couldn't breathe. I choked. Stinging bile ran out my nose. My legs, bent at the knee, hung out of the car. My head was wedged under the lower rim of the steering wheel.

My panicked mind raced from one thought to another. Screaming is useless. Men at cockfight can't hear...too far off road for anyone to hear...have to get this beast off me...why did I stop...why didn't I listen to Will?

The brute was so intent on the assault that his hand slipped off my mouth and I took a breath before spitting vomit at him.

He wiped at my mouth and clapped his hand down harder.

Rapid-fire thoughts flew in and out of my mind. The faces of my boys flashed. They smiled. Then cried. Will's face loomed. I was consumed with a ferocious need to be there for them. Survival was uppermost in my mind. I rolled my face away from the offending stench, only to be stricken with the odor of linseed oil and solvent from his work clothes. *The smell of the school.*

A monster's white visage loomed from the periphery of my vision as Jimmy thrust against me with renewed violence. Stabbing hot pain shot through my body, pulling me back into the moment.

Jimmy's body shuddered. He let out a low moan and pulled himself away.

The pressure from his hand on my mouth eased. Hot sticky liquid oozed against my thighs. I had a fleeting thought that he had not made a full penetration—or at least pulled away before it was too late. My mind played tricks. Was it possible he hadn't emptied himself inside me? That unrealistic hope was all I had as I plotted my escape.

Jimmy partially stood and released the pressure on my body. He grasped the edge of the open car door with his right hand and removed his other hand from my face, reaching to wipe the vomit off on the coveralls that were around his knees. His hideous member hung limp against his leg. "Don' scrm. Wuv oo. Wuv oo," he gurgled, looking down at me with tenderness.

Suddenly able to catch my breath, I spotted a space between his body and the legs that had pinned my thighs beneath him. I sucked in air, pulled my legs up, planted my shoes in his groin, and unleashed coiled anger in one solid thrust. Jimmy, already off-balance, was propelled over the embankment and into the thick thorny growth of mesquite shrubs. I heard him cry out as he fell. I hoped he'd die there. I pulled my legs into the car and scrambled to sit. I grabbed the passenger door and yanked it shut.

Jimmy hollered in pain from the thorns impaling him.

I heard him thrashing and trembled with cold fear as I slid behind the steering wheel. To escape I had to crank start the car. Terrified that he would untangle himself and make it up the bank before I could get going, I gritted my teeth, kicked the door open, and jumped to the ground.

I grabbed the hand crank and raced to the front of the car, dragging my bloomers through the dirt. I shook my foot to get them off, but they stayed wrapped around one shoe. My hands shook so hard I could barely hold them steady enough to get the crank on the receiving rod. My teeth clattered and my arms ached. I felt detached from my body as I pulled straight up and then forced down with everything I had. "Go, go, go."

Lizzy did not disappoint. I pulled the crank loose, raced to the open driver's door, and tossed it onto the passenger seat. I would have a weapon if Jimmy crawled up that bank. I pressed the floor pedal as hard as my shuddering foot would allow. I pushed the accelerator lever with my right hand and cranked the wheel hard to my left to get the car righted and back on the road. Nothing happened. *The parking brake!* I released the handle, pressed the accelerator, and sped toward safety.

I was in shock as I approached the house. The only sound I could hear was the faint roar of men cheering the winners and cursing the losers in the cock barn. The loud cheering broke my concentration and jolted me back to reality. My thoughts jumped here, then there, as I struggled with what had happened. I clenched and unclenched my jaw until it ached. My entire body was shimmying as if the temperature had dropped forty degrees.

I parked the car outside the fence. My mind raced with irrational thoughts as I tried to maintain my composure. If I tell Will what happened, he'll get his gun and kill Jimmy. There won't be any reasoning with him. This was my fault. He told me to stay away from Jimmy and I stopped anyway. If I'd followed his advice this never would have happened. What if he can't love me anymore knowing another man ravaged me? If Will kills Jimmy, he'll go to jail. What would I do then? How would I take care of the kids? I can't tell the sheriff. Everyone in town would know. I could never hold my head up.

I needed to clean Jimmy off me and clear my head. I felt the sticky mess all over my thighs. My bloomers were wrapped around one leg. When I kicked Jimmy down the bank only one foot came clear and I had dragged them through the gravel and dirt. They must be filthy.

Vomit stuck to my neck and my blouse was glued to my back. I felt disgusting. I was disgusting. I hated Jimmy. I hated myself for thinking he needed help.

The soiled bloomers and what to do with them emerged as the most critical issue. To reach the house I would have to walk across the yard. I couldn't be dragging bloomers. I had to get rid of them. I had to look and act like nothing happened. What if Will sees the car and comes to greet me? What will I tell him?

I pulled the gear lever into the center position and jerked hard on the parking brake before I cut the motor. Maintaining control of my routine was essential.

The soft glow of lantern light came from the chicken house, where at least a dozen men laughed, shouted, and cheered for their fighters. The sounds rang in my ears as if from a great distance. I was lightheaded, frightened, and ashamed.

Resting my forehead against the big steering wheel to steady myself, I reached down and pulled the bloomers off my other leg, wadding them into a tight ball. I tucked the bundle against my sore rib cage, opened the car door, and set foot onto the running board before stepping to the ground. I was determined to maintain my composure and not do anything that would give away my condition. My focus was on making every movement, every detail of my arrival appear normal.

I glanced down the lane to make sure Jimmy hadn't followed. Seeing no movement in the gathering dark, I took one faltering step toward the back porch of the house, about thirty yards away. When I passed the privy, I ducked inside and dropped the bundle down the hole. The bloomers would disappear into the muck, and I would never have to think about them again.

Dry-eyed, I gathered myself and walked into the house with my head high. When I saw Katherine my stoic resolve evaporated, and I collapsed against her.

"Maidee! What happened to you?"

I was unable to respond. I trembled and sobbed and shook my head, gulping air.

"I'll get Mr. Will," Katherine said.

"No!" I blurted with such fierceness it stopped Katherine cold. I shook my head. I couldn't think. I needed to wash and get myself ready for bed.

Finally, I lifted my head, set my jaw, and looked Katherine in the eye. "You're going to help me now, and you will never say a word about this to anyone. Do you understand?" My tears had stopped as suddenly as they had begun.

Katherine nodded and stared, her face a palette of confusion, worry, and fear.

"Heat a kettle of water and bring a washbasin to my bedroom. I need soap, vinegar, a douche bag, a clean washcloth, and a towel. Can you do that for me?"

She whispered, "Maidee, what happened to you?"

"I won't tell you. Not now, not ever. Do you understand me? I will never talk about this night again. And if you know what's good for you, you won't either. Am I clear?"

Katherine turned to get the kettle started. She opened the back door and stepped out to dip water from the barrel. Hearing the merriment coming from the cock barn she hesitated. I could tell she was wondering if she should run and get Will. She glanced inside at me, huddled on the chair with my arms clasped about my shivering body. Our eyes met.

"No," I mouthed, "you help me."

Katherine put the water to boil on the woodstove and gathered the items I requested. She brought the washbasin to me. "Did you miscarry?" she asked.

Stunned, I processed the question. My mind cleared, and I looked at Katherine as though she had spun gold dripping from her lips. "Yes! Don't tell Will. He didn't know I was expecting. This would kill him. No one knew."

Katherine enveloped me in her arms. "I won't tell," she said. "I'll never tell anyone." The stench from my hair and clothing gagged her. "Did you throw up on yourself?"

"Yes. All over myself and the car. I could barely drive myself home after. I stopped just over the bridge and got out. Oh, Katherine, it was so painful and so horrible. I can't bear to think of it."

"What did you do with it?"

"Most of it was in my bloomers. I threw them in the privy."

"You poor thing. Are you sure you don't want Will to know? He would want you to see the doctor after something like this."

"No. Never. I can't explain but I don't ever want him to know. Will you to do one more thing for me tonight?"

"Of course. Whatever you need."

"Would you mind cleaning the car seat where I puked? I don't want Will to have to smell it, and if he sees it he'll start asking questions. I wouldn't ask if it wasn't important."

"I know you wouldn't. Sure. I don't mind. I'll go right after we get you cleaned up so you can rinse your hair and get your nightshirt on."

Katherine set about cleaning me and removing my clothing to be laundered. I could tell from the look in her eyes she thought I wasn't telling the truth. I could see her mind spinning like a top trying to imagine what it could be. When she stripped my blouse off, she gasped, her hands hovered in the air and quivered like a pair of hummingbirds. "Oh, Maidee, whatever happened to you? No miscarriage ever left a woman looking like this."

"What? What do you see?"

"You're all bruised. Your whole chest and stomach are red and turning black and blue. Your arms are bruised. You look like you've been in a brawl with a bear!"

I looked at Katherine. I pondered another lie but couldn't find one that was fitting. All at once, my throat closed, my breath came in gulps, and my body heaved up a wail, so mournful Katherine dropped to her knees and flung her arms around me. Tears flooded over the rims of previously dry eyes from both of us. We clung to each other like bark on a tree, shaking, and weeping, and attempting to keep our voices from waking the children asleep on the other side of the thin wall.

"He ravaged me. I stopped...to help...and he...ravaged me." I croaked out the confession between rasping gulps and stifled sobs.

"Who, Maidee? Who did this to you?"

"Ji...Ji...Jimmy."

I buried my face in Katherine's hair and swallowed another onslaught of tears, my shoulders convulsed, and her chest heaved.

"Jimmy Calvert did this to you?" Katherine's voice broke through my gulping and sobbing.

"Yes. Yes. You can't... tell Will. No one...can...ever know." I lifted my face from Katherine's hair. Mucus streamed from my nose and my eyes were swollen and red.

Katherine took the washcloth she gripped and wiped my face. "Can you tell me what happened?"

"No! I can't talk about it. Swear you'll never tell anyone! Especially not Will."

"I swear. You said you stopped to help, and he attacked you? Maidee, you need to tell the Sheriff. Someone like that shouldn't be allowed to run loose. If he did this to you, he could do it to someone else."

"No! If Will finds out, he'll kill Jimmy and he'll go to jail. Then what would I do?" My desperate, irrational words spilled free.

Katherine held me close and whispered in my ear. "Maidee, if you tell the Sheriff, he can keep Will from taking the law into his own hands. You need to think of who else Jimmy might do this to."

"I can't. Everyone in town will find out if I tell the Sheriff. I'll never be able to go out in public again. My pa has already disowned me. How much more humiliation can I take?"

The two of us rocked in each other's arms, neither satisfied that we had resolved the situation. At length, we parted, and Katherine continued cleaning my tender, sore, and violated body. While she finished the gruesome task, each touch of her hand and the washcloth caused a jerk, a twist, a small cry swallowed down a dry throat, or fresh tears to spill over red rims. She slid a clean cotton nightgown over my head and tucked me into bed.

Will staggered home well after midnight, drunk from the moonshine and with his pockets full of winnings. I never allowed him to touch me when he was in this condition, but tonight I made an exception to be certain that whatever seed might have been planted this night was the right seed.

When he entered our room, I opened my eyes, steeled myself, and greeted him with a smile.

A wide grin spread across his narrow face. "I won. Big time." He slurred his words.

"Well, why don't you crawl in here and tell me about it?" He looked startled, but in the manner of any drunken man, he was quick to undress and roll into the bed beside me. I pressed my body to him as bile rose in my throat.

My husband was thrilled with my attention and responded in just the way I wanted. If he noticed that I was detached, or that my body tensed and recoiled as he entered me, he was too drunk for it to register. He finished and rolled off, clumsily patted my cheek, and fell into a deep sleep.

I spent the night in terror. Every time I closed my eyes Jimmy's face loomed, and a chill washed over causing goosebumps. His grunts and garbled words invaded my mind. I replayed the scene over and over. The size and color of his member grew darker and bigger with each replay. If I drifted off, his earthy smell, coupled with a mixture of cleaning solvents and linseed oil, rose to fill my nostrils and bring me instantly conscious. My body was coiled tight as a watch spring and hurt everywhere. The brutal slamming had bruised me badly and I felt every slight movement of the bed as warning of a new assault.

CHAPTER 50

MAIZELLE

When dawn finally broke, I climbed out of the warm bed and shuffled to the kitchen to stoke the fire. I usually left this task to Will, but I needed to be busy and prepare to face my children and husband this morning.

There was much to think about. My body went through the motions, and my brain was in a fog of remorse, regret, anger, and confusion. What did I do to make Jimmy think he could have his way with me? My mind gave me no peace.

The boys scrambled out of bed and spilled into the kitchen as soon as they heard me up and about. They were noisy, out of sorts, and unusually clingy and demanding. As I tried to settle them, I thought, it's funny how they pick up on your mood.

Katherine heard us and came into the kitchen to help me get breakfast. Her face was drawn, and her eyes red and puffy, like she hadn't slept a wink. I knew I probably looked worse and put on my large-brimmed sunbonnet to keep from making eye contact. I didn't trust myself not to lose my composure.

"Mama, why are you wearin' your sun hat in the house?" Charles quizzed.

"My head feels chilled. I need it to keep all the heat in my body from escaping."

My attempt to sound cheerful and teasing fell flat. Charles looked at me with grave concern. He wasn't buying the explanation. "Mama, if your heat all 'scapes, I'll help you catch it up and put it back."

I tousled his blond head and kissed him on the forehead. "Thank you, my big, brave boy, but I think this ol' bonnet should do the trick."

I caught Katherine looking at me like I'd just landed from the moon. I scowled and gave a slight shake of my head. All I needed this morning was for Will to figure out there was something between Katherine and me that he wasn't in on, and I was none too soon.

Will poked his head around the doorway and said, "Is the coffee on?"

I was sure he had a headache from his night of revelry and said, "It's perking. We'll have it ready in a few minutes."

"I have to go to the shop this morning. What's for breakfast?"

"I'm making flapjacks," Katherine piped in, "they'll be ready in about fifteen minutes."

"Sounds like just what I need to settle my stomach," he said before disappearing into the bedroom.

Katherine sidled up to me and whispered, "The bruises on your face are beginning to show. You should go put some powder on as soon as Will's out of there."

I nodded my thanks, poured Will some coffee, and took it to the bedroom. I was looking down and almost collided with him.

"Whoa," he said, "is that for me?"

"Yes," I said, passing the coffee to him and pressing past. "I need to finish getting washed up. I didn't want to disturb you earlier."

He took the cup from my hand and stepped out of my way.

I rushed in, closed the door, ripped my bonnet off, and examined my face in the small mirror on the bureau. Faint yellow patches were emerging where Jimmy had held his hand over my mouth. I gasped and grabbed my face powder, opening the jar with shaky hands. I dipped a cloth in the water pitcher on the dresser and dabbed a corner in the powder to make a tinted cream to apply around my lips and cheeks. I was able to conceal the spots well enough that I thought I could go back to the kitchen without Will noticing.

I relieved Katherine at the stove and kept my back to Will and the boys.

Will wolfed down his flapjacks, gave me a quick peck on the cheek through my bonnet, and said, "I'll try to get back before five."

I bobbed my head and went right on tending the flapjacks on the grill. "That would be nice," I said, "have a good day."

"Why you wearin' a sunbonnet in the house?"

"I was going to go out to the chickens before everyone got up this morning, but y'all were up earlier than I expected. I just got busy and forgot to take it off."

Will pulled the tie and peeled the hat off my head. "Here, I'll hang it on the peg for you," he said as he turned and walked out the door.

As the day wore on, I went through the motions. I ached everywhere. I hurt in places I didn't know you could hurt. Walking hurt. Sitting hurt. Breathing hurt.

I strolled out to the chicken house to gather eggs. I asked Little Dubbya' E if he wanted to go with me. If I took short steps and lots of time, I could make walking appear normal.

Dubbya' E managed to pick up the eggs from the nests and place them in my gathering basket without breaking a one. That spared me having to bend over. I pulled him close and said, "aren't you getting to be a big boy. You didn't break a single egg."

He beamed with pride and ran ahead of me to the barn to check his rabbits.

I took my time walking the short distance between the chicken house and the rabbit hutch behind the barn, letting the warm sun penetrate my body that felt chilled to the bone.

When I rounded the corner to the back of the barn, I expected to see Dubbya' E standing by the hutch, but he wasn't there. I shouldn't have been surprised. He's a precocious toddler, curious, and always into something. "Dubbya' E? I called. He didn't answer. "Where are you, Dubbya' E?" Fear clutched my throat. Where could he have gone? If he ran into the barn, I think I would have noticed. "Dubbya' Eeee," I called again and again, but the sound blew back at me with no response.

I am usually a very calm mother, not given to unprovoked worry, but this morning my mind raced back to last night's horror. I could only think that Jimmy lurked in the shadows and grabbed my precious child. My voice rose to a hysterical pitch, and I screamed Dubbya' E's name.

I raced to the rabbit hutches. Every step jarred my body. I thought I might faint from the stabs of pain. I ran around the row of cages. Looking everywhere my eyes could gather light. As I rounded the row of hutches for the third time, a slight movement under one of the pens caught my eye. I stopped short and bent down to peer into the dark shadows and fresh mounds of rabbit dung under the hutch. My boy, my precious Little Dubbya' E, sat on a pile of pellets with fresh pee running off his blond head.

I shrieked and grabbed him. Dubbya' E looked up at me, unconcerned. "Dubbya' E," I shouted, "whatever are you doing under there?" And without waiting for an answer, "just look at you. Rabbit pee running off your head. Your coveralls dirty. What am I going to do with you?"

I reached for his arm to drag him out from under the hutch, and a stabbing pain shot through my rib cage. I fell to my knees, gasping for breath.

"Oh, well, dat don't matter, Mama," my child reassured as I dissolved in a heap on the ground. I covered my face with my hands and wept.

Dubbya' E bent over and peered under the broad bill of my bonnet to see why I was so distressed. I grabbed him and pulled him to my breast. I squeezed so tight he wriggled and howled, "Let go! Let go!"

When I managed to stem the flow of tears and get partway under control, I loosened my grip, rose with difficulty from the dusty ground, and shook my petticoats.

Dubbya' E scrambled to his feet and bolted, but I caught a chubby arm and pulled him back to my side. Without thinking, I gave him a hard swat on his behind. "You stay with me, you hear?" I hissed into his upturned face. "Don't you ever go running off like that again. You scared the pee waddin' out 'a me."

Dubbya' E, used to few reins and much freedom, stared at me in wonder. I'd never struck one of my children. *What had possessed me?* The sting from the swat told him this would not be a good time to argue, as guilt washed over me like a flash flood on the Sabinal.

I clasped his hand in mine and marched toward the house much faster than the walk to the barn. Holding tightly to his hand, I half hauled, half dragged him onto the back porch, where I peeled off his clothing and dropped them in the washtub.

"Katherine," I hollered at the back door. "Katherine, come help me."

The urgency in my voice brought her running. As the screen banged shut behind her, she stopped short and stared.

Little Dubbya' E, Katherine's favorite of my three boys, stood buck naked with his hair matted to his head and covered with dried rivulets of yellow crackling liquid on his face, chest, and back. He cried when he saw her, and Katherine's first inclination was to reach out and hug him.

"Don't touch him," I snapped as she stepped toward him. "He's got rabbit pee all over himself."

And for the second time in less than twenty-four hours, I asked Katherine to get me a clean washcloth and a basin full of warm water. She turned on her heel and disappeared into the kitchen without a word.

When she returned, we set about giving Dubbya' E his weekly bath. This meant he got clean water and wouldn't have to share the Saturday night tub with Aaron and Charles. It also meant he wouldn't be allowed to play outside the rest of the day.

"Katherine, please keep an eye on Charles and Aaron for me. I'll take Dubbya' E." When he was clean and dry, I took him and my guilt inside and offered to read him a story. I sat in the rocking chair and removed my sunbonnet. Painful as I knew it would be, I let him climb onto my lap. The insides of my thighs ached, and my right shoulder shouted in protest.

Dubbya' E clutched his favorite well-worn storybook, *The Tale of Peter Rabbit*. I smiled at the irony of his choice, given where he was when I found him.

He looked up at me and noticed a tear slip down my cheek. "Don't cry, Mama. Mr. McGregor won't get me. I'll be good."

"Oh, Dubbya' E, you are good. I don't know what's gotten into me. Losing track of you put a fright into me, I guess."

He gazed up and reached a chubby hand for my cheek. "You have dirt on your face, Mama."

I glanced at my image in the mirror hanging opposite my chair. I could see the faint yellow bruises where Jimmy's hand clasped my mouth shut and held my head down. A bitter taste flooded my mouth, and my body jerked with an involuntary tremor. A chill spread from my feet to my head as my body reacted to the memory.

I pulled Dubbya' E's head down against my breast and held him close as I tried to compose myself to get through the day. He squirmed against my tight grip and strained to lift his head. "Read, Mama. Read Peter to me."

I released his head and opened the book. I stared at the page, but nothing came. My impatient son grabbed the book and turned to the illustration of Peter Rabbit running from a hoe-wielding farmer McGregor. The image triggered such intense fear and disgust that I wretched, dumped Dubbya' E from my lap, scrambled to my feet, and headed for the chamber pot in my bedroom.

My body heaved as I tried to eliminate the memory that dogged me. I knew Katherine could hear me from the back porch, where she prepped vegetables for canning and watched Charles and Aaron at play.

Dubbya' E gave up on me and ran outside. I heard his little voice say, "Mama's sick. She can't read Peter. You read, Kath'in," he demanded, unwilling to give up his moment of special privilege for a story in the middle of the day.

I heard a stool scrape. "I'll go see how your mama is doin' first, Dubbya' E, then I'll read you the story." She called to Charles, "bring Aaron into the house now. I need to go inside."

My loud heaving had stopped by the time Katherine reached the bedroom. She found me collapsed on the bed, exhausted and spent.

"You okay? Can I get you anything?"

"Sleep," I muttered, "I need sleep.

CHAPTER 51

WILL

Our family rarely missed church. I fought my way to consciousness Sunday morning, rolled over, and reached for Maidee. My arms hit empty space, and I realized she was already up. Her absence jolted me into believing I had overslept. I threw the covers back, jumped out of bed, pulled my trousers on, and stepped into the front room. My wife was curled up in the rocking chair like a kitten, wrapped in a quilt Ma made.

Katherine stood next to her wiping her forehead with a wet cloth.

"What's wrong? She under the weather?"

"She doesn't feel well. She doesn't want to go to church with us this morning."

I crossed the room and muscled Katherine aside, looking down at my girl. "What's the matter, Sugar?"

She pulled the quilt over her face and barely moved her eyes when she glanced at me. "I don't know. I hurt everywhere, and my stomach is turning somersaults." Her voice was weak, and her face pale. "You and Katherine should take the boys and go. I think I'll lie down again."

"I don't want to leave you by yourself. We can all stay home."

"No. I need some peace and quiet. I'll be fine. Please, just take Katherine and the boys and go."

"Let me help you back to bed." I reached for her, and her body stiffened.

"No! Please don't touch me. I hurt everywhere. I can get there on my own."

My temples still throbbed from yesterday's hangover. Going to church and leaving her alone was the last thing I wanted to do, but her mind was made up. Katherine dressed and fed the boys while I drank strong coffee. When they were ready, Katty and I loaded the kids into the tin Lizzy. She climbed up on the running board and lowered herself onto the seat next to me, holding Aaron in her lap.

"Katherine? What's troubling Maidee? Is she mad at me for having the cockfights here?"

"I can't rightly say," Katherine said through pinched lips.

"You keep an eye on her for me, okay? I don't know what I'd do if anything ever happened to that girl. If she's still sick tomorrow, I'll make an appointment with the doctor in Sabinal and drive her up to get checked."

Her voice was near a whisper when she answered, "Yes, sir, Mr. Will. It's sure too bad her daddy won't see her."

We fell silent and stayed silent all the way to the church. When we got back home, Maidee had moved to the bedroom, closed the curtains, and was asleep. I reached down to stroke her hair, and she flipped over and shouted, "Get your hands off me!"

"Maidee. Maidee, it's me," I said. "You must be havin' a bad dream."

Her eyes were wild with fear—as if she'd never seen me before. Once she recognized me, she burst out cryin' and fell back with her hands covering her face.

I sat on the edge of the bed and reached for her shoulders, drawing her to me. Her body went stiff. It felt as though I held a chair in my arms. "I'm taking you to Sabinal, to Doc Wilson."

"No... no," she whimpered. "It was just a bad dream. I'll be fine. Let me sleep."

I laid her back against the pillows and brushed wet hair stuck in salty tears, out of her eyes and off her cheeks. "Okay. For now, I'll let you sleep, but if you aren't better in the morning, I won't take any argument from you, hear?"

"I hear," she murmured, closing her eyes.

MAIZELLE

I got up on Monday and told Katherine I was fine as frog's hair. I could tell from her expression she wasn't convinced.

She hugged me and whispered, "Maidee, I love you. You are my best friend in the whole world. If you need to see the doctor, you let me know, and I'll make sure Mr. Will drives you up to Sabinal."

When I stepped back, I saw tears the size of Texas raindrops burst from her eyes. I wrapped both arms around her and said, "Katherine, you are my only friend. I will need you to be strong and help me through this. Please don't cry. They'll fall apart if Will or the boys see you cry." I hustled her into the bedroom to keep anyone else from noticing.

She wiped her eyes and pleaded, "You have to tell him. He's worried about you. He thinks you're mad at him over the cockfight. You should see the doctor. You might be losin' blood."

"No," I said. "Just leave me be. I'll be fine. You promised not to mention this again, and I expect you to keep your word. I don't have anyone else to talk to, Katherine. You have to help me. And Will can't find out."

Katherine didn't understand how I could keep such an important secret from my husband. But she recognized the terror in my voice, left me to myself, and went to the kitchen to feed my hungry brood. "You stay here then," she said. "Ever' time I look at you, I want to cry."

We knew Will and the boys were waiting at the table. Katherine would have to make an excuse for me, and she did. I could hear her bustling around, putting kettles on the stove, cracking eggs into the frying pan, and setting dishes in place for the meal. She kept herself extra busy, so Will wouldn't press her about my absence.

I heard the coffee cup bang down on the table, and Will's voice reached me through the thin wall.

"How's she doin' today?"

"Fine. Far as I can tell."

"Why didn't she come out for breakfast?"

"I think she felt a little wobbly and is takin' a minute to get her legs under her."

Then the talking stopped. I heard a chair scrape and Will's voice. "I should check on her."

Katherine spoke—a little too quickly, I feared. "No need, Will. She just bent over to lace her shoes, and when she straightened, she felt dizzy. She hasn't eaten much in the past couple days. I'll have her out here for some breakfast before you finish your coffee."

Charles piped in, "Daddy, can I ride on the running board to the edge of the bridge?"

"Not a chance, Charles. Your poor mother would have a fit and fall in it if I let you do that."

"Hunh unh. She wouldn't care. Besides, she couldn't see if she was in the house."

"No. And that's final." Will's voice was firm.

Charles knew he'd lost when Katherine said, "Sit down here, Charles, and finish your breakfast."

I had to make an appearance to calm Will's fears and help Katherine make good on her promise to have me out there before Will finished his coffee. I dabbed tinted powder on my face and appeared in the doorway as Will stood to go. I managed a weak smile and said, "I wanted to get my goodbye kiss before you got out of here."

Will took two long-legged strides across the floor and planted a kiss on my lips. "I wouldn't have left without kissing you," he said. "You feelin' any better?"

My eyes flitted toward Katherine. "Sure. Yes. I am. I must have had a little touch of the flu. Katherine will make sure I get something on my stomach. When you come home tonight everything will be better. I promise."

"It better be, or I'm takin' you up to Sabinal to the doc."

I nodded.

But everything wasn't all right when Will came home that night. You could have cut the tension between Katherine and me with a knife. We spoke in a false voice covering the true meaning of everything we said. When Will asked about my well-being, I said, "Fine, just fine," and Katherine said, "Not too well." We exchanged glares.

Will looked from one of us to the other. When he tried to clarify what we'd said, we spoke over each other until I dismissed Katherine's concerns as "nonsense."

He caught Katherine's eye, and she turned away, but not before he saw something that gave him pause. I knew he'd try to get her alone to find out what I was holding back.

I turned my face up for his welcome home kiss, lifted his hat off the table where he'd dropped it, and hung it on the peg by the door.

Katherine busied herself with the routines of the kitchen and dinner.

I plastered on a false smile and said, "I'll be out back peeling potatoes."

Whatever was between us befuddled Will, and I guess he decided it was best to let us work it out. I made a real effort to appear to be moving without difficulty, even though each motion of an arm or a leg shot stabbing pains through my body.

Will seemed satisfied that I was recovered and diverted his eyes to Charles and Little Dubbya' E, who tugged on his pant legs, demanding attention. It was easy to be distracted by the commotion and leave Katherine and me alone to resolve our differences.

Two weeks after the assault, I realized I was pregnant. The ravishment was perfectly timed to catch me at the most vulnerable time of my cycle. When my monthly visitor failed to materialize, I tried to convince myself that lying with Will after the cockfight was the reason. I kept the news from Will and Katherine, unable to reconcile how to justify my secret to Katherine and equally unsure of what to tell Will.

The dark thoughts that gripped my mind pestered and hounded me day and night. I didn't want this baby. I wanted to die. I wanted to kill Jimmy. I didn't want to hold my boys because when I held them, I loved them, and I didn't want a reason to live.

Wracked with guilt I didn't earn, I wore old clothes with long full skirts and petticoats instead of the straighter, less cumbersome dresses we had all taken to wearing after the war. I was convinced that the slim, thin fabric dress I wore on the night of the attack was why I could not protect myself.

It wasn't until I was well into my second trimester that I could no longer conceal the obvious. This was my fourth pregnancy in under six years, and my body had not bounced back after Aaron's birth. There would only be sixteen months between Aaron and this new baby.

By the time I entered my sixth month, it was clear to Will and Katherine that I was expecting.

WILL

I followed Katherine to the hen house one morning before the place came alive with children and breakfast activities.

"Katty," I whispered, trying to catch her attention without waking anyone, "is it my imagination, or is Maidee expectin' again?"

"Ain't your imagination, Mr. Will," she said, "we're getting' us another young'un 'round the time the Blue Bells pop, by my guestimation."

"She say anything to you? I mean…is she happy about it? Or is that why she's been so shut up in herself?"

"She don't mention it, and neither do I. She's so jumpy these days I'm afraid to say anything. She acts scared of her own shadow."

I shoved my hands deep into my overall pockets and kicked a clump of dirt, tryin' to get up the courage to say what was on my mind. "Something's happened to her, Katty. She wakes up at night, screaming."

"She ever tell you what she's dreamin' 'bout?"

"No. When I reach for her, she pushes me away. She's never been like that. Last night she woke, and her body was shaking so hard the bed rattled. When I tried to comfort her, she beat my chest with doubled-up fists."

"She ain't much better in the daytime, Mr. Will. She jumps ever' time I come into the room. She acts like I'm a stranger...and won't let the boys sit on her lap. That's the worst of it to me. She's shuttin' those little boys clean out'a her life."

"And me," I said before I turned and headed to the house, leaving Katherine to finish gathering the eggs with my parting comment to chew on.

As for Maidee, she had crawled so deep inside herself I couldn't reach her. She shunned conversation, seemed burdened with fear and anxiety, and flinched at the slightest noise or touch.

Katherine told me she wouldn't even go to the chicken house alone. Katherine and I both came to dread the nights when she woke screaming. The more I tried to comfort her, the more she pushed me away. Her face had such a tortured appearance it tore a hole straight through my heart, but I was helpless to explain her behavior.

Our lives had always been open and full of trust. Now she didn't trust anyone or anything. She was broken.

CHAPTER 52

MAIZELLE

I no longer reached for Will when we went to bed. My emotions hung on a razor's edge, and a pall settled over our marriage and the household. Will questioned me about my dreams, and I cried and turned away. I needed to tell him something, but what? What could I say to explain my dark mood? How could I ever face him again, knowing another man had ravaged me? No excuse I offered could explain what I was going through.

One night I felt Will's manhood press against the small of my back. The odor of Linseed Oil and sweat rose in my nostrils. I jerked my body away and gagged into the pillow.

That was the last straw for Will. He slammed his feet on the bare floor and sat upright on the edge of the bed with his head cradled in his open palms. "Maidee, this has got to stop. You've quit me as a wife. You've quit the boys as a mother, and you've quit Katty as a friend. What has gotten into you? How can I fix it if you won't tell me what I've done wrong?"

"It's not you, Will. You haven't done anything wrong."

"Then what in *God's* name is it?" His voice rose so that I was sure Katherine could hear. "I'm sorry I got you pregnant again so soon after Aaron. I'm disgusted with myself for getting drunk at the cockfight and thinking you wanted to make love. I'm sorry. I don't know what to do about it. Seems to me like we're going to have to live with it."

The guilt on his face ripped me apart. How could I explain? "It isn't you, Will. It can't be helped. It's as much my fault as it is yours."

"Then why, Maidee? Why won't you let me touch you? Why do you pull away or stiffen when I reach for you?"

"I don't know," I whispered, shaking my head, teardrops plopping into my lap. "I don't know. I just can't seem to help it."

"What about these nightmares you're havin'? They happen almost every night. What are they about?"

"I can't remember when I wake. I've tried, but all I see is a monster with no face trying to hurt me. I guess this pregnancy isn't like the others. I've never felt this way before."

"Katty says you're sick all day long. Spend half the day hangin' over a bucket on the back porch. If I'd known you were going to be sick like this, I'd never have come to our bed that night."

"I know. I'm sorry. Please be patient with me. I don't know what I'd do if I lost you."

"Lost me? You aren't ever going to lose *me*. I'm just tryin' to figure out how I lost you."

I reached for Will and pulled him down to the bed. I steeled myself against the revulsion I knew would bubble up and nestled my body next to his. I fell asleep that night with my head resting on his shoulder, and no nightmares invaded our momentary peace.

The next morning, Katherine collared me as soon as Will left for work. "I heard you and Will discussin' last night. Did you tell him?"

I pulled my sleeve from her grip. "No. I didn't tell. I never will. Remember, Katherine, you promised."

"I remember, alright. Ever' time I close my eyes and try to sleep knowin' that beast is lurkin' out there just waitin' to get to you again—or me."

She twisted away and went outside, where the boys were fussing over who got to ride and who had to pull the wagon. The easy chatter we'd always engaged in was gone. She went about the daily routines in a trance of her own.

I heard Katherine snap at Charles because he was the oldest, and she thought he should pull the younger boys. I ignored it.

After a bit, she brought all three boys into the house. When Dubbya'E and Aaron tried to climb onto my lap, I pushed them away. I couldn't stand to be touched.

I stayed close to home throughout my pregnancy. I refused to drive, using the excuse that I was uncomfortable driving when I was expecting. I only ventured out in Will's company and stayed in the car whenever possible.

We quit attending church during my confinement. This puzzled Will at first because I had always been the one to push going to church to raise the boys right. Honestly, though, he didn't mind in the least. Church wasn't his favorite activity, and we both knew it.

Few in town realized I was with child. This pregnancy was difficult. Morning sickness visited all day long for the entire eight months I carried. Cooking was near impossible, and if it hadn't been for Katherine, I'm not sure if Will and the boys would ever have had a meal.

I wouldn't have made it out of that darkness without her. She fulfilled every responsibility I had as a wife and mother, except meeting Will's needs as a married man. A truer friend no woman ever had, yet I couldn't bring myself to share the details of the assault or my nightmares. I refused to let her tell Will, the Sheriff, or anyone else.

I sat hunched over the bucket on the back porch. My body and mind tried to throw the baby out with every wretched heave I took.

Katherine said, "The light has gone out in your eyes. Please let me tell Will."

I shook my head.

When I finished heaving, I went inside and curled up in the rocker. A deep sadness that exceeded anything I had experienced settled around me. It was worse than losing my mother... worse than having Papa disown me.

Katherine followed me inside and tried again. "Maidee, I love you more than anyone else in the world except your boys. I can't stand to see you hurtin' this way. The boys don't understand why you won't hold them. You won't look at me or talk to me. I don't know what to do."

"There's nothing you can do. I can't talk about it."

"If I asked the midwife to come talk to you, would you tell her what happened? I think she could help you."

"No, Katherine. I'm not talking to anyone. It's too late for the midwife to do anything that would help me. I waited too long. I couldn't allow myself to believe it was real."

"I didn't mean that, Maidee. I just thought she could help with something for the sickness and give you someone else to talk to about how you feel."

"No. I don't want to talk to her. I'll try harder, I promise."

My ability to engage with my boys was reduced to near zero. I made the motions to get through each day, still breastfeeding Aaron until my seventh month. The one night I slept on Will's shoulder was the only close human contact I allowed myself. My belly grew.

Will quit trying to make love to me. He stopped touching me.

I left the house less and less.

Will thought I was embarrassed to be pregnant. "You've lost your chatty nature," he said.

I smiled and went back to my knitting.

"Is there anything I can do to help you feel better?" he asked.

What could I say? *Yes, kill Jimmy Calvert? Tear this growth inside me out by the roots?* Instead, I shook my head and went on doing whatever I was doing, often without even glancing up.

I was overcome with shame and the urge to cry if I met his eyes. Sometimes he caught me with tears falling from beneath the large-brimmed sunbonnet I always wore—even in the house. From his doleful expression, I knew his heart ached, thinking he was responsible for my misery. There was nothing I could say to salve his wounded feelings and nothing he could do to make me feel better.

CHAPTER 53

MAIZELLE

My labor began in late January, a full month earlier than expected. There was tremendous relief in the household. Everyone, from the children to Katherine to Will, was anxious to meet the new baby who had caused so much grief and difficulty, no one more than me. I wasn't expecting the baby this soon and was unprepared.

My first thought was *it must be Will's.* My eyes flew open in disbelief when the first contraction gripped my body. *How can it be? It's too soon. Does this mean the attack didn't cause this?* My mind ran helter-skelter like a chicken scared off the nest.

Katherine spent her nights in the house now, as her fear of Jimmy had blossomed into full-blown terror.

Will thought it was because the weather had turned cold and gloomy, but she told him it was so she could be on hand if I got sick in the night.

I slipped from the bed and woke her at the first signs of labor. I didn't want to disturb Will. I feared this baby like nothing I had ever feared in my life. What if it came out looking like Jimmy? Then what?

"Katherine?" I bent over the pallet to whisper. "The baby is coming. I need you to walk with me."

Katherine roused, trying to puzzle out what I said. "Coming? Isn't it awful early?"

"Yes. Too early. You need to send Will to get the midwife...but not yet. Let him sleep until we know if this is the real thing."

WILL

Around six, I woke and reached for Maidee. The bed was empty, and it startled me conscious. I rolled out and pulled my trousers on. When I stepped into the living room, I saw Katherine walking with her arm around a hunched-over Maidee. I whispered, "Is she alright?"

She looked over her shoulder. "Yes, Mr. Will."

The two women stopped moving, and Maidee let out a long, mournful wail.

Katherine said, "This young 'un has decided to join the family. Her pains started at two, and they've stayed 'bout the same since. She don't think she needs the midwife yet, but you'd best let Mrs. McDonald know we'll need her soon."

I grabbed my shirt, stepped into my boots by the back door, and headed for the Lizzy.

Mrs. McDonald was up and about when I got there. I could see the light on in her kitchen when I pulled up. "You'd better come quick," I shouted through her back door.

She grabbed her bag and climbed into the car.

Maidee's labor was long and arduous. After all she'd been through over these last months when we thought her body was trying to get rid of this baby, now it was as if her body didn't want to let this child into the world. Her other deliveries were all routine and relatively brief. This time her body struggled for almost thirty-six hours to give me another son.

I suffered with every pain that clutched at her body and lifted her off the bed. I sat with her and held her hand. She wouldn't look at me.

When her labor took a turn, Mrs. McDonald told her to push. She sat up and shouted at me to get out. "Just go! I don't need an audience."

I was shocked because when Dubbya'E and Aaron were born, she didn't want me to leave her side long enough to have a smoke.

Katherine took my arm and steered me out of the room. "Let's give her some privacy," she murmured. "She doesn't want you to see her sufferin'."

This didn't seem right. My girl had always wanted me close. What changed to make her shun me like this? I went out on the porch to smoke, but the questions kept creeping into my mind like weeds in a garden. What had I done to make her push me away?

MAIZELLE

When my new baby made his entrance, I was exhausted from my long labor. Yet, the moment Mrs. McDonald put him to my breast, I felt the same overwhelming love I'd experienced for the other three. I examined the tiny body in my arms to make sure he was whole. Satisfied that all his parts were in the right place, I nuzzled my face against his downy white skin and kissed him with welcome relief. Tears slipped off my cheeks onto his.

He squinted and squirmed. It was apparent there was something very different about this baby. His skin was so pale I felt I could see through it. His little head was covered with long hair, the color and consistency of new corn silk. His eyes were blue like his brothers' but were so pale they looked almost colorless. He had fine, silky white down on his arms and back. He was delicate in his construction the way Charles had been.

Because he was a month early, he was smaller than my other babies. Even Charles, as frail and sickly as he was as an infant, seemed robust compared to this one. I took him to my breast, and my heart swelled with love for this unwanted but welcome new child.

Once Katherine settled the other kids, eager to meet their new brother, Will led them into the room where I lay spent, cradling my newborn. He looked at us with the same wonder I saw in his eyes after the births of each of our boys.

He brought them in turn and introduced them to Lynch Davidson. They each touched the downy white hair on his head and put a finger in his tiny hand, thrilled when his fingers curled around theirs. Will stepped back to let the boys get closer.

Our eyes caught, and I saw the same Jones pride shining on his face as I did each time I delivered him a new son. The fear and trepidation I harbored deep in my soul released with a sigh, and my shoulders relaxed into the pillow in a way I hadn't experienced in many months. *He doesn't suspect.* The thought flashed through my mind and was gone.

Katherine herded the boys back into the front room, leaving Will and me alone with the new baby. Will perched on the edge of the bed and stroked Lynch's face with one finger as our son suckled on my empty breast. He reached up and brushed the matted hair off my forehead.

I smiled. I think it was the smile he had hoped for all these dark days and weeks because he mouthed the words I was so desperate to hear. He said, "I love you. Thank you for this beautiful boy." He leaned down and kissed my lips.

I didn't flinch or pull away for the first time in a long time. "I love you too," I said. "I was afraid you'd be disappointed this wasn't your girl."

Will grinned and said, "Umm, a smidge. But after I saw him, I was just as happy as I was with the others. We'll get our girl someday."

I turned my face away. "Not for a while, Will. I'm not sure I could survive another pregnancy."

"I'm sorry for all the pain I caused," he said.

"Please don't ever say that again. What's done is done. We have a new son now, and I have a lot to make up with the other three...and you," I whispered.

He squeezed my shoulder. "You get some rest now. I'll be right outside if you need anything."

CHAPTER 54

MAIZELLE

Katherine was changing the baby's diaper when she commented, "That albino streak must run strong in Will's family. This here little one looks a lot like Jimmy Calvert."

I froze. My face went cold. I was without words.

Until this moment, we had been steadfast on our pact, never to mention his name. Katherine had honored my request not to speak of the attack, though keeping the promise caused an unresolved rift between us. The two of us held a powerful secret. Katherine believed it should be shared with the Sheriff and Will. I remained resolute that no one ever know.

Would Katherine break her promise now that Lynch was here? Paralyzed with dread, I forced myself to put one foot in front of the other and walked to where Katherine stood, pinning a clean nappy on my baby. I pondered him with interest as though the thought that he might be albino had never occurred to me. My voice sounded quizzical and detached when I gathered the courage to speak. "I suppose it does. Things like that seem to run in families, don't they?" Gazing at Lynch with feigned interest, I held my breath to see what Katherine would say next.

She stared at me, my face as bland and expressionless as I could make it. Her eyes narrowed a bit, but she held her tongue, and the moment passed.

I reached for Lynch and carried him to the rocker for a feeding. He nursed, staring up at me wide-eyed. His eyes closed in sleep as he released my nipple, a satisfied smile tickling the corners of his mouth where milk seeped.

I kissed his downy head and returned him to his bassinet, where I stood watching him sleep and thought, *how could anything this tiny and innocent be the cause of so much pain and anguish?*

Katherine stood folding diapers, her lips pinched and her jawline tense.

A storm was brewing, and we both knew it. We couldn't go on living under this cloud of fear and uncertainty. Lynch was not like the other boys. The only explanation was that he was Jimmy's child.

I couldn't reconcile my feelings for him with my feelings for Jimmy. I wanted Jimmy dead. I had not seen him or heard his name since the night of the attack.

Katherine's comment caught me off guard. I had considered the possibility but dismissed it the moment it entered my mind.

Following Lynch's birth, I sometimes lapsed into introspective moments of deep despair, which Katherine chalked up to a case of baby blues to mollify Will's fussing and concern. During these times, I would ask Katherine to take over the care of the boys and the household and escape to my room to be alone with my dark thoughts. These were the times I contemplated what had happened and the result. I resolved that Lynch's arrival, almost a month earlier than expected, was proof that he was Will's.

It was clear that when Lynch made his debut, Katherine took in his unusual appearance and drew her own conclusions. She alone knew what had happened. She stood by me throughout the unwelcome pregnancy and the difficult delivery, steadfast in her help to our growing family. I couldn't have asked for a better or more loyal friend. But until today, if she believed Lynch was Jimmy's spawn, she had kept her peace.

Sometimes I would catch her looking at me, and I knew she wondered if the deep sadness that had covered me like a heavy quilt for all these months would ever lift. I wanted to reassure her that I would be okay again—things would return to normal—but I could never make the words come out of my mouth.

Spring was upon the Sabinal Canyon, and the weather fluctuated between frequent deluges and warm sunny days punctuated by the fresh aroma and colorful displays of wildflowers. Lynch was sleeping, and the three older boys were busy gathering blossoms from the field in front of the house. Katherine and I sat on the front stoop watching. I enjoyed the closeness as we sat shoulder to shoulder and pondered her presence in our family.

It dawned on me that she might return to sleeping in the barn soon. "If you need help moving your pallet back out to the barn, I'd be happy to help you."

Her response brought me out of my reverie like a lightning strike. "I will *not* go sleep in that barn again and leave myself open to an attack by that monster!"

Her fierce response shocked me. That was the first time I noticed my animosity and hatred for Jimmy had begun to recede. There were days when Jimmy didn't enter my mind, but I wasn't the only one suffering.

I turned to her and saw angry tears glistening. I'd never seen Katherine so incensed nor so frightened. I threw my arms around her and pulled her close. The tears she had held back all these months poured out with a flood of words.

"You never gave a thought to what it was like for me. I tried to sleep, but I couldn't let myself. Ever' sound, ever' creak that old barn let out made my eyes pop open and my whole body tense up. I dreamed Jimmy was creepin' around the barn just waitin' to prey on me like he preyed on you. I'm leavin' you, Maidee. I can't live under this roof knowin' what I know, lyin' to Mr. Will, bein' afraid ever' single day. Watchin' you avoid your young'uns and hurtin' your husband. If Mr. Will hasn't made the connection yet, he soon will. I don't want to be around when that happens."

My mouth gaped open. *Leaving me? What would I do without Katherine?* "Leaving me? You don't mean it. Where would you go? Haven't we been good to you?"

"'Course you been good to me. You know that. I think I'll go to California. I want to get as far away as I can from these nightmares and this secret. I saved all the money you and Mr. Will give me. I have enough to buy a train ticket and head west. And I ain't sleepin' in no barn again—ever!"

I grabbed both her hands to hold her in place. "Katherine. Dear Katherine, of course, you were afraid. You're right. I've been so caught up in my own darkness I never gave a thought to how you were feeling." My eyes brimmed, and I pleaded with her from the inside out. "Please don't go. Please stay and help me—help us—get our feet under us again. The boys would be lost without you. I'd be lost without you. Of course, you can stay in the house. I'm sorry. So very, very sorry."

We clutched each other and wept. Lynch let out a wail from inside the house, and my heart swelled with love for my new son as milk seeped through my blouse to Katherine.

"I love you, Katherine," I said, wiping my tears and nose with my apron. "Please say you'll stay. I promise to try harder to get back to normal. I've left everything on your shoulders, and it wasn't fair. Thank you for staying with me. And thank you for keeping your promise."

"It's okay, Maidee. I won't leave right away—if I can stay in the house. But I still think you should tell Will what happened. If this baby isn't his, he has a right to know."

"I don't think Lynch is Jimmy's. He came almost a month earlier than we figured. I know that's what you think, but I just can't believe it."

"I still think you should tell Will what Jimmy done to you. What if he comes back to try to get at you again?"

"I'll think on it. I promise."

And I did think on it. I played the conversation over and over in my mind, weighing each word, and each of Will's possible reactions, until I came to believe I *had* had the conversation with him.

CHAPTER 55

MAIZELLE

The dark episodes I suffered grew farther apart with time, and I grew more confident about going out again, although never by myself. I doubted I would ever again go anywhere alone. I made a genuine effort to reconnect with my boys and Will.

It was easier with the boys. I held them close, laughed with them, and played silly games. They cherished their new baby brother, making my feelings for him seem natural. He was less rambunctious and a bit more timid than the other boys, but he adored me and clung to my skirt as he learned to crawl and walk. He was never far from my side.

Will made a swing to hang in the live oak off the back porch, between the privy and the root cellar.

The boys took turns sitting on the board seat, and I pushed them until my arms ached. Their laughter was the best medicine I could have swallowed to bring a feeling of life back to my bones.

Will and I had a bit more trouble being close again. I wanted to put things back the way they were, but it was awkward since so much time had passed without any physical relationship. If I touched him in bed, he took it to mean I was ready to make love. When my body stiffened at his advances, he felt rejected again. I couldn't explain why my body recoiled from him, so he continued to blame himself. In time, he quit trying. I knew if our marriage was to survive, I would have to be the one to initiate the lovemaking.

The arrival of Spring gave me a feeling of tranquility. My body and my mind responded with a primordial connection. As a child, I was given to daydreaming when the season approached and accused by Julia and Papa of getting "spring fever." Something about the season's arrival this year gave me hope. My body felt different. I found myself remembering the pleasure I experienced making love with Will when I was a new bride. I revisited the night we made love in the river when we were building the bridge. The memories sparked a flood of new sensations that stayed with me all day, invading my thoughts at odd times, causing pringles up my spine and goosebumps on my arms. I felt lighter and more resilient. Maybe tonight.

After the children were tucked into bed, Will and I sat on the front porch side by side as night fell and stars rose in the clear sky. Katherine had gone into town for an overnight visit with her family. We watched with amusement as she scrambled into the waiting car when her pa came to pick her up in his new automobile.

"Bye, Katty," Will called after her.

"Bye-bye, Katherine," I said. "Come back soon, ya hear?"

Katherine leaned out of the rear seat window and waved her whole arm in our direction. "Back tomorrow," she shouted as her pa drove away.

We all needed a break. It had been a long year, and Katherine bore the brunt of the work both physically and emotionally.

Once the O'Brien's car cleared the bridge, I reached for Will's hand. The same thrill I experienced as a fourteen-year-old, the first time we locked eyes, raced through me. The sensation startled me, and I chuckled.

Will's eyebrows knit, and he said, "What you find so amusin'?"

"Nothing," I said, "I just got a little thrill like I used to when we were first sparking."

I felt the heat rise in my cheeks and stared at my hands; a woman's hands now, with calluses, red and cracked cuticles, skinned knuckles, and broken nails. The sight alarmed me. *Had I let myself go this badly?* How could Will ever love me the same way after all that had happened? Four babies in six years were strong evidence of his desire, and I squeezed his hand. "Shall we call it a day?"

He stood and tugged on my arm to help me from the chair. I turned to him and raised my eyes. Willingness and desire rose in a way I had not felt since the attack.

Will didn't say anything, but his eyes questioned me. I felt timid and shy and ridiculously foolish under his gaze. I nodded my head, and we stepped inside to our bedroom.

My heart pounded. I willed my body to respond to his touch without recoiling. My mind flashed between images of Jimmy's white visage and the gentle, loving countenance of my eager and excited husband as he undressed me.

Will shed his clothes and rolled onto his side beside my naked body.

I waited for the involuntary tensing. When my body remained still and relaxed, I reached for him. "I've missed you," I whispered, my lips against his ear.

"And I've missed you."

I closed my eyes to the darkest days of my life and concentrated on the love I shared with Will. My hope was to let that love erase Jimmy from my mind.

CHAPTER 56

MAIZELLE

I began my studies to join Eastern Star when I turned twenty. The attack stopped me in my tracks, but I thought if I wanted to have a normal life again, I should resume. I insisted that Will drive me to study with Elizabeth and Emma. No amount of arguing convinced me to take the car on my own. In a short time, I finished the process of becoming an initiate.

Julia, also in Eastern Star, was thrilled when she learned I was to be initiated, and she approached Sam about buying a dress for me as their gift. I told her I had several I could choose from, but she insisted, so I sent her the page from the Sears Roebuck Catalogue with the dress I wanted. The ceremony would take place on Tuesday, March 25, 1924, and I would wear the beautiful new outfit I chose, and Julia bought.

I had selected a Crayon Blue flat crepe silk that featured a simple darted silhouette suitable for my curvy figure. It had long sleeves, a jewel neckline, and a hip band adorned with rayon embroidery. In the fashion of the day, a large flat bow graced the hipline. My new dress ended mid-calf and showed my narrow ankles and slender legs. The magazine advertisement asked, "Could you imagine feeling other than your best in such an attractive frock?"

If Julia and I had been anywhere close to the same size, she would have showered me with her recent discards, but the reality was that Julia was tall and slender with an athletic figure, and I was short with ample breasts and shaped like an hourglass. The new straight styles were advantageous to her figure but much more challenging for me.

The dress I chose had a shaped bodice that draped seductively over my curves. I modeled it for Will.

He sucked in his breath, and his eyes grew wide. My new svelte figure showed off the stunning dress to great advantage. He said, "It's easy to forget what a beautiful girl I married when you're pregnant or nursing a baby. I like seeing you in something besides practical clothes. A string of pearls would go with that dress, wouldn't it?"

"Yes, I suppose. It's called a jewel neckline, but I don't have a string of pearls. I thought I might make a ribbon neckband to compliment the dress."

On initiation day, I was hunkered over the sink while Katherine washed my thick mane of hair. Dubbya'E burst into the kitchen and tugged on her apron. "Juwia, Juwia," my four-year-old babbled. "Big car! Come see, come see!"

"Oh dear," Katherine said as she wrapped my hair inside a clean towel and piled it atop my head. "I'd better go see what Dubbya'E is prattlin' on about."

I followed and was greeted by the bright yellow Handley-Knight automobile parked in front of the porch. Will wasn't home from work yet, and the arrival of guests was unexpected. Chaos erupted with a flurry of activity.

The boys were delighted to see their Aunt Julia, especially Charles, who had developed a genuine bond with her. They corresponded with each other since Charles now knew his letters and attended primary school. He threw himself around Julia's legs and gave them a mighty hug.

Dubbya'E stood with two fingers in his mouth, gaping at the tall, elegant woman standing with her arms outstretched to him.

Aaron padded around the front yard in his diaper, covered with dirt, enjoying a few minutes of freedom from Katherine's watchful eye.

We left fourteen-month-old Lynch strapped into the wooden highchair in the kitchen, where we had been preparing for the evening.

Julia ran up the steps and shouted, "Surprise!"

I looked at my sister in shock. "Julia! Where did you come from? What...why... is Sam...?" My voice trailed off in confusion.

"Oh, Honeybee, you didn't think I'd let your initiation ceremony pass me by, did you? Sam and I are so proud of you and Will for joining the Lodge. We wouldn't have missed this for the world!" She bent down, hugged me, and air-kissed both cheeks. "We want you and Will to ride with us in the Handley to the ceremony tonight. Nothing but the best for my baby sister." Julia stepped back and looked at me, radiating love and excitement.

I gazed in wonder. "Where are you staying?"

"At Papa's," Julia said with a *where else* tone of voice. We both knew that Sam and Julia couldn't stay in our little house.

"He knows we're coming but thinks we're arriving late tonight. That way, we can attend the ceremony without offending him. I want the whole afternoon to help you prepare. We can dress here, can't we?"

I looked Julia up and down. "Dress here? You look to me like you're already dressed for an audience with the Queen. But of course, you can dress here," I hastened to add when I saw her crestfallen face. "We don't have cooties as far as I know."

The sound of Julia's dismissive laughter rolled over me like pellets of ice. I had never felt less than—or like my life was in any way inferior to my sister's—until this moment. This moment, when Julia, already regaled in the finest and most expensive clothing I had ever seen, announced her intention to up her game for the ceremony. We might be members of the same fraternal organization, but Will and I would never equal the McGaverns in social stature.

I touched the towel atop my head and said, "I have Katherine to help me get ready. Perhaps you could entertain the boys while we work on my hair." I knew this was the worst possible job I could have suggested.

Julia's smile froze in place, and I saw Katherine turn away so Julia wouldn't see the sheer delight and amusement that played around her lips. For me to choose her help over my sophisticated sister made up for any slight she felt the first time Julia visited.

"Well, sure, I suppose I could mind them for a while," Julia managed to say as her smile faded. "I just thought since tonight was so important, you'd want *me* to help you get ready."

I could hear the pout in her voice and knew Julia's feelings were hurt. It was my own tender heart that wouldn't let me continue the charade. I looked at Katherine and said, "Katty, would it hurt your feelings if Julia did my French braids? I know you were getting anxious about lunch for the boys. This might be a good time to get them fed."

"Sure, Maidee," Katherine said. "You know I'm all thumbs when it comes to French braiding. Besides, those young 'uns need their lunch."

Julia's eyes lit up anew, and a smile of relief swept across her face. "Let's get started then!" She clapped her hands and snatched the towel off my head, letting my hair fall heavy and wet down my back. "Oh my, you've let it grow clear to your waist. This is going to take a while."

She stuck ten fingers into my locks and lifted as she gave a disparaging glance at Katherine's long cotton skirt. "I'm glad we came when we did," she said, "I was so happy to get rid of long skirts flapping around my ankles and a wad of long, hot hair hanging down my back. I don't know how you girls can stand either one."

Katherine and I lowered our eyes to avoid giving away our amusement at Julia's haughty attitude. We were of one mind about this intrusion into our day.

CHAPTER 57

WILL

I got home an hour earlier than usual, shocked to see the Handley parked by the front steps. I knew what it meant. Sam and Julia McGavern were here and planned to insert themselves into the evening I had planned for my wife. I took the wrapped box of Sears and Roebuck pearls and carried it into the house through the back door.

Katherine was busy preparing dinner, and the table had two extra places. "Hi, Katty," I said, looking around the room to see if anyone else was within earshot. "I see we have company."

"Yep," she said. "We sure do have company. If you want to see Maidee alone, you'd best hurry to the bedroom 'cause Julia's fixin' to be in there with her as soon as she gets herself dressed. She's in the boy's room with Sam right this minute, doin' just that."

"Thanks, Katty," I squeezed her arm. "You're the best."

I opened the door to our bedroom and watched Maidee applying lip rouge as she sat in her chemise in front of the small mirror on the dresser. She didn't see me, and I drank in the sight of her slender figure, white shoulders, and neatly braided hair. Her neck looked long and inviting, with her hair pulled up in the twist of braids. I couldn't resist stepping over to sneak a kiss on the satiny white surface.

She heard me and turned into the face of a man lusting for her in a way she hadn't seen for a long time. "Will, you're home early!" She sounded surprised and pleased. "You may have noticed we have company. Julia and Sam drove up to attend the initiation."

"I figured as much when I saw that bright yellow car out front. I'd like to give you something before the boys discover I'm home." I handed her the box and watched as she untied the ribbon and lifted the necklace from the tissue.

"Oh, Will, they're beautiful. They're perfect for the dress. Thank you." Her eyes glistened with gratitude and love as she held the pearls.

When she looked at me, my heart swelled. She stood, wrapped her arms around my neck, and kissed me on the lips.

Julia opened the bedroom door and saw Maidee in her undergarments, her arms around me, and our bodies pressed together in an intimate embrace.

"Oh!" She exclaimed as she pulled the door shut.

Maidee laughed and let go of me. "It's okay, Julia," she called through the closed door. "You can come in."

Julia timidly reopened the door and stepped inside, careful to conceal Maidee from Sam, waiting in the living room. "I'm sorry for walking in on you," she sputtered, "I had no idea Will was home. Hello, Will."

"Hello, Julia. This is a surprise. Is Sam with you?"

"Yes, of course, silly. I don't drive. Only my brave baby sister sports around in a motorcar by herself."

"Well, any wife of mine has to be able to drive if she ever wants to go anywhere," I said, thinking, *at least, that's what I used to believe.*

"Sam and I brought you a little present, Maidee." Julia slipped a small box from behind her back.

"Thank you," Maidee said, "but you've done enough by sending me the dress and shoes." She lifted the lid on the box and let out a little gasp before snapping it closed. When her eyes met Julia's, they were full of panic. "I can't accept this," she said.

"Why ever not?" Julia asked. "We wanted you to have something special to wear."

"I already have something special," Maidee said, "Will gave me pearls."

Julia blanched as her eyes went from Maidee to me and back again. "I'm sorry. I didn't know." She reached for the box, and Maidee handed it to her.

I was confused by the exchange but didn't say anything. I decided it was best to let them work it out, whatever it was. "I'll get out of here and let you finish dressing," I said, making a quick exit.

MAIZELLE

After the door closed behind Will, I turned to my sister and said through clenched teeth, "Will has never given me a piece of jewelry of any kind. He bought me a pearl necklace for tonight, and I'm wearing it. You should keep your expensive gifts for someone who has a use for them. The pearls are beautiful, and I'm sure they were expensive, but I'd rather wear the Sears and Roebuck pearls Will gave me than all the finery you display like a...like a... peacock."

I was embarrassed by my outburst. I didn't know why Julia's gesture made me so angry, but I didn't stop there. "Don't assume, because we live a simple life, that we're impoverished, and don't assume that Will doesn't love me enough to buy me gifts. I'm not joining the Eastern Star to please you; I'm doing this because it's important to Will. You need to take those pearls and get your money back. They're too expensive for the likes of me. I would never hurt Will's feelings by wearing them."

My angry diatribe shook Julia, and she tucked the jewel box into her pocket.

I should have let it stop there, but something in me broke loose. "You chose one kind of life, and I chose another. I'm happy in my *little* house. I'm happy wearing cotton skirts and blouses, and I like my hair long because Will likes my hair long.

It isn't any of your business if I have long hair. I like it this way, and I like my life this way." I turned away from my sister's stricken face and plopped down on the edge of the bed.

"Honeybee..." Julia began.

"And stop calling me Honeybee! I'm not a honeybee. I'm not a baby, and I wish you'd quit treating me like one. You blow in here like loose tumbleweed, bouncing off every part of my life. Will and I don't need to ride in your showy automobile to feel important. We have a perfectly good car that gets us where we want to go when we want to go."

"I..." Julia started, but I jumped from the bed sobbing and threw my arms around her neck. She held me, not knowing what to say.

"I'm sorry," I choked out between gulping sobs. "I know you were just trying to make this night special. It's just that Will and I had planned this evening for the two of us."

That wasn't the real reason I was crying; seeing Julia again had dredged up horrible memories from the last time I saw her, the night Jimmy attacked me.

"It's okay. I understand. Let's each take our car to the Lodge, and then Sam and I can go straight to Papa's after."

The thing was, she *didn't* understand. I hadn't seen Julia since that night, and I'd never spoken of it to her. Seeing her again had jolted me backward in time. The reference to Papa caused another eruption. "I'd give anything for Papa to be there tonight to see me in this beautiful dress and see how happy I am. Why is he so hard, Julia? Why can't he be happy for me and enjoy his grandsons?"

"I don't know, Honeyb... I don't know. He won't talk about it. If I mention your name, the whole room goes silent. I guess your eloping made him feel like he failed as a father. He pinned all his hopes on us after Mama died and wanted what he thought would give us the best life."

"And you lived up to every dream he had. I've been a complete failure and disappointment. I shouldn't have had to choose between Papa and Will. It wasn't fair. I didn't want what you wanted. I wanted to be Will's wife and the mother of his children, and I'm happy with my choice." I slumped against Julia and dabbed my eyes.

Julia, realizing her silk crepe dress would soon be spotted with tear stains—if it wasn't already—eased me away. "Let's get you into that new dress and join our husbands." My sister was very careful not to disturb my neat hairdo as she lowered the dress over my head.

When we arrived at the Lodge, the strain between Julia and me wasn't apparent to our husbands, but Elizabeth immediately picked up on it.

I smiled at Elizabeth, the Worthy Matron, but there must have been something in my smile that let her know I wasn't my usual self.

Elizabeth caught my eye and questioned me with a quizzical expression. I gave a barely perceptible shake of my head and looked away to let her know this wouldn't be the time to talk about it.

Julia carried herself regally, but I felt awkward and uncomfortable in my chosen dress.

Elizabeth gushed that we both looked "stunning." Julia greeted her with air kisses and a light hug that looked insincere. I'm sure she realized Julia's usual exuberance was missing.

I was presented, along with two other young women, to the assembly of invited guests and members of the "Utopia Masonic Lodge and the local chapter of the Order of the Eastern Star."

As I stood and walked the length of the long aisle to the dais, I caught Will's eyes surveying me with unabashed admiration and love. My heart quickened, and my cheeks grew warm. I lowered my eyes to the floor in front of me as I finished the long walk.

The Worthy Matron welcomed me and handed me a long-stemmed red rose and a small white satin cushion with a gold ring tied to the top. The ring featured the Eastern Star emblem and held my initials on either side.

I learned later that since I didn't have a wedding ring, Aunt Elizabeth had encouraged Will to let her order this for me. Neither of the other initiates received one.

"I'd like our brother, Master Mason William E. Jones, to step forward and place this ring on our new sister's hand," Elizabeth intoned, sounding like an officiant at a wedding.

Will beamed.

My eyes filled with tears of joy. My sister was here to see me in this moment that, for me, was as close to a wedding ceremony as I would ever get.

Emma, Bobby, Elizabeth, and Robert were here to witness Will slip a ring on my finger.

Papa and Katherine were missing, and I swallowed a lump when I thought of them.

When the ceremony concluded, Elizabeth invited everyone into the anteroom for refreshments.

Julia pulled me aside and said, "Maidee, I could see the love in Will's eyes, and the devotion in yours as he put the ring on your finger. I know in my heart your marriage is a true love match."

I hugged her. "I'm sorry I jumped all over you earlier. I know you meant well. I think the anxiety over the initiation caught up with me. I'm truly sorry."

"It's okay, Maidee. Today, when you said, 'you chose one kind of life, and I chose another,' I finally understood. Then seeing how you and Will looked at each other tonight, I choked up and had to swallow hard to keep from crying. When Sam noticed, he squeezed my hand. I blinked back my tears and felt grateful to have such a kind man for a husband, and I'm thankful you found happiness with Will."

I think tonight was the first time she realized how much I love Will. I wish that I had my sister closer. I could have told her what happened to me, and it might have been easier if I hadn't tried to carry it alone. I hugged her tight and thanked her for coming, knowing I would never share the true reason for my outburst.

When Will reached for me in the quiet of our bed that night, I responded in the old way. I was open, willing, and eager to make love to him.

CHAPTER 58

MAIZELLE

Following the initiation, I kept busy with activities for the Eastern Star and enjoyed social contact with the other women. I felt my old confidence returning. It was slow at first but grew as time passed.

As Lynch grew and gained strength, so did I. My emotions gradually returned to a pre-pregnancy level, and I felt stronger and could step outside the confines of my self-imposed exile. My relationship with Eastern Star renewed my faith, and I wanted Lynch baptized. I was learning to pray again and trying my best to forgive God for what had happened to me.

One Sunday, I was up before anyone else in the house. I sat on the front porch and looked down the dirt track leading to the river and the bridge, thinking, *he's out there. I feel him. I know if he catches me alone, he'll ravage me again. I can't let him ruin my life. Will's here to protect me at night. Katherine and the boys are here during the day. I doubt he would approach the house. I refuse to live in fear. I must put this behind me. My family needs me, and I need them. If Katherine decides to make good on her dream to go to California, I'll find someone else to help. I need to forget what happened. I'm safe here.*

When Will wandered out and stood by my chair, I said, "I think we should all get dressed for church."

He stretched his arms over his head and inhaled a deep lung of morning air but didn't say anything. He placed both hands on my shoulders and squeezed.

I was about to say something when Katherine joined us.

Will looked at her and said, "Maidee thinks we should go to church."

I saw the glance between them, wondering if this was a one-time thing or if we would begin attending regularly.

Katherine nodded her head my way and said, "Well, if we're goin' to make it on time, we'd best get those young 'uns fed and dressed."

I followed her into the house. "You start breakfast," I said, "I'll get the boy's clean clothes ready."

Everything happened in a flurry, and once the boy's faces were washed and their hair combed, we rushed to get them dressed in clean overalls and long-sleeved shirts. Will put on his suit and tie and got the car ready.

Not long after the initiation, he purchased a new car that was big enough for all of us. It was a Ford Touring car, and I'd never driven it, which gave me an excuse not to start driving again.

I sat beside Will on the large front seat, with Katherine next to me, holding Lynch in her lap. The three older boys sat side by side on the back seat as we rolled down the lane toward town.

Going to services again was a huge step for me. When we arrived at the Methodist church, Will parked and came around to open the doors. He got the boys out with Katherine's help while I held Lynch.

When she was free, I handed him back and took Aaron by the hand.

Charles and Dubbya'E each held one of Will's hands as we walked up the pathway to the small sanctuary with Katherine and Lynch close behind. I felt myself swell with pride.

We took seats near the back, and as I looked toward the front, I saw an unmistakable crop of snow-white hair on top of a very pale pink neck. The head had not turned, and I knew he hadn't seen me. My stomach contracted, and the taste of bile filled my mouth.

Panicked, I pushed Aaron at Will and fled toward the open door, brushing past Katherine. Once outside, I doubled over, held my stomach, and retched.

My sudden departure surprised Will, but he settled Aaron onto the pew and followed me. I heard him tell Kathrine to watch the boys as he pushed past late-comers with puzzled expressions. A woman grabbed his arm and said, "something's wrong with your wife."

He pulled away and rushed out the door as I slumped to the ground, sobbing. Will knelt beside me, slipped one arm around my shoulder and the other around my waist, lifting me to my feet. As I rose, our eyes met. When he saw my face, he nearly lost his grip. He guided me toward the car, leaned close, and whispered, "What happened? What frightened you?"

I gulped air and shook, weeping uncontrollably. "Go home," I gasped between sobs, "go home." I left no room for argument.

Will helped me into the car and leaned inside. He held me close to his chest while I cried. When the sobbing slowed enough for me to wipe my nose and catch my breath, he asked, "Will you be okay here while I get Katherine and the boys?"

I nodded and fell to my side on the seat so I would not be visible to anyone who happened by. "I'll be fine. Just hurry!"

He rushed to get Katherine and the kids out the door and into the car. He slipped behind the wheel, and I pressed myself against him and turned my head away from Katherine's inquisitive eye.

We rode in silence except when a worried Charles said, "Momma, why'd we have to leave? I wanted to stay."

Dubbya'E cried and kicked the back of Will's seat. Will was so sharp with them when he answered that it silenced them.

When we got home, I fled to the bedroom.

Katherine and Will could hear me retching, and Katherine came into the room with a cool cloth to bathe my forehead. My sudden illness so disturbed her that she hovered over me like a mother hen.

I wouldn't talk and averted my eyes when she entered the room. I let her bring Lynch to me for his feedings instead of getting up and sitting in the rocking chair. I wouldn't discuss my breakdown.

Late in the afternoon, Will came in and sat on the edge of the bed. "Maidee, was seein' Jimmy what upset you? 'Cuz, when you ran out, he gave me a glare like he wanted to kill me. When I went back to get Katty and the kids, everyone turned to see what was happenin', and I noticed him glarin' at me with pure hate. I didn't give it much thought at the time, but it left an impression. I was just wonderin' if he looked at you the same?"

I wanted to tell Will what happened, but the words stuck in my throat. I nodded my head. I thought about the attack I endured at Jimmy's hands and relived the horror.

Will saw tears in my eyes and tried to cheer me up by joking that I hadn't even let the minister get started with his sermon before I started throwing up.

I couldn't muster a laugh, dabbed my tears with the corner of the pillowcase, and looked at him with dead eyes.

Katherine poked her head in and asked if I was ready for Lynch's feeding.

I was happy for the interruption and took him. I looked at my latest son with mixed emotions. His appearance and presence in my life served as constant reminders of what I now accepted was the result of that single violent act. My attempt to convince myself Lynch's birth resulted from seducing Will the same night was a fool's errand. My memory of the event was so vivid that just seeing his head of hair triggered a response so vile and violent I could not cope.

I spent the next five days in a deep slump, unable to eat, startled awake by visions in my sleep, powerless to talk to those who loved me and set apart from my four beloved sons. On the sixth day following the ordeal at church, I climbed out of bed, weary and weak, and made my way to the kitchen to sit at breakfast with my family.

My boys stared at me as if I were a ghost.

Katherine feigned a cheerful demeanor and tried to act as though nothing untoward had occurred.

Will studied me with a furrowed brow and concern. "Feelin' better?" he asked.

"Better," I answered, pushing food around on my plate in a half-hearted attempt to eat but barely denting the portion Katherine served.

Will had to leave for work and pulled Katherine aside. After he was gone, she told me he said, "I don't know what I would have done without you this past year. I can't thank you enough. Keep an eye on her, and I'll try to come home early to relieve you."

Katherine said she seized the opportunity to say, "Will, I've been here for four years. It might be time for me to think 'bout makin' my own life. I'm eighteen and want to go to California—see a bit of the world. There's nothin' for me in Utopia. I can't live with y'all forever. I won't leave 'til we know Maidee's okay, but you need to be lookin' for somebody else to help."

She hugged me and said, "I felt relieved once the decision I'd been ponderin' was off my chest, but Will looked dumbfounded, like he couldn't believe I would ever go."

"I warned him awhile back this might happen," I said.

"All's he said was, 'I see,' before he ran to the car. As if by runnin' away, he could pretend he hadn't heard."

"It's okay, Katherine. I know you can't stay forever. You need to get out and find a husband before you're an old maid."

"It's not that, Maidee," she said, "it's just that I can't see spendin' my life takin' care of someone else's babies. It don't seem right somehow."

I moved through the following weeks as if I lived inside a cocoon that nothing could penetrate. I only spoke when it couldn't be avoided and left all the care of the house and the children to Katherine. It was as if I wanted to see how much more I could get out of her before she up and quit me.

When Will approached me in bed, I stiffened and turned my head away. I could pretend he wasn't there if I couldn't see him. I sat for hours staring out the window toward the river at something only I could see.

When Will or Katherine caught me shedding silent tears, which I concealed by wearing my sunbonnet again, it reminded them of the earlier time. The sudden onset of this illness, and the melancholy that followed, were reminiscent of those days. They kept a close watch for any signs of a swelling belly.

Alone on the porch in my rocking chair, nearly four months after the incident in church, I stared down the dirt track to the bridge concealed in the tall branches of the Cypress Trees. I patted the new baby inside me with a loving tenderness I never allowed myself to feel when I carried Lynch.

Lynch turned one. I weaned him, and life began to return to normal. I had more energy and took joy in the rambunctious antics of my brood. I initiated conversations with Katherine and laughed with her again. I even approached Will, startling him with pleasure I'm sure he had forgotten he could have.

The deep despondency that had enveloped me over the past months seemed to lift of its own accord. Katherine and Will must have been relieved that they no longer had to walk on eggshells. The figure I had enjoyed for a short time was gone again. Now, carrying my fifth baby—the one Will and I hoped would be the daughter we longed for—I looked and felt womanlier.

Katherine said I had "a youthful glow," and Will always made me feel beautiful.

CHAPTER 59

MAIZELLE

All four boys, now six, five, three, and almost two, were thrilled with their new baby sister. As she grew from infant to toddler, Will added a chair swing to the live oak that shaded our long back porch, using a seat from a discarded highchair he found along the road.

When Katherine was away, I often worked on the covered back porch. I watched the boys play and kept my eye on Maisie. My precious little girl was just over a year old when we began to use the swing. Maisie loved the motion and the attention and would sit for hours as her brothers took turns pushing the swing and doting on her every smile, gurgle, and delighted squeal.

Maisie was a sweet-natured child with curly dark hair and dark brown eyes. Her appearance stood in stark contrast to Lynch's, with his snow-white hair, pale skin, and dancing light blue eyes. She was such an easy baby that as soon as I weaned her at twelve months, Katherine reduced her time with us to two days a week.

I sat on a three-legged stool preparing fruit for preserves, peeling potatoes for the evening meal, sewing, and mending the children's clothes. The devotion my boys showed their baby sister gave me great joy. I felt safe here, hidden from the road and surrounded by the joyful sounds of my babies. The darkness that had engulfed me for so long had lifted. It was still light out on this warm April day when I saw the car coming up the road. A comforting peace came over me, knowing Will was home early. He always tried to make it home early when Katherine wasn't with me.

When he started toward the porch, I hollered, "Will, help me carry this bucket of potatoes inside, please." I missed Katherine's helping hands and took advantage of Will.

Katherine had found a new boyfriend, and the two decided to make good on her dream of visiting California. She wasn't here this past week and won't be this week either. I marveled at how far behind I was without her to do laundry and help with the children.

Will picked up the heavy bucket and followed me. "I have to go to the Fosters and fix Al's crystal radio set. He called this afternoon. That's why I came home early."

"Oh, is that the reason," I teased, "and here all along, I thought you just couldn't wait to see me."

"I can never wait to see you, Sugar. You should know that by now," he said, plunking the bucket down next to the sink.

I smiled and batted my eyes at him like a silly schoolgirl. I reached into the bucket of water for a potato. Slicing the vegetable into four pieces, I slipped it into a boiling pot on the woodstove and reached for another. "Nooo," I drew the word out. "With five little ones under the age of eight and another one on the way, how would I ever guess?"

Will slipped up behind me and wrapped his arms around my growing abdomen. "I hope this one's another girl. We need a playmate for Maisie."

"If your ma was still here, she could tell us, but since she's not, we'll just have to take beggars' luck."

"True, but beggars' luck has been good to us, so I don't have to worry."

"Not much, anyway," I said. "I think we need to get Lynch's eyes checked, though. It seems to me he sees less and less every day. He squints his little face until his nose wrinkles, and he sets to wailing every time the others get more than a few feet from him."

"You're right. I'll call the doc in Sabinal tomorrow and make an appointment."

Finished with the potatoes, I turned to face my husband, who still had his arms clasped around me. I wrapped my arms around his neck. "How late do you think you'll be? It makes me nervous being here alone with the kids after dark. With Katherine in California, I feel even more anxious."

"Silly girl. Do you think the boogeyman will come all the way up here? He'd have to cross our narrow bridge, and you'd have plenty of time to hide when you saw him coming."

He kissed my neck, and a chill ran down my spine. I shoved the fear down and nestled my head against Will's shoulder.

"I love you," he whispered against my ear. "I'd never let anything happen to you. I won't be late. I just need to put a new cat's whisker on his radio. It won't be much after dark if it's after dark."

I removed my arms from around his neck and pushed against his chest. "I know you think I'm silly, but it scares me to be here alone. Just promise me you won't get to drinking whiskey with Al and forget to come right home."

"No whiskey for me tonight," Will chuckled. "Just a quick service call and straight back to my beautiful wife."

His words were reassuring, but the fear I was fighting pushed back. *Not now*, I thought, *don't give in to the fear*.

Will hurried through his dinner of venison backstrap, boiled potatoes with gravy, and home-canned green beans. When he put the last bite in his mouth, he said, "Great dinner, Sugar. Where'd you learn to cook like this?"

I handed him a look and turned my face up for a kiss. He gave me a peck and said, "I promise to come right back. I shouldn't be gone more 'n an hour."

A chorus of "bye, Daddy" filled the air as each boy tried to outshout his brothers.

I lowered my chin to keep from laughing at their antics. I caught Will's eyes, and we shared the moment in silence. "You be quick now, you hear?" I called after his bony frame as he hurried to the car.

CHAPTER 60

JIMMY

Jimmy had noticed the change in the family's routine. He knew their comin's and goin's as well as they did. He had hideouts to watch from without them knowing.

When he finished work each day, he stopped at home to check on his ma and grab a hunk of cheese and a piece of bread before he headed downriver to the Jones place. They didn't know about the little cave at the top of the hill between the house and the river, where Jimmy watched everything Maizelle and Katherine did.

He waded across the river in a shallow spot at the curve below the bridge, then went behind the hill between his Aunt Sarah's old house and the house Will built. He scooted under a rock overhang where he could watch Maizelle and the children. Sometimes the pictures of Maizelle in his mind took over. When that happened, his body reacted as it had the night he watched them make love in the river. He relieved the discomfort in the usual way.

Jimmy hid in the rocks every day until he saw the lights of Will's car. Then he crawled out of the rocks and slid down the back of the hill where they couldn't see him.

He recognized that Maizelle was pregnant, which meant another child would soon join the family. It made him angry because he knew she wouldn't leave home without Will when her belly swelled.

W'll keep pressin' her, like in river. Now she stay home. I want show I love her.

When Jimmy realized Katherine was not there every day, he sneaked closer to the house to get a better view.

Soon he knew each of the children and their names. He was particularly fascinated by the one called Lynch. It was not lost on Jimmy that Lynch looked more like him than the rest of his family. He also observed that Lynch wanted to be close to the older boys. If they ran off, he tried to catch up and often fell. The big one—the one called Charles—always came back to help him.

This reminded Jimmy of experiences he observed at the Galveston Children's Home, which often meant a child had poor eyesight and would be given spectacles, as he had. It was another way he related to the youngest boy.

Jimmy left school early on this particular day and crawled into his hideout to watch Maizelle and the children. It was raining and had rained hard enough during the day to raise the river level to make crossing difficult.

He noticed that Will's car was parked by the gate.

W'll never be home this early.

Jimmy watched as Will sat on a stool by Maizelle. He talked to her while she peeled potatoes and rubbed her belly. He kissed her and bit her neck like he did that night at the river.

He watched as she laughed and looked at Will in the way he remembered.

That look mean W'll goin' press his neckid body on her. Make her cry.

The more he watched, the more excited he got. His insides felt all mixed up. His agitation grew until he believed he had to stop Will from hurting Maizelle.

He scooted from the small cave and slipped down the muddy hill to the river. Mud caked his boots. Rain had made the river deep in the spot he usually crossed, and when he waded in, water overtopped his boots. The waterlogged boots and his cold feet made him angry. He slogged up the bank and pulled them off to empty the water. His anger was directed at Will.

K'll W'll. Gun. Get Pa's gun. K'll W'll.

When Jimmy got back to his cabin, he was shivering from the cold, angry about his boots filling with water, and knew he had to stop Will.

Inside the cabin, his pa's Winchester rifle rested in a rack above his bed. He'd never fired it. His Uncle Irvin had shown him how to load and lock the action. He stared at the gun, remembering what Irvin had said. *This ain't a toy Jimmy... Don't ever play with it...Never point the gun at anyone unless you mean to kill 'em... only use this to protect your ma's life.*

He remembered the instructions and had never touched the weapon. He lifted the heavy, cold gun from the rack and poured bullets from the ammunition box. He pulled the lever down like he'd been shown and loaded six in the chamber, one behind the other. He closed the lever and recalled Irvin saying, *when you lock this lever, Jimmy, the gun is ready to shoot.*

He put the gun on his bed and looked at it. Irvin told him to carry it pointed at the ground, so he didn't accidentally shoot someone.

Jimmy put on dry socks and struggled to pull his wet boots over them.

Not let W'll hurt M'zl. K'll W'll. Not go in water. Use bridge.

Jimmy's head filled with pictures of Maizelle. He loved her. He wanted to show her he loved her. He lifted the gun off the bed.

He did his best to avoid the thorny mesquite bushes as he picked his way through the brush along the river trail. His memory of getting stuck in that particular schrub was not pleasant. It was his only bad memory of the night he showed Maizelle he loved her.

He remembered that Maizelle hadn't cried when he put his privates inside her. He decided that meant she liked it, and even though he had been advised not to put it near girls, he hadn't been able to stop himself once he had his arms around her. He wasn't sure exactly what had happened or how, but he knew the relief he felt afterward was something he wanted to experience again.

I touch her top parts. Why she kick me? I want say I love her. Fall in bushes like when Will push me in barb wire.

Jimmy had many cuts and scratches from both experiences that bled. In a rare act of kindness, his mother put Iodine on his cuts. She fussed that it would sting or burn, but Jimmy hadn't noticed. Sarah had told her Jimmy didn't feel pain the same as other people. His mother never asked him what happened to get him so scratched up.

Jimmy plodded along the tangled trail, trying to keep the rifle pointed at the ground the way his Uncle Irvin had shown him. It was hard to keep it pointed down, and when he stumbled on a tree root, he nearly lost his balance and the gun.

He heard a car cross the Jones's bridge and head downriver, but he didn't see who it was, and it didn't register that it might have been Will.

He concentrated on staying upright, and when he saw the bridge, he felt happy.

Tonight, I shoot him.

He walked toward the house picturing how happy Maizelle would be to see him. He fantasized that she would be his wife. He would never hurt her the way Will did. He would work hard and take care of all her children. He thought when he killed Will, she would be able to visit her father again. In Jimmy's mind, everyone would be happy.

Don't see no one. Fixed on one thing. I see how it happen. Pound the door. W'll come. He say, "Yes, Jimmy?" to get rid of me. I don' matter to W'll. Point gun at W'll. Pull trigger. W'll fall down. M'zl hear bang. She come. W'll dead. Smile. She 'preciate me.

He climbed the stairs and knocked.

CHAPTER 61

April 12, 1926
MAIZELLE

I finished dinner, and Charles helped me clear the table. The baby was in her highchair, and I sent Dubbya'E, Aaron, and Lynch to their room to get ready for bed. I heard insistent rapping on the front door and lifted Maisie out of her chair, settled her on my hip, and went to answer.

Who could that be? Katherine would come to the back door unless her boyfriend was with her. Probably just Elizabeth and Robert dropping by to see Maisie.

The insistent pounding came again.

Maybe Will had an accident.

My heart skipped a beat, and I felt the blood drain from my face as I imagined the worst. I reached for the doorknob as the door cracked open from the forceful knocking.

Jimmy's pale face and white hair glistened in the gathering dusk.

I screamed and slammed the door, but he was quick and stuck his boot in the opening.

I turned sideways, pressed my shoulder against the door to hold it closed, and shouted, "Get away from me!"

"W'll, W'll," he insisted.

"Get away!" I screamed again, and all the boys came running to see what was happening. "Go away!"

"W'll, see W'll."

"No!" I pushed against the door and stomped on his foot.

Jimmy raised a gun barrel and stuck it through the narrow opening, using it as a lever to open the door.

The children cried out, reacting to the terror in my voice and face. Bedlam ensued.

Charles stomped up and down, saying, "Mama, what's wrong? What's wrong?"

Dubbya'E and Aaron copied Charles, flailing their arms and screaming in alarm.

A gunshot rang through the night. The pressure I had on Jimmy's foot was released as I slumped to the floor. A searing pain tore through the side I had pressed into the door. It felt like my insides exploded, and my abdomen burst open. The sound barely registered in my brain but instantly stopped the boys' hysteria.

I was holding Maisie on my other hip and lost my grip when I fell. She tumbled and bumped her head, letting out an indignant wail.

My body slithered down and lay against the door. With the strength I had left, I used my shoulder to try to close the door. I clasped my stomach to hold my unborn baby inside.

After the initial shock from the loud gunshot, all four boys resumed screaming, stamping, and running in circles.

"Get away from the door!" My voice was raspy, but my fear penetrated their hysteria and silenced the room.

Jimmy looked at me through the narrow crack. Our eyes met.

His face contorted. "No, no," he muttered, "k'll W'll, k'll W'll."

I watched as he slowly pulled the rifle barrel out of the doorway. A large pool of my blood flowed past the opening. When the gun came free, my body rolled against the door, and it closed.

My boys all fell to the floor beside me, clutching my arms and legs, crying, "Mama, Mama." Their wails were the last thing I heard before the agonizing pain overtook me and the room drifted away into darkness.

CHAPTER 62

JIMMY

Nothing had turned out the way Jimmy imagined it in his mind. He failed to recognize that Will's car was gone when he approached the house.

Maizelle did not look happy to see him when she answered his knock. She said Will was not there. Jimmy inserted the gun barrel into the narrow opening and used it as a lever to pry the door open. When he put his foot into the space, she stomped on it, and the gun went off.

The sudden explosion frightened him, and he almost dropped the gun. He looked through the small opening and saw Maizelle looking at him. She had slumped to the floor, her face contorted in shock and pain. He watched as a pool of dark liquid crept past the opening. He thought it might be Maizelle's blood. Jimmy didn't know what had happened.

Gun shoot. Jump in my hands. Make loud boom. Shoot M'zl. Accident. Not want to k'll M'zl. Head hurt. Can't think. Run. School. Hide. Burn gun. Burn school. Burn me.

Jimmy knew that if Maizelle died, he wanted to die. His head throbbed. He pinched his eyelids to make the shocking picture of Maizelle's face disappear. He squeezed his nostrils shut. The smell of gunpowder and blood assaulted him. He didn't want to kill Maizelle.

When the pressure on his foot lifted, he pulled it out of the doorway and slowly pulled the gun barrel free. The door shut, and he wasn't able to push it open. He stumbled off the porch and jammed the barrel of his pa's gun into the dirt to stay upright. It was then he noticed that Will's car was missing.

W'll not home! Run. Hide. Take gun. If W'll come back, he catch me. Shoot him before he see M'zl.

Jimmy crawled down the riverbank and hid in the thick undergrowth. He held the gun and waited for Will to return as he formed another plan. He would stop Will and kill him before he could reach the house.

Wait long time. Water cold. Mud cold. Body shake.

The darker it got, the more frightened he was. He wondered if he could point and shoot the way Uncle Irvin had taught him. He was afraid he might do it wrong and create another accident.

Gun maybe shoot on accident again. Feet wet. Shiver.

He tried to make the shaking stop. His hands quivered. He couldn't hold them still. The longer he waited, the more unsure he was about carrying out his plan.

Feel sick. Where W'll? When he come back?

Jimmy crawled through the bushes, looking for a place to cross the river where his boots wouldn't fill with water. The rain had stopped hours ago, and the river flow had returned to normal. He looked for another hiding place where he could see a car coming, but that meant moving to higher ground, and he feared that someone might see him.

Time meant nothing to Jimmy. He didn't know how long he waited by the river for Will to return, but the cold and wet had done more to weaken his resolve than cause him discomfort. He sneaked through the bushes, looking for a shallow place to cross. Holding the gun high with one hand and grabbing exposed tree roots with the other, he hauled himself up the opposite bank.

The moon was merely a sliver this night and shed almost no light. Jimmy emerged cold, wet, and muddy into a big field from where he could see a faint glow from the school's bell tower. It was a long walk to the school, but he knew he couldn't go to his ma's place and he couldn't go home. Aunt Sarah was gone, and his only refuge was the school.

Not wait for W'll. Fire school. Burn me up. If M'zl die, I want die. If she not die, she tell W'll. Put me in jail. I never see her.

Jimmy laid the gun on the wet grass and grabbed his head to make it stop pounding. Planning was hard. It made his thinking fuzzy, and his head hurt. He stomped to warm his feet, realizing that nothing had happened the way he had planned.

He picked up the gun and ran toward the school. He was careful to avoid any place where he might be spotted. He dropped to his belly and crawled the last 100 yards between the edge of the field and the school's front door.

Nobody here. Use janitor key.

He leaned the gun inside the door and rubbed his hand along the wall, searching for the basement staircase. When he reached the bottom, he lit a match to find what he needed.

The cans of linseed oil he would use to refinish the floors and desks after school let out for the summer were stacked against the wall on the far side of the room, away from the furnace. He grabbed two cans and hurried upstairs to the top floor, feeling his way along the banister rail. When he reached the upper level, he lit another match and opened one can. He carried the open can to the room farthest from the stairway and poured oil along the floor next to the wall. When he drained the can, he returned for the other one and emptied it in the second upper-level room.

Head sweating. Chest hurt. Throat scratchy. Can't swallow. Head pound. Hands slippery.

Jimmy made a second trip to the basement, feeling his way along the banister railings, and brought two more cans of linseed oil upstairs. His heart hammered so rapidly he could see his chest pumping. His hands shook and slipped off the cap of the new can. He spilled the oil, splattering his coveralls and shirt sleeves, righted the can, and hurried to the remaining two classrooms.

He wiped his oily hands on his coveralls, struck a match, and tossed it into the room farthest from the stairs. He raced to the next room and flung a match inside. The oil ignited immediately, and flames burst up the walls.

Jimmy's hands were slimy from perspiration and oil. He couldn't grip the handrail and slipped and slid to the bottom. The fire upstairs went fast. Jimmy could feel the heat and hear the crackling sounds it made as it ate everything it touched.

I go to basement. Fire take me. Take Pa's gun.

The fire spread so rapidly that he could only light one room on the ground floor. Pieces of the upper floor rained down around him. Everywhere he went, he dodged burning hunks of the upper floor. His clothing was soaked with oil. He knew he needed to escape the inferno before it was too late.

Fire bell clang, clang, clang. Bad taste in mouth. Smoke choke me. I stay. I die. I run.

CHAPTER 63

MAIZELLE

I drifted in and out of consciousness as I lay bleeding from the wound. When I could open my eyes, I felt unnaturally strong and calm. My instinct was to protect my children. I tried to sit but couldn't make anything work. The boys wailed in terror.

"Charles, stop screaming and crying. It won't help. I need...you...to be...man, you hear?" I wasn't sure if I spoke aloud or if I imagined speaking.

Charles ceased wailing. Tears and snot ran free-fall down his face as he looked at me wild-eyed. "Aren't you dead, Mommy?"

"No, I'm...not... dead...but...need...help." My voice sounded weak and distant. My eldest nodded and leaned close. "Go for help. Go to Fosters and get Daddy. Can you do that? Hurry. Saddle Mona and go through the old place...doctor." My head lolled to one side, and my eyes closed.

"What about Dubbya'E and Aaron?" Charles asked.

I forced my eyes open a slit and said, "too little... slow you down... go alone. Need doctor." My voice was so feeble I wasn't sure he heard me until he ran from the room.

I drifted away. I floated above the scene. I could see the boys huddled together, crying, and Maisie patting her hands in a pool of blood near my body. I wondered if I was dead and if I could just watch over the children from up here until Will got home. What was to be our next child—we hoped for a second girl—lay lifeless against me. I tugged on my blouse to lift it so I could see.

Dubbya'E leaned close and said, "Mama, somethings crawling out of your belly."

I wanted to answer him, but I couldn't make any sound. I was still thinking, I was still feeling, but I wasn't able to make words. I moved a finger out and touched Dubbya'E's arm as he helped pull my blouse free. I rubbed my finger up and down on his skin. I don't know if he felt it or not.

Aaron lay next to my legs, hugging them to him, sobbing. In my mind, I reached for him and cradled him against me.

The crying and wailing from all three of my boys continued. A fat little hand patted my cheek. Maisie had crawled over my back and was smatting blood onto my face.

I'll look a fright when Will gets home. Where is he? Why hasn't he come back? I sent Charles to find him, He's been gone too long. If he doesn't hurry, it will be too late. I need to tell him...I want him to know Jimmy did this.

"Mama? Mama, are you dead yet?" The concerned voice of my second son penetrated the fog as I drifted in and out.

"No," I said, "cold...so cold."

"Should I get covers for you?" Dubbya'E was doing his best to be a grown-up and help. I must have nodded my head because he scrambled away. I couldn't hear anything but the children's crying. I wanted Will. I knew I was dying. I didn't want to die without him.

CHAPTER 64

WILL

I whistled as I crossed the narrow bridge to home. It seemed to me that it had gotten dark earlier than usual. The moon was just a sliver peeking through the covered sky giving everything an ominous cast of black shadows. I drove up the lane pleased with myself for finishing the repair job post-haste. I looked forward to the happy expression on Maidee's face when I came in sober and in good time.

When our house came into view, I noticed no lanterns were glowing. I squinted, leaned over the steering wheel, and peered into the dark, thinking maybe Maidee was in the kitchen where I couldn't see the light. I knew the boys would be in bed and reminded myself to be quiet. When I parked, I saw the kitchen was dark, too.

I stepped through the back door and crossed the empty kitchen to the living room, where four pairs of terrified eyes turned as one to look at me.

Dubbya'E jumped to his feet and flung himself at me. A mournful sob escaped his throat with the word "Mama."

Aaron sat rocking next to a crumpled figure by the front door. He stared at me as if at a stranger. There was no hint of recognition in his eyes.

Lynch lay curled next to the body on the floor. After looking at me when I entered the room, he pushed his face deep into the back of the person he was curled against.

Maisie was spatting her hands in a dark pool of liquid by the body. A faint odor of…what? Gunpowder and blood?…drifted up my nose.

I could not comprehend the scene. A coldness swept through me that brought a deepening fear closer to reality. "Maidee?" I said, "is that you?"

I pulled Dubbya'E off my leg and knelt beside her. From this position, I could see her face and a bloody mass of clothing bunched around her belly. I placed my hand on her shoulder and tried to roll her toward me. Her eyes fluttered open, then closed again. "What happened? What happened to you?"

Dubbya' E tugged on my arm. "The bad man shot her."

I couldn't make sense of what my son said. The words were clear. There was no mistaking *what* he said. My brain simply refused to accept what I heard. I looked at Dubbya'E and back at my wife.

"I put a cover on her, Papa. She's cold."

I reached for her again, stroking her face as I swept the hair out of her eyes. They opened at my touch. I lifted Lynch away from her body and rolled her onto her back.

She grimaced in pain, but her eyes met mine and held. "What happened? Who did this to you?"

Maidee's eyes looked hollow and dead, but something else was there like she had summoned the strength to live until she could tell me. "Jimmy," she whispered. "He came for you…" Her eyes closed, and she appeared to shrink into the floor. "Cold," she said, "so cold…baby gone." Her head lolled to one side, and she opened her eyes. "Charles…?"

"What about Charles?" My voice rose to a shrill timbre. "Dubbya'E, where's Charles? What's she saying about Charles?"

"She told him to take Mona and go to Foster's to find you."

"I never saw him. Didn't he come back? When did this happen? Did she say Jimmy did this?" I peppered my traumatized five-year-old, never pausing to get an answer.

Dubbya'E's chin trembled, and he began to cry. The volley and intensity of my questions pelted him like an accusation. "I didn't do nothin', Papa. The bad man shot Mama."

I clutched him to my side. When I stood, the room swirled.

Aaron still sat on the floor, silently rocking.

Maisie patted her fat little hand in the thickening blood and smeared it like a child's finger painting.

Lynch whimpered as he crawled back to his mother's side.

Maidee's face was smattered with blood. I couldn't think. I had to get help. I didn't know what to do.

Charles is missing. If he rode Mona to the Foster place to find me, I'd have seen him on the road. This madman must have my son too. I leaned over Maidee to assess the damage but couldn't see enough in the dark to know what I was dealing with. I took the kerosene lamp off the hook by the door and pulled a cigarette lighter from my pocket to light the wick.

The lamp flared to life, and the horror that faced me rolled through the room like a thundercloud over the Rio Grande. The bullet had entered Maidee's side and exited through her belly. Our new baby hung through the opening, blue and grotesque, like a naked bird fallen from its nest. I could see her clothing had staunched the bleeding from her abdomen and womb.

I gagged and grabbed hold of my throat. Acrid bile filled my nostrils as it rose and subsided in my mouth. I fell to my knees beside my love and lifted her shoulders. "Dubbya'E help me. Bring the rocking chair over here. I need to get her off this floor." I barked the order.

Little Dubbya'E ran to the other end of the room and tugged on the chair. His crying reached a new pitch as he dragged and pushed the heavy rocker closer. It tipped over when a foot caught in the hooked rug. He tried to lift the arm as it lay on its side, attempting to right it. He wasn't strong enough or big enough to do the job and fell to the floor sobbing, "I can't. I can't."

I laid Maidee back on the wood floor and jumped to my feet, taking the distance between my wife's body and the upside-down rocker in two strides. I grabbed the arm, pulled it upright, and dragged it across the rug to where she lay.

Dubbya'E's howling filled the room. "Shut up, now! Just shut up with the cryin'. Get over here and help me with your Mama."

My boy stood, tears streaming, and ran to me. Once more, he launched himself, wrapped his skinny arms around me, and buried his face in my pant leg. His little body was wracked with sobs, and he trembled like a leaf tossed in the wind.

I patted him on the head, took him by the shoulders, and stood where I could hold him still and look him in the eye. "Dubbya'E, you and me, we've got a problem here. I need you to be a big boy and help me get your Mama into this rockin' chair. You're the only one big enough to help, and I need you to stop your wailin'."

Aaron stopped rocking and looked at me with recognition for the first time. "I can help, Daddy. I'm a big boy."

"Yes, Aaron. You too. Come on, boys. We have to move Mama to this chair."

I knelt and slipped my hands behind her shoulders to raise her upper body. Her eyes shot open, and she cried out. I nearly dropped her but held fast, sliding her toward the chair.

"Aaron and Dubbya'E, y'all get Mama's legs. When I lift, you slide."

The boys each took a leg. I eased Maizelle into the rocker, and they raised and dragged her legs for her.

The chair rocked backward, and I said, "Dubbya'E, go back there and hold it for me while I get her situated."

He let go of her leg, ran behind the chair, and pressed his weight against it.

I lifted again, and the chair slid forward under her as Dubbya'E pushed from behind. I let her down, and she cried out as I settled her body against the cushioned back. The bloody mass from her abdomen was grotesque in a way that would stay with me for the rest of my life. I pulled her clothing over the opening in her belly and tucked it as tight as possible to slow the bleeding.

"Cold," she muttered. "So cold." She shimmied in pain and response to the loss of blood.

The room wasn't cold, and I knew she was rapidly losing her life. "Aaron, go get a quilt. I need to cover her, so she'll stay warm."

Aaron ran to the bedroom and returned dragging the heavy coverlet my ma gave Maizelle when she left for the Gulf. I grabbed the blanket and tucked it securely around my dying wife.

She moaned and reached for me with her eyes. "Thank you," she said. "Jimmy came...kill you." She sucked in a breath, and her lungs rattled. "I tried...keep him out." Her eyes closed, and she struggled for another breath. The determination I had seen in her eyes was present in every breath and attempt to speak.

"Put barrel...crack...force door." Her face had no color, and each word was more effort than she had life left to utter. Her eyes drifted shut, and she said, "Love you... care...my babies." Her head lolled, and I feared she was gone. Her eyes fluttered again, and she said, "Maisie...? Where...Maisie?"

I lifted Lynch from the floor and placed him next to her in the rocker. I took Maisie from the pool of blood she played in, wiped her hands on my trousers, and carried her to her mother. I put our daughter in the chair with Maidee opposite Lynch.

"Dubbya'E and Aaron, you sit right here beside your mother's legs and make sure she stays in the chair. I'm going to town for help." I leaned over and kissed her on the lips. "I love you, Maidee. I'm going for the doctor now. You stay strong for me. I'll be back before you know it."

"Don' go... Tell ..." What life was left in her eyes implored me.

"Don't try to talk. Tell me when I come back." I stroked her forehead.

"Jimmy..." Her head drooped. I lifted her face and righted her as best I could. "Ravage..." Her eyes opened a slit and fluttered closed, "...s-s-sorr..." Her voice trailed off as she lost consciousness.

What is she saying? Ravage? I stuck my hand into Maizelle's knitting basket next to the rocker and plucked out a rolled-up ball of yarn to tuck between her ear and shoulder for support.

"I'm goin' for the doctor," I said to my sons, clinging to their mother's legs, "stay put until I get back." The door banged shut as I ran for the car.

I reached to open the car door when I caught a movement out of the corner of my eye. I stepped away from the car and peered into the dark toward the barn, thinking it must be Jimmy. A horse materialized, and someone slid off its back and ran toward me, shouting, "Pa, Pa."

It was Charles, and I flew to him, gathering him in my arms. "What happened? Where have you been? I didn't see you at Foster's." My questions fired like bullets.

Charles trembled, sobbing. "I...I...I," he gasped between sobs. He lifted his head from my shoulder and said, "He won't come."

"Who won't come? Did you see Jimmy Calvert?"

"No, Papa, Doctor Clarke won't come."

I hoisted Charles and got a better grip on him as I ran to the car. "I need to get to town to find the doctor for your ma." I tossed my boy onto the front seat and slid behind the wheel. I pushed the electric starter and said, "Tell me what happened while we drive. Stop your crying. We don't have time to waste." I looked over at my son and said, "Well?"

"Mama sent me to find you at Foster's, but she said she needed a doctor. I thought it would be faster to go to town and find him if she needed a doctor. I rode Mona across the river and along the trail to the doctor's house. I didn't mean to disobey Pa, but she told me I had to be a man."

"How'd you know where the doctor lived?"

"Aunt Julia and Uncle Sam took me there once, and she said it was the doctor's house. They made me wait in the car. I'm sorry, Papa. All I could think was, Mama needs help, and there ain't no doctor at Foster's place."

"Don't say ain't. You know better. What happened when you got there?"

"I ran up the steps and pounded on the door real hard. No one answered, so I pounded again and yelled. 'Help. I need help.' A big lady answered. She looked at me and tried to shut the door. I knew she recognized me, and I put my foot in the opening so she couldn't close it."

"How do you know she recognized you?"

"I saw her watch me from the window that day Julia brought me. It was the same lady.

"She leaned out and whispered, 'What do you want? You shouldn't be here. Go on home now.'

"I started to cry. I couldn't help it. I said, 'Mama's been hurt bad. I need a doctor! Please.'

"She said, 'He won't help you,' and tried to shut the door. I pushed it open and ran past her. I shouted, 'I need help. I need a doctor.'"

"That's good, Charles. What happened then."

"Doctor Clarke heard me shouting and came to see what was happening. When he saw me calling for help, he rushed forward and said, 'What's happened here? Who needs my help?'

I said, 'Mama's been hurt bad. She needs a doctor. Please come!'"

He said, "Who's your Mama? Where is she?"

"The lady said, 'His mother is Maizelle Jones.' The way she said it gave me shivers. Dr. Clarke looked real mad. He stared at me with mean eyes, Pa. No one's ever looked at me like that before."

"Did he say anything?"

"No. He just turned around and walked away. The lady said, 'You need to go now and tell your daddy if he needs a doctor for Maizelle, he should take her to Uvalde.' Then she opened the door wide so I could pass."

"What else did you say?"

"I said, 'He isn't home.' I ran out and untied Mona. I heard the fire bell clanging as I boosted over her back. It was still ringing when I crossed the river behind the church. I looked toward town and saw a red glow. I wondered what was burning, but I came straight back to Mama."

"You did the right thing. You made a man-sized decision and took action. I'm proud of you, son. No matter how this turns out, you did the right thing."

CHAPTER 65

JIMMY

The fire pushed through the roof, and flames tickled and licked the night sky before erupting in a furious wall of red. Jimmy ran to light the oil by the front door. The floor above continued to drop burning chunks of wood. The fire burned fiercely and wildly, spewing debris into the sky. A large piece of fiery timber fell at his feet, startling him. He dropped his box of matches, and the whole thing burst into flame.

I hide. Basement cement. Cement don't burn. Fire can't get me there. No oil in basement. I safe.

The unrelenting clang of the fire bell interrupted Jimmy's thoughts. He knew he had no more time to make a decision. Men would soon be there to put out the fire.

They catch me. I run. They won't know. Should run.

The smoke was black and thick. Jimmy gagged and coughed. His eyes watered, and his nose dripped. He knew if he went to the basement, he couldn't change his mind. If he stayed, they would know he set the fire.

In an instant of clarity, he grabbed the gun and ran. He kept running across the field toward the river. He knew his only hope was to get far away from the school. Everywhere he looked, he saw men running to fight the fire.

Cars came from every direction. Headlights bounced in the dark sky creating ghostly shadows as they jostled across fields, along little-used dirt roads, and in both directions on the highway. Flames licked at the sky, and the school walls crumbled as Jimmy bolted for the river.

CHAPTER 66

WILL

I pushed Lizzy as fast and hard as I dared. The night sky glowed red. I knew something big must be on fire when I pulled off the bridge and headed for town. A roadblock was in place to the school's West to keep any traffic from slowing the progress at containment. I couldn't get through.

"You stay here," I said to Charles. "I'll be back as soon as I find help."

I jumped from the car and ran toward the bedlam. I had to find Doc Clarke.

I dodged men coming at me from every direction. I shouted, "Has anyone seen Doc Clarke?"

Men just shook their heads and kept running. Volunteers raced into the garage where the lone fire wagon was parked and donned their firefighting equipment. Everyone could see the school was ablaze. Those who weren't regular volunteers ran from their houses, grabbed buckets and hoses, and made their way toward the inferno.

I watched as the fire burned out of control. No one could get close enough to train a hose on the blaze.

Flames leaped from the two-story building, sending fiery projectiles spewing through the air onto nearby buildings. The flaming pieces of wood were so hot they ignited one structure after another. There was nothing in danger immediately around the school, but the wind set up by the raging blaze carried burning hunks of wood over the roofs of businesses on the opposite side of Central Street.

Men shouted, "Here. Over here! Another fire just took off!" The flames spread like a fever along the main street of Utopia. I ran until I had to stop to catch my breath. Near the Clarke home, I passed a pair of men going house to house, pounding on doors to get more help and alert people of the danger.

Men ran every which way. Shouts of "Here! Over here! Another one is going up!" rang through the night. I took the steps in a single leap and pounded on the door. My heart raced and hammered until I thought my head would burst. I beat on the door with doubled-up fists. I was under no illusions that my effort would be any different than my son's.

Leila opened the door.

"Doc Clarke," I said between gasps of breath.

"I told your son to tell you to take her to Uvalde or Sabinal. Doctor Clarke is busy."

"There isn't time. She's been shot. If I don't get help right now, she'll die. Does he want that on his conscience?"

"It doesn't matter whether he wants it on his conscience. He isn't here. He grabbed his bag and went to help out at the fire."

"Where? Did he say where he was going?"

"No, he said something about this being a 'big one,' and his 'services would be needed,' as he shoved past me."

"Where does he usually go in a situation like this? Does he go to the firehouse?"

"I don't know. He never tells me. I felt sorry for your boy. He's a hard man, Will. Sometimes I don't think he has any feelings."

I jumped off their porch and ran for town, operating on pure adrenaline as I entered the fire hall. A well-dressed figure bending over a cot, tending someone's wounds, caught my eye. Doc Clark. I gathered my courage to approach.

"Doctor Clarke," I called. "I need you to come. Maizelle's been shot." My voice caused the man to turn. It was not Doctor Clarke.

The town undertaker stared at me. "I'm sorry...I thought you...I thought you were..."

"I know what you thought," the man said calmly and quietly. "Doctor Clarke went back home to get more bandages and supplies. We have a couple of pretty badly burned and injured men here tonight. Did you say someone's been shot?"

"My wife. Maizelle. Doctor Clarke's daughter. I can't get through the roadblock with my car. I need to get back to her. She'll bleed to death if he doesn't get to her right away."

"Who shot her? How bad is it?"

"It's real bad. She's pregnant. I mean, she was pregnant. He shot the baby too. It was Jimmy Calvert. He's the janitor at the school."

"I know him. You go on home, Will. When Doctor Clarke gets here, I'll send him straight to your place. If God forbid you need me, you know where to find me. I expect I'll be here all night." He turned back to the injured man, who moaned in pain.

I left the fire hall and ran to my car. The door was open, just as I'd left it. Charles sat staring blankly at the chaotic scene.

I jumped behind the wheel, pressed the starter, and Lizzy roared to life. I made a U-turn in the wide street and drove faster than I should. When I turned left onto the bridge approach, the wheels spun out from under me, and the car swerved in a wide arc, threatening to overturn. I cranked the wheel in the opposite direction of the skid and got control just as the tires mounted the narrow bridge.

Charles bounced against the door and then off me. "Slow down, Pa. We almost flipped."

My heart raced, and my stomach was in my mouth. A sense of panic swept over me, raising goose flesh. I talked myself down as we sped off the bridge and up the lane.

I skidded to a stop by the rear gate and barely remembered cutting the engine before I ran to the back porch.

Charles was on my coattail as I flung open the door and heard sobbing, crying, and moaning from the front room. I hurried across the kitchen and glanced around the living room before I moved toward the rocking chair.

I bent over and put my face close to Maizelle's for any sign of breathing. Nothing came from her face. I laid my head on her chest, listening through the heavy quilt for any hint of a heartbeat. There was none.

I lifted Maisie off her mother's lap and sat her on the rug. I removed Lynch and sat him next to his sister. Dubbya'E and Aaron were where I left them, each clinging to a leg of her cold body with tears dropping into their laps.

Charles's dry gulps of air punctuated the stillness of the room. All the air had been sucked out of the house.

I couldn't breathe. I felt faint and helpless, yet I knew I had five young 'uns that were now my responsibility. I kissed Maizelle on her cold blue forehead and pulled the big quilt up to cover her beautiful face.

I sat in the darkened room with my dead wife and five children, all in shock, barely aware of the knock on the front door.

Charles raised his head. "Daddy, someone's here."

"Don't answer!" Dubbya'E said. "The bad man's back!"

Aaron screamed in terror and cowered behind my chair.

Jolted back to the present, I stood and moved toward the door. Despite the insistent pounding, I passed by and continued to the bedroom, where I removed my carbine from the wall rack. I returned to the door and called through. "Who goes there?" No one answered, so I said it again.

"Donald Clarke," came back at me. "I'm told you need a doctor."

My blood ran cold. I didn't respond.

"Mr. Jones, let me in so I can help her."

"Too late. She's gone." My voice was flat.

"Open the door. I want to see her."

"Too late. You should have come sooner. Send the undertaker."

I turned away from the door, my rifle at my side. I wondered if it would make me feel better to shoot him. I went into the boys' bedroom and watched from the window.

Doctor Clarke rested his forehead against the door. I saw him take a swipe at his eyes. With a shake of his head, he turned, went down the steps, got in his car, and drove away.

CHAPTER 67

WILL

I saw another car coming up the road as the doctor drove off. The two vehicles stopped, and I saw one man get out of each and exchange words. The second car continued, and Dr. Clarke left. It was Bobby, and I let him in around ten o'clock.

"Will. What happened? The Sheriff said that Jimmy killed Maizelle. I ran into Doc Clarke on the road, and he said it's true."

"It's true. She's gone. Jimmy came lookin' to kill me and killed her and the baby."

"Maisie?" Bobby asked, looking around the room.

"No. The one she was expectin'." My eyes were dry. I turned my back on Bobby and paced the room. I touched Maidee's face with each pass to see if she was really gone.

Charles, Dubbya'E, and Aaron all sat curled at her feet. Lynch was asleep on the rug, and Maisie lay with her head on Lynch's legs, sucking her thumb. The arrangement might have seemed to an onlooker like the children were being read a bedtime story.

"I'll stay with you tonight," Bobby said. "Doctor Clarke said he'd send the undertaker to get her."

When the undertaker pulled up, it was quiet and dark. I saw the lights from the hearse inching closer and knew the time had come.

I fell to my knees beside her body and buried my face in her hair. A mournful wail emerged from somewhere deep inside me as the shock that insulated me from reality peeled away, exposing the raw wound.

All the kids set to cryin' when they heard me wail, and bedlam reigned by the time the undertaker got to the front door.

He rapped, and Bobby let him in.

"Excuse me," he said, over the cryin' and wailin'. "Mr. Jones? Dr. Clarke said I was needed. Are you prepared to let the body go?"

I shook with silent heaves. My shoulders lifted and fell as tears spilled down my twisted, misshapen face. The agony of my loss consumed me.

He reached for me and squeezed my shoulder.

Bobby pulled me to my feet.

I shook my head and faced him. I reached for the arms of my children to hold them away while a stranger took their mother.

We watched as the undertaker and Bobby lifted my beautiful broken girl onto a stretcher. They covered her with a white sheet. Before they carried her out, I asked the undertaker if he had spoken to Dr. Clarke.

"I did," he said.

"What did he say?"

"He came to the Firehall and said, 'I'll take over now. You're needed at the Jones place.' It looked like he had more to say but thought better of it. I waited a minute and said, 'I'll just go then.' But when I started to leave, he called after me. He said, 'I'll want to examine the body when it arrives.' I said I'll call you as soon as I get back."

"That's it? That's all he said?"

"Yes."

"I don't want him to see her body. He disowned her; he refused both his grandson and me when we went for help. No. I won't let you take her body if you're going to let him see her."

The man gave me a look of pity. "I know you must be hurting something awful, but he was her father. Don't you think it would be good for him to say goodbye?"

"I don't care what's good for him. He never wanted to see her when she was alive, so why should he get to see her dead? I mean it. I'll put her in a pine box and nail the lid shut if you don't swear you won't let him near her."

"I swear. We need to take her now so I can prepare her for burial. We only have thirty-six hours before we get rigor mortis, and decay starts right away. I don't have cold storage for the body."

I pulled the sheet back from Maidee's face and touched her lips. Cold. I pulled it up again and let her go. I held onto Charles and Dubbya'E's arms as Bobby and the undertaker took her out of the room. All three of the older boys cried.

Aaron screamed, "No. Don't take Mama. Don't let them take her, Pa." He grabbed the undertaker's arm and tried to pull him back as they threaded the stretcher through the doorway.

I let go of Charles and Dubbya'E and went to Aaron. I lifted him off the floor and held him tight. "We have to let her go now, Aaron. Mama's gone."

Aaron wailed and kicked, calling, "No, no, no," after the trio as they disappeared out the door and down the steps to the waiting hearse.

Bobby came back inside, and we watched the car make its way down the road and out of sight.

"Help me get the boys into bed," I said.

I put the three oldest in my bed.

Bobby brought Maisie and Lynch to the room Maidee and I shared.

I lay Maisie and Lynch on the bed with the older boys and tucked a blanket around all of them.

Bobby and I went into the kitchen and sat at the table.

I said, "Tell me what happened in town."

"Well, the fire burned the school to the ground. About five other businesses, plus the library, went up too."

I shook my head in disbelief. "Did you help fight the fire?"

"Yeah. I was fighting with Roger McDonald, who lives close to the school. When Roger heard that a madman murderer was on the loose, he lost it. He dropped the hose we were using to play water on the smoldering remains of the library and shouted, 'I have a six-year-old son, a two-week-old daughter, and a bedridden wife at the mercy of that madman.' He took off for home, and I ran to find the Sheriff."

"Where was he?"

"A crowd had gathered in the field behind the burning school, where he was talking to them. I got as close as I could and heard, 'We don't know where the killer went, but we know that the fire started sometime after the murder. Calvert's the janitor and would have access. He could'a burned hisself up in that inferno, but the site is too hot for us to look for a body. Until we can, we have to figure he's still on the loose.' He asked for volunteers to join the posse. I wanted to volunteer, but I thought I should check on you and the kids to see if what he said was true."

"Has the posse gone out yet?"

"Yes. The Sheriff picked six men. I went home to tell Emma to lock the doors and not let Jimmy in if he came around, then headed out here."

"That was good of you, Bobby. Thanks."

"Word spread fast, and attention shifted from the fire to a search. The Sheriff and that retired Texas Ranger who lives here joined up to hunt Jimmy."

When he told me what he knew, Bobby said, "If you think you'll be all right until morning, I'll go and let you rest. Mother and Emma will come in the morning to help with the kids. I'll make burial arrangements for Wednesday."

When Bobby was gone, I dragged a chair from the kitchen and sat by the bed to watch my kids sleep. Something deep inside told me I couldn't leave their side.

My mind was numb. Maidee was gone. Katherine was away. That only left me.

Random thoughts formed as the instincts of survival took root. I knew I had to stay with the kids and protect them from the madman. I wanted to go on the hunt for him. But how? *They're helpless. I can't leave them alone while I hunt the bastard.* Nothing in my world made sense.

I vaguely remembered Dr. Clarke coming to the house...too late to save her. Had I let him in? I couldn't remember. I remembered Bobby saying someone would come to help after daybreak.

I stared at the innocent faces of my five children, huddled together in the bed in which all of them except Charles were born. Grief swept through me like a hot, dry, East wind. My eyes burned when I closed them. I couldn't take them off Maidee's babies. They were my responsibility. No tears fell. I felt dead. I wished I was dead. There couldn't be any life without Maidee.

CHAPTER 68

JIMMY

The school blazed with a wild fury all around Jimmy. The chaos confused his already twisted mind. Should he stay and risk being captured by those who would hunt him, or should he run and take his chances at escaping discovery?

Making any decision was difficult in his present state, but he had little time to ponder the choice.

He stepped outside the front door, and the decision was made for him. Beams from car lights bounced willy-nilly into the sky. Vehicles came from every direction, across pastures, along narrow dirt roads, from the main highway, and beyond. Everywhere his eyes fell, more evidence of the onslaught of people met his gaze.

The clanging fire bell reached far into the surrounding countryside. The telephone exchange was alive with calls between and among those with one. Everyone was coming to fight the fire.

I run. Run for river. Go back same way. No one see.

Violent red flames licked the sky. Every time Jimmy stopped to look back at the school, he could see more fires in more places.

I only want to fire school. Not town. I hide in bushes by river. I scared. Body shake. Can't make shaking stop. Crawl through brush by river. Listen. Press my ear on ground to hear. If they huntin' me, I can't hear nothin' yet.

Tummy growls. Cheese and bread used up. Thirsty. Chest hurt. Eyes sting. Water come out. Stinky smoke in air. Slip on muddy bank. Almost fall in water. Grab branches to keep out of river.

Jimmy spent a long, cold, wet, and grief-filled night picking his way along the recently flooded Sabinal River. He used the hiding nests he had previously made to spy on Maizelle and get occasional rest. His head pounded with confusion about what had happened. He couldn't remember why he needed to kill Will Jones, but he understood that something had gone terribly wrong. He thought he might have killed Maizelle, but he wasn't even sure about that. His only comfort as he crawled through the brush was to conjure the pictures of Maizelle he held in his mind.

I see my cabin. It dark and quiet. No one here. Ma's house dark. Press ear to ground. Don't hear nothin'. Don't know if they huntin' me. Maybe they not know I fired the school. Maybe M'zl die before she tell Will I shoot her.

Jimmy crawled onto his small porch and leaned his pa's rifle against the wall beside the door. He removed his mud-covered, linseed oil-soaked clothing, and stood naked in the chilly air. Grief and remorse overtook him, and he wept uncontrollably. He gulped smoky air, picked up the gun, and went inside.

He fell onto the bed, stuck his face into his dirty, smelly pillow, and cried. He used the pillow cover to wipe off the mucus and tears that ran free-fall over his face.

M'zl. M'zl. Sor'e. Sor'e. I think I done somethin' bad, like when I hit W'll with wood hammer. Aunt Sur'a scold me hard. This feel same. I want to die. If M'zl die. I die. Sleep.

When Jimmy woke again, it was four o'clock in the morning. He put on clean coveralls and looked around for the gun. His head was clearer now, and he had a plan. He wanted to die. He needed to die. There was no reason to continue living if his love was gone.

He remembered the small bottle of Iodine his ma had given him the night Maizelle kicked him into the prickly mesquite. He remembered her warning that it was poison and that he should never put his fingers into his mouth after applying it to his scratches and cuts. She had told him it would make him very sick and he could die.

Jimmy dug around in the small night table next to his bed. His fingers found the small square bottle full of dark orange liquid and lifted it out. He stared at the bottle and wondered what dying would feel like. Wounds never hurt. He wasn't even sure what it meant to hurt. The poison might kill him, and he might not feel anything bad. It seemed like a good plan. The gun scared him when it went off, and he didn't think he wanted to try to shoot himself. What if he missed and the noise brought people to see what happened?

He had no way of knowing what would happen to his body. The convulsions, the cramping, the burning throat and eyes. Iodine was not a gentle way to die, but it was effective.

He opened the bottle and drank the poisonous liquid in a single gulp. Within moments his body convulsed. Snot ran out his nose, and he caught it with his tongue. His body cramped and bent double. His vision blurred. His throat grew raw and burned. He gagged and crossed his arms across his belly to stem the cramping. Nothing worked to make his limbs stop jerking, and his body convulse.

He picked up the gun and staggered to his bed. His mind played tricks on him. Objects in the room seemed to run away, then rush toward him. He flopped onto the bed and dropped the gun beside him. His body burned from the inside out. He rolled onto his side and pulled his coveralls off to let the heat escape. Nothing worked.

Footsteps on porch?

Jimmy's mind thought he heard footsteps. Then it told him someone was standing by his bed. He lifted the gun with his jerking, twitching hands and swung it wildly toward the intruder. He put his finger on the trigger, just as his Uncle Irvin had shown him, and pulled. The loud bang startled him. His body flopped uncontrollably, and he dropped the rifle to the floor.

Side hurt. Side hurt bad. Touch. Fingers go in gooey hole. Maybe bullet in here.

Jimmy's wound oozed blood. He remembered seeing blood run past the crack in the door when the gun shot Maizelle.

If M'zl got hole, she hurt bad. She die. I die.

Jimmy's body gagged, and he vomited orange foam straight up. It fell back to his chest as bubbles of yellow and brown that fizzed and popped. He watched in fascination, coughed, gagged, and gulped air.

The convulsions slowed with the elimination of Iodine from his stomach. He leaned over the edge of the bed and picked the gun off the floor. He thought he might need it if the Sheriff came looking for him.

CHAPTER 69

April 13, 1926
WILL

Someone opened the back door and stepped inside.

I heard footfalls but couldn't bring myself to consciousness. The house was quiet. I heard whispering.

Footsteps moved through the kitchen and into the living room. The steps stopped at the door to the children's room. I wondered if it was open. It didn't matter; no one was inside.

The door to my bedroom was closed. I forced my eyes open and watched as the doorknob turned and the door opened enough to peek inside. Eyes stared at me, then shifted to my five children asleep on the bed. A throat cleared, and someone whispered, "Will, Emma, and I are here to help. Would you like us to start breakfast?"

It was Elizabeth. I stared in her direction. I understood who she was and what she said, but I couldn't respond. After a few seconds, I turned away to look at the children. Three little boys with tear-streaked faces. One white-haired child curled in a fetal position with red smears of dried blood on his chubby legs. My curly-haired little daughter, with streaks of blood on her cheeks and forehead, as if costumed as an Indian warrior.

Aunt Elizabeth pushed the door open and stepped inside. She put her hand on my shoulder. "I'm so sorry, son. I don't know what got into Jimmy for him to do such a thing. You should try to get some sleep. Emma and I will care for the children until we can help you figure out what to do." She squeezed my shoulder and looked past me at the kids.

I blinked and tried to remember what had happened. Why was I sitting in a chair with all the kids on our bed? Elizabeth said I needed to figure out what to do. I didn't know what she meant. Where was Maidee?

I rose and left the room. I did not speak. I did not make eye contact. I did not feel. I put one foot in front of the other until I reached the mattress on the floor in the children's room, dropped to my knees, flopped onto my stomach, wrapped my arms around my head, and covered my eyes.

It was almost noon before the commotion in the house woke me. I heard the boys fighting. Someone screamed. The sound pierced my brain and brought me alert in a single jolt. The scream sounded just like last night, full of terror. I sat up and crawled to my feet. I heard laughing, crying, and voices coming at me from all directions.

I opened the door and stepped into bedlam. The boys clung to Emma and Elizabeth's legs, bombarding them with questions. They wanted their mother, wanted Katherine and asked for me.

When Charles realized I was in the room, he flew at me and clutched my legs. "Daddy, where's Mama?" I had no idea how to answer. I stiffened, pulled his hands away, and looked into his upturned face.

Emma said, "Come here, Charles. Let your daddy get awake before you go peppering him with questions. Can I get you some breakfast, Will?"

"Nah, that's okay. I'm not hungry. Where's Maisie?"

"Elizabeth put her to bed in your room. She's had a rough morning."

"How so?"

"You know, scared, wanting her Mama, calling for Katherine, refusing to eat. They're all pretty shook up."

Elizabeth wrapped her arms around me and hugged me like there was no tomorrow. "Son, I am so sorry. Emma and I will take the kids home with us so you can get more rest. Bobby will come by tonight and discuss the arrangements."

"Arrangements?"

"For Maizelle. For the service and burial."

I stared dumbly.

"Do you want me to try to reach your folks? I called Eula and Eloise last night. Eula and Fred will drive up today. I'll call Julia when I get back to town."

Try to reach my folks? Why would she want Ma and Pa? The horror of what had unfolded in my living room roared back as the question flashed through my addled brain. I felt like I'd been struck by lightning. I mumbled, "Sure. Thank you," as I fished in my pocket for my tobacco and started toward the porch. I was numb.

Emma opened the door. I noticed a dark stain on the floor and paused.

"We scrubbed the blood up as best we could," she said, "you will probably want to put something stronger on it to get it all up. All we had was vinegar."

"Blood?"

Elizabeth followed me outside and said, "We left you some dinner in the root cellar so it would stay cool. We're taking the children for a few days. Bobby and your Uncle Robert are taking care of the funeral arrangements. I think the plan is for her to be buried at noon on Wednesday in Jones Cemetery." She waited for a response. I made none. "Will," she said, "are you going to be alright by yourself?"

I blinked and shook my head, trying to process everything. "Yeah, I'll be okay. Thanks, Aunt Elizabeth. I don't know what to do."

"I know, honey, I know," she soothed. "We'll help you work it all out in a few days. You just rest now. There's no need to plan anything just yet. Give it some time."

I nodded my head and turned back to the house. "I better hug the kids before you take them. Let them know I'm still here." I stepped inside and called the boys.

I hugged each one and whispered into his ear, "You'll stay with Emma and Aunt Elizabeth for a few days, but I'll come for you soon. Try to be brave, and don't cry unless you have to."

When Emma handed me Maisie, I lost it. The tears I hadn't shed flooded my cheeks. My little daughter wiped them with her pudgy fingers and said, "Papa cry." I handed her to Emma and rushed to hide in the bedroom.

The next thing I knew, Bobby stood over the bed, shaking me. At first, I didn't understand why he was there. When my brain fog cleared, I looked at him with more questions than he could hope to answer. No one would ever be able to answer why.

"I need to know a couple of things before the service in the morning. Did you eat the dinner Ma left?"

I shook my head and sat up.

"You need to eat. I'll get it for you. Splash some water on your face and come into the kitchen."

When I cleared my eyes and went to the kitchen, Bobby peppered me with questions about Maizelle. What was her birthday? What was the exact date we got married? How old was she when she moved to Utopia? When was she baptized? He wanted the full names and birthdays of all the kids. I wanted to know about Jimmy.

"Bobby, is Jimmy still out there? I need to get my gun and go find the son-of-a-bitch."

"No need, Will. The Sheriff got up a posse last night, and they hunted him to ground. He died in a shootout with them."

"Where?"

"His cabin. Sargent Wilson said they searched on foot and horseback all night with hounds. They found several hiding places where he holed up along the river between your place and his. They finally tracked him back to his cabin."

"Who's Sargent Wilson?"

"He's that Texas Ranger who retired here last year. The one with tracking hounds."

"You talk to him?"

"Yeah. Pa and I were cleaning up the pharmacy after the fire this morning, and he came by."

"Did he tell you how it happened? Who shot him, I mean?"

"He said they heard a gunshot from inside the cabin just as they were about to enter. They backed away and used their gun barrels to push the door open. He said it was a gruesome sight."

"How so?"

"There was a naked man on the bed holding a gun pointed at the ceiling. His face was splattered with orange foam, and his eyes darted like he couldn't focus. He had a bleeding wound to his side and looked like a ghost. Wilson says he shouted, 'Drop the gun,' but the guy was having some kind of fit. He held the weapon over his head, and his arms flailed around like they weren't attached.

"Wilson shouted a second time, 'Drop the gun or I'll shoot,' but Jimmy swung the gun back and forth like a majorette's baton. He said whatever kind of fit had hold of him had him in a firm grip."

"Is that when he shot him?" My gut clenched.

"No. He said Jimmy lowered his arms as the fit eased and pointed the gun right at him. Wilson aimed his pistol and fired. The bullet hit Jimmy in the back because he rolled onto his side just as the gun went off."

"I wish it had been me that shot him." I rested my head in my hands. Remorse flooded me. I left her alone. I should have listened. I didn't understand what she was afraid of. I would never forgive myself.

"Wilson said after he shot, the rest of the posse rushed in, and someone shouted, 'He's going to shoot'.

"Jimmy fired a wild shot into the ceiling. Several men got shots off, and he was hit more than once.

"Wilson told us Jimmy reared up, roared, and swung his rifle at the men standing near the door. They fired another round, and he slumped backward. Wilson thought for sure he was dead, but when he approached, Jimmy opened his eyes. The Ranger said, 'Jimmy Calvert, did you shoot Maizelle Jones?' and Jimmy said, 'Y's, H'rt M'zl.'"

"What was the orange stuff on his face?"

"Poison. Wilson said an empty bottle of Iodine was on the table by the bed. They pulled the bed sheet out from under Jimmy and covered him before they put him across the saddle of one of the horses. He said the bloody sheet didn't do much to hide the gruesome load, so he said, 'Cover him with a blanket from the cabin. We can't take him in like that.'"

Bobby and I sat awhile after he told me Sargent Wilson's account of Jimmy's capture and death. I wished that a bullet from my gun had done the job. I'd have emptied the chamber. Then I might have torn his limbs off and fed them to the dogs. I imagined cutting his throat. I'd never been so filled with hate. Now he was dead, and I could not expel my rage.

Bobby turned the conversation to the arrangements for Maidee's service and burial. He pulled me out of my black thoughts and back into the kitchen. He said the minister at the Methodist Church would hold a service at ten in the morning, and then everyone who wanted could go to the cemetery for the burial.

I couldn't get my head around the idea that I wouldn't ever see my wife again. "I'm tired, Bobby. I think you should go. I'm too shot to talk anymore."

"If you're sure," he said. "I'll be by for you in the morning in time for the service at nine. Do you need me to do anything before I leave?"

"Nah. I'm going to walk out and pick up the eggs and feed the dog. I'll be fine."

When he closed the door, I got a bottle of whiskey off the top shelf and poured myself a cup. I intended to get drunk and stay that way until I quit seeing Maidee's face everywhere I looked.

CHAPTER 70

April 14, 1926
WILL

When Bobby arrived to take me to town for Maidee's service and burial, I was passed out on my bed, an empty whiskey bottle on the floor. I wasn't dressed. I hadn't bathed. I reeked of stale smoke. I looked about as bad as it was possible to look.

My cousin wrestled me into my suit and shoes, half dragged, half carried me to the car. When we reached the church, he hauled me out of the Packard and shoved me toward the open door.

I staggered and almost went down.

Bobby grabbed my arm and hung on tight until we got inside. He guided me to a pew at the front of the sanctuary, where he stood me and let go.

I flopped down and looked to my left. I wasn't prepared for what greeted me.

Eula and Fred stared at me with looks of horror. Julia and Sam managed weak smiles before they turned their gaze to the minister.

I cautiously turned my throbbing head and peeked behind me; a sea of black, every seat in every pew was occupied.

I faced the front and waited.

The minister began his incantation, words meant to explain the inexplicable and console the inconsolable. People nodded and sniffled and let go of the occasional sob.

I don't remember much of what he said. Blessedly, he kept his comments short.

The congregation sang "Shall We Gather at the River," one of Maidee's favorite hymns, and the pastor said a prayer for her soul.

My angel didn't need a prayer for her soul to get into heaven. That much I knew. I struggled to keep the tears in my eyes, but they wrested their way free and fell onto my crooked necktie.

When the pastor finished, he invited everyone to the Jones cemetery to join the family as we laid her to rest.

I struggled to make sense of what he was saying. I tried to stand but fell back onto the hard pew.

Bobby stepped over to assist.

Suddenly, Eula's arms were around me, and my head was pulled against her shoulder. She held me close in a fierce hug, and her body was wracked with sobs.

Fred tugged on my left arm, and Bobby pulled me free by hanging on to my right. When the church was empty, they helped me to the door.

When I sucked in the fresh air, my stomach tossed, and whiskey spewed on the hallowed ground. I was too drunk to be embarrassed and let Bobby and Fred drag me to the car.

They drove straight to the graveyard, where Maidee waited in a simple pine casket. I let them help me out and guide me to the open grave.

The crowd looked even larger than the one that filled the church.

As we approached the front of the gathering, four men lifted the top of the coffin, and I caught a glimpse of Maidee's angelic face with her hair loose around her shoulders. A gut-wrenching wail emerged, and I fell to my knees in front of the casket, weeping her name.

Eula says I cried, "No, no, no. Don't go without me. What will I do? How will I take care of our babies?" I can't personally attest to that. I don't remember. She said Uncle Robert and Bobby each took an arm and lifted me to my feet, pulling me away from her casket. They guided me to an empty chair near the grave and gave me a fresh white handkerchief. My four boys sat in a row next to the empty chair. Aaron reached for my hand and patted me.

Eula, who held Maisie, says I pressed the linen over my eyes and shook with sobs before I lost consciousness and fell out of the chair. I don't remember anything, don't know who brought me home, didn't see them lower Maizelle into a grave.

They let me lie where I fell until the service ended, and everyone left.

I only know what Eula and Julia told me later, that the crowd grew until it looked as if every resident of Utopia, past, present, and future, gathered to mourn Maidee's passing. If Doctor Clarke and Leila attended, I never saw them, and Julia didn't mention them.

After the burial, the family was welcomed at Aunt Elizabeth and Uncle Robert's house. Julia, Sam, Eula, Fred, Bobby, Emma, and all the children. Ma and Pa couldn't make the trip. Elizabeth said it was too far, and Ma wasn't in any condition to travel.

They put me to bed in Bobby's old room to let me sleep off my drunkenness and disgrace. And while I slept, they made plans for me.

When they went, Julia and Sam decided to take Charles back to San Antonio. They said they would raise him as their own if I agreed. Eula and Fred offered to take Maisie and make her a part of their family. Since neither couple had children of their own, everyone seemed to think I would agree to this arrangement. To argue it, I would have had to be present and of sound mind. I was neither; and it was too late by the time I came around.

Sam had business, and he and Julia made a hasty departure. I'm told Charles was eager to go with them. Julia held him close and offered him something I couldn't give him, something that felt like a mother.

Eula had never met Maisie, but she loved my wife wholeheartedly and extended that love to our daughter without hesitation. She told Elizabeth to make sure I understood that if she took this little girl to raise, I couldn't come back and reclaim her later.

She would take her until I decided on my future, but I couldn't take her again if I didn't claim Maisie within the month.

My sister and her husband left that day with the daughter, Maidee, and I had struggled so hard to have, who brought light back into our lives after the dark time.

That left the boys. Three towheaded, blue-eyed, rambunctious, and seriously disturbed boys. Elizabeth kept Aaron and Lynch, and Emma took Little Dubbya'E. They made it clear it was temporary until I had my "feet under" me again.

When I finally roused, sober, and grief-stricken, Aunt Elizabeth called Bobby to drive me home. She explained the arrangements with my sister and sister-in-law and encouraged me to accept that it was the best possible solution for two of my children.

I couldn't think, and I didn't want to.

She told me she and Emma would look after the boys for "a few days" to give me time to figure out what to do next.

As Bobby drove me through town on the way to my place, I could see Upton's Pharmacy had survived the fire but sat alone next to smoldering ruins on either side, its walls soaked with water, its merchandise damaged or ruined, and sporting a gaping hole in its roof. I saw that my garage had been spared. It stood dark as we passed.

Everyone but me realized Utopia was lost. Not just the private utopia Maidee and I had constructed out of our troubled beginning, but the whole town.

The school that was the center of our community and all its activities lay smoldering in the arms of the cement basement walls that had given Jimmy purpose, refuge, and protection.

Five businesses on the main street were ashen piles on the ground. The library that provided solace and inspiration to so many no longer existed.

Maidee's service was so much more than the loss of one person, however tragic. Utopia buried itself that day.

CHAPTER 71

April 19, 1926
WILL

I awoke from my drunken stupor and groped for my whiskey bottle in the dark. I tipped it to my lips and poured the liquid down a raw throat. It burned going down, and it burned coming up, as my empty stomach hurled the offending liquid back. I crawled to a sitting position and wiped my mouth on my shirt sleeve. The rancid odor of sweat mixed with stale whiskey, cigarette smoke, and vomit assaulted my nostrils.

Hungry and disgusted, I pulled myself up and staggered out of the bedroom with the near-empty whiskey bottle in one hand, dangling by its throat. I blinked rapidly to clear my eyes as I looked across the living room to the far end. The sun was only beginning to rise, and the room was still dark.

I stumbled across the braided rug and flopped into my easy chair. My arm with the whiskey bottle dropped over the side, and the bottle hit the floor. The noise jolted me to a different level of awareness, and I lifted the bottle to take another swallow. Empty. The realization cleared a spot in my fogged brain, and I felt anger rise in my throat along with the bilious liquid my stomach could no longer tolerate.

I saw the rocking chair facing me as my vision cleared in the dawning light. I glanced from the empty seat to the mirror Maidee and Katherine placed on the wall behind it to give the room more depth.

A primal scream rose from somewhere in the bowels of my being as I hurled the empty whiskey bottle at my image. The mirror shattered, and shards of glass fell to the floor. Pieces hung in the edges of the frame. The center was gone. The slivers of glass reflected fragments of memories.

The chair where I last saw her alive sat still and empty. A contented reflection no longer looked back at me from the mirror's frame. I stared at the tableau of my broken life. The fog gradually lifted from my alcohol-anesthetized brain when the tears finally came.

I don't know how long I wept. Sunlight filtered into the room from windows at each end of the east wall. Rays fell on my head and warmed the back of my neck, where I sat slumped in the easy chair. I didn't know the time. I was lost and alone. My stomach growled, reminding me that I was still alive.

I stood and went to the kitchen. Wrapped plates of food sat untouched on the table. I vaguely remembered Bobby coming by and leaving something. I wondered if these meals were what he had brought. I chose the plate closest to the edge and removed the waxed paper from Emma's fried chicken, cold mashed potatoes with gravy, and beets.

I picked up a chicken leg and gnawed, went to the drawer next to the sink, got a fork, returned to the table, and ate a few bites before my stomach heaved. I bolted for the back door.

The warm morning smelled fresh until my stomach lurched again, and I retched up the chicken, potatoes, and beets. I thought I heaved blood until I realized beets were the culprit. A whole week of nothing but whiskey left my stomach aching, sore, and raw. Holding food down was near impossible.

I walked the length of the porch and looked toward the barn. I surveyed the area. Unsure what I was looking for, I stepped off the riser and wandered toward the chicken house, letting the sun reach for my bone marrow.

From somewhere, a thought emerged, telling me I needed to bathe and get presentable. I remembered Aunt Elizabeth telling me she and Emma were taking the children. *When was that? How long had it been since I'd seen them?* Charles's kitten—now a full-grown cat—rubbed against my leg.

As the sun warmed my body, my mind began to function. What would I do now? Where would I go? How would I care for five children and hold down a job? The only answer I could find was that Maidee was dead, and I was alive. The children were my responsibility, and I needed a plan.

When Bobby came by that evening—ten days after Maizelle's murder—I was sitting on the front porch. I was clean, dressed, hungry, and trembling from alcohol withdrawal.

"Will," he called as he approached. "Good to see you up and about." He climbed the steps and offered his hand.

I took it without standing, raised my eyes, and nodded. I didn't smile. I made no verbal acknowledgment of the greeting.

"How ya feelin'? Are you ready to go see your boys?"

My face felt like stone. I shifted my eyes to meet his, and they filled with tears.

Bobby didn't know what to say. Men never cry in front of other men. He had no way of knowing what my grief felt like. He stepped toward me and clasped me on the shoulder. "Look, man, I'm sorry. We all are. I can take you to see the kids if you're ready."

I shook my head. "Not yet. I need a few days to get straight. Thanks for the meals." It was the first I'd spoken in days.

"I'll leave your dinner on the table in the kitchen." When he returned, he sat next to me on the top step. "It's good to see you up and sitting outside. I've come by every evening since the funeral and found you passed out drunk. You couldn't stand, talk, or walk. I'd bring you a fresh dinner. I'd tell you to eat, and the next day I'd find it still covered and sitting on the table."

"Sorry, Bobby. I appreciate it."

"I wasn't sure you'd ever get right again. I'd pick up the plates, leave the two most recent, scrape the rest into the scrap barrel out back, or toss it to the dog. I hated wasting good food, but I didn't want Ma and Emma to know you weren't eating."

I rolled and lit a cigarette. Bobby stood. He squeezed my shoulder and stepped back. "You better have some supper. See ya tomorrow."

"Sure."

CHAPTER 72

WILL

Two days after Bobby's visit, I bathed for the second time in as many days, dressed, and opened the front door.

An empty and silent expanse of field stretched between the porch and the Cypress-tree-lined river. Pungent lime green grass announced the birth of spring. Volunteer bluebells dotted the pasture, waving their cascades of blossoms as if to beckon me out of the house.

Stepping over the sill, I stood where Jimmy stood and felt a chill rise from the bottoms of my feet until it reached my chest. My body shuddered.

I moved onto the steps and inhaled the fresh morning air. I let the rising sun warm my wasted body and broken soul.

I drove to town and turned down the street where Maidee had grown up. I pulled to a stop in front of O'Brien's house. Katherine was in California with her new beau when Maidee died, but she was home now. Bobby told me she'd been to see the boys and offered to help if she could. She wanted to come see me, but he told her it wouldn't be a good idea.

I climbed the front steps and knocked.

Katherine answered.

We stared at each other as strangers might.

"Will."

"She's gone." I reached for the young woman in front of me, and the two of us fell together in a desperate embrace. Neither of us knew what to say.

When the moment passed, Katherine stepped back and dropped her arms. "Will, I'm so sorry. So sorry I wasn't there."

"I'm the one at fault. I knew she was afraid to be alone, but I thought she was being silly."

Katherine looked at me, and tears welled in her eyes. "I shouldn't ever have left her, not after...."

"After what?"

Katherine raised her eyes, and I knew it was the secret between her and Maidee I always suspected.

"She tried to tell me," I said. "I couldn't understand what she was saying."

"I begged her to tell you. If she had, none of this would have happened."

"What was it, Katty?"

"Come in. I don't think you want to hear this standing out here." She held the door for me.

I sat in a small chair. Katherine faced me from the sofa. We looked into each other's faces for a long time before she spoke.

Tears slipped down her cheeks. "I swore I'd never mention it, Will. I wouldn't tell you now if I didn't think it might help you get over feelin' like this is your fault." She sucked in a big gulp of air. "It happened the night you had the rooster fights at your place. She never would tell me how it happened, but Jimmy stopped her on the road right after she crossed the bridge. He raped her, Will. The word she used was 'ravaged,' but no matter what she called it, it was rape."

My blood ran cold. The flesh on my face chilled, then flushed hot. Rage filled me. I buried my face in my hands, unable to look at Katherine. My shoulders slumped, and my body crumpled into itself. I felt broken in a way I'm sure Katherine had never seen in another human being.

The look on her face held pity, fear, and the hopelessness I think we both felt. "The dark time, Will. The rejection of you and the boys. The sickness that fell on her like stink on a dog was all from what happened to her. I begged her to tell the Sheriff. I begged her to let me get you from the coop. She wouldn't have it. She made up her mind no one could ever know."

"Why? Why couldn't she tell me?" My distress came from a place so deep inside that I felt naked.

"She didn't think you could love her if you knew another man had ravaged her. She wouldn't tell the Sheriff because she didn't want anyone else to find out. She thought you'd kill Jimmy and go to jail if she told you. She was humiliated. I tried, Will, I tried. I couldn't convince her."

We sat quietly for several minutes.

"The pregnancy," I said, "...did she think Lynch wasn't mine?"

Katherine paused ever so slightly before she raised her eyes to mine and said, "No. I wondered after he come lookin' so white and fuzzy, but Maidee said 'no' he was your boy."

I knew. She knew. There was nothing more to say. I stood and walked out the door.

CHAPTER 73

May 10, 1926
WILL

A month had passed since I'd seen my boys. I knew Charles and Maisie were safe in San Antonio, but I still had to decide what to do with the other three.

My garage stood closed and dark, just as it had the day after she died. I couldn't go back. I couldn't stay in Utopia.

Everywhere I turned, I saw her. Nothing but whisky dulled the pain, and I knew it would kill me if I kept drinking at this pace. There were things I needed to do, and I had to leave to do them.

I stood on the porch and looked toward the river, the bushes where the coward hid, and the town that lay in ruin. There was nothing left for me here.

I went inside, lifted a valise with my clothes and a box with the children's clothes, and carried them to the car. On my second trip, I picked up a small wooden chest filled with a few of Maidee's keepsakes. It held the ring I gave her when she was initiated into the Eastern Star and a pair of Charles's first shoes.

The undertaker had removed the ring and given it to Aunt Elizabeth to return to me. I placed the little chest under the front seat and drove down the lane without looking back.

I parked outside the cemetery and entered the grounds on foot. The day they buried her was a blur. I remembered almost nothing of it.

I walked past the graves of my great-grandmother, Elizabeth, and my great-grandfather, the Reverend Irvin Jones, Sr.

As I rounded the small hillock in the center of the graveyard, I could see the freshly turned dirt at the lower corner to my left. New blades of grass and a few bluebells were scattered across the mound.

I turned toward her grave, lowered my head to my chest, and stared at the ground as I hurried down the incline.

When I reached her resting place, I knelt and bent over to press my forehead against the freshly turned earth. My shoulders shook, and tears fell.

Someone called my name. I raised my head. Embarrassed to have anyone see me in this state, I grabbed my handkerchief and attempted to control my emotions.

I heard the voice again and strained to hear. I couldn't see anyone, but the words came as clearly as if she was sitting across from me in the rocker.

"Promise me you will take care of my babies. I can't go until you promise."

"Don't go," I said. "Where are you? Take me with you."

"I can't, Will. You need to stay and take care of our babies. Promise me you will."

I searched the area for her. I couldn't find her. My eyes filled with tears.

"I promise," I said. "Please let me see you."

"Remember your promise." Her voice drifted away as a slight draft touched my ear.

I stood and brushed the soil from my knees, inhaling the smell of fresh dirt as I scanned the cemetery. Nothing stirred but a few bluebells quivering in an unseen breeze.

Four weeks after I buried my wife, I set a sober foot on the town's main street. I saw the charred remains of Utopia that now served as a metaphor for my life. My first inclination was to retreat with a new stash of whiskey. Instead, I put a "**For Sale**" sign on the garage, leaving Bobby's number to contact.

Few people talked about what had happened in our midst. No one mentioned the deep unease that swept through the community. People were afraid to make eye contact with me. It looked like everyone felt guilty about something. Those whose businesses survived felt guilty; those whose businesses had burned buried them with Maidee. Those who referred to Jimmy as 'the mute' wondered if their slight put him over the edge.

It seemed everyone had lost something. Children lost their innocence, parents lost their footing, and businesses everyone counted on were gone for good. The community lost its school. People lost their jobs. I even heard that Leila and Doctor Clarke were divorcing.

Men were injured fighting the fire. People lived through a night of terror unlike anything our community had experienced since the Indian wars, and the list went on.

I learned that a second pine box was lowered into a grave outside of town, in Wareville Cemetery, on the same day we buried Maizelle. Anna Mae Calvert stood alone to watch the box go into the grave.

None of it mattered to me. None of what was lost by anyone else came close to what I lost.

This is tough country. People don't spend much time on pity. True love matches are as rare as the Spanish gold coins that wash out of the shallow caves on the canyon rim and find their way to the riverbank. Marriage matches are made for practical reasons, not emotional ones. Ours was an exception.

Death is a part of life in the Sabinal Canyon. One might say in Utopia, the tough hide of the West got thicker that day. Life would go on.

Charles and Maisie were safe. I missed them both with an ache that wouldn't salve itself. I went first to Elizabeth's, then to Emma's, hugged and kissed my three little boys, put them in the big car with the dog and Charles's cat, and headed for San Antonio to keep my promise.

THE END

AUTHOR'S NOTE

This project began thirty years ago as a biography of my grandmother. I had never met her and only knew my grandfather until I was around two years of age.

All I knew was what I had heard from my mother over the years, as a conduit for information she gleaned from my father, rarely a font of revealing conversation.

I knew my father's mother and father had eloped. My father believed his mother was fifteen at the time. I knew she had been murdered, but not why. I knew that she was murdered by a relative of her husband and I had been told her murderer was an Albino, deaf mute.

The only reason ever given was a vague recitation of "a dispute over a fence line, or a dispute over livestock." Questions elicited no more information than this.

My research into the family history revealed a much different set of circumstances, conflicting newspaper accounts, a variety of ages for the assailant, his relationship to my grandfather and no clear answer as to why.

I also came to understand that the murderer was severely Autistic, although that word or diagnosis was not in use at that time; nor was he an Albino. I have tried to create a somewhat sympathetic character out of my fictional assailant as I could not help but feel sympathy for the actual murderer.

I have always felt sad and cheated not to have known the mother my father so obviously revered and adored. The town of Utopia, TX became a substitute for the grandparents I missed knowing.

A trip to Utopia in 1997 revealed many long buried secrets, some of which are included in the book, some of which remain mysteries.

It is my sincere hope that you will enjoy this book as a work of fiction inspired by three verifiable incidents: a youthful elopement, a murder, and a fire. Everything else is a figment of my fruitful imagination.

ACKNOWLEDGEMENTS

Thirty years ago, the muse visited. An unknown force prompted me to write about a place I'd never been and a story with a sad end.

In 1997 I traveled to Utopia on a journey of discovery.

I owe a debt of gratitude to many people: Rusty Redden, who directed me to Katherine Redden, the Holy Grail in my search; Frances McNair, who led us to the home where my father and his sister were born; Anna Lee Burns for the history of Utopia; Beth and J.R. Davenport, for a first-person account of the night the school burned; Edra (Clark) Crow who told me more than she realized in our 20 minutes together; William (Bowen) Clark for the photographs that gave my father a childhood.

The Burns Oregon Writers group and the Writers of The Purple Sage; The Henderson Writers Group in Las Vegas, NV, for three years of tough, loving critique and friendship; The Sin City Writers Group, Las Vegas, who listened, taught, and encouraged me to believe; my early readers, Marlene Rose, Dana Wand, and Dana Dickey, for your encouragement, and liking my book. It meant so much. Jenny Ballif, for a fulsome developmental edit and the guidance I needed to "kill my darlings" and take the story to a higher level, and for crying in the end!

Beta Readers Paul Atreides and Sue Thornton offered insights and opinions to make the book stronger, richer, and more readable; Chris Jensen and Sharon Richter suffered through every version I inflicted on them and gave the feedback and encouragement that kept me going; My daughter, Stacey, who always believed in the story, and me, with love, honesty, and insights that let me carve off big slices of my treasured prose without hurting the story.

And my friend and loving young mentor, best-selling author Amanda Skenandore. She has been my touchstone, rock, idol, and friend, but most of all, she has been the best Beta Reader and cheerleader I could ever have dreamed. I feel honored that she trusted me to want to be better.

Sheryl Rhoades, for the excellent cover design. It truly does tell the story and keep the promise.

My loving husband, Dennis, without whose unfailing support I would never have accomplished my dream.

And finally, to the writers, friends, and critique partners of Sisters Writes. You sustain me.

A READING GROUP GUIDE

FINDING UTOPIA

ABOUT THIS GUIDE

The suggested questions included are to enhance your
group's reading of Linda Weber's **FINDING UTOPIA**.

DISCUSSION QUESTIONS

1. Did the age difference between Will and Maizelle cause you discomfort?

2. Did the fact that Maizelle was the initiator of the romance make a difference in your opinion?

3. If you were initially uncomfortable with the age difference, did your opinion change as the story progressed?

4. Do you think Maizelle should have followed Will's instruction to avoid Jimmy since she had never had a troubled relationship with him?

5. Was Maizelle's descent into depression a result of her poor decision-making? In what ways? Was her climb out of depression realistic?

6. Do you think Maizelle was wrong not to tell Will what had happened to her? If she had told him, how might her life have been different?

7. The book title implies that the couple was in a happy, healthy relationship. How did you view their relationship?

8. You watched Maizelle grow from a young girl into a mother and wife. Do you think her journey to womanhood and motherhood was a happy, successful transition?

9. In what ways did Maizelle grow as a person outside of her role as mother/wife?

10. Did Will change from the beginning to the end of the story? In what ways?

11. How did you feel about Jimmy? Did you ever feel sympathy for him?

12. In what way did Katherine's role in the family change over time?

13. Who was your favorite character, and why?

14. Did the end give you hope for Will and the children's future?

If you would like to know what happened to Will and the children, watch for my next book, **SURVIVING UTOPIA**.

ABOUT THE AUTHOR

Linda (Jones) Weber is the granddaughter of William Echols Jones (Will) and Maizelle Clark (Maidee). She is the daughter of "Little Dubbya'E."

Linda writes Historical Fiction and Memoir. Her personal non-fiction essay, "Katherine," based on an interview with Katherine Redden in 1997, won first place in the Writers of the Purple Sage writing contest in 2010.

She is retired and lives in Sisters, OR with her husband, Dennis, their dog, Jilly, and cat, Houdini.

Reach Linda at **novelistlindaweber@gmail.com**

www.novelistlindaweber.com
www.talesfromthesabinalcanyon.com

LinkedIn: **Linda Weber**
Instagram: **Linda Weber**
Facebook: **Linda Jones Weber**
Twitter: **@LindaJonesWebe1**